SAVAGE NOIR

THE COMPLETE ADVENTURES OF FRANK SAVAGE

GREG NORGAARD

PRO SE PRESS

A Pro Se Press Publication

Cover Photography by Michael Cabrera Photography
Cover designed by: Roy Torres Cover Design and Michael Cabrera Photographer
Cover Models: Kit Nordmark, Roy Torres and Greg Norgaard

Book Design, Layout, and Additional Graphics created by Sean E. Ali

Edited by - David White
Editor in Chief, Pro Se Productions - Tommy Hancock
Submissions Editor - Barry Reese
Publisher & Pro Se Productions, LLC - Chief Executive Officer - Fuller Bumpers

Pro Se Productions, LLC
133 1/2 Broad Street
Batesville, AR, 72501
870-834-4022

proseproductions@earthlink.net
www.prosepulp.com

SAVAGE NOIR

THE COMPLETE ADVENTURES OF FRANK SAVAGE

To Paul—
Your Savagery
Knows No Bounds—

TABLE OF CONTENTS

A SAVAGE RETRIBUTION

★ ★ ★ ★ ★

PROLOGUE

The plains of the Nebraska Territory tend to be just that: plain and flat. Albeit not the best place for a hiding spot, Frank Savage found his. He found a location just outside a rundown and desolate cowboy town. A surprise to him, he was able to find a secure area.

Frank had become situated among some rocky hilly terrain that afforded him with just the perfect location. He could hide not only himself, but also his horse. Frank crouched down at the base of a dusty cliff with an overhang that could provide cover if it were raining. His colt grazed on some nearby grass on the downwind side of an obtrusion that extended away from the steep but short hill. The position allowed him a convenient venue for his inevitable meeting with a dangerous gunman, his notorious adversary, Victor Danvil. It granted him a situation in which he could watch and listen for the killer headed in his direction.

With the advantage of being on the high ground, he waited. Frank prayed he would catch Victor Danvil by surprise. He needed all the help he could get.

Alert with his Henry repeating rifle in hand and loaded, he eyed the entrance to the shallow valley that led to his hideout from the west. The sun was going down, but it wasn't below the ridgeline yet.

Frank liked his Henry rifle but it was a new gun, and it had a shiny receiver that reflected too much sunlight. Anyone who wanted a gun that couldn't be seen for miles had to disturb the shine, which Frank had already done. The rifle was a bit slow to load and during firing it became hot to the touch. He overlooked these imperfections because with a Henry rifle in his hands he was an excellent shot.

Frank's horse shuffled her hooves and rotated in place. He knew she sensed something or someone was approaching. Ever vigilant, Frank cautiously tilted his head around the left side of his hideout where he anxiously awaited. Thinking ahead so that he wouldn't be seen, he had removed his brown flat brimmed hat and set it to the side so as not to provide a bigger target.

The sun was beating down furiously upon his head causing beads of sweat to drip into and burn his eyes. With the air still, he was able to hear his heart pounding in his chest. He thought if he had planned this capture better, maybe he would not be so uneasy. Frank wished he had a partner he trusted to watch his back. He sorely needed a friend to aid in the seizure of Victor Danvil. The trek to Omaha with a captive in hand would be difficult for one man.

After three hours of sitting and waiting in the excruciating heat, Frank felt a disturbance. Attempting to stay focused, he strained his ears. After a moment he could hear the clomping of horseshoes on the rocky dusty ground. Attempting to judge the distance by the sound was difficult because every sound he heard echoed off the walls that surrounded him.

If I look too soon or too late it'll be the death of me, he thought.

Danvil was well-known, not for his skill with a pistol, but for his aim with a rifle. This killer Frank pursued would be wary, for he knew he was a wanted criminal in many states.

Frank fought hard to concentrate on the task at hand. He had to be ready to capture someone who more than likely would rather be shot dead than hung. To be hung wasn't a glorious way to go. He would fight for his life. Or he would die a warrior's death.

There was no other option. It had to happen now. Peeking around the corner, Frank squinted into the sun that sat at a forty-five degree angle in the sky. The glare made it difficult for him to see.

Damn, that's bright.

He saw a tall rider on a black horse that was definitely his target, and a second rider accompanied him. Rightly confused and slightly off-guard, Frank hesitated. He'd heard Danvil had worked with another, but Frank had recently received intelligence information that he was traveling alone. Savage quickly worked out a new plan of attack to allow for the best chance of success, and to ensure his own survival.

Danvil was aware, too aware. He shifted in his saddle and reached for his rifle and eyed Frank's hideout. It was as if he knew somebody was looking to take him out at that moment. The man on a black horse with carbine in hand squeezed off his shot. The sound banged loudly off the rocky surface of Frank's temporary fort. The blast stung his ears. The bullet hit directly in front of Frank's roost, spraying a handful of pebbles into his face that felt of a dozen needles, a clump of dirt shot into his salty bloodshot eyes.

Moving quickly, Savage pulled his rifle to his shoulder. Using every muscle he could muster, he jumped four feet to his left. Exposed, he fired off two quick piercing rounds. He dropped to the dusty floor at his feet. A plume of dust flowed up from the ground into the space around him. Frank squeezed his eyes and blinked furiously to rid them of the debris that blurred his vision.

Lying under a cloud of powder that floated around him, he remained still. His eyes were irritated. With hazy vision he attempted to focus on his intended targets. It was as though he was looking at a mirage through an out-of-focus eyepiece. His left eye was so agitated it was useless. Using only his right eye, he could see a dust devil dancing off in the distance on his left. The twister rotated vigorously, but remained stationary. On the right, he could make out two dark objects in the background that were slowly coming into view.

The tall man on a black horse was sitting straight up in his saddle. He just sat and stared. Their horses were surprisingly impassive. It was dead silent. Frank was confused as to why there was no movement from the two riders he had just shot. He wondered if he'd completely missed both, and if he had, then why didn't they turn-tail and ride?

The tall criminal ever so slowly listed to his right side, all the while looking straight ahead still holding his rifle. Creeping farther to the right, he was now tilting so far in his saddle that gravity reached its hands out, it gripped the tall wretch and pulled him to the ground with a thud and a burst of earth.

Frank's gaze fell upon the unknown rider, Danvil's companion. The man had a small frame and was an average height. He swayed slightly. His right hand reached out. It was suspended about a foot or so above his knee as he sat upon his horse. The stranger's hand slightly slid side to side then moved in little circles that were barely perceptible, as if searching for the pummel of his saddle. Frank had never seen such a reaction before, and he had shot and killed others before the day had started. The small man's left hand hung to his side as his horse calmly stood in the now welcomed breeze.

Frank stood and walked toward the stranger who sat on his horse. He moved within about a dozen feet, and he could see into the eyes of the scared one, whose hand continued to search in the air for something.

Frank stopped to ponder the situation and could see the man was facing death as he sat. The injured man was crying quietly. Then his body started to let go. His lower back gave out first, causing his frame to shift. His hand never found the pummel, and he slipped out of his saddle with an audible whimper. His horse lowered its head to the injured rider.

Frank felt his world closing in on him as he stood and watched the man crumble to the ground in a heap. He picked up his pace, but he continued to be leery of Victor Danvil who remained motionless. He took a quick look to make sure he was dead. He inspected the still corpse. Frank scanned the body. Victor Danvil had been shot straight though the Adam's apple. The bullet shattered his neck on its way out of his body.

Moving to the second gunman, Frank noticed that there appeared to be no gun. No weapon was visible either in a scabbard or a holster. Stooping down to straighten out his victim, Frank discovered he was still alive. Blood was trickling out his mouth, nose and eyes. The man's gaze was deep with sorrow as he reached for air with his damaged lungs. The bullet wound was directly in the middle of his sternum.

Frank was an excellent shot, but he knew his second shot was all luck. Bad luck.

Trembling, with quiet breath, the fallen cowboy said, "Why?"

Frank's heart was beginning to cramp in his chest. He had reached the depths of the pit in his core before. Frank experienced a broken heart and the loss of a family member, but this was a deep bottomless sadness. A place he had been to only once, and he would have traded places with this man, for he now knew he shot Victor Danvil's hostage. An innocent person was about to die. The tears that had welled up in Frank's eyes pushed the last of the dust out.

Choking on his words, Frank mumbled, "I didn't mean to. I'm, so sorry." Frank cradled the dying man's head and held his hand.

The desperate stranger looked up and said, "Tell, I don't want to--"

Frank could see the life he held in his arms was drifting away. The eyes showed it all. This poor gentleman was slipping away deeper into nothingness, taking Frank's own soul with him.

CHAPTER 1

John Campbell just turned sixteen years old. He was a stout and hard working lad who woke up early every morning. Sure, everyone woke up early. When you worked on a ranch, you had to. But John didn't need much sleep, and he was up before the animals.

It was always dark when he readied the kitchen for his mother who wouldn't be up for another two hours to make breakfast. John not only got an early go of it, but he was a fast worker as well. He required few breaks as he moved through the day. He would have a normal man's full workday completed by noon, and he was only half done. His folks tried to tell him he didn't have to work so hard. But John knew he did.

John's half brother, Jim, was different. He was more adventurous and followed a slightly different path in life. Jim was more like his father, but not as evil. His dad had left the scene before he was born to fight in the war and never returned. The man's whereabouts were never discovered, and Jim's mother and step dad seemed happy that Jim had no desire to find his father. That didn't keep their son out of trouble. It wasn't that Jim was a bad fellow. He just ran with a trouble-seeking group of young men.

Jim was friendly with a clan of cowboys that promised him excitement by way of illegal activities, and the initiation to enter the gang was to steal a horse. He was not wise in the ways of horse stealing. Jim fumbled up the robbery and got in a tiff, while in the act, with a local cowhand who helped run a dude ranch. Why he chose a horse that lived so close to home is anyone's guess. It was probably due to his inexperience and laziness. In the ruckus of stealing the horse, he got into a fight with Hank Zimmermann, and they fell into a horse pen. Hank received a kick to the head from a frightened mare, and he died three weeks later in his bed.

If Jim had had the wherewithal to stop stealing the horse and run for the town's doctor, he would have just been looking at a fine and some jail time. He was sentenced to hang for Hank's death. After the trial,

Jim's mother blamed herself and did everything in her power to keep the household together for her youngest. If she could just keep her John on the right track, life could go on.

The sun had another hour left in the sky, and a storm loomed off to the west when John swung by Cindy's place of business.

Cindy ran a sundry store and was a friend of the family. She had offered to make some meals for Jim while he waited in the town's jail. Cindy had shoulder-length brown hair. She was well known for her strong tall figure, but it was still feminine. She was a well-liked girl who had come out west with her parents to start life anew and open a general store. By the time she was twenty-one, the business had done so well that her parents continued westward to California to open a new store in a new town. Cindy, wishing to stay, took over running her parents' shop and ran it with aplomb.

Before John stepped into the doorway of the store, Cindy cried out, "Now, John, I certainly hope you're not going to track in some more of that mule crud again."

John stopped abruptly, put his hands on his hips and replied, "How in the world do you know I'm coming? Every dang time. And I know you don't have a window on that side of the building. I just can't figure it out."

Grinning on the left side of her face, and almost in a whisper, she said, "Why, John, any woman with any sense can just feel your manliness approaching before you even enter a room."

"Oh, stop teasing, Cindy. You know I don't believe that. It's some kind of sixth sense or something, I don't know."

"Well, anyway, how are your folks? Are they handling the ranch okay without Jim around?"

John removed his hat. "They both just feel miserable," he said looking down. "Mom cries all the time and Dad buries himself in the work." He tugged on the brim of his hat and held his breath a moment.

Cindy walked behind the counter. She pulled up a tray and started assembling the food she made earlier that morning.

"I'm sorry I'm not a better cook. I did put a piece of Mrs. Fairchild's chocolate cake here, so at least he can end the meal on a good note," said Cindy.

John, fighting back a tear, remembered how coming to the store used to be the highlight of his day. Flirting with an attractive girl like Cindy would make any teenage boy happy. The last few weeks had been different. He still looked forward to seeing her, but it was a different feeling. It allowed him to be optimistic about his future. Maybe if he finished school and worked hard, he could someday find a woman like Cindy and settle down, and be happy again.

John said, “Thank you, Cindy.”

Cindy replied, “Well, it’s my pleasure. Let me know if Jim thinks my stew is getting better. I’m trying to kick up the spice a notch.”

“I mean,” John said. “Well, thanks for what you’ve done for us during this time, but, thanks for being you, for being my friend.” John choked on his words. “I’ll always cherish the time you took out of your days to be with me. Just to talk and hang out. You always knew I was coming.” He smiled through a tear. “I don’t know how you knew, but you make me smile every time you holler out to me. I will find a girl just like you sometime and make her as happy to be alive as you do for me.”

Cindy pulled John close and gave him a hug. “You’re all grown up now, John, and your parents should be so proud of you, as am I.”

John picked up the tray of food. He exited the front door and headed to the jail to see his brother one last time.

Sitting at a desk in his dusty unkempt office, Sheriff Shayne jerked up in his seat when he heard some loud banging on the front door. With a scowl and a perturbed look on his face, he glanced up.

“Sheriff, are you in there?” John said through the door. “I have Jimmy’s dinner. Lunch and dinner for that matter.” He trailed off with some obscenities that Shayne couldn’t understand.

“I’m coming, stop the banging,” Sheriff Shayne snapped as he pulled his large frame up from his seat using his arms with his hands on the top of his desk. The sheriff walked to the door wearing two pearl-handled Colts, with the butts facing forward, holstered high on his waist.

Bearishly Shayne said, “What the hell you got there? Smells like ass, and I don’t mean donkey. Did you cook that?”

“Sheriff you’re always a joy. Can I see my big brother now or what?”

“John boy, don’t you get smart. You know I have to inspect the food.

Besides, you shouldn't take it so personally. It's true that I hate you, and your family for that matter. The deal, mind you, is that I hate everyone with equal amount."

Sheriff Shane Shayne dug his forefinger and middle finger of his right hand rigorously around the food on the plate. Smelling the substance that was stuck to his fingers, he let out a grunt of disapproval and a face full of disgust.

Shane snapped his head in short lurches from side to side, he said, "If we let your brother eat this, maybe we won't have to hang him in the morning. Better yet, if he does die of food poisoning, I won't have to sit here guarding him all night babysitting him."

John followed the sheriff to the door that led to the two cells of the jailhouse.

"Johnny, it's damn good to see you little brother," Jim said as he jumped up from his seat.

Jim was a lot like his brother in looks. Both were short and broad in stature. He was surprisingly clean-cut for a member of the local outlaw faction. Jim was to be hung first thing in the morning for stealing a horse and for the murder of Zimmermann, the ranch hand. The fact that he had unintentionally committed murder was inconsequential. Horse thievery was a hanging offense in and of itself.

"Cindy cooked up some grub for you, Jim, so don't expect too much, but it does come with good intentions."

John could feel that Jim was happy to see him. A sense of sadness did fill the cell, though. The sheriff opened the cell door, allowing John to step in and place the tray of food on the bed. John stepped out of the cell, and Shane locked the door directly.

Shane said, "Well, I tell you what, you sit right there by the door where I can see you. You can talk with your brother for a while. I'm going to have me a smoke out front."

"Okay, Sheriff." John took his seat by the door as the sheriff grabbed a cigar out of his desk and stepped out the front. John noticed that Shane's twitching head was growing more prevalent.

Jim watched the sheriff until he was clear. Jim stood up and looked at the front entrance through his cell bars. He said, his voice firm, "John, the keys to the cell are in the desk, on the right side, second drawer down, in the back, hurry."

"I don't know. Do we have enough time?"

Jim continued, "The Sheriff has the same routine every damn night. He leaves to take a smoke and flirts for twenty minutes with the gals walking to dinner. Do you understand I am going to die tomorrow?"

John didn't say anything.

"Do you want to spend the rest of your life with the thought that you could have saved me? I'm your big brother. Do as I say, and do it now." As Jim spoke, John could sense the desperation that permeated from his voice and eyes.

John ran over to the desk and found the keys exactly where his brother had told him to look. On his way back to the cell he stumbled and fell down. With nervous energy he fumbled with the lock until Jim grabbed the keys and unlocked the cell himself. Once the door was open, Jim moved to the gun rack at the back of the office.

"Jim, I think I heard someone outside," John said. He was scared and wanted to cry. John hesitated with all his movements.

"Calm down, it's going to be okay. I promise you, I have a plan. The stable out back has six or so horses. Two of them are already saddled and ready to go at all times in case of an emergency." Jim continued to struggle with the gun rack while his brother watched out the front window.

"Jim, I, I don't see him no more," John said. His hands shook.

Ignoring his brother Jim blurted, "Shit, shit, shit." After much exertion on the gun rack, he unlocked the shotgun from its housing. "Finally."

"Grab the shotgun shells from the desk. They should be in there somewhere," Jim dictated to his younger brother. John was sweating and visibly troubled.

"I can't find them, Jim. I just can't!"

"Okay, forget them. Let's go out the back. Now!"

Jim tossed the keys back to his brother and followed him toward the back door in a mad dash to escape. John hastily unlocked the door. They started to run to the horse corral. Soon after their escape they heard a voice.

"Yo, boys!" The sound boomed off the surrounding buildings.

Stopping abruptly caused Jim to slide in the dirt on the soles of his boots. He staggered, but stayed upright. John stumbled and pulled himself straight with his hands in the air.

Time seemed to slow down for John as the two young men got their bearings. John's lower lip began to quiver. He had his back to the man with the powerful voice. He stared straight ahead. He saw his shadow on the side of an old wooden wheel barrel. It was at that point that he recognized the man's voice.

As John was looking at his shadow, something overcame him. Death was imminent, and he could feel it as he slowly turned with every sense on high alert. His motion was surely quick, but his time lapse was such that he could see the trees just a few feet away with leaves fluttering in slow motion, and birds that flew about as if they were hovering in place.

As his view continued to turn toward his adversary, he heard a female gasp that was then abruptly stifled. He came to a head staring down evil, and it had guns.

They both faced Sheriff Shane Shayne who stood wide-legged with an unlit cigar hanging from a smarmy grin, both guns drawn, one pointed at each brother.

John thought to himself, *Shane knew?*

"I'm sorry, John," Jim whispered.

John cried, "What?"

Without any reservation, fury was unleashed as each pistol blasted fire, one after the other. Jim was only conscious long enough to know that his brother would die, too. The first shot hit Jim square in the heart. He died instantly, but the sheriff's shots were too quick, and he was hit two more times before he impacted the ground. He fell straight down with his knees buckling under him.

The second gun rang true as well, but it allowed the poor younger brother time to know what was happening before he fell. Disbelief and a cry for help overcame his eyes. But there would be no one to heed his desperate plea.

Shane grinned and chuckled. There was no hesitation, doubt, or wavering in the act. Another and another followed each explosion, even after both young men were bleeding into the dirt.

The murderer, Shane Shayne, sauntered over to the two dead brothers with a smile that seemed to intensify with each step. His head no longer twitched. Shane leaned over, pulled a bone-handled knife from his boot and tossed it to the earth next to John's corpse.

Jacob Sanders stepped into Cindy's store through the back door exactly as the front door had slammed shut. With a heartfelt smile for the love of his life and a childlike wave hello, he stepped into the rear of the store. When he walked by the aft counter, his arm clumsily bumped into a stack of candy bars that went spilling across the countertop. As he reached out to prevent the chocolate from falling, he kicked over a pile of magazines that were neatly stacked on a chair, causing a dozen to go sliding across the floor to Cindy's feet.

Embarrassed, Jacob replied, "Sorry, Honey."

"Darling, you never have to be sorry with me, you know that," Cindy said with true affection.

"Was that John who just left? I really wanted to say hello to him today. Tomorrow is going to be a horrible day."

"Yes, you just missed him, but if you hurry you might be able to catch him," said Cindy.

Jacob carefully stepped over the magazines scattered about the floor and opened the front door. Looking up the boardwalk he said, "Darn, I missed him. He has other things on his mind. You know I have to go over and shoe one of Shane Shayne's horses today. I could probably catch John on his way home." With a smart aleck tone he continued, *"Shane Shayne,* what an evil man with a dopey name."

Laughing, Cindy joined in and said, "He has the face of a bison's rear quarters and the breath of the same."

"I don't like violence, Cindy, but someone, someday, is going to have the courage to take that man out of this life and in the process save others. I know he kills without hesitation, and we need to get together as a town and do something before someone else gets killed," Jacob said, redness flushed his cheeks.

"Darling, please don't get so upset. Life is not long, and it's not worth the precious time we have to waste it getting so angry."

"Okay, but I was hired to do a job for the town today, and that's to shoe the posse's horses. I'm going to do that now. Do you want to walk over? It's almost lunchtime, and you could keep me company while I work." Smiling ear to ear, he continued, "I only have one shoe to work, and they have all the supplies I need so I can do the job on the spot." With a wink he added, "You know I love showing off my best girl around town."

Sternly Cindy replied, "Your best girl? I think, Mr. Sanders, you meant to say your only girl."

"Isn't that what I said?"

"No."

"Well, I'm pretty sure I said 'only', but if I didn't, I'm certain that's what I meant."

Jacob reached out and pulled his girlfriend into a hug. He said, "Now, how about a kiss, Sweetness?"

"Well Mr. Sanders, if you say so." She kissed Jacob with hesitated passion and then pushed him back. "We better get moving. I know you all too well. Once we get going somewhere, there's no turning around and no detours."

Cindy placed a closed sign on the front window and locked the door. They proceeded to the stable where the horses used by the sheriff and subsequent posses were kept. As the two walked they spoke quietly and flirtingly to each other, mostly unaware of any other pedestrians.

As they rounded the boarding house situated next to the sheriff's office, they sauntered between the two structures to the back. Behind the jail was an open courtyard with a few trees around the perimeter and an old wheel barrel that looked unused in over a year. On the backside of the courtyard was the stable that could house about a dozen horses along with their saddles and bridles. In front of the pen of horses was a small area that allowed enough room to saddle or shoe a horse. Between the corral and the courtyard there stood an old oak tree and some bushes.

Cindy said, "I love that old tree. I remember when I used to come here when your Dad was the sheriff, and we used to play in this very spot. I miss your father."

"Me, too. Someday I'll find out what happened to him. I sometimes dream about that day when he went out with that posse. I somehow think that if I stay in this town and keep coming back here to this stable, maybe something will come to me. Maybe an answer will show itself."

Cindy threw up her hand and said, "Wait. Quiet, something isn't right." Pausing for a moment and grasping Jacob's hand, she pulled him to a squat. "Do you hear anything?"

"No, I don't," Jacob said while looking around intently.

Everyone in town learned to trust Cindy and her instincts. The last few years had shown that when Cindy had a feeling, it was best to believe her.

Jacob was not a gunfighter, and he didn't carry a weapon at Cindy's request. Jacob whispered, "I should be carrying, shouldn't I?"

Cindy swallowed hard and said quietly, "Yes, this time, yes."

As they looked over the bushes into the jailhouse courtyard, they saw Shane standing by the back of the jail. He had two weapons drawn and a cigar hanging low from the corner of his mouth.

"What the?" Jacob said just as John and Jim came bolting out the back door of the Jailhouse.

"Yo, boys!" Shane hollered.

The brothers stopped running immediately, they almost lost their footing. Jim dropped his shotgun, and John was obviously unarmed.

Cindy knew what was about to happen a moment before Shane pulled the trigger on his left-hand Colt.

Everything moved too fast for the two brothers. Cindy went to cry out just as Jacob's protective instinct took over, and he grabbed her by the arm to drag her away from the shooting. They were downwind from the violence, and a round came within a few feet of them. Jacob tugged on her arm, and they tried to stay low. The ricochet sound of gunfire filled their ears from every side.

Cindy pulled up on her arm, causing Jacob's grip to fail. They both stood behind the oak tree to look on at their fallen friends. Cindy's mind was fully aware of what had happened. She couldn't comprehend as to why.

Shane arrogantly slipped his left pistol into its housing and meandered over to John. He seemed to notice John had no gun on his person. He slyly bent over and with his free hand pulled a knife from his own boot. He placed the knife by John's now deceased body. Shane paused a moment as he watched the dirt soak up his victims' blood.

Still holding his pistol in his right hand, Shane then went to remove the hat from his head with his left. There was no sound as he removed his cover and wiped the sweat from his forehead with the sleeve of his forearm.

A shot sprang out from the deathly silent scene. A quick sharp discharge broke into the courtyard with as much fervor as the previous slaughter. Shane hollered out. Blood shot from his hand. The squirt sprayed with a rate that matched his heartbeat.

The bullet had entered between the knuckles of the forefinger and middle finger of Shane's right hand. The lead drilled a path severing tendons, veins, arteries, and nerves all along the way. The ball finally came to rest in the bones of his wrist. It shattered and destroyed all the tissue in its wake.

White-faced and with a look of confusion, Shane stood shaky-kneed staring at his hand as the blood continued to flow. The dark red thick fluid moved down his fingers onto his gun. It streamed over the barrel uninterrupted and overran the end of his pistol to his feet.

Jacob went to grab Cindy to run. As he turned and looked, he bumped into the tree. His jaw dropped. Cindy stood with an outstretched arm. She held a single shot Marlin Derringer, and it was smoking from the barrel.

The murderer looked up and glared at Cindy who was standing by the oak tree with a weapon in her hand. Shane stepped forward towards her. Walking briskly, he leveled his pistol in Cindy's direction. With total and utter hatred pasted across his mug, Shane attempted to kill the woman who had shot him, and who was a witness to his atrocity. But his hand failed him. Shane couldn't pull back the hammer. Not only was he unable to fire the gun, he couldn't even release it from his grip. Shane yelled in disgust as he reached for his second gun with his good hand. At that instant Jacob swung in and escorted Cindy off at a flat-out run.

As Jacob and Cindy turned the corner between the two buildings where they passed earlier, a crowd started to work its way into the courtyard on the other side of the jail.

A professionally dressed, and visibly agitated man barked, "Sheriff! What the hell is going on?"

Prying his gun from his bloody hand, Shane replied scornfully, "Mayor." He grimaced from the pain. "They were trying to escape."

"Are you hurt? Do you need a doctor?" asked the mayor as more people swarmed into the courtyard.

"Can't get much by you, can I?" Shane answered with contempt.

Shane wrapped his wound with his tie. "Oh, and by the way, where the hell is Odekirk? I want to see him. I have a job for him," Shane uttered. He sneered, looking over his shoulder in the direction that Jacob and Cindy had escaped.

Staring down the street, Shane noticed that a scruffy looking man with a missing front tooth stepped into his field of vision.

"On time, as always, Odekirk. You'll earn your pay with this one," said Shane

"What's all the ruckus about?" Odekirk asked.

"Get your horse and your knife and your gun, and everything else you enjoy killing with," Shane said. He attempted to hold back the pain from his wound. "I have a killing for you to do."

"A job I can surely handle, Mr. Shayne, and with pleasure," Odekirk said.

Shane said, to his accomplice, “Cindy, and her boyfriend Jacob. Kill them. And do it, slow.”

Odekirk smiled.

CHAPTER 2

Cindy was trailing behind Jacob as she rounded the corner onto Main Street. At that moment, she caught a glimpse of a bright flash of light in the corner of her eye.

"Did you see that?" Cindy hollered.

"Hurry, Cindy," Jacob said. He reached for her hand.

Cindy looked back over her shoulder to see a luminous cloud coming into view from the west. A dramatic storm was brewing, and it was beginning to darken the sky. The storm's anvil hung high with a blackening horizon at its feet. It would be the perfect cap to an imperfect day. The massive squall line was bearing down on the town and was about to wash away all the blood that had been spilled.

Cindy could hear the treading of their footsteps as they darted past the many onlookers, most of whom were more interested in getting to the jail to see what the ruckus was about than to even notice the two runners. Cindy looked at the faces as she ran past, and she knew that they would never be able to see these people again.

"Do you know what we have to do?" Jacob said with heavy breath.

"Yes, I do." Cindy choked up on her words.

The pace slowed as they approached Cindy's store. The run seemed long, especially for such a small town. Jacob led the way, and with little delay he opened the front door and closed it immediately after Cindy had entered. They proceeded to get busy gathering goods and supplies. They moved about the store simultaneously as if they had a plan and were thinking as one.

"We'll gather only the necessary items, then we'll split up," Jacob dictated.

"Understood," Cindy answered laconically.

"Yeah!" Jacob said excitedly to himself. There was a hint of a devilish grin as he eyed the rifle he had removed from the enclosed case that sat behind the counter. "We might need this carbine if they catch up with us. We can both head to the house and then I'll run over to the stable and saddle up our horses. You go home to gather some clothes and pictures and what not."

Rain started to fall, and it came down in heavy sheets. Jacob turned as a horse blazed by the front window. It was gone as quickly as it had arrived. He thought aloud. "Why would anyone be out riding in this weather?"

Cindy moved about in a mad rush to garner up foodstuffs for the trek that lay ahead. She walked deliberately to the back room. Next to the wall, she pulled a wooden plank from the floor and removed a metal box.

Cindy announced, "I have the box of cash and the deed to the store."

"Great," Jacob replied. "Hopefully we can get our money that's in the bank when we get settled."

"What about the store?"

"We can get a lawyer, someone we trust, to do the sale of the store. That is, when the time is right. It's more important for us to get out of town before Shane can get to us."

"Toss me that gunny sack," said Cindy. Jacob heaved Cindy a sack. Cindy moved all the supplies she had gathered into it. When she was done, she noticed the ceiling was starting to leak. She grabbed two buckets along with a pot and strategically placed them so that they would catch the water leaking through the roof. Jacob watched, but didn't say anything. He looked as if he had fallen in love with her all over again as he relented to a small smile.

"Okay, ready?" Jacob said as he moved to the door and peeked outside. "I want to make sure we have a clear path farther up the street." He loaded his rifle with four rounds and shoved a handful of shells into his pocket.

"Ready," Cindy answered.

Jacob grabbed the sack from her and threw it over his left shoulder with the carbine in his right. They gave each other a quick kiss and sprinted out the door up the street. The two runners were instantly wet. Darkness was slowly slipping onto the small community.

Cindy had been renting a two-bedroom house on the edge of town. It was cattycorner across the street from the stable that housed Jacob's horses. As the two structures came into view, they separated.

"I'll be there as quickly as I can. Wait for me inside," Jacob yelled as he veered right, running across the road to the livery stable.

Cindy was only a short distance from the front of her house when the clouds cracked intensely, jolting her senses. A torrent of rain bombarded her as she sprang up her front steps. She had her key in hand and opened the door with a swift and smooth motion. She was halfway into the room when she heard the door close behind her. She stopped. With quiet breath she stood. She made no movement except for a silent shiver as water crept down her skin. She could hear the rain slamming against the windows and an explosion of thunder from the storm that loomed over the town.

Her dress, normally bell-shaped, was heavy with water, and it drug along the ground under her feet. She felt, as she moved in the wet and heavy garment, that it restricted her movements.

She listened carefully but all she could detect was silence. She realized she had made a grave error. She was vulnerable in the middle of a dark room. The only light she could see emitted into the living area from the windows. The solitary illuminated spot was a picture above the fireplace of her with her parents and little brother. She looked away so that thoughts of her family wouldn't cloud her mind.

In the torturing silence of her home she knew she wasn't alone. There was a disturbance, but she couldn't pinpoint its source. It left a revolting image stamped on her psyche. Cindy's instincts told her it was close. She then concentrated on her senses one by one.

She looked for any movement in the dark. *Maybe*, she thought, *I can catch a shadow or something out of place*. Lightning lit the sky and beamed into the room. Every piece of furniture, every chair, table and even the paintings on the wall looked like a person. Her mental image showed her that one man lurked in the dark. Somehow, she remained calm.

She concentrated on her hearing. She held her breath as she listened for any snippet of sound she could wrap her ears around. Nothing.

She focused on scent. She could smell the stew she cooked earlier in the day, as well as her candle. Something was off, though, and it wasn't the change in weather. Cindy knew that smell and liked it. This odor made her uncomfortable. This was a stench that caused the hair on the back of her neck to stand up and the adrenaline to move through her body.

She targeted the kitchen with her senses and could feel the danger that prowled in her home. She knew there was only one hiding in the shadows, but she also knew he was vicious.

Jacob was worried. It was dark as he approached the stable. His initial concern was to get out of town before the storm hit. With the horses at a full gallop, he planned to leave without ever being seen. During such time, he hoped, everyone would have taken cover of the storm or would be distracted by the commotion that had occurred behind the jail.

Jacob wanted to hole up in an adobe block house that had been abandoned. Only a few people knew about it. It was located about a half mile up the road, then farther along on a lesser-known trail. He was optimistic that the storm would cover their tracks, possibly even slow down the sheriff and his posse.

Jacob's intent was to stay in front of Shane Shayne and his henchmen. The sheriff was a heinous man, and Jacob hated him. Shane had the city council and mayor under his thumb. He was able to control the townspeople with fear. He had connections with nefarious friends who used malicious and destructive tactics. It was rumored that at his ranch lurked some revolting fiends whom nobody had seen. Jacob had no desire to be introduced.

On most days Jacob was clumsy, and he knew he was. But now he was steady, and he moved as if Cindy's life was at stake.

"Mr. Masters, Mr. Masters, are you here?" Jacob bellowed, then whispering to himself, "Of course you're here. You never leave this place." He continued his search. "Mr. Masters, it's me, Jacob. I need my horses please."

"I'm coming. Hold your horses," Masters said with a laugh, he spoke with a coarse, but jovial voice. "Oh, I never get tired of that one, oh my. I do find myself amusing, don't I?"

Joe Masters was a waif of a man, but he wasn't one to push around. He was short and had a bit of a hang to his shoulders, and he could make himself chuckle. "What is it, lad? Going for a little night ride with your sweetie? Oh goodness, how do I do it?" Joe grinned with self-adulation. He moved slowly as he exited his office inside the stable. He walked using small steps.

Jacob was saddling his horses, and he worked feverishly.

"Well, son, I'm not one to pry, but what in tarnation are you up to in the middle of this storm? We got ourselves a squall moving through. I knew all along because of my damn knee, and my elbow, hell, all my joints hurt. Oh, dad-blast it, they always hurt, rain or shine, who am I kidding? You know what I mean? I never was the type--" Joe trailed off with his monologue, knowing his words fell on deaf ears.

"Joe, here's what I owe you," Jacob said while handing him money. Two horses were saddled and the third was ready for carrying supplies and such.

Jacob said, "Now if anyone asks, Joe, you know what to say."

"I don't know where you are, and I hadn't seen you. Right?" Joe said.

Jacob added, "That ought to do it. You could add that--"

Joe interrupted, "Now don't go and beat a dead horse about it. A dead horse. I'm funny, yes sir, I am." Joe was smiling as he walked back to his office.

"Alright, Joe. I don't know of too many people who know where I keep my horses anyway. You take care," Jacob said.

Jacob patted his horse on the neck and whispered, "That's one good thing about living in this piss-hole town. No one gives a damn what you do."

Jacob ushered the way with a tug on the reins of his lead horse. The remaining two followed close behind tied in trail. He stepped into a wall of water and the drops made a heavy thumping on the brim of his hat. A flash of lightning spooked his horses.

"Whoa! It's okay," Jacob said with a calming tone and a reaffirming hand on the neck. "There's nothing to be afraid of. I don't want to be out here anymore than you do. This will pass soon. It always does."

Picking up his pace he ran the horses into a small barn in the back of Cindy's home. After making some room in the barn for a temporary sanctuary, Jacob closed the barn door and looked over to the house. He noticed a hole in the corner of a window with shattered glass on the flowers below in the back of Cindy's home. Jacob gasped, "Oh no."

Cindy felt she was at a crossroads in her mind. She was debating whether to stay put or move. She thought that if she moved, she would make too much noise. She would have to do something eventually, it was too dangerous to stay in the house.

A bombardment of thunderous explosions shook the floorboards under her feet. She saw an image of a man in her mind. A rush of air whisked by her. She felt the movement with a flicker of her hair that hung in her face.

The air was being pushed violently, and Cindy visualized that someone was forcing himself in her direction. An image of her perpetrator's face became apparent to her.

Instinctively she ducked in a linear motion downward just as a fist flew over the top of her head. Always aware of her position, she maintained her balance as her aggressor lost his footing.

Cindy couldn't stop herself when she hollered out, "Odekirk!"

Odekirk fell flat on his face on the hard oak floor. Rolling forward toward the front door, he whacked his head on the doorknob.

Cindy was now at the top of her game, and with a smirk she moved with purpose.

Odekirk scowled and growled and rubbed his forehead. His head snapped left and right as he scoured the room for his prey.

Desperation permeated from his pores as Odekirk reached for his gun. His hand stopped abruptly and he slid his pistol back into his holster. He slowly pulled a knife from a sheath that hung from his belt.

Pitch-blackness enveloped the entire room as if everything had been swallowed up by the night sky. Odekirk reached out in front of his face with his free hand into the darkness of the room. His hand circled searching for where his quarry may have hid. He found some cloth lying on the floorboards and he grasped it tightly. He pulled the clothes with all his strength and flung his entire body forward with his knife, swinging. He flew through the middle of the room.

Odekirk was right, it was Cindy's dress, but Cindy wasn't in it. His homicidal rage pushed him too far, and he had entered into the arena of self-destruction. As he flailed headfirst through the empty space of Cindy's living room, he impacted a writing desk with his chin. When he settled to the floor, his body fell onto his knife. It dove into his guts. He squeezed Cindy's dress as he gnashed his teeth. His eyes rolled into the back of his head. As he sat with his back to the wall and a six-inch blade sunk into his intestines, blood began to pool up in his crotch. He sniveled slightly. Cindy heard him.

Holding the blade with both hands, Odekirk slowly pulled the weapon from his body. His eyes fluttered and almost shut, permanently. He began to apply firm pressure to his gaping wound with the empty dress he still held tight in his hand. Stomach acid streamed into his mouth and leaked out the corners.

Cindy was lying on the floor in the kitchen listening to Odekirk. After shedding her dress, she had dashed to the back door, but in the darkness she didn't see the table that had been moved to block the rear exit. She impacted the wood solidly just below her waist with all the force she was using to flee her opposer. She lay on the floor with legs aching. She heard another groan come from the front room. An intense heat rushed to the back of her neck when she came to the realization that she ran into a table that she knew was already there.

Cindy sat up and paused. "I have got to get moving," she whispered to herself. "Think, damn you. Trust your instincts."

With the back door blocked, she committed herself to escaping out the front door. She thought, *Where is Jacob?*

Cindy calmed her nerves and subdued the pain in her legs with her will. As the pain slowly evaporated, so did her anguish, and she was quickly up on her feet in one fluid motion.

Standing in the middle of the kitchen, she could see a sliver of light shining through the front door window. In her undergarments, Cindy dominated her surroundings. Her muscles twitched showing a lean and muscular body in the narrow beam of light that reflected off her still and wet figure.

Strong willed and unwavering, she stood and studied her primary exit: the front door. Cautiously she stepped forward. She could see that there were only a few quick steps to the entryway. The living room was all that separated the kitchen from her freedom. The thunder was sounding from the east as the storm was moving away.

Cindy closed her eyes. She could see Jacob. In a split-second decision she rushed forward, and just as she was passing through the entryway to the living room, her antagonist lurched from around the corner. One hand was holding his stomach and the other hand swung around with the gun pointing at Cindy's face.

She moved decisively to the side just as the gun went off beside her head. The barrel was too close to her right ear. She felt the burning discharge from the blast and a deafening bang that slammed on her eardrum and caused it to rupture. The pain was excruciating, and her hair caught fire.

Desperately she grabbed a handful of her hair with her right hand to quash the flame before it spread out of control. With her left hand she took hold of the barrel of the gun that was still in Odekirk's hand. Just as she grasped the pistol, it burst once more with a bullet exiting out the kitchen window. Even though it was hot to the touch, she was able to hold on and pull down, ramming her knee into the brute's stab wound. Odekirk cried out in agonizing pain. He yanked back the gun and fell into the kitchen on one knee.

Jacob screamed with torment from outside, "Cindy!" The agonizing voice of her boyfriend sent a chill through her body.

Cindy saw her opportunity, and she took it. She darted towards the front door. As she opened it and exited the front of her house, she knew she was being pursued.

"Cindy!" Jacob cried out again as he was running around the corner from the side of the building at full bore with rifle in hand.

Jacob's feet splashed through the small flood that flowed through the yard as he held his rifle. In a smooth and flowing motion with one hand, he cocked the rifle with the lever-action.

A bullet in the chamber and ready for use, he tossed the weapon, butt end first, to Cindy who was on the porch. Catching the gun with both hands, she swiftly turned to her attacker and unloaded a round into the house. With determination, she maintained her attack. In quick succession she worked the lever action of her rifle, unloading all four rounds into the dark house.

Moonlight was now breaking through the cloud cover and Cindy noticed the motion of a man standing in the darkness with pistol in hand.

Rotating the gun around and holding the piece by the barrel, she stepped back inside. She swung the hard wooden end in an upward motion like a battle-axe. She smacked Odekirk solidly under his jaw. His head snapped back, his muscles relaxed, and he dropped unbending to the ground. As his two hundred-pound body fell, his weight caused a leg to break with a loud snap.

Cindy stared into Odekirk's vacant face and said, "You were dead the minute you stepped into my house."

Jacob said, "Cindy?"

She turned, let go of the rifle and ran to him.

Rushing into each other's arms, Jacob noticed blood coming from her ear. "Are you okay?" he asked. His hands held her wet face.

"I think so." She touched her neck and wiped some blood and looked at her fingers. "He blew out my eardrum," she replied.

"I'll never leave you alone like that again. I promise," he said as he grabbed and pulled her close to his chest.

"He underestimated me." She sighed.

"He won't be doing that again anytime soon, or ever, for that matter. And where in the world did you learn to take care of yourself like that?"

Cindy looked into his face and said, "Your father taught me."

"I wonder why I didn't learn anything."

With a grin, and holding her ear, she said, "You, my dear, were too busy falling in love with me."

Jacob gripped her arms tightly and kissed her.

CHAPTER 3

Frank Savage rode his horse aside his friend and colleague, Derek Wright. They had been riding for three hours when they came across the small town of Sabotage. The sun set atop a cloudless blue sky, and it was a calm crisp spring day. They were beginning to see the outskirts of their destination. Frank watched the wisps of clouds as they rolled over the tops of the roofs of the dirty brown structures of Sabotage. It wasn't an official city, not anymore. It was an abandoned village. It had grimy dilapidated wooden structures that might have one day grown into a town if the railroad had not sidestepped around it.

Working their way slowly into the deserted hamlet, they kept their horses abreast of each other. The two cowboys had always worked well together. Frank, at one time, was a counterpart of Derek's.

Frank was trying to move away from his violent past. In his attempt to start a normal quiet life, he bought a store with a nice elderly couple in North Fork. After the store was up and running, he received a telegram from his old boss. It informed him that his friend and old partner, Derek, was beginning a new mission, and Savage was needed. Derek's new assignment required Frank's presence to establish a foothold on the case.

There were no 'ifs, ands, or buts' about it; Frank was going to help. He didn't really enjoy spy work, but he was successful at it. But, when you work for the government, you understand that they may make leaving a bit of a challenge. And Frank was quitting the best way he knew how. Besides, if his friend had asked for his help as a favor, he would have done it without question.

Frank and Derek had known each other about a decade. They met while fighting for the Union with the 7th Kansas Cavalry Regiment. They rode alongside the likes of Bill Cody. Having saved each other's lives multiple times, they trusted each other implicitly.

Frank's new orders were to introduce Derek to his first contact. Then he would be left alone to retire.

"Thanks again, Frank. You know, you could have passed the secret knock and passwords to me, and I would have been fine," Derek opined.

"I think my presence will guarantee a safe passage, and you won't be mistakenly shot," Frank responded with a roguish smile.

"And to that, I am truly grateful." Derek tipped his hat. "We'll continue to take it slow," Frank interjected. Derek nodded his concurrence, and he pointed with his eyes to the first building on the right. An odd gangly looking man stood from the porch of the first house and walked toward the two men who were approaching his fort on horseback.

Frank removed his hat. "I need them to recognize me. I don't want us to get shot before you even get started. I know this guy. He tends to take his job a little too seriously."

They continued forward into the abandoned town as the man walked down their right side with rifle in hand. He looked at them with a suspicious gaze. He was in a position to turn and fire. Frank rode with one hand on the butt of his rifle that was still in its scabbard, and Derek had his gun hand resting on his pistol.

Derek said, "I don't like this guy. You are sure we're in the right place, right?"

"Yep."

"Frank, I told you I should have brought you a pistol," Derek said with concern.

"I won't need it. It's okay. He just doesn't recognize you," Frank replied calmly. "This is how you'll always approach the town. Even when this case is concluded, you'll be back here again." Then whispering to himself, he added, "Whether you want to or not."

Gradually the man walked past, but Derek kept his eyes and body turned to the stranger as they progressed forward.

"We're in the clear. He's the watch, and he knows who I am," Frank told his friend. "This is the place."

They dismounted in front of a large, square, three-story structure and tied their horses to the hitching post out front. Frank collected his rifle, walked to the front door and opened it with Derek following closely behind. Inside was a foyer with another door that appeared locked. Frank had been here before.

The flaking wood on the door and smell of mold in the entranceway brought back many memories for Frank, some not so good, but that was the business he'd been in. He never pursued the job in the first place. He was recruited when he left the service.

Frank Savage was well respected for the work he did while in the military. Most of his undercover work had been for the Union during the war. His decision-making was beyond reproach. When it came to life and death, he always seemed to be the one left standing. Oftentimes, he stood over more than one corpse.

Frank never considered himself to be the best shot or the best fighter. He just seemed to always find a way to get the job done. Sometimes it wasn't pretty, but successful nonetheless. Savage was hired for his proficiency.

"This is more than your first contact, Derek," Frank said with all seriousness. "This is the safe area you've heard about, but never knew where it was. It seems you've been promoted. Congratulations. I guess."

Frank faced the inner door. He whispered to Derek, "The secret knock is--" He knocked with two quick knocks. He paused for a moment, and then rapped three more times in succession.

Frank whispered again, "The password is--" Then speaking into the door, he said, "The day is torrid."

"I concur. Is your horse famished?" a voice replied from the other side of the door.

"I have no horse. I'm Savage, and I have a friend who needs water," Frank said.

"He may enter with caution." The person behind the door unlocked the door, but it remained closed.

Frank turned to Derek and said, "Okay, buddy, this is where I leave you. I kinda wish I could stay on this with you, but I have my own work to do. They're good guys, you'll be fine."

"Thanks, Frank. We'll see you later and have a beer sometime when I join you in retirement."

"Sounds good, Derek," Frank replied solemnly.

Derek paused, then said, "Frank." He wasn't quite sure what to say. "Take care of yourself."

"You too."

The two friends shook hands. Derek entered the establishment, and Frank rode off out of town at a gallop. As he rode, Frank felt a feeling of uneasiness creep through his bones. He had a sensation that he would never be able to walk away. Not with so much unfinished business to take care of. Too many evil men continued to walk the earth.

Frank was getting close to the train depot. He made it just in the nick of time to catch a ride home. He was anxious to be back in his own bed and excited, too. It was only a half day's train ride back to North Fork.

After returning the horse he rented, he walked to the train station. Frank carried his rifle, and his bedroll slung over his shoulder. He strolled over to the ticket counter and bought passage back to North Fork.

Frank was about to board the train when he recognized an old friend, Sam, the train's engineer. He had gotten to know Sam over the last six months while going back and forth between North Fork and Lasso City.

"Hello, Sam!" Frank hollered.

The engineer was sheepishly milling about by the locomotive section. Sam Buckshot was a stocky man in greasy overalls with a beard. He was a good friend, and Frank enjoyed talking to him.

"What's up with you, Frank?" Sam had an infectious smile.

"I was just in the area for business, and I'm going back home today," Frank answered.

"How is the store doing?" Sam asked.

"Everything is flying off the shelves. The town is starting to grow now. In the six months I've been there, it's made some considerable progress. By the way, how is 'the situation'?"

Sam frowned. "Well, things got out of hand. Let's just say I barely made it out alive."

Frank heard the conductor yell, "All aboard," and noticed most of the passengers were saying their last goodbyes before boarding the train.

"Well, Sam, you might want to start dating single women from now on," Frank said with a warm and crooked smile.

"I know, but--"

"You know what?" Frank interrupted. "Actually, you might be addicted to the drama."

"What do you mean by that?" asked Sam.

"I think, now don't take it personal but, you're addicted to the rush of the affair. I'd be willing to bet you get a high out of seducing married women and you enjoy the danger of the chase. Both chases."

"Both? What do you mean both?" Sam asked with concern.

"Chase Number One and Chase Number Two. You see, Chase Number One is you chasing the gal."

"Okay, I understand that one." Sam rubbed his chin.

"And Chase Number Two is her husband chasing you with a sawed off shotgun." Frank laughed and added a friendly but firm punch to Sam's arm. "I'll see you around, Sam. You be careful now."

Sam walked off in thought. Stroking his bearded chin and with a bit of a sulk Sam said, "See you, Frank." He mumbled to himself, "Now, why in the world would I want to be chased with a sawed off shotgun?"

Frank worked his way to the passenger car. He was one of the last people to board. As he progressed through the car looking for his seat, he noticed a heavier-set woman take a seat near him. *I hope I don't have to sit next to her. She takes up too much space. I won't be able to move my arms.*

A little girl holding onto her mother's hand said, "Mommy?"

"Yes, dear?" her mother responded.

Pointing at the portly woman, the girl said, "That lady ate too many potatoes, didn't she?"

Frank smiled, but was also embarrassed for the rotund looking woman.

Working his way towards the front of the passenger-car, he noticed his empty seat, and more importantly, he noticed that it was positioned across from a very lovely and busty girl. Next to her was a small boy of maybe ten years old, and next to Frank's seat was a man.

Frank put his belongings into the overhead bin and said quietly, "Drat, married."

She had dark brown eyes and soft brunette hair with a hint of blonde, but Frank wondered why all women kept their hair up when it was much sexier to leave it down.

"Hello, ma'am," Frank said, tipping his hat to the pretty girl. He noticed she had some nice cleavage. He whispered, "Ouch."

"Hello," she responded with a smile.

The gentleman sitting next to Frank's seat stated matter-of-factly, "Kelly, that's that man from the store in North Fork."

Frank extended his hand to everyone and introduced himself, then took his seat in front of the attractive Kelly.

Catching a peek at Kelly's bosom, slightly aroused, Frank thought, *ten months isn't so long to be without. It clears the palate, right?*

In an attempt to maintain his situational awareness, in case violence was to break out on the train, Frank continued to keep his eye on the entire car. As the train pulled from the station, he introduced himself to some of the passengers across the aisle. He always made friends wherever he went. On more than one occasion he needed one, especially in his line of work, that is, his previous line of work.

"Did you say your name was Savage?" asked Troy, the man who accompanied this bodacious work of art.

"Yes, I did," said Frank.

"Weren't you the bounty hunter who caught that man who murdered twenty or so men? I can't think of his name," said Troy.

"Victor Danvil was his name," Frank answered, "and I wasn't a bounty hunter. I was working for the government when I was hunting down Danvil."

"Yeah, that's it. Didn't you mistakenly kill his hostage?" Catching himself he said, "Oh, I'm sorry. Honestly, I'm not trying to say you were at fault."

"It's alright," Frank said. He paused, and then continued, "I'm learning to live with my mistakes. I don't do that kind of work anymore. I'm in sales, trying to expand my business. That's why I'm here. And how about you folks?" Frank changed the subject hoping they wouldn't ask any more questions. He fidgeted with his hat and caught a glimpse of Kelly's eyes just as she looked away from him.

"Well, first off, let me say my son Jeffery here thinks quite highly of you," Troy added.

"Is that so?" Frank said.

"Yes, sir. I know all about the many different criminals you've apprehended," Jeffery said. "You have a pretty good record."

Frank smiled. "Thanks, Jeffery, that means a lot to me," Frank continued speaking to the group. "I unfortunately had to kill quite a few as well. You mentioned that hostage. Well, the problem with law enforcement is that one mistake can ruin not only just your life, but many others as well. That man who was Danvil's hostage had a wife and children, and I took him away from them."

Kelly said, "But Danvil was an evil man and had to be stopped."

"Some people believe that if you have to kill a man, then you have failed. I guess that makes me a failure. It seems it's something I'm good at," Frank admitted with a crack in his voice. "So, where are you all headed?"

"We don't live in North Fork," said Troy. "We take the train to North Fork, and then it's about a three hour ride out to our ranch."

Frank nodded with a grim grin.

"But my sister here lives in town," Troy added excitedly, "and she's single."

Frank and Kelly looked at each other and smiled, Kelly's face flushed.

Frank opened his store six months earlier with a nice local couple who also owned a hotel in town. They had always wanted to expand their business. When Frank invited them to join him in opening a store, they said yes.

The town already had a general store, but the surge in growth demanded another. Frank's plan was that at a certain point, after he had saved enough money, he was going to buy the other half of the business from his partners. He enjoyed working and was able to make a little extra money by managing the commerce and running the books.

It was early on a Saturday morning, and Frank had only been open for a few minutes when his first customer of the day came in, or so he thought. His name was Toby Gibson, and he was the Deputy Sheriff.

"Frank, I am so sorry, but the Sheriff sent me over and he needs your assistance," said Toby.

Toby Gibson was a young up-and-comer in the world of law enforcement. He had a lot to learn, but was a quick study, and was well liked.

"What seems to be the problem?" Frank asked.

At that moment, Cassandra Jones, a pretty girl with short blonde hair in her late teens, came in the front door. She threw her arms up and blurted, "What the heck is going on down at the saloon, Toby?"

Toby shuffled in place. He said with urgency, "Well, that was why I came in here to talk to Frank. It seems a young punk and his buddy were on the outskirts of town getting drunk all night, and they decided to continue the party when the saloon opened up. Everything was fine until the two got into a fight, and the loser got himself all fired up. He's holding the saloon patrons as hostages. Or they're just too scared to move."

"Toby, I'm afraid I don't see what that has to do with me," Frank retorted.

"Yeah, what do you need Frank for?" Cassie asked.

Frank's look of confusion changed to that of understanding and he interjected, "I think I can answer that question for the deputy. You see, I've been known to help out the sheriff's office on occasion because the Sheriff likes how I do business."

Cassie wrinkled her brow.

Frank said, "If violence breaks out, I'm good at it, most of the time."

Cassie crossed her arms.

"I'm a people person."

Cassie said, "Yeah, I bet."

Toby still excited, said, "That's exactly it. The sheriff has already poked his head into the saloon and almost got it shot off by the damn idiot. But the sheriff believes the kid doesn't want to hurt anyone. He just needs a way out."

Frank replied, "Okay, let's head on down to the saloon, and you can brief me on the way. Cassie, do you mind watching the store for a bit?"

Cassie said, "No problem, but I think this isn't your job. You should start getting paid for these shenanigans."

"Good idea."

Cassie blurted, "And do you know if Nathan will be coming by anytime?" She turned a pinkish red.

"He does most days sooner or later. I appreciate your help."

The deputy and Frank Savage stepped out the door and headed up the roadway toward the saloon. Frank could see the sheriff and a few others step inside the hotel located across the street from the bar. One person of concern was Al Turner, who just happened to be on the city council. He was also an actor in the local plays that performed on the weekends.

Not too happy about seeing Al, Frank groaned, "Dang it. That narcissist thinks he knows everything about everything."

Toby chuckled.

"Brief me on the situation, Deputy. What's the scoop?"

"The kid really is only about sixteen or seventeen years old, tops. His buddy, who split quick and in a hurry when his partner pulled his gun, said they had been doing some odd jobs for the railroad. They had just completed a two-week job and they planned, I guess, to have a little fun and burn off some steam."

"Okay, I think I've got the gist of it."

The two walked to the hotel that sat across the street. Frank asked the deputy, "Who else is in the saloon?"

"I'm sorry, not real sure who else might be in there. Sheriff Clark will have to update you on the rest."

When they stepped into the hotel's front lobby, Brad, a slightly balding man with a nice face and a medium build hollered, "Mr. Frank, good to see you. Damn, you look good. You been getting some sun? Look at that full head of hair. I think I'm going to have to shave that in your sleep some night so you know how the rest of us feel." Everyone looked at Al Turner. He had the least amount of hair of anyone.

Brad, a friend of Frank's since he had moved to North Fork, was always smiling. He worked a lot of odd jobs, but mostly drove the stagecoach when people or goods needed to be moved to towns that didn't have the railroad. He was always on the move, and Frank trusted him.

Frank walked past Al Turner who acted like he had something he wanted to say. Frank smiled and extended his hand to his friend. "Bradley, what are you doing here? I thought you were running a stage to Laraby."

"Once I got there they told me to head straight back here to meet two coaches, six horses each, to make a pick up and head west. Some important shipment is to leave here in a couple weeks. I was actually hoping to ask you for some help with this one."

"Bradley, you know I don't carry a gun anymore," Frank said sternly.

"I know, but--"

Sheriff Clark interrupted, "Frank?"

"Oops, I'm sorry. Brad, this will have to wait," Frank said. "What's the job I'm being asked to do?"

"The deal is we have a drunken cowboy who, I feel, wants a way out. For some reason he doesn't want to talk to a sheriff. He claims his dad was hung by an unjust law enforcement officer," Sheriff Clark said.

"I see. And who else is in the saloon?"

"Jack the bartender, and a table of poker players numbering four. They've continued to play, I imagine in hope of not antagonizing this kid who is dead set on garnering some attention. Oh, and his name is Curtis Smalls."

"Sheriff, you're an honorable man, and you know I would do anything for this town. But someday I'm going to have to say no." Frank looked at the floor and said, "But today isn't the day. I'll go in. I want someone to make an announcement that I'm walking in before I get *my* head shot at. Any volunteers?" Frank looked around the room.

"I'm your man, Mr. Frank," Brad announced enthusiastically.

Frank grinned, but he wasn't surprised. "You are the man, and make sure he hears my name."

"Not a problem. Are you sure that's prudent?" Brad asked.

"Yeah, I'd be willing to bet if this guy is in his late teens, and if he's from this area of the country, he's heard of me," Frank said with his hand on Brad's shoulder as they turned to the back door.

"Now, Sheriff," Al Turner interrupted. "Are you just going to let Mr. Savage go in and incite further violence?" He pointed at the ceiling as he spoke. "You know this man Savage has killed before, and I believe that once a man has killed, he gets a taste for it."

"What is it that you do again?" Brad said in a brash and sardonic tone, "Oh, right, you're an *actor*. So, you think that if you play a lawman in a play, then that now makes you an expert. You know what, Mr. Turner? People like you are watchers and pretenders. You *watch* the rest of us *do,* and then you pretend to be a doer. And when all is said and done, you try to tell us what it's all about. I'm fed up with the likes of people like you."

"Bradley, it's okay." Frank gripped his friend's arm. "Us doer's have some work to do. Let's go."

"Al, barring an unfortunate accident, you and I are going to finish this," Brad roared back as they stepped out the back door. Frank attempted to contain his grin.

The two friends walked around the back of the post office, then across the street. They positioned themselves to stay out of view of the windows of the saloon. All sounded quiet inside the bar. Brad walked over to the side of the porch within yelling distance. He remained out of sight. He hollered into the front swinging doors of the saloon, "Curtis Smalls, are you in there?"

"What do you want?" an agitated voice answered.

"Mr. Frank Savage is coming in, so don't shoot him."

"What's he want?"

Brad looked over to Frank with an unsure look on his face.

Frank shrugged and replied, "I'm thirsty."

Turning back to the bar Brad answered, "He's thirsty."

There was no answer from the bar. Frank asked, "You think it's safe?"

"You know not to ask me that. I have no stinking idea," Brad said, he paused, then, "Sorry."

Frank nodded and proceeded to the door. Slowly with both hands he swung the doors inward and stepped into the saloon, unarmed. Looking around, he did his best to take note of everyone in the room.

He first noticed the table of four gamblers playing cards. He recognized the players and thought they were safe enough not to cause the dilemma to escalate.

Frank nodded and smiled towards the table and said, "Good day, gentlemen."

Frank had been here many times before, and he knew the layout. He was also aware that it being a weekday, it would be quiet and with no music.

Frank reminded himself that there might be a man or two with the gals upstairs, so he kept an eye on the doors that hugged the balcony. He knew the bartender kept a scattergun under the bar. And if the need so arose, he could get to it.

Walking slowly to the bar, he scanned the room from right to left. He stopped his scan on Curtis who stood at the far end of the bar with a drink in his hand. His gun rested on the bar top, with his other hand close by. Frank sighed with the realization that Smalls was not pointing the gun at anyone.

Curtis downed a shot as he eyed the newcomer. He swayed slightly. Jack, the bartender, nervously stood at his post. In a poor attempt to seem busy, he cleaned the bar, frantically. Frank guessed Jack had been wiping the wooden rest stop for the last thirty minutes.

He cautiously and confidently stepped up to the bar and removed his hat.

"Hi, Jack, I'll have a scotch and a water chaser please," Frank asked politely.

"Sure, Frank."

Jack poured the scotch, then some water into a separate glass and set them gently on the counter top. He moved back a step. Frank took a sip of his scotch and followed with a drink of water. He looked into the back mirror behind Jack and could see an inch of walnut that was the base of the stock of the shotgun under the bar.

"What is up with the water?" Curtis asked in an irritated tone. "Sounds like something a woman would do."

Frank took another sip of scotch and followed it with a drink of water. With a laugh he replied, "It is, isn't it?"

"So, why do you do it? I would think a ma--" Curtis said adding a belch. He stumbled back a half step just catching his fall with both hands on the bar's edge.

Savage held back his smile as he cocked the hammer back on the ten-gauge shotgun he held leveled at Small's chin. Curtis finally realized he was looking down the barrel of a scattergun when Savage used his free hand to slide Small's six-shooter down the bar. Jack collected the gun and stuffed it into his belt.

"Continue," Frank directed, while setting the shotgun down and picking up his scotch.

"Mmm, I think a ma . . . man, person of your reputation would drink whiskey," Curtis said. He tried desperately to look sober.

"Well, I know it's not that manly, but the deal is I have a reaction to liquor where it irritates the lining of my stomach and the bottom of my throat," Frank calmly told him.

"You don't say?" Curtis asked, actually curious now. "I get that burning, too, especially with hot spicy food." He hiccupped and wiped his chin with his forearm.

"Yep," Frank continued, "it's some sort of medical condition and my doctor said I can't drink alcohol, coffee or eat chocolate."

"Well, them's the best damn things in life, except for women, of course." Curtis seemed to have completely forgotten what had just happened over the last hour.

"Exactly my thoughts," Frank said while moving closer to Smalls. Jack the bartender was starting to calm down, along with the poker players. The tension in the room evaporated.

"I like the taste of scotch, so I just add a little water to help with the burn, because I don't think life is worth living if you can't partake in its pleasures," Frank said with a smile.

Jack threw Frank a confused glance.

Frank continued, "Someday, when you sober up, I'll buy you a scotch."

Brad, Toby Gibson, and Sheriff Clark stopped pacing around in the street when they took a peek into the saloon. Brad poked his head in the door with Toby looking over his left shoulder, and Sheriff Clark looking in over his right shoulder. They watched Frank as he talked to Curtis by the bar.

Toby whispered, "They're just in there shooting the shit."

"Frank?" Brad calmly inquired.

"What?" Frank answered.

"What you talking about?"

"I was just telling Curtis here about scotch whiskey and its origins."

"Can we come in?" Clark queried over Brad's shoulder.

"Of course you can come in," Frank said.

"Hey, Sheriff, I'm sorry about all the ruckus. I really wasn't aiming at you," Curtis remarked.

The three men entered into the saloon. Clark walked over to the two at the bar and said, "Frank, this town is growing. I sure could use your help full-time." Frank just smiled.

"Alright, Curtis, you are going to come and spend the night in jail," Clark said calmly, but sternly. "And you're gonna pay for that hole in the wall."

"Okay, I'm coming." Curtis tried to down another drink, but the glass was empty. The Sheriff and Toby escorted him to his jail cell for the night.

Brad ordered a shot of whiskey. Frank changed Brad's order from a shot of whiskey to a glass of scotch.

CHAPTER 4

After the two friends had finished their drinks, they headed back to Frank's store. Nathan, Frank's godson, was at the store's counter with his elbows on the countertop. He was smiling and flirting with Cassie. Nathan was just an inch or two shorter than Frank, putting him at about six feet. Cassie was tall and beautiful.

"Uncle Francis, did you save the day again?" Nathan said. He welcomed his godfather with a smile.

"Oh, don't call me Francis. You know I hate that."

Brad interjected beamingly, "Yes, sir, your godfather prevented bloodshed once again in our fair city."

Nathan gave Frank a hug. "You're my hero, Uncle Frank," Nathan added with an air of teasing.

"Yeah, yeah," Frank replied blushing.

Brad walked over to the sweets that rested on the countertop. He casually snaked his hand into the large candy holder and nabbed a piece of hard candy. He said, "Hey Nathan, you still riding in the horserace this afternoon?" Then he winked at Cassie.

"Absolutely, I hear Mr. Turner has some money bet against me. I can't wait to see the look on his face when I cross that finish line first," Nate said cheerfully.

"Well now, it seems we have a bit of a predicament on our hands," Brad retorted.

"How's that?" Cassie inquired.

Frank interjected, "Nathan and Bradley are both entered in the race this afternoon."

"I certainly hope after I win that you and I can still be friends," Brad said, putting his arm around Nate's shoulders.

Nate blurted, "We'll see about that. We'll see. Your arrogance just might be your undoing."

Cassie covered her smile with her forearm. She said, muffled, "Oh, Brad, you know Nathan loves his horse."

Brad said as he was readying to leave, "I think I'll go get my horse saddled up. What time is the race again?"

"It's at five o'clock," Nate answered. He looked down to the floor.

"Uh-oh, that wasn't very sportsman like," Brad said, continuing to rib his young friend, "I think I recall the race being at four o'clock. If I didn't know any better I might think he was trying to get me to miss the race." He turned and looked at Frank with one eyebrow raised. Brad mused, "What do you think? You think he was trying to mislead me so I would be a no-show?"

Frank was enjoying the act Brad was putting on. "I reckon."

Brad turned to Nate, grinning ear to ear with a piece of stick candy jutting out the corner of his mouth. He casually tipped his hat to the top of his forehead and crossed his arms. "I'll see you at four o'clock."

"Yeah." Nate perked up. "You'll be seeing my backside, and I'll be giving you a dust sandwich. Just a bit of a heads up to you, Maggie and I will play hell with you if you get too close."

"Well done," Frank added.

Brad chuckled as he stepped out the front door on his way to saddle and ready his horse. Nathan turned his attention back to Cassie. "You'll be there, right Cassie?"

"I wouldn't miss it for the world," Cassie replied with tenderness.

"Cassie, isn't it your birthday this week?" asked Frank.

"Yes, it is," Cassie said. "Actually, my birthday is today." She frowned at Nathan with narrow eyes.

"Whoa, baby, what's the fuss about?" Nate asked defensively.

"I'm turning eighteen today, and you forgot," Cassie blurted. She tapped her toes and thrust her lower lip out in a mock pout.

"Here's the package you ordered, Nate." Frank pulled a large heart shaped box of chocolates out from under the store's counter. Nate quickly recognized that his godfather was saving his bacon, and he wisely decided to play along. Walking over to pick up the chocolates, he remarked, "See? I couldn't forget your birthday." When Nate grabbed the box, Frank gripped it tightly and held out his other hand palm up. "That'll be one dollar."

"One dollar!" Nate blurted. He caught himself but it was too late.

"Yes," Frank emphasized, "you asked for the Swiss chocolates. I recollect you actually saying, 'only the best for my Cassie', remember?"

"Yes, of course I remember," Nate mumbled while digging into his pocket. He handed Frank some change. "I'll get the rest to you after I win the race for Cassie. Which, by the way, I aim to deliver as the second half of her birthday gift."

Frank smiled and nodded his approval.

"Can you believe Cassie is the same age as me now?" Nate asked.

Cassie retorted with disapproval, "For only three months, Nathan Hanson."

"I'm sorry, Sweetheart. Here's your present. Happy birthday," Nathan said, hugging his girlfriend. "I have to go and get Maggie ready for the race." Nathan uttered an abrupt goodbye to Frank and rushed out of the store.

Frank sat shirtless at the side of the bed. He was pulling his boot on when Kelly threw back the covers in anger.

"I don't like to read?" Kelly snapped as she quickly covered her naked body with the sheet she pulled from the bed.

"Well, I didn't mean you don't like to read. I meant you don't read as much as I do." Frank sensed he was about to be put in his place.

"You're trying to make me feel bad on purpose." Kelly was seething.

"No, no," Frank said, quizzically shaking his head. "That isn't, or wasn't, my intention. I am sorry."

"I don't like people trying to make me feel stupid!" Kelly barked as she moved briskly around the room.

"Now, wait a sec. I said, I didn't mean it that way," Frank said calmly. "I meant that I'm an avid reader. Most people don't read as much as I do, that's all." He continued and was trying to add a little bit of a smile in the hope she might find the humor in the situation.

Frank had always been good at reading people. He knew Kelly was becoming more and more agitated. Not a place he liked to visit. He was also good at diffusing most difficult situations with men. He knew all too well that his abilities in diplomacy did not translate to women.

"That isn't what you said," she said sharply. She attempted to dress herself in a manner that wouldn't allow Frank to get another glimpse of her nude figure.

"That is what I meant, and you know it."

"No, I don't," Kelly spit back.

"I truly am sorry. I should have thought before I spoke. Can you please accept my apology?"

"I will not put up with you saying I don't like to read," Kelly said, ignoring Frank's plea.

Frank couldn't understand how her voice could get any louder, but it did. He asked, "Will you stop yelling at me, please?"

"I'm not yelling!"

"Okay, my perception is that you are yelling," Frank replied. He was starting to become irritated himself.

"Well, I'm not yelling, and you said I don't like to read. You want me to feel uneducated." Kelly burned holes in Frank with her eyes.

"Hey there, slow down. I never said that, and may I add something?" He paused for a two count, then said, "Why is it that you were the one who canceled our date for Nate's race, and for dinner tonight, but it is I who is being yelled at?" Frank threw his hands up in frustration.

Kelly turned and pointed her finger at him. She said, "Oh, and now I'm supposed to feel guilty because I have to work?"

Frank was trying to stay calm, but he felt as if he was being forced into a corner. He was starting to believe that maybe she was doing all this on purpose. Maybe it was a test, or could it be that she just 'got off' on being angry?

"Nice way to spend my lunch break. At least I got laid, I guess," he mumbled under his breath.

Frank stood, walked to the door, and turned toward Kelly with his shoulders squared in her direction. He was attempting to stand his ground because he had already apologized. He was well aware that it didn't matter anymore what he said. Kelly's anger was nourishing itself. With a mind all its own, her emotions took over. She had lost all ability to think straight and was now only agitating Frank, just because.

She continued to berate him. "You have some nerve. Why did you say that?"

"Hey, I said I was sorry, but you continue to give me a tongue lashing, and I don't like it. At a certain point I'm going to stand up for myself. I'm not going to take anymore of your abuse," Frank said. He was visibly angry and his voice was louder.

"I have to work today and you are just trying to get me upset," Kelly said, pacing the floor.

"You know, I think we need to take a break, maybe a cool down period or something. I feel that if we don't take some time out, we're going to say something we regret. I think you should take a look into your heart and try being honest with yourself. I get the impression you don't even like me. I feel if you think it over, you'll agree with me. You know . . . that you don't like me."

Kelly stomped over to the back door of her room. She opened it, and without saying a word she slammed it shut behind her. Frank put on his hat, snapped the front brim down, and left the room. On his way out he noticed that he felt sad, but he also felt relieved.

"She's got issues," he mumbled. "Good luck with all that."

A small smirk came across his face that lasted only a fleeting moment. It was then that he realized he had left his books behind.

Nathan loved horses, and he personally owned six. So, when deciding which horse to race, he had to determine which one he deemed most appropriate for such an event. He also wanted to ride an animal with which he had good chemistry, one that he trusted. That horse was Maggie, and he'd been riding her for a couple of years now. He started practicing with her on the first day of spring to prepare for the race.

Maggie was a beautiful Appaloosa that from the front looked like a bay. A stunning and shiny brown coat covered most of her body except her hindquarters. Maggie's brown coat had some dark red mixed in, and the red would really shine when she stood in the sun. Her hindquarters had the colorful spotted coat patterns that helped distinguish the Appaloosa from other horses.

Maggie had another distinguishing physical trait; she had one hazel eye and the other was blue. It was widely accepted that the reason for the spotted coat was that the Spanish Conquistadors brought with them wildly colored and decorated horses when they came to North America. Whatever the reason, Maggie had such a distinctive look that people could pick her out of a large herd and could also see her coming from a hundred yards away. She was tall, with long legs and a muscular but lean look.

The Appaloosa was regarded as a good runner in shorter races, so this made the day a bit more interesting. The event was a little longer than what suited Maggie, and Nathan considered this. He felt she was full of determination. She possessed a spirit that you could see in her bi-colored eyes.

Maggie's hazel eye showed intelligence about her. You didn't know what she was thinking, but you would swear she was deep in thought. Her blue eye showed her empathic and loving side. She would not be the biggest horse physically racing today, but she had the biggest heart.

Nate enjoyed riding Maggie because he appreciated her personality. All horses tend to have a personality, but not one so close to that of a person. It always appeared to everyone that she knew what people were saying. She often would turn her head to you if you were talking about her, whether you mentioned her name or not. Maggie also seemed to know when you asked her a question, because every time you asked her something, she would whiney as if answering. Adults and children loved her, and on the day of the race they all showed up to greet her when Nathan came trotting into the proceedings. They had arrived early for the racers' introductions.

As Nate and Maggie loped their way through the crowd, all the kids came running while saying her name in unison and jumping with excitement. Nathan dismounted, and a group of six or so children came up to Maggie. She lowered her head as if to greet them. One at a time Nate helped the kids pet her mane, and when someone talked about her, she would turn to them. Every time a child would ask a question, she would whiney as if responding to their query and it caused everyone to cheer and smile.

Nathan was aware that his surroundings were filling up with more spectators. The town seemed excited for the horse race that was scheduled to commence within the next thirty minutes.

Nate analyzed the track. He noticed that the race itself was to start out on a somewhat straight road with no trees that would eventually bend around a small lake. The site was the same every year because it allowed spectators to view the entire race without any obstacles to obstruct the view. The only obstacle along the track was one tree at the turning point halfway through the race. Upon circling the lake, the track would bring the racers back, facing the finish line. The final stretch would have the racers charge up another straightaway that would end where the event had started.

Tables of food filled the banner decorated field where the race was to start. Frank rode up to Nate who was holding Maggie. She was still surrounded by a gaggle of people, mostly kids.

"Hi there Uncle Frank. I heard you met a gal on the train. Do you know if she's coming to the race today?"

Frank dismounted and tied his reins to the hitching rope that was strung up for the spectators' horses. "Well, she was supposed to, but when I went to pick her up, she said she had to work."

Nate sensed his godfather's disappointment. "Oh, I'm sure she must be busy then. Being that there is so much to do in this town."

"Yeah, right, and this is the second time she's cancelled on me, and she doesn't seem too bothered by it."

"Don't get sucked into another relationship with someone who doesn't treat you the way you deserve to be treated," Nate said, a little fired up. "Like that one you spent six years with. Mom and Dad are worried about you. They say you're a self-loather, whatever that means. You deserve the best, Uncle Frank, that's all I'm saying."

"I'll be alright. She wasn't right for me, just a diversion. I'm just pissed because I left some of my things at her place."

"Well, you can say goodbye to those," Nathan quipped, he patted his uncle on the shoulder. Nate took Maggie by the reins and walked her over to the starting line where the other racers were already assembling.

Brad waited in front of the pack as he inspected his saddle. He worked the tension on the girth strap. He looked up as Nate approached. The two shook hands and mounted their respective horses.

The crowd moved away from the food tables, most carrying pieces of pie, to find a comfortable spot to watch the race and enjoy the day. As Brad was getting into position, he eyed Al Turner who was speaking to two of the other racers. He was holding some bills in his hands and looking in Nate's direction.

Brad whispered, "And what in the hell is he up to? Horseshit, that's what."

A race official announced, "Mount up," and the remaining cowboys mounted their horses and lined up along the starting line. Frank found a good position to observe the day's event while looking for a piece of apple pie to snack on.

Nathan was speaking to Maggie when the sorrel on her left side attempted to nip off her ear. Maggie responded with a puff and a nod as she stomped her front hooves in the dirt.

Nate smiled. "Oh, you shouldn't have done that. You're in for it now."

The sorrel's rider scowled and grunted. "I doubt it."

The racing official was holding a gun in his right hand that was pointed to the clouds overhead. He bellowed, "Racers take your positions." The discharge from his Colt sent all six cowboys down the first stretch at breakneck speeds. Nate was working the middle of the pack. He was trying to get into a position on the right-hand side. He hoped to get to the inside of the track as they rounded the far side of the lake. The group of horses seemed to move along heavily and clumsily for a moment. But once the riders got some distance between themselves, the pace quickened.

Frank was picking up a large slice of warm apple pie off the pie-table when he heard the bang of the starting pistol. Just as he looked up from under the brim of his hat to watch the start of the race, he noticed he was looking right into the face of his railroad buddy Sam.

"Sam-dog! What in the Sam-hell are you doing here? You should be halfway to California by now." Frank reached out and shook his hand.

"Well, Frank, you know I haven't been feeling so well lately. I decided to stay in North Fork to see the doc. I told him my dad passed at a young age, and I don't think he understands. He can't find nothing, but I don't think I got much time left," Sam said with genuine concern.

Frank, knowing his friend was a bit of a hypochondriac, thought he would use the moment to tease him a little bit. He said, "Well, I guess you better make the best of what time you got left."

Sam, a bit taken aback, replied, "What?"

Frank could feel his muscles in his face about to give him away with a grin. Turning away from Sam and forcing his smile to the opposite side of his face, he said, "I reckon it's too late for you to quit smoking then."

Sam was starting to fidget when he finally saw the grin on Frank's face. He lowered his head, kicked the dirt with his foot, and said, "Dad-blast it."

A well-dressed slightly older woman interrupted the conversation. "Frank Savage, you're standing here jibber-jabbering and your godson is out there racing with all he's got, trying to make you proud of him, and you pay him no mind."

Frank replied pleasantly, "You are right, Mrs. Simpson. I should be watching the race. But I would much rather keep my eyes on a beautiful woman such as yourself."

"Your charms may work on the rest of the ladies here in North Fork, but not me." Mrs. Simpson winked at Frank with a sly smile and went back to cutting pies.

Sam said, "Frank, I overheard someone say that Al Turner has two riders with instructions to keep Nathan from winning the race today."

Frank looked out into the direction of the raceway and said, "I'll tell you what. Those two riders had better have done some research on Nate because he is awful crafty. If they haven't done their homework, they're about to find out how difficult he can be."

Nate could feel Maggie was in the zone, and he knew the other horses would be hard pressed to beat her. The first turn that would take them around the lake was quickly approaching as the racers pushed hard on the opening straightaway.

The corner had a large maple tree with two thick limbs reaching out and up marking the first turn and checkpoint. Aiming for the tree and planning his turn, Nate could feel Maggie was at a slower pace than her introductory surge. He knew that their current pace was to keep the lead, but to still have some reserves for the final sprint home.

The clumping of horse hooves was almost deafening, but Nate could still hear a rider gaining on him alongside his right. Hesitating on pushing Maggie any harder, he was trying to figure out the best way to keep his position without burning Maggie out. She was running hard, and Nate was staying low over her withers. They were working as one as they kept the pace.

Nathan was holding the reins so tight he thought he was going to squeeze juice out of them. He told himself, *relax, this is supposed to be fun.*

He glanced back briefly under his right arm to get an idea of how close the other rider was getting. As he looked he saw that the horse was the sorrel that nipped at Maggie at the starting line. He also noticed the rider had a short black stick in his hand. Nate could feel that the rider had his sights set on him. He turned to face forward with concern on his brow. As he rode, the wrinkles on his forehead faded, for he had a plan.

Galloping with purpose and headed for the first turn, Nate pulled ever so slightly on Maggie's right rein. Maggie felt a mite of a tug on the right side of her bit and she responded famously.

The sorrel's rider was adamant about knocking Nate from his saddle. So entrenched in what he was doing, he was shocked to find himself airborne. The sorrel stopped running so abruptly that she slid on her hooves a good five feet in the dirt.

The cessation of motion was so drastic that the rider completely left his saddle a split second before he planned to swing his club at Nathan.

Maggie had hugged the turn around the Maple tree. The sorrel had no desire to run smack dab into the tree, so she did what came naturally. She halted. The sorrel's rider landed flat on his face at the base of the tree. He glided forward on his stomach, eating dirt all the way.

Nate howled over his shoulder, "How's that taste? Try watching where you're going next time."

Nathan quickly rounded the far end of the track. The road curved around the lake and led the racers back towards the finish line.

Brad was just now getting control of himself because he was laughing so hard at what he had just witnessed. His horse was accelerating for the final stretch of the race as Al Turner's second rider, who was riding a black, was picking up speed.

Dust was everywhere on this side of the track because some wind had picked up. All the riders where forcing their way into the wind, squinting to keep their eyes clean of dirt.

Nate hollered, "Let's go, Maggie."

Maggie heeded his call, and Nate felt the surge.

"Jesus, you almost left me behind," said Nate.

Brad was again laughing as he was purposely staying in front of the rider on the black, preventing him from advancing on Nate.

Brad bellowed, "Go, Nathan! Go, Maggie! Yee-haw!"

Nate moved with his beloved horse, and they continued to increase the distance between themselves and the other riders.

Frank was the first to congratulate Nate on his win. A crowd formed around the winner and his horse with congrats coming from all directions. There had been no doubt in Frank's mind as to the outcome of the race.

Frank said, "I saw a little incident down on the far end. What happened?

The doc is on his way out there right now in the medical wagon."

"One of Mr. Turner's riders was carrying a black club and was fixing to wrap it around my head, so I just heeded what you always taught me. Use your head and never--"

"Never hesitate?" Frank interrupted.

"Never hesitate, and I didn't. I just knew that I had to do something. Especially since I didn't want to give up my lead. I don't want him dead, though. That was never my intention. I just didn't want him to hurt me, or to win the race by cheating, that's all." Nate turned his attention toward the medical wagon kicking up dust off in the distance on its way to the downed rider.

"Don't worry, Nate. It's not your fault. If he dies, it's survival of the fittest if you ask me," Frank said. He noticed Nate seemed concerned. "Oh crap, here comes the devil himself."

Al Turner was working his way through the crowd in their direction. Nate was expecting some sort of backlash, but it never came. Al walked up to Frank and asked if he could talk to him in private. Frank reluctantly followed him to an area away from the crowd.

Talking fast, Al said, "Mr. Savage, I have a proposition for you that I think you might be interested in."

"Yeah? And what might that be?" Frank asked suspiciously with a raised brow.

As Al spoke he paused often between his words. "We, I mean the town council, has arranged for a cross-country trip. An exhibition of sorts, you know, to show off a new stagecoach line. The stage will arrive in town in five days. I'm here on behalf of the city of North Fork and Southwest Stagecoach Travel to offer you a job to ride shotgun on one of two stagecoaches."

"I'm a little caught off guard here. I was expecting you to be pissed about your rider getting launched into a maple tree. And while I'm on that topic," Frank said getting red in the face. He turned his intimidating frame to face Al. "Your rider pulled a club on Nathan, and he was planning to take a swing when he screwed the pooch and almost killed himself. What's the deal with you siccing your men on him?"

Stepping back one short step at a time with Frank bearing down on him, Al said, "Now, Frank, calm down. I didn't want my boys to get violent. I just told them I had a little money riding on them and, that's it. I don't authorize or condone violence, I assure you."

Brad rode up alongside and swung out of his saddle. "What the hell, Al? What was all that horseshit? Nate could have been killed."

At the moment, two tall perturbed cowboys were hanging over Al as he finally backed into a picnic table and fell into it with his hand in a blueberry pie.

"Now, fellas, you don't understand. Seriously now, it was just a bet, that's all. Those two must have had some money down, too, and they may have made a decision that I had no part of."

The medical wagon was now just pulling up with the doc and the injured rider.

"I deserve more for this shit," Al mumbled to himself.

"He's hurt pretty bad, but I think he should be okay," Doc yelled. "He would have walked away from the fall, but he fell on a club of some sort he was carrying. Broke a couple of ribs looks like. As long as he didn't puncture a lung, he'll live." Doc snapped the reins and drove the wagon back to town with his injured patient in back.

Al Turner stood back up, wiping his hand on his shirt. "I'll come by the store tomorrow, Frank, to talk over the job."

Frank was calm now, but he still showed his dislike for the man. "Answer is no. You better soak that shirt." Under his breath he added, "Jackass."

"You think on it. I'll stop by tomorrow." Al scurried off like a frightened rabbit eluding a predator.

Brad interjected. "I'm on that job."

Frank was surprised, but he didn't show it. "I'm listening."

Brad said, "It's a new stagecoach line. The coaches are a brand new design. There will be two coaches that'll be led by six horses each. It pays well, and it's from here to Lasso City and then onto Sawmill."

Frank nodded.

"It's a short ride, just a few days. Once at Sawmill, a new crew takes over, then we come home. It's a big deal, I reckon. Al Turner had the stage's route changed so that it would come through town. It would be great if you'd join us, Frank. Whad'ya say?"

Frank said, "Doesn't the carriage company have their own employees? What do they need us for?"

Brad said, "I'm the employee representative on the trip. It's kind of a publicity tour, and your presence would help things. That's about it. Oh, and Nate has already taken the job to drive the lead stage."

Frank sighed.

"Al Turner talked him into it."

Frank remained silent as he stood with his arms crossed staring into the distance.

CHAPTER 5

"Nate, you better get ready. Supper gets eaten with or without you," Marie yelled up the stairs to her son.

"Coming, Mom." Nate hurried himself along combing his hair and buttoning his shirt. He had barely stepped out of his bedroom door when he heard Frank say hello to his parents. He moved quickly down the stairs, taking two steps at a time.

Nathan showed up in the dining room in the middle of a conversation. Frank was speaking to Ed. "That rider had had Nate dead in his sights." Everyone turned when Nate stepped up to the table.

"Well, here's the man of the hour himself. I was just telling your folks about your race today," Frank said, patting Nate on the back.

"That was quite a race, wasn't it?" Ed asked.

"Yes, sir," Nate said.

"Sorry we weren't at the race. Your Uncle Karl has taken a turn for the worse, and we--"

Nate interrupted, "You don't have to explain. I wanted you to be with your brother today. You don't need to worry about me."

"Let's eat," Frank barked with a smile while placing his hat on the hat rack, he took his seat at the table.

Ed was dishing up some potatoes. "Frank, we heard about Nate's new endeavor, and we wanted to talk to you about it."

"Brad did mention something about Nate accepting a job to take a loaded coach to Sawmill," Frank said while looking at Nathan with a cocked brow.

"I think Nate figures that this is something you two would have done in your younger days. Following in your footsteps." Marie said.

"From what I gather," Ed interposed, "Al Turner and the town council have worked out this trip to help bring some attention to the city. Do you happen to know the cargo and destination?"

Frank took a bite out of a roll and answered, "From what Brad Simon has told me, it's mostly paperwork destined for California, and there will be a few passengers getting on here and some more in Lasso City. No dignitaries and no money, though. They don't want this trip to be a target for would-be robbers. From what I've been told, Al would go along to Sawmill. At that point he, along with the crew of the coaches, will be replaced for the remainder of the trip."

Nate added, "Along with Mr. Turner is a man named George Cummings. He's a gambler I think. I was told that he's pretty good at it, too. Also, we're to pick up a newlywed couple in Lasso who are trying to get to California. From what I understand, Mr. Turner made all the arrangements."

"Sounds like quite the adventure," Marie said.

Nate said, "And Cassie's going."

Ed dropped his fork with a clang on his plate. Marie started to cough as she choked on her food, and Frank tried to hide his smile under his napkin.

"Why-why on earth is she going? Are you two--" Marie said with a hushed tone.

"No, mom, we're not running off to California to elope," Nate announced. "I told Cassie I wanted to do this, and she said she wanted to come because she has a sister in Sawmill. She wants to visit her sister and her family, that's all. Once the job's complete, we're going to stay with her sister for a couple of days. Then we'll catch a stage back to Lasso and ride the train from there."

Ed was visibly relieved. "You know, Nate, we love Cassie. Your mom and I just feel that if--"

"I know dad," Nate said. "We should give it a couple of years until we're a little older. Hey, let's stop talking about me. What of Uncle Frank and his girlfriend, or girlfriends, should I say?"

Marie said, "Your Uncle Frank's problem is he likes 'healthy' women."

Nate said, "What's wrong with wanting someone who is healthy?"

"Well, they just aren't always the nicest," his mother answered.

"Does healthy not mean what I think it means?" Nate asked.

"She means I fancy opulent ladies. You know, curves where curves should be," Frank explained.

"Oh, okay, I understand," Nate said, winking at his godfather. "Why is that anyway? Why aren't they very nice? I've noticed that, too," Nate spoke between bites of steak.

"That seems to be the quandary of all men, son," Ed said. "Some men believe that women with large attributes have always gotten what they want, mmm, whenever they want it, without ever having to work for it. I lucked out with your mother being so beautiful and nice at the same time because, I think it was her wonderful family. To be perfectly honest, both of her folks believed in a loving home. And they valued education and smarts above beauty."

Marie blushed. She smiled at her husband and added, "Cassie's parents have the same value system as we do. I think that as long as you two don't rush it, you have a good catch there, too. Who wants some pie?"

Nate blurted, "I do, please."

Frank and Edward each devoured a slice of the dessert and continued to enjoy the evening while Nate ate two large pieces of pie. After they were finished, Ed asked Nate to help his mother with the dishes. He then motioned to Frank, and they exited to the front porch for a smoke.

Ed rolled a cigarette, and Frank lit a cigar while they stood on the front patio. Frank cherished the feeling of a light cool breeze and the smell of a good cigar. Frank, out of the blue, questioned his friend on what he wanted to talk to him about.

"What makes you think I need to talk to you about anything in particular?" Ed asked suspiciously.

"I can tell your mind is preoccupied, so I just thought you might have something you wanted to talk to me about."

Ed grinned. "You are one-hundred percent correct, Mr. Savage. Sometimes I forget you used to be a spy."

"Out with it then. I'm all ears," Frank said while taking in the aroma of his cigar.

"I had a long talk today with Marie about Nate," Ed said, then, "You do understand why Nathan is going on this trip?"

Marie quietly unlatched the front screen door and stepped out onto the porch. "Nate's going to finish cleaning the dining room and the dishes." Marie turned to Frank and said, "He told me to tell you good night, and he'd see you tomorrow."

"It's a bit early for bed, isn't it?" Frank asked.

"He reads those books by Jules Verne you gave him," Ed replied. "And then he cleans his guns, if he practiced that day, before going to sleep. He stays up pretty late, actually. Nathan doesn't need much sleep. He didn't get that from me." With a suspicious grin he gave his wife a look. "But for some reason, I never seem to get to sleep when I'd planned to."

Frank said, "I'll order some more books for him then." Frank continued to puff on his cigar. He told his body to relax his shoulders and enjoy the evening as he looked at the stars.

Marie said, "You see, Nate views this as his opportunity to head out on his own. He believes this is something you and Ed would have done at his age."

"It's hard to debate that," Frank replied.

"Oh, absolutely, and we're not planning on stopping him," Ed admitted. "I would rather he stay and work here on the ranch with me, but--"

Marie interrupted, "Nate's a man now, and he's moving out. He has plans to marry Cassie, someday."

"If he wants excitement, being married is going to hinder that," Frank said.

"We know, but he'll have to make his own decisions and learn for himself," Ed said. He walked over to Marie and put his arm over her shoulders. "Frank." He paused to collect his thoughts. "Marie and I would feel better if you went along."

He wasn't surprised, but, still, sadness crept onto Frank's face. They never talked about his demons.

Marie said, "Ed could go."

Ed added, "Marie can handle the range without me for a few days. We have an outstanding foreman leading a great crew. We are letting Nate go, but if you were along for his first job--not to baby-sit, mind you--if you worked on the ride, we would sleep better. That's it."

Frank was in thought and finally said, "Of course I'll go."

"Thank you," Marie said, then, "What's up with this Kelly girl? I thought you were going to bring her with you tonight."

Frank knew this was coming and grinned. "Oh, well, she couldn't make it. She's angry with me. When she cancelled on me, I wasn't really sure we had made plans, officially. So, before I said anything about her always canceling on me, I asked her, 'did we have plans tonight?' You know, to make sure I didn't have things wrong. Make sense?"

Ed and Marie both nodded.

Frank continued, "Anyway, when I asked her that, she got all fired up and was accusing me of 'trying to make her feel bad.' She started yelling at me out of the blue."

"What?" Ed asked.

"Oh, that's just ridiculous," Marie opined.

"I thought so, too," Frank said. "It didn't make much sense to me that I was the one cancelled on, but now I'm the one getting yelled at." Frank wasn't too terribly upset and was laughing it off. "We worked through that argument, I thought. She then became upset with me again about something I said. Walking on eggshells around someone all the time is not something I enjoy. I don't want to bore you with it. Thinking about it has grown tiresome for me."

Marie mused, "I did read a psychology book that talked about something called 'anger illness.' maybe she has that. Women do get upset easily, but she yells at you for the stupidest things."

"Maybe," Frank said, "I think she just doesn't like me. Either way, I don't appreciate being yelled at. Too much drama. If that's what she's all about, well, I'm done with her, period." Frank shook his head back and forth confused, tossed his cigar butt to the floor, and stepped it out with his boot. "She certainly was healthy, though."

"It's probably best you found out now," Ed said, laughing. He put his smoke out on the porch rail.

"Thanks for a lovely evening. I have to get going now. I'm meeting Brad at the saloon for a drink." Frank said his goodbyes to his friends and added, "Tell Nate not to come to the store tomorrow. I'll meet him here, and we'll shoot for practice around noon time or so." He mounted his horse, then heeled her to a gallop back to town.

The gloaming arrived with little fanfare, and the shape of the moon notified Frank that it was about three or four days from being full. The evening sky was bright, and it lit the town as Frank rode up to the saloon. He swung from the saddle, tied the reins loosely to the hitching rail, and stepped into the beam of light shining out the door of the bar. He could hear some laughing mixed in with the clanking of coins, all coming from within. He stepped through the swinging doors. They squeaked in unison and fluttered shut. There were two tables of card players, and Brad sat alone with a beer at a table in the middle of the room.

Frank sat at the table with Brad and ordered a beer from the waitress. Frank always looked forward to talking with his friend about the day's events. It gave him another man's perspective, and it cheered him up.

Brad started to tell a story from his day. He always had one that he thought Frank would appreciate. "So I'm walking in front of Tom's stable," Brad said enthusiastically while sitting on the front of his seat, hanging over his beer, "and I was on my way to speak to Al about our trip, right? And then I notice this beautiful gal walking in front of me."

Frank perked up.

"Well, I thought she was beautiful. She had gorgeous long wavy red hair down over her shoulders that looked great with her fit frame. Lovely backside, her dress fit her perfectly. And I'm thinking this is either the new nurse that Doc said was coming to town or a new teacher, so I'm excited."

Frank intervened and said, "And with so many men about and so few respectable women, you wanted to make a play before some other lucky bastard got in there."

"Right."

"Yeah, so what did she say?"

"Hold on, I'm getting to it. So, I want to get a look first, and I decided that I would follow her for a bit. My hearts going a mile a minute now, it's pounding harder and faster as I'm walking. I'm trying to relax and think of something witty to say."

Frank nodded.

"So, I notice that she slows down to look into a window. Now's my chance. I figure I'll look into the window and catch her reflection as I'm walking by and . . ." Brad paused for effect.

"Well, what?" Frank said anxiously.

"Man alive, how can a woman look so good from behind and up front just, just--"

"Not."

"Yeah, not! Poor gal," Brad replied.

"I guess you dodged that bullet then."

"Oh, we're goin out," Brad said matter-of-factly as he sipped on his beer. His eye actually twinkled.

"You and your lack of standards," Frank said, laughing heartily.

"At least my women show up," Brad said.

"That was low, even for you."

"Why don't you just get yourself a lady of the night? Mandy's kinda cute, no?"

Turning to Brad, Frank said, "I am not going to pay for it."

"When don't we pay for it? You always pay for it in some form or another."

"That you do." Frank tipped his glass and took a drink.

Brad's eyes grew round like something had just bit him. "I'm percolating," he said with anguish.

Frank looked quizzically at him.

"I have to see a man about a horse," Brad explained. Hurriedly he pushed his chair back and darted for the back door.

"Dude," Frank snapped in disgust, having sniffed something foul. "Check your britches while you're at it. Scratch that, no need to look, just burn them." He fanned the air with his hat.

As Brad stepped out the back door to the outhouse, one of the card players stood from one of the card table and walked over to the back corner of the saloon. He placed his hat on an empty table, then laid flat on his back on the floor parallel to the wall. Shortly thereafter, Al Turner stepped into the barroom and walked over to Frank's table.

Al said, "Hello, Frank."

"Evening, Al."

"May I have a seat?" Then under his breath he talked to himself. He said, "It's Allan."

Frank thought he heard it, but wasn't one hundred-percent positive. He said, "Be my guest." Frank waved his hand towards the empty chair.

When Al went to pull the chair back from the table, he looked at the sleeping cowboy in the corner. He asked, "What's wrong with that man?"

One of the card players said, "He's drunk. He always does that. He'll be back playing cards before morning."

Another player mumbled, "What do you care?"

Frank said while looking at the sleeping card player and grinning, "He ain't staggering." He turned and took a drink from his beer. "He must not be that soused."

Al waved to the barmaid. "It sure is a nice night," he said, as if he were testing Frank's mood.

"If you say so," Frank answered curtly.

"Frank, I wanted to talk to you about this Southwest Stagecoach line that's coming through town."

"If you must." Frank stared into his beer.

Al said nervously, "Yes, okay, I was still hoping you'd ride shotgun on the second coach."

"Let me ask you something, Al. Did you go to Nate and offer him the job? Or did he come to you?"

Al was moving around in his seat, fidgeting with his hands. "I was told that Nathan wanted to go, so I then went to him. I didn't force him,

Frank. I know what you're thinking. You think I went to him to get you to go. Now, I can assure you that is not the case. We just want the best men we can get, and Nate has a good reputation with horses and with a six-shooter."

"Uh-huh," Frank said suspiciously, but he was listening. He was annoyed, but calm. "I'm not real sure why you would go out of your way to get me to go with you. Our displeasure for each other is well known in three counties."

Al sat anxiously for a moment then ordered a whiskey with a beer chaser.

"Relax, I'm going along," Frank said between drinks of beer.

"That's great, Frank. The pay is real good for such a short trip. You'll get half now and half--"

Frank interrupted, "I'm not doing it for the money. Please tell me the specifics of the job while you're here."

"Well, first off, the job is that you'll ride shotgun on the second stage," Al said. Frank tried to hurry him by waving his hand. He'd already heard this part. "Your driver will be the deputy, Toby Gibson. The lead stage will be driven by your godson, and Brad Simon is riding shotgun on that one."

Brad meandered into the saloon through the back door. He stopped to talk to some of the ladies who worked the rooms upstairs.

Al continued, "As of now, there are only two passengers in your stage along with some papers, mostly mail, no gold or money. We don't want to be a target on our first cross-country run." Al forced a nervous smile.

"Al, I'm not going to shoot you. I don't even carry a gun, so relax, please."

"Okay," Al said. He swallowed the remainder of his drink and took a breath. "The lead stage will have some more documents with one passenger, Nathan's girlfriend Cassandra, and we'll pick up a newlywed couple in Lasso. I didn't want Cassie to go, but Nathan insisted."

Frank nodded.

"The newlyweds just happen to be on their way to California. And, oh, I almost forgot, the other passenger in your stage will be George Cummings. He's a gambler, and as a matter of fact, he's playing cards at the table on the right. He's the one wearing the short brimmed black felt gambler's hat on the right side near the window. He's not from here."

Frank turned to look at George the gambler just as Brad rejoined and took his seat at the table. Frank thought, *I know that guy.*

Frank asked, “Okay, and what’s the plan once we get to Sawmill? How are we getting back?”

“That will be up to you. I plan to rent a horse and ride to Lasso and pick up the train coming back. I assure you that your pay will cover any hardships.”

Brad had overheard part of the conversation. “Are you going along, Frank?” Brad asked, casually attempting to hold back his excitement.

“Yeah, I’m coming,” Frank answered with some reluctance, but he started to smile when he saw how happy it made Brad.

Al said, “Alright, fellas, I’ll see you Friday morning. The stage should arrive around eleven, and we’ll exchange the horses and be on our way when you gentlemen see fit. I bid you two good night and thank you.” Al tipped his hat with a shallow bow and exited the front doors.

Brad said, “Boy, you sure do make him nervous. He’s worse than ever.”

Frank squinted and said, “I’m not so sure it’s me that’s making him so nervous.”

“How exciting is this?” Brad turned to the bar and said, “Another round over here. We’re celebrating.” He then punched Frank in the arm.

“I wouldn’t celebrate just yet. Maybe when we get back we should throw a shindig or something,” Frank said.

“That’s a great idea, but that doesn’t mean we can’t have a drink tonight.” Brad handed Frank his fresh beer, and they toasted to the trip.

Nate was waiting in a small pasture on his parents’ property. He stood next to a homemade wooden stand. On the stand was resting his gun and some ammunition. He watched Frank slowly work his way up the straightaway that pointed to town. On the back of Frank’s horse was a large gunnysack clunking about as he rode up.

“Hey, Nate, I’ve got some more targets for you,” Frank said.

“I’ve got our usual targets all set up,” Nate said.

“I know, but I’ve got something else for you.”

He jumped from his horse and removed the sack that was tied up to the back of the saddle. “We’ll start with our normal practice, then we’ll move on to something a little more difficult.”

Frank walked over to Nate and emptied the bag onto the ground. The bag had four coffee cans tied together with some thin rope. Each can was about three feet from the one tied next to it. On the end of the first can the rope extended out about twenty feet.

Nate had taken some time to prearrange multiple targets. Some were cans sitting on the ground at differing distances. Some were empty coffee cans, and some were smaller tomato cans. A few targets were up higher on fence posts and on the sides of trees for the distance shots.

Frank had Nathan start with a warm up. After a bit, he had Nate increase the speed of his shooting. Between shots, when Nate was reloading, Frank stopped him so he could talk.

"Okay," Frank said, taking the gun from the table and inspecting the chamber. "I may be repeating myself today, but I want to reiterate what we've talked about. First off, you're doing quite well, just as I expected. We've spent some time talking about guns and hunting. Although, I haven't talked much about shooting a person."

Nate listened intently. Frank's tone was grave. Frank had been in a lot of difficult situations where he had to use a gun. This was the man to learn from, so, Nate took it all in.

Frank continued, "You're going to come across some evil men at some point in your life. Our times have few people to enforce our laws right now, and many men are going to try and take advantage of that. Desperate hideous men are going to use the lack of the law against us. You'll see this if you go into my line of work. I mean my old line of work."

Nate nodded.

"Anyway, when you come across such ruthlessness, you will have to be able to recognize what you're facing. First off, if you don't learn to see these people for what they are, you're going to get yourself hurt, or someone you care about will get hurt or killed. It's important that you understand what this person is capable of. These individuals are few and far between, but they are dangerous."

Frank looked stern. "An evil man's only concern is to put you and everyone you know six feet under at any cost. Understand what I'm saying?"

"Yes, sir, I think so."

"There are those who will do whatever it takes to kill, just because. There is absolutely no reason at all sometimes. It might be for money or to rape or for revenge because of a deep-seated hatred. For some, it's just their nature. A villainous man will shoot you in the back of the head because that's the easiest way for him."

Nate added, "They are cowardice and weak."

"Exactly, and they show this when they kill unarmed women and children. Some have been known to cut you just to watch you bleed. I've seen the burned down homes, and I've helped with wounded women who had been raped just because they were there. I worked a case when a man killed an entire family because he didn't want any witnesses to him stealing a horse. The reason I'm telling you this now is because you're leaving home and going on this job."

Nate asked, "Did Mom ask you to talk to me about this?"

Frank said, "No, she didn't. I believe that this experience will be the first of many, and I want you to be prepared. The only thing stopping these people is individuals such as me and your dad, and you."

Nate listened intently.

Frank said as he pointed his finger, "If you ever come across this man, you must not hesitate to wipe him from the earth. This person will try to trick you by talking to you. He wants you to look away or to say something back in anger. Do not fall into this trap. Your best hope is that you see who he is, and understand what he's planning to do. If you're lucky, he'll be arrogant and underestimate you. And when you strike, don't go for the wound."

"Okay."

"You shoot to kill. Take him out, end of story. Now, that doesn't mean to kill every threat. You'll learn through experience and using your head to tell the difference between the man who is trying to destroy you, and the drunkard looking for attention. Your instincts will sharpen, and you'll learn to trust them. I think you know what I'm saying."

"I do, Uncle Frank," Nate said sincerely.

"Okay, I want you to think about what I said later, but now, I want you to shoot at something new I rigged for you."

Frank walked over to the roped coffee cans he had brought with him from town. He dragged them out about twelve paces from where they stood and lined them up across the shooting range. Frank took the end of the rope that was tied to the first can and walked to the left edge of the homemade shooting range. He was now positioned out of the pathway of where Nate would be shooting.

"Today is about small targets," Frank said. He stood in a position to pull on the rope. "No different, except these will be in motion. I want you to learn to aim quickly."

Frank paused to wipe the sweat from his forehead.

Nate said, "It's hot out."

Frank whispered, "I hate the heat." Then, he said, "Okay, I know you can hit a stationary target. You need to learn to hit multiple moving targets without thinking. You may be confronted with a handful of offenders close in, and you'll need to be able to aim and shoot instinctively. I'm going to pull the rope. When you see the cans start to move, I want you to pull your weapon and use six bullets to hit four cans. After we practice this, we'll have you shoot at the cans after I throw them out onto the range. Ready?"

"Ready," Nate answered. He turned his body slightly and positioned himself to draw quickly, just like he was taught.

Frank walked at a slow pace away from the range, and Nate drew his gun and began shooting. He hit three of the cans, with two of his shots hitting the dirt.

"Nice," Frank said. "Go ahead and reload. Always remember to keep-
-"

Nate interrupted, "Your gun loaded." Nathan began reloading as Frank smiled and repositioned the cans for another round.

"Sometimes you may have to be moving, too," Frank added. "Like a run for cover and shoot. We'll work on that in a little bit."

"Sounds good, Uncle Frank," Nate said smiling.

Frank said, "This is fun, right?"

"Absolutely," said Nate.

"Okay, with each pass I'm going to increase the speed."

Frank worked with Nate for about another hour. He tried to keep his teachings fun. Nate was already an excellent shot, and he learned quickly. It wasn't a surprise to Frank that he would ace this test as well. Frank did hope that Nathan would never have to use his skills with a gun. But he also knew how unrealistic that was.

CHAPTER 6

Frank decided to use his day off to get ready for the trek to Sawmill. After having retired from law enforcement, he sold most of his firearms except for his Henry rifle and an old pistol which he used for practice. Frank knew it was best to arm himself with some new weapons. Since he worked in a general store that sold guns, he already knew what he was going to buy. His business partner Mr. Evans was working the store as he often did when Frank took the day off. He was a gentle, but capable elderly man.

"Hello," Mr. Evans said. "Isn't it your day off today?"

"Yes, sir, I'm not here as an employee today. I'm here to make a purchase," Frank said as he stepped up to the customer side of the counter. "Things look mighty different on this side."

"That's probably because you work too much. What can I help you with?"

"I need to purchase some new firearms," Frank said. He looked down through the glass case at the handguns.

"Need a new hog-leg, do we?" Mr. Evans remarked while unlocking the gun case from his side of the case.

"Yes, I do, and what exactly does 'hog-leg' mean anyway? I never understood that one," Frank inquired.

"I don't rightly know," Mr. Evans said as he stopped to ponder the question for a moment. "Maybe it's, no, that doesn't make any sense. Good question. Anyway, what is it that you had in mind?"

"I'm going to purchase two weapons today, one being that Colt 44." Frank pointed at a Colt that had a seven and a half-inch barrel. It was a handsome gun with checkered hard rubber grips. The gun was clean looking and had the Colt logo on the top of the grip.

"Aw, the Frontier Six Shooter, nice gun and quite popular. I thought you had a nice gun," Mr. Evans inquired.

"It's decent, I guess. Well, it's always gotten the job done, that's for sure. But I'm intrigued by the caliber of this Colt. With both weapons using the same cartridge, I'll be able to carry just one size of ammunition. Less chance of putting the wrong shell into the wrong gun." Frank chuckled.

"Oh, I hate that, don't you?" Mr. Evans replied, then somewhat surprised, added, "But you said both weapons?"

"I did," Frank answered. He pointed to the back room. "If you would, Mr. Evans, please grab the package that's on the second shelf from the top. I set that aside for myself."

"You know, I was wondering what that was. It's been sitting there for quite some time now." Mr. Evans moved slowly and carefully to the storage room.

"Yeah, I wasn't sure I would need it. Kept changing my mind on if I should keep it for myself, or if I should just sell it," Frank said.

Mr. Evans now knew what was in the package and was excited to get it open so he could see it. He tried to move as quickly as he could while Frank checked his new Colt. Frank spun it in his hand, and then paused to feel the weight and balance of his new hog-leg. Mr. Evans brought the package into the storeroom and proceeded to open it, revealing a brand new Winchester rifle.

"Oh, it's a beaut, Frank," Mr. Evans said, taking the rifle into his hands and looking down the top of the barrel through the sites.

Frank loaded five rounds into his handgun and holstered it with a spin. "That feels better. It's a tad embarrassing walking around with an empty holster on your hip. I do hope I don't have to call on this."

Mr. Evans handed Frank the Winchester. As Frank looked it over he said, "I'm going to need a couple boxes of ammunition as well."

Mr. Evans wrapped up some ammunition and returned to the counter with a pencil and paper to tally up the total.

Mr. Evans said, "The total comes to, with the ammunition, forty-eight dollars."

"That sounds a little light," Frank said.

"I'm not going to charge you more than what we paid, Frank. There is absolutely no reason why we should make money off of each other for these necessities. What's the point in being an owner if you can't buy the goods at retail for yourself?"

"Thanks, Mr. Evans." Frank handed him the forty-eight dollars. "See you when I get back."

Frank smiled and walked out the front door. He was smiling as he walked up the boardwalk, then he noticed Kelly approaching in his direction. *Ah, shit,* he thought. He also noticed her notice him. Frank recognized the eye aversion she dished out to him. He knew what that meant. She recognized his presence by not recognizing his existence. Frank could feel her anger as they passed, and he tipped his hat to her. *What rage*, he thought. *Life is too short. Let it go*. He debated whether or not he should ask for the books that he had lent to her. He knew she wasn't going to just give them back. Common sense helped him with his decision.

"What a beautiful day," Nate announced as he rode up with Maggie. Maggie nodded.

Frank was early to the stagecoach station. It was a temporary station that had been set up in front of the telegrapher's booth and post office.

"Morning," Frank replied. He looked around, then up to the blue sky. "It is a great looking day, but it's a little early for me. I like to sleep in. My reason for being up late is not a good one."

From across the street Brad came walking out of the Sheriff's office with Toby Gibson. They each had a cup of coffee in one hand and a cigarette in the other. They seemed to be of good spirits, and as Toby walked, he bounced on his toes causing his long bangs to bob up and down as he walked.

Brad yelled across the street, "Yo, Mr. Frank. I have a feeling that the stage will be arriving early. Think we can make it to Lasso City by sundown?"

"I reckon I'm willing if you are," Frank answered. "You got some more of that coffee?"

Toby said, "We do if you got a mug."

Frank spoke as he walked. "I think I can round a couple up. Keep it hot for us. We'll be over directly."

Nate tied Maggie to the hitching rail, and Frank ran into the telegrapher's office. He came out with two coffee mugs he had borrowed from the telegrapher. Frank could feel the excitement brewing in his soul, for he was happy to be hitting the road with his friends. He had forgotten how much fun a stagecoach trip could be when things went well.

Toby poured Frank and Nathan some coffee.

"Toby, I'm heading to the corral to gather up our horses," Brad said. He stepped out through the front door.

"Alright, we'll be along shortly to help you," Toby answered. Then, smiling, he whispered to Frank and Nate, "Let's see if he can gather up twelve horses by himself and make it back here without any help. What do you say?"

"I wouldn't put it past him," Frank said as he took a sip of coffee. He drank too much and burnt his lip.

"Put some money on it?" Toby said with a grin.

"I'll take that bet," Nate answered while digging into his pocket. As he pulled some coins from his pants pocket, he noticed Frank was carrying a sidearm. "You're freaking me out with that flame-thrower hanging off your belt. I'm not used to seeing you armed to the teeth like this. You expect to run into a cougar or some killer rabbits?"

"You know, I actually feel more comfortable with it. Scary, uh?" Frank replied.

Frank stepped back outside as Toby and Nate laid their money on the sheriff's desk. He saw his friend Sam from the railroad. Sam was carrying a big bag as he walked up the street. He was red from the effort.

"Frank," Sam yelled.

"Sam, what in tarnation are you doing here?"

"I'm hoping to come along with you, but Mr. Turner said I can't come. I got the money for it," Sam said in desperation. His eyes sought some reassurance from his friend.

Frank said, "It's okay with me. You can go if that's what you want."

Sam shook his hand. "It is, and I'm mighty obliged to you."

"Why do you need to go with us?"

"I'm going to head to Sawmill. There's a doctor there who might be able to help me," Sam said, choking on his words.

"What's the scoop, Sam? Cause you're worrying me a little."

"I don't want you to worry about me. I don't want to burden others with my problems, but the doctor isn't sure. I'm having real bad headaches, and I need some relief," Sam said, touching his forehead.

"Okay, it sounds important to you, so you absolutely can go," Frank said, patting his friend on the back. "But, you know, I think you're fine."

"Thanks."

"I got to get my stuff and welcome the stage, and it looks like it's getting close," Frank said, looking up the street at the far end of town. He could see a disturbance in the road that showed the stages were arriving. "I'll see you on the stage."

Frank walked back across the street and couldn't help but note an uncomfortable feeling in his gut when he saw Al Turner. Al was waiting at the post office with the gambler George Cummings who looked like he had been up gambling and drinking all night. Frank still felt like he knew him from somewhere, but couldn't place where. Maybe it was the mustache that threw him. There was something familiar about his eyes.

"Hello, Al. How are you this morning?" Frank asked as he greeted the actor turned politician.

Al replied, "Morning, Frank. This is George Cummings. He's the one I mentioned to you the other night."

"Hello. Nice to meet you," Frank said.

They shook hands. Frank noted that George had a firm but sweaty grip.

"The pleasure is all mine, Mr. Savage," George said, keeping his eyes just under the brim of his hat.

"How far are you going? But first, don't you ever sleep?" Frank inquired.

"Oh, Frank," Al interrupted. "George signed on with a no questions asked request. I do hope you understand."

The gambler stepped away while the two men spoke.

"Sure, not a problem. I will add, however, if Sam Buckshot wants to come, he is coming," Frank said.

Al started to rise on his hind legs to say something, but was cut short by Frank when he said, "No questions asked." He smiled and turned his attention to the two coaches that had just turned around the final bend on its way into the city. Dust kicked up around the horses' hooves.

Both coach drivers bellowed, "Whoa, whoa!"

After pulling the parking brake, the driver of the first coach said, while tipping his hat to the back of his head, "I hope you have cold beer in this town."

"It wouldn't be a real town if we didn't," Frank said.

The cowboy who was riding shotgun barked, "Great." He then leaped from his seat as he found his new purpose in life. "Just give us an hour, and the coaches will be all yours. We'll run our horses over to the livery stable. Once we sign the paperwork, the goods will be your responsibility until Sawmill. Sound like a plan?"

"Absolutely," Frank announced with an increased vibrancy. He smiled ear to ear.

Toby yelled, "Look." He pointed at Brad who was coming up the street on top of a Cleveland Bay. He had eleven more trailing behind him.

Toby grumbled. "Well, I'll be a son-of-a-gun, he did it."

The road they traveled was dusty and polluted with a few bumps and divots. With a blue sky for cover and green trees on each side of their path, Frank settled into his position of riding shotgun. He was admiring the weather when they hit a bump. The bounce was so abrupt it made Frank and Toby laugh.

"Man, I forgot how uncomfortable these seats are," Frank complained to Toby.

"Actually these are the nicest seats I've ever seen on a stagecoach. They're new, with leather, and a bit of padding. Mighty fancy, I must say."

"It may be nicer, and don't get me wrong, I do appreciate the effort, but my ass is killing me," Frank said. He stretched out and rubbed his lower back. "Actually, I think I'm just not used to it, and I have a bad back."

"You're getting old." Toby chuckled. "We've only been riding for a few hours."

Frank said, "I am so glad this is only a three-day trip. Although, about the time I start to get used to it, we'll be there."

The stagecoaches were beautifully built and were a dark reddish brown color. Nathan was driving the lead stage as planned, with Brad Simon riding shotgun. In the cab were Cassie and Sam Buckshot.

Toby Gibson drove the second stage as Frank rode shotgun. Frank had his Colt on his hip. He also had his Winchester in a scabbard behind his left shoulder and a scattergun in a sheath on his right. Al Turner and George Cummings sat in the cab.

Maggie trotted along behind the stage on the right side with a tether attached to her. Brad also had his Quarter horse, Corduroy, along. Corduroy was rigged to follow abeam Maggie on the left side. Nathan had rigged a harness that would make Maggie's trip a bit more comfortable. This way she wouldn't have reins tugging at her bit. Frank would look back every so often to make sure the two were okay. He caught a glimpse of the two walking closely, rubbing against each other. *Maggie has a new friend.*

With twelve beautiful Cleveland Bays working hard, they were sure to make Lasso City just before nightfall. The ride between the two towns was about twenty miles and was well ridden. It would be a smooth trip.

Al sat in his seat and stared at a sleeping George Cummings. George's head would frequently bounce and sway with the rhythm of the prairie wagon. Mr. Turner glared at George as his head rocked with the stage. He scoffed as George lay on his bench in an effort to get more comfortable. He rolled his eyes when the snoring started. Then the stage hit a moderate bump and George's sleeping body bounced to the floor. Al looked down upon him. George didn't wake, and snored louder than ever.

Toby was telling a story to Frank while driving the Bays. "I was on an old beat-up wagon about three months ago," Toby said. "And there was no leather cover to the seat, and the wood was old. I mean, this hunk of junk was aged. Can't believe I trusted my life to that thing getting me anywhere, let alone the long journey we were on. Anyway, the wagon couldn't handle the turns very well, and when we took a corner I slid in my seat. You know that happens all the time, but this wood splintered into my ass."

Frank cringed.

"I'm not talking about a little finger splinter. I'm talking about a six inch piece of wood."

"Oh, man, that's hurting me just thinking about it," Frank added, smirking.

"Tell me about it. I screamed out like a little girl, and Brad about falls off the wagon laughing when he heard me."

"So, how'd you get by with that?"

"We had to pull over. And in front of all our passengers, I had to pull my pants down while Brad took a pair of pliers and yanked the damn thing out. You wouldn't believe how much it bled. It was ridiculous."

"I bet he'll never let you live that down," Frank said.

"He told my girlfriend in front of her parents." Toby cupped his hand and yelled up to Brad on the lead coach, "Yo, Bradley! You're an ass!"

Brad turned in his seat. He thought someone might have yelled up to him. All he saw was Toby and Frank laughing.

"Did you hear something?" Brad asked.

"No, why? Did you hear something?" Nate responded.

"Thought I heard someone yell my name." Brad turned to his right and yelled into the cabin, "How are things down below? You all okay?"

Sam hollered out the window, "We're just peachy!"

"Now tell me how you and Nathan met," Sam said.

"Oh, that is a funny story, but I'm not so sure he wants me telling people," Cassie admitted.

Sam winked. "I won't tell anyone if you don't tell anyone about my girlfriends."

Cassie laughed. "It's a deal."

The coach hit a bump, and the two bounced in the air. Both reached out to grab their seats. They also happened to be wearing safety-belts across their laps, which kept them from hitting their heads.

"Whoa, that was quite a bump," Sam said with a snicker. "This is fun."

"It sure is, but I don't think I would want to do this for very long," said Cassie.

"Tell me about how you two met."

"Okay. Oh my, he would kill me. It was about two years ago. I had been in North Fork since I was a little girl. Nathan's family had just moved to the area and bought some land right next to my folk's ranch. I was about sixteen, and Nate had just turned seventeen."

Sam nodded as he listened.

"They hadn't been in town but more than a few days when they needed some supplies. I had gone into town with Pa to collect some things for the house. We had just finished loading the wagon when Nate came bounding into town on Maggie. Some kids saw Maggie and just fell in love with her and ran over to meet her. When he pulled up to the hitching rail at the storefront, he started to swing out of his saddle. At that moment something caught his eye." Cassie stopped telling her story.

"And what might that have been, I wonder?" Sam said.

"Why, that would be me, of course," Cassie replied. "I smiled at him just as he was swinging his leg around to dismount, and his knee gave out, or his foot slipped or something, and he fell."

"Oh, no." Sam snickered. "And he's so proud of his horses."

"Yep, and he fell hard, too. He landed such that he hit his head on a horse trough. He knocked himself out cold."

"Ouch, not good."

Cassie continued, "No, and I felt so bad for him. Pa and I ran him over to the doc's office, and he patched him up. I had to stay up all night with him. We've been together ever since. I never tell people about the falling off the horse thing, so please don't mention this to anyone."

"Not a word," Sam promised.

Sam and Cassic were having a good laugh when they felt the wagon bounce suddenly. It wasn't a bump. The jolt felt different, more like a twisting motion.

"Whoa, whoa!" Nate bellowed. Once the horses came to a stop, he threw on the parking brake. "Did you hear that?"

"Yes, yes, I did. It was like a sharp crack or a snap sound," Brad answered.

Nate swung down to inspect the wagon.

"What happened?" Frank asked as he walked up to the stage to help assist.

"I don't know," Nate replied, looking under the frame of the stage. "The road was smooth enough, and I didn't see any rocks or holes. We felt a bump as if the frame twisted. We heard a crack sound, but I don't see anything."

"Boy, that could have come from anywhere," Frank responded. He gave the stage a quick look over. They spent the next ten minutes inspecting the wagon, but found nothing.

"Well, we better get rolling if we want to sleep in a bed tonight," Brad said, trying to push things along.

"Alright, let's move. We can look things over again in the morning," Frank hollered over his shoulder as he started his walk back to his stage where Al sat and George still slept.

The sun was down, and the moon was up, but the clouds were blocking most of its light from reaching the small town of Lasso City. Frank, Brad and Sam had just cleaned up at the hotel and were on their way to the saloon for a drink.

They walked along the boardwalk toward the saloon, tipping their hats to the fairer sex as they passed. They all had to get up relatively early, but as a group they had decided to enjoy their trip and relax with a couple of beers. Al decided to lock himself in his room, and Nate chose to spend some time with his girlfriend. Besides, Nathan didn't drink alcohol, and he promised his mother he would stay out of the gambling rooms.

Frank felt uneasy about the trip through Lasso and onto Sawmill when he had first contemplated going. Recently, though, he noticed how relaxed he felt, and was now actually enjoying the trek. He was remembering how fun being on the trail could be. But his fun would be short-lived.

"Sounds noisy tonight," Frank remarked. Concern popped into his fore mind. They stood in the middle of the dirt-covered street. Nobody said anything for a moment. Frank was once again feeling some apprehension. His casual air was evaporating.

Frank broke the silence and said, "I've been in this town on at least a dozen occasions, and it has never sounded this rambunctious."

Brad scoffed, "Ah, Frank, it's probably no big deal. There are just some local cowboys in town burning off some steam. And, why did you take your gun off?"

Frank replied, "I'm not at work. I know this town, and there is no reason to walk around armed. Someday Bradley, no one is going to carry a gun."

Brad patted the gun on his hip. "Well, until that day, I'll never go without mine."

"I'm starting to agree more and more with your line of thinking," Frank said. "Let's have a drink, but before we go in," Frank turned to Brad and continued. "You have to promise me you'll raise your standards on the ladies, just for tonight."

Brad paused in thought, then said, "You know, I could promise you that now. I'm just worried that once I have a few drinks, I'm afraid that'll just go out the window."

Sam laughed, pushed the two friends to the front entrance of the bar and said, "Let's go, fellows. We don't have all night to dilly-dally."

Stepping into the saloon, Frank noticed right off how smoky it was. There didn't seem to be any more people than normal. However, there were some new faces. There existed some grubby unfriendly mugs, one of whom eyeballed the three as they worked their way to the bar. When the man's eyes got to Frank, his face shone with recognition.

Savage saw two tell tale signs of a man who had had too much influence from the bottle. Glassy eyes and lazy lids pasted on an ever-prevalent grim expression.

There were four players at the table where the grim one played cards. Only one player from the group did Frank recollect. His name was Henry, and he was a friendly, affable local farmer who enjoyed gambling on a

Friday night. That was the night his wife would allow him to divulge in his vices.

Frank didn't like the other three. He knew trouble traveled close behind wherever they roamed. The dirty drunkard had a full beard, and they all had a similar crude look about them. Frank kept his vision on the drunk and his buddies. He scanned the man's gun-belt, but was unable to see what he carried, or how.

The grim-one brought the attention of his two friends upon the three newcomers. A scantily dressed woman sat on his lap as he played cards. She was attempting to woo him upstairs.

"Three beers, please," Brad dictated to the bartender. The bartender nodded and said hello to Frank, for he recognized him.

"Hi, Thomas," Frank said, then quietly he continued, "different crowd tonight."

Thomas poured the drinks as he spoke with a hushed voice. "The bearded one is three sheets to the wind and an asshole."

"I gathered that," added Frank"His name, which I just overheard a few minutes ago, is J.D. I don't know much about them, but what I have heard ain't good. They're hired gun hands, and I don't rightly understand why they're in Lasso, but I wish they'd move on."

"Do you know the other two?" Sam interjected over Brad's shoulder.

Thomas said, "The man with his back to us, his name is Kelton. You can't see it, but he has a black patch over his left eye."

"How quaint, a fashion statement I reckon," Frank joked.

Thomas smirked and said, "Don't make me laugh. They'll think we're making fun."

"I'm sorry. To each his own, I guess."

Thomas continued, "The third fellow, the larger bald one, I have not heard his handle yet. He is surprisingly polite and follows the orders of the other two. I also overheard J.D. say he was looking to give someone what for. From what I can see, guys, he seems to have his eyes on you, Frank."

Frank turned sideways to the bar to face Brad and Sam. He could still see some movement through the mirror behind the bar. He moved slowly in an attempt to not provoke any unwanted attention. Glancing into the mirror he could see J.D.'s hat, but he could not tell how well armed he was.

Thomas whispered, "This is so bizarre."

Frank sat still, he said, "Yeah?"

Thomas said, "As soon as that man walked in, I thought to myself, 'I wish Frank Savage was here'."

"Get off me, you withered old woman." J.D. pushed the woman off his lap with a shove that caused her to bounce on her bum off the floor.

Frank made a check toward the table to see what was going on and J.D. saw it. "Yo, *Salvage*!"

Frank took a sip of his beer and continued as if in conversation with his friends.

The ruffian blurted out again, "I said, yo, *Salvage*. I'm talkin to you."

They all continued to ignore the drunken obnoxious troublemaker. Frank smiled as he drank, knowing full well that he was more than likely agitating the fool. Frank said to his friends, "I can't believe I followed you two in here."

"I'm sorry, Frank. I didn't know," Sam said regretfully.

"It's not your fault, Sam. It's Brad's," Frank said, poking a finger at Brad.

"Look, man," Brad replied defensively, "the trouble follows you, not me."

"Frank, we're here for you, but I'm not carrying either," Sam added with concern.

"When we throw down, Sam, step back out of the way," Frank directed.

The screech of a chair being pushed back across the floor reverberated through the saloon. Then, it was quiet. Everyone seemed to be frozen, awaiting the next move. Two of the smarter gamblers managed to sneak out the front door without making a sound. One of them was Henry. Everyone else could feel the tension building but chose to stay, in order to view the excitement first-hand.

"I'm talkin to you, *Salvage*!" J.D. bellowed again as his one-eyed partner, Kelton, attempted to get him to take a seat. J.D. was having none of that.

Frank remained at his stance perpendicular to the bar face to face with Brad so he could take a peek into the mirror when need be. Brad was in a position that he could keep his eyes on their new adversary. Frank calmly looked into the bar's mirror and saw that his newfound enemy was a big and somewhat round man. He was still unsure how armed he was. Frank was slightly taken aback when he saw Nathan come in the front door of the saloon. *Shit, I promised his folks he'd be okay.* Frank then turned his back to the gunman.

"You didn't just do that," J.D. roared angrily as he started to approach the bar.

"Gun," Frank stated to Brad.

"Left hip, cross draw," Brad answered calmly.

"Diversion please," Frank said. He acted like he was still enjoying his drink.

The chubby bearded man was almost breathing down Frank's neck.

"Not a problem, buddy," Brad said slyly.

Frank set his beer down and saw J.D. go to shove him into the bar. Brad dumped his beer onto the oppressor's feet. J.D. looked down, and at that moment Savage turned to his left. With one continuous motion he had un-holstered the gunman's pistol, cocked it, and pointed it directly under J.D.'s chin.

"I warned you, you fool," Kelton snapped. Kelton and his bald companion simultaneously dropped their hands to their waists to arm themselves. Brad had them beat, so they hesitated, and in that fateful moment of indecisiveness they became aware of Nate's Colt as he flipped back the hammer. His instincts suited the moment. He had them covered from behind.

"It's Savage," Frank said. He walked forward forcing J.D. to step back. "Say it," Frank ordered.

"Savage," J.D. uttered under duress.

"I don't think you'll make that mistake again. Take a seat," Frank commanded.

J.D. didn't budge. He just eyed his new enemy with anger and frustration. His hands were shaking as if he wanted to move them, but he didn't know how.

"That sure is a nice hat you have on." Savage pushed the gun farther into the soft spot under his chin. "I'd hate to have to put a hole in it."

"Take your seat, J.D.," Kelton said firmly. "That's an order."

An order?

It was only then that J.D. stepped back to his table and reluctantly took his seat. He continued to stare down his opponents.

Frank stepped back to the bar and unloaded the six-shooter and discarded the shells into the dirty spittoon that was resting by his feet.

"Why, you," J.D. spit out through his clenched teeth.

Frank handed the gun to Thomas the bartender.

"Do not give this to him until we're gone."

Thomas held the gun and said, "You got it, Frank."

Frank noticed a flash of motion in the mirror and heard a cry of warning. A shot rang out. The flash he had seen was J.D. who had bolted from his seat as Frank had handed Thomas the gun.

The shot was from Nate's pistol. Upon seeing the attack, Nate shot the leg off a chair. It sent the big bald gunman sprawling to the floor with his arms flailing.

"Don't shoot," Frank dictated to Brad.

Frank moved fast in response to his attacker. He shifted his body to the side. J.D. ran into the bar chest first, knocking the wind out of his lungs with a grunt.

Kelton spun around as he attempted to go for his gun a second time. Brad grabbed a chair and tossed it to Kelton's feet, causing him to trip on it. Kelton fell flat on his face and lost his pistol on his way down. Nate was overshadowing the bald man after having disarmed him. He covered his downed opponent so his godfather could take care of business on his end.

Savage grasped J.D.'s right forearm and twisted it. He then put his leg behind his attacker and pushed him over backwards. The heavy gunman fell on his back. Savage continued to twist with his right hand as he choked J.D. with his left. With J.D. on his back, Savage slowly tightened his grip on his throat.

Everyone in the bar was motionless, watching. Nate's eyes were taking everything in. He had never seen his godfather like this. It was as though he was a different person. Nate watched a much darker man. It made him cringe as he held tightly to his pistol.

J.D. tried to swing with his free arm, but to no avail. Everyone could hear his neck gurgle and crunch. He tried to gasp for some air, but was unable to. J.D.'s face was bright red and his eyes bulged as if they were either going to come out of his head or explode in their sockets.

Savage sat on his chest with his knee and bent over to whisper in the dying man's ear. Only J.D. could hear him. "Thank you. I would much rather kill you with my bare hands."

J.D.'s partners, as well as everyone else, watched with dropped jaws.

"Frank?" Brad said quietly.

At that instant, Frank released his grip and stood. It was quiet except for J.D.'s coughing as he attempted to breathe. Frank took a slow look around the saloon as he worked to slow his heart rate. The watchers in the bar all seemed to be waiting with baited breath.

Frank said, "Well, enough of the pleasantries." He turned to Nate. "I want you to escort these two to their horses and make sure they leave town."

Nate replied, "Yes, sir."

"Brad, will you take this one down to the Sheriff's office for me?"

Brad said, "Sure thing."

"See you next time, Thomas. Sorry about the ruckus." Frank exited the saloon as if nothing had happened.

Thomas waved, nodded, and whispered, "Okay, next time." His voice cracked.

Brad looked down as J.D. was starting to get his bearings.

Brad said, "You truly are a moron. You want a little advice? First off, do you see that mirror?" Brad spoke as he pointed to the back mirror behind the bartender. J.D. slowly got to his feet. Brad continued, "You can see everything going on behind you. Pretty neat, Huh?"

Brad belittled J.D. further. "Secondly, why would you mess with Frank Savage? I bet you don't do that again. You know what? You're so stupid that I should shoot you right now just to keep you from spreading your idiot seed. What'd ya think about that? Good idea?"

Brad escorted J.D. to the jailhouse. He said, "It's a shame, you're more than likely only gonna spend the night in jail. At best, you'll be forced to pay a twenty-dollar fine for disorderly conduct."

As Brad handed J.D. over to the deputy he said, "You might want to lose the key to this one. Better yet, an accidental discharge of a firearm into his face might work."

The deputy locked J.D. in a cell. After he closed the door, J.D. stammered, "I'll get you. I'll get you--" Brad halted the new prisoner's speech by executing a punch to the mouth through the cell's bars.

The deputy said, "Now here, you can't be doing that."

Brad said, "That was for Frank Savage."

The deputy replied, "Savage?"

"Yeah, Savage," Brad said with his arms crossed.

"Oh, well, okay then."

CHAPTER 7

The last flame had flickered across the night sky hours ago. A small camp rested quietly in a hollow surrounded by trees. The first glimmer of sunshine was beginning to spill over the horizon. It was still dark, but the sky was lightening in the east while the stars were still visible to the west.

The gunman snapped up from his slumber to a sitting position with his gun pointed, searching for a target that wasn't there. He sat with his eyes darting around as he attempted to see through his haze. Breathing heavily, he slowly calmed down. A realization came to him, he'd been dreaming. The gunman's dreams were more often than not, quite violent. He slept with a gun in hand and sometimes with one eye open.

Conrad Bovis was a handsome man who always wore a black hat that he matched with a black vest and slacks. He remained aware of his surroundings, which was why his dreams startled him so much.

The wind warbled through the trees, and Conrad noticed the sun would be pushing its way into his world within the hour. It was time to get up. *Coffee sounds good*, he thought, *and some bacon*. The nervous cowboy shook away his nightmares and got out of his bedroll. He kicked his two partners awake. They were none too happy about it, but he was the boss.

"Jesus, Bovis, you don't have to knock me conscious," the now awake Sherman said. "I can wake up just fine with a, 'hey Sherm, time to get up.' Or, how about throwing some coffee on the fire and letting the smell arouse me? This isn't the military, for shit-sake." Sherman cleaned the sleep out of the corner of his eye with his knuckle.

Bovis replied, "I reckon not, but I got me some nervous energy built up inside, Sherm."

"You always got nervous energy. You're wound up like a Swiss pocket watch," Sherm snapped.

"Do you see the likes of Kelt, J.D. or Hector?" asked Bovis.

Sherman looked about and scratched his head. He sealed his nostrils with a finger one at a time and blew snot to the ground.

"What the hell?" Bovis barked.

Bovis stood with his hands on his hips and then walked to the wood pile.

"Styles," Bovis said as he threw some wood on the fire he had just lit. Sparks and ash flew up and evaporated into the air.

"Yes, sir," Styles replied. He attempted to get to his feet in the midst of a sleepy state. He stumbled clumsily out of his bedroll.

Bovis asked, "What was Kelt's plan if we didn't see them this morning?"

"He assured me they would be here before we woke," answered Styles.

"Alright." Conrad Bovis stood in thought. He was an intelligent, but troubled man. And for now, he had a one-track mind. "We'll wait."

"How long?" Sherm asked.

Bovis looked at the ground and said, "Haven't decided yet."

Bovis felt a bolt of pain flash through his skull. He said, "Get some more wood for the fire. Start packing." *Damn that hurt*, he thought. He then ordered, "Water the horses first." Bovis turned away so the others couldn't see his face.

"Aye, aye, captain," Sherm said. He followed up with a half-assed salute.

Styles finished rolling his bedroll, and then cleaned out his coffee cup with sand. Bovis had forced himself to put some bacon in the skillet. He had a cigarette in his mouth that hung from his lips with a long ash.

"You don't really talk much," Styles said.

Casually Bovis responded, "I ain't got much to say."

"We are getting paid pretty well ain't we?" Styles said nervously.

Bovis had a powerful reputation as a man you do not want to cross. The deal was that Bovis didn't treat them disrespectfully.

Bovis knew Styles and the others had a tough time understanding him. Most guns for hire had a certain way about them. They were despicable and untrustworthy. Bovis was different.

"I'm not doing this for the money," Bovis remarked.

"The boys and me were talking about that the other day," said Styles.

"Oh yeah?" Bovis remained stoic. He attempted to relax, but with little success.

Styles continued, "Yeah, we know about you and your reputation with a gun and ah . . . we just wanted to know."

"Okay, go on."

"You want us to capture, but not to kill. That is, unless you say so."

"Kelt's got the list," Bovis said matter-of-factly.

"Well, why can't we take out Savage? He's too damn dangerous to leave alive."

Bovis said, "Because a higher authority says so. I'm following orders just like you." He started to eat some bacon he'd been frying. He left some in the pan for the others. "Besides--" He took another bite.

Styles waited for Bovis to finish, but he didn't. So Styles asked, "He's yours, ain't he?"

"The deal I made doesn't concern you." Bovis took his last bite.

"You're gonna shoot him down."

Pensively Bovis whispered, "Something like that."

Styles shook his head and shrugged. "Okay, I think I understand, I guess."

A disturbance in the direction of the horses caught their attention. Sherm shot out of the trees and said, "We got company."

Bovis, in a blink of an eye, stood with two pistols drawn. He paused in thought. "Wait," he directed. "I'll take a look." He holstered his guns and pulled a telescopic eyepiece from his bag. He moved to the entrance.

There were two ways into the camp, one for the entrance and another in case an escape was needed. Bovis looked through his lens at the entry road that approached through a narrow valley. He saw two riders. He recognized the gait of the horses. Bovis lowered his head and looked at his partners with disappointment. "It's Kelton and Hector."

"No J.D.?" Sherm asked.

"No, he's not with them. Let's finish cleaning up."

Sherm and Styles had the camp about cleaned up when they heard Kelton.

"Hello the camp," Kelton yelled as they got within earshot of the campsite.

"Come on in, Kelt," Styles hollered back.

The two demoralized and tired riders dismounted. Their heads hung slightly, and their eyelids drooped.

"I'm listening," Bovis said. His hand was never far from his gun. He looked sternly at Kelton.

"J.D. got himself arrested," Kelt said, looking tensely at his boss.

"I can't say that I'm surprised. I knew we hired an idiot when we took him on. You get what you pay for." Bovis was grim, and he still worked to calm himself. His head hurt.

"He, uh . . . well that's not the worst of it," added Kelt.

"Go on, please." Bovis placed a hand on his head then jerked it away abruptly.

"We ran into Savage, and J.D. was drunk and--"

Bovis interrupted, "Just answer one question. Is Savage alive?"

"Oh yeah, he's very much alive." Kelt slipped his thumbs in his belt and half smiled as he spoke.

Bovis said, "Well, that was a dumb question. Okay, I lied, I have two questions. Does Savage know of our plans?"

"No, sir, they just think J.D. was a drunkard," Kelt answered. "You should have seen this guy. I've never seen anything like it."

Bovis walked away agitated and uninterested in what Kelt had to say.

Kelton continued telling his story. "He almost killed J.D. with his bare hands. It was weird, too. It was like, he wanted to, but he knew he shouldn't. He's just too deliberate and fast. I hope you guys understand what we're up against. I am not looking forward to what we have to do. How about you, Hector? You looking forward to this?"

"No, sir," Hector replied courteously.

"See? No way, no how, can this all turn out good." Kelton shook his head. "It might be fun trying, though."

Styles and Sherman just stood there listening and soaking up every word.

"You planning on quitting, Kelt?" Bovis bellowed.

"Well . . . no, I ain't quit'n. I'm just say'n--"

"I know what you're saying. I want Sherm and Styles to take some gold coins and ride into town. I want you to be respectful and pay whatever you have to pay to free J.D. As dumb as he is, we need six to pull this off. No drinking, none. Do you understand?" Their boss pointed with his finger as he spoke.

"Yes, boss," Styles said. "We'll do right by you. You can count on us."

Bovis stood rigidly and said, "We'll meet at High Ridge Pass. When you head out, don't take the road, they'll have almost a half a day head start on that road. You won't be able to get around them without them seeing you. If you can't get J.D., leave him. Remember that you must beat the stages to the pass or this will not work. I want you to take the

Stampede River. It's the most direct route. If you hustle, you should make it, with some time to spare. Get fresh horses in Lasso and that should help. Now move!"

Styles and Sherm swung into their saddles and lit out for Lasso to free their partner.

Bovis stood still as he watched his two men ride off. He felt like he was losing control. A part of him didn't seem to mind. He looked up at the now lit sky and said, "It's going to be a full moon tomorrow night".

Kelton turned to Hector and said, "That Savage is a dangerous man. Isn't he, Hec?"

"Yes, sir," Hector replied courteously.

Kelton slid a finger under his black eye patch up to the knuckle and scratched the inside wall of his eye socket. He grumbled, "Damn, J.D., he kept me from getting laid. I'm all worked up."

Bovis stepped away from the conversation and turned his back to the campsite. His head dropped violently forward, and he put his hand on his temple. He knew the touch wouldn't halt the hurt that lurched through his head, but it was all he could do.

Bovis picked up his pace and walked into the woods. Ducking and swerving, he worked his way farther into the brush until he felt he was out of hearing range of the others. He dropped to his knees and held his head in his palms. Panting, he pushed harder and harder on his temples. He rolled forward onto his face. His hat fell aside. He whimpered, and spit sprayed out of his mouth as he breathed.

Breathing deeply, Bovis sat back up and put his hand on his gun. He rested his hand there for a few moments, and then cocked back the hammer. Continuing to hold his head with his left hand, he pulled the gun from his holster. He glanced down at the weapon with his eyes vibrating rapidly back and forth. He spun the cylinder slowly with his thumb. Looking at the weapon that had killed so many people, a shot of his pain moved down his spine. Losing control of his body, he fell to his back. He looked up through the leaves of the trees that fluttered overhead. It was then that Conrad Bovis could see his family from his youth.

Conrad whispered, "I'm sorry. Please forgive me." His lip quivered as he spoke.

Conrad pulled the gun up in front of his face and stared at the brilliant shine of his most prized possession. He focused on the muzzle. His arm began to shake. Tears rolled down his temples and over his ears to the ground.

As Bovis lay, his tears evaporated. A sneer crept to his face. The pain was there, but now he felt no hurt. Grinding his teeth, he sat up and holstered his weapon. He glared straight ahead, but was not seeing what was in front of him.

It was a nice enough room. A soft warm bed sat on a dark brown wood floor with a plush rug that matched the burgundy-colored walls. Frank sat at the side of his bed with his feet comfortably resting on the delicate rug, he didn't notice. He eyed a chair in the corner of the room. Next to the chair was a partially open window. The cream curtains flowed effortlessly with the cool morning breeze. Frank stared, but could only see what he was dreaming about. Images in his brain flashed from his past.

He could see his old house. He'd only been home from his service to the union for a few days. His wife sat in the living room. She was a pretty blue eyed blonde. She had seemed aloof ever since he had arrived home.

Frank had hoped that when he returned from the military that their connection would not have been lost. He found a letter in the dresser drawer of their bedroom. It had been written by his wife, but not yet sent. Maybe it was for him and he had returned home before she could send it to him. He did love her.

As he read, he could all but keep his eyes open. Frank dropped the letter to the floor. He lowered his head to his knees and put his hand on his forehead. He moved to the living room after sitting for awhile. His wife Pamela cried when he showed her that he had found the letter. It was a letter about a rendezvous in New York. Frank sat down and looked into Pam's face. He knew the tears were not genuine, but secretly wished they were.

Brad bellowed as he knocked on the door. Frank jolted to and wiped a tear from his cheek. He answered his friend's query. Brad's footsteps could be heard clomping down the stairs of the hotel as he left.

Frank could see her face when he closed his eyes. He hated himself for it, not being man enough to let go. No woman should be allowed to have a hold of you like this. His eyes flowed. The room was so cloudy. He stood briefly, and then sat back down on the bed. Frank felt betrayed by his best friend in life. He knew she didn't love him, never did, and never could.

He sulked. *Chemicals in the body, that's all this is*, he thought. Frank believed that he was going to live a long life, alone. He had the conscious perception that he would have a good life, but it would be isolated and without. He knew that in his final years, he would be void.

Frank washed up, dressed, strapped on his gun, picked up his Winchester and put on his hat. He arrived at the diner in time to share some breakfast with his companions. He paid for everyone's meal, ignoring his friend's cries of dissent. He did this in lieu of feeling the pain in his chest.

On the walk to the stagecoach, Nate told them of his morning. He had arrived to pick up Maggie and Corduroy from the stable and noticed how close the two were standing. Nate's story was interrupted. At that moment they all smiled when they saw Corduroy at the hitching rail with Maggie, she was resting her head gently over the crook of his neck.

Frank took his post at the door of the stagecoach with Toby. They welcomed back Al and George, as well as the two newcomers.

The two additional passengers were a man and his wife. Frank took note that they were almost the same height. Not that the man, Jesse, was short. It was that his wife, Cathy, was pretty tall. Jesse stumbled off the last step of the boardwalk, and his foot stepped off the path when he attempted to catch himself. His foot landed in mud. Frank wondered if these two were going to be a handful. He smiled at Toby, embarrassed for the man. Cathy, who was wearing bloomers, assisted her husband. *I bet she rides a horse like a man.* Frank was impressed with a woman who rode a horse like a man. But he did prefer women who wore dresses.

Frank was beginning to forget the events from the previous night as well as his melancholy from earlier in the morning.

With the stages all loaded, Nate and Toby took the reins of their respective teams and snapped them forward. With a moderately paced trot they moved along kicking up dust until they were out of sight of Lasso City.

Everyone was still waking from a deep slumber. Jesse and Cathy held hands. Al rolled his eyes. Cathy scowled at Al's disdain for them. She threw a quick glance to George Cummings, who was still a bit standoffish.

Cathy whispered to her husband Jesse, "This might be a long ride."

J.D. was brooding in his cell when he heard a knock on the front door of the sheriff's office. The deputy was on duty.

"Who is it?" inquired the deputy.

"It's Mrs. Anderson, I have dinner for you," Mrs. Anderson said cheerfully.

J.D. could almost smell the roast beef with gravy and taste the pie, he was so hungry. The deputy unlocked the door. At that instant Mrs. Anderson screamed. J.D. stood rapidly to catch a glimpse of the activities in the office. He saw Sherm barge in with a shotgun. Sherm swiftly pointed the scattergun at the deputy. Next to Sherm appeared Styles. He had lifted Mrs. Anderson with one arm wrapped around her and a Colt extending from the other. They charged into the jail so dramatically that they sent the food splashing to the floor.

"What the--" said the deputy. He stepped backward a step with his hands in the air.

Sherm said, while pulling a bag of coins from his pocket, "Now, I was told to be respectful, so that means I ain't gonna shoot you. That is, unless I have to."

Styles laughed. Mrs. Anderson started squirming in his arm and yelled, "You let me go, you degenerate smelly oaf!"

She worked herself free, stumbled and straightened herself to respectability. Styles smelled his armpit.

Sherm directed a smarmy grin at the deputy. "Like I was saying." The deputy couldn't take his eyes off Sherm and his misaligned and bi-colored teeth. "I was instructed to get J.D. out of jail. Respectfully, how much?"

"Um, well, disorderly conduct is twenty dollars," the deputy said as he attempted to keep his composure. "Can, can I put my hands down, please?"

"You may, sir." Sherm waved his gun. "But slowly, please." He pulled twenty dollars worth of coins from his bag and laid them on the desk.

They stood there looking at each other. Mrs. Anderson was starting to get antsy.

Sherm nodded. "Well?"

"Oh." The deputy pulled the keys from his belt and unlocked the cell.

Sherm pulled another coin from his sack and laid it on the table. "This is for the dinner we respectfully ruined. I am truly and respectfully sorry, ma'am." He took his hat off and nodded to Mrs. Anderson. She huffed.

J.D. said, "Thanks, boys." He bounced out of the cell.

"A respectfully good evening to you," Sherm said, walking backwards out the door. He tipped his hat to Mrs. Anderson. On his way out, J.D. scooped the pie from the floor and ate it in one bite.

J.D. said to Mrs. Anderson, "Nice work. Thanks." He gave her a thumbs up. He then burst out the front door after his partners. They hustled around to the side of the jail.

J.D. inquired, "What the hell does degenerate mean?"

Sherm looked over at Styles for an answer. Styles shrugged.

Sherm replied, "Don't rightly know, J.D. It can't be good, though. I agree with her in that Styles wouldn't be hurt by a bath."

J.D. said matter-of-factly, "We all could use a good bath."

Three horses waited around the side of the jail. The three outlaws mounted simultaneously. They heeled their horses up the street on their way to a meeting. And they mustn't be late.

The glow of orange and yellow flashed upon Frank's face as he sat looking upon the fire. He had built the fire while the others readied the camp, watered the horses and prepared supper. He sat on a log with George Cummings on his left. Frank spoke quietly, as if he didn't want the others to hear. "I frequently look back on my life, and I try, almost desperately, to figure out how it's all going for me."

George sat silent. He had settled in an uncomfortable position, but remained still as Frank spoke. He held his plate of food when it was handed to him, but didn't eat. He was hungry but he only looked at his food as he listened. The gambler had to relieve his bladder gravely, but he held it. His eyes darted about under the brim of his black gambler's hat.

Frank continued, "Some days I feel proud of my accomplishments. I think of my service to my country, and I know it's something I should be proud of. I feel deep down I should feel some self-satisfaction even though most people aren't all that impressed."

Frank smiled as he accepted his meal from Cathy. "Thank you." He paused in thought.

Everyone was seated around the fire eating and watching the glow, fixated on the hypnotic glare. Brad was trying to listen to what Frank was talking about, but could only catch a word here and there.

Jesse tried to straighten out his pants to get comfortable and fumbled with his plate. He almost lost it to the fire. His fork fell into the ashes at the edge of the ring. "Dang-it!" He rustled up a stick and attempted to retrieve the utensil. Cassie smiled at Jesse's wife, Cathy, who was watching her husband clumsily work the stick on his fork. Feeling the heat, he almost fell backwards over the log he and Cathy were sharing.

Cathy said to everybody in earshot, "My husband works best under pressure."

Frank turned his head to George, who still hadn't taken a taste of his food, and said, "You'd think people would be grateful. It doesn't work that way." He stopped to take a bite of his biscuit, and then continued, "Other days I don't see accomplishments. On those days I see only disappointment and failure. As hard as I try, though, I cannot remember a specific day. Just flashes in my mind of a visual event like scenes in a play. I frequently wonder if some of my memories are real. They seem to blend in with my dreams sometimes."

Frank glanced back at George who just sat there looking at his plate. "I know you're tired, George. I can see that. It's in your manner, and it's visible in your eyes."

Underneath the brim of his hat George could see Cathy looking at him. She was listening.

"I am also concerned with the fact that you're running from something."

George jerked his head.

Frank said, "But I do not know why you're on the move. I'm not sure what you are running from or from whom. I do know, however, that I have seen you somewhere before. I reckon I might remember before the trip is over, or maybe not." Frank paused. "Maybe you'll let me know where I've seen you before. I'm aware that you remember me, but you're afraid for some reason."

Frank took a bite of ham and a spoonful of beans in one scoop.

Frank said to the crowd, "Outstanding, Cathy. Thanks again."

George nodded and sat sullenly, looking off into the distance. His food was cold before he finally took a spoon and began to eat.

Nate added, "That's a fact. Great vittles, Cathy. Thanks."

Cathy smiled. "Thank you and you're all welcome."

"Yep," added Jesse, "my wife has become one hell of a cook. It wasn't always this good."

Cathy tapped Jesse in the ribs with her elbow.

Nathan finished his second plate and some of Cassie's. He then whispered to his girlfriend, "I'm going to go check on Maggie." He gave Cassie a kiss on the cheek. As he went to walk away, she held onto his hand. When she didn't release his grip, he turned back to her. As he looked into her face she said, "I love you."

Nate stammered but his instincts quickly took over. He moved behind her and put his left palm over her left cheek. He bent down with his lips touching her hair. George noticed the shine off of Nate's eyes.

Nate whispered into her ear, "I love you, too, Sweetheart." He kissed her neck and slowly pulled away into the trees.

The camp was only a few yards away from the horse pen that Nate had roped off earlier in the evening. Once again, Maggie and Corduroy stood together. Their noses were gently touching, as if they were resting on each other.

CHAPTER 8

Sherm, Styles and J.D. rode the path they were instructed to by Conrad Bovis. They moved deep into the night before resting for a few hours. Once they arrived at the river they slept and ate. They departed at first light and advanced quickly. The group galloped along the river with their hooves kicking up mist. The liquid moistened their chaps in the cold damp air. Surprisingly there were no complaints.

Another individual who was surprisingly quiet was Al Turner. The stagecoach camp awoke with the sun, and after a leisurely breakfast, the group hit the trail.

Everyone was in good spirits, seemingly with no concern. Everyone except Frank and Cathy felt comfortable. Frank was worried about his night in Lasso City when he had met a drunken cowboy by the name of J.D. He was also distraught with the fact that he could not remember where he had met George Cummings. He could only recall that he knew him from a case he had worked on years earlier. Frank thought that maybe it was when he was in Montana. He was certain, though, that he never met the man during his military days.

When two events came to the forefront in his mind at the same time, he took it seriously. He took it as a sign. As the two events were worked over in his head, it triggered in Frank a state of disquietude.

Cathy, too, moved about with furrowed brow. Only Jesse was conscious of what was bothering her because she shared her thoughts with him the night before. As Frank's stagecoach rolled across the ground in the early hours of the morning, another campsite was close by, and underway.

Conrad Bovis sat in his saddle. He scanned the landscape from the top of a short, steep edged, dusty hill with Hector and Kelton. Bovis was deep in thought about his plans and how they were to be carried out. His location was perfect, and his weapons were loaded. All that was needed was the rest of his gang. Their three partners were in route, he hoped. His only other concern was that he would need the element of surprise to take Savage alive.

Bovis looked over his list of names and descriptions one last time. At the top of the list was Frank Savage. He ordered Kelton to do the same. He was sure Kelt would listen. It wasn't that Kelt respected him, but Bovis knew Kelton was fearful of their employer. The man they worked for had a wrath that you would not survive if you were in its path.

Kelt never would've taken the job from this man in the first place if he had been told who they would have to capture. Savage would not be an easy man to trap.

Kelton was an evil, almost despicable individual who also carried fear deep down inside. It would rear its ugly head from time to time. But he was the smartest of the lot whom Bovis had to work with.

Kelt would not have taken the job if he had known who the boss was either. But, once he said yes, there was no turning back, and he knew this.

Bovis was not told who he was to catch at first hire. He took the job for the money. But he stayed with the job because of his target, Savage. The target was a man he knew. His head hurt more and more with each day, and this was going to be his time. His destiny was here. Bovis was approaching a place and time where he would once again meet the man he had personally taught everything he knew.

After a short break to rest their twelve Cleveland Bays, one Appaloosa named Maggie and one Steeldust named Corduroy, they were once again on the move.

Nathan bellowed, "Roll 'em, ho!"

Frank's trepidation was getting worse. He had thought about turning back to Lasso City. They were already past the point of no return, over the halfway mark, so he decided against it. Besides, nobody else would support or agree with his decision. If they did support it, they more than likely would think he was crazy or overreacting. Al Turner would throw a conniption fit.

Frank figured that if they traveled about twenty miles a day on said road, they would need to spend one more night on the trail. That would put them in Sawmill by tomorrow afternoon, a few hours ahead of schedule.

"Sam?" Cassie said breaking the silence in the jostling cabin.

"Yes," Sam replied.

"Is your last name really Buckshot?" she asked.

"Um," Sam answered with hesitation while fidgeting with his hat, "No, it's more of a nick-name."

"Why? Do you carry a shotgun or something?"

"Oh, I knew you'd ask. It's something altogether different."

Cassie looked at him with her big round eyes expecting him to continue.

He did continue, reluctantly. "Well, I've been shot once with a shotgun."

Her fingers over her lips, she gasped. "Oh my, what on earth happened?"

"Uh." Sam shifted his position. "Well, I've had relations with some married women. Please, don't think too badly of me."

He looked at Cassie, he waited for some disappointment or understanding. The only response he got was an unassuming quizzical look. She was so innocent.

Sam continued, "I for some reason have found myself to be attracted to women who have husbands." Sam's explanation was clunky to say the least. "Sometimes when a husband finds his wife in bed with another man, he lets his anger get the better of him. Twice I've been chased away with a shotgun. One night the gun I speak of, well, went off."

"Oh?"

"Yep, I was lucky. Only a portion of the buckshot got me in the hindquarters. The doc laughed the entire time as he plucked the pellets from my arse. The fellows at the railroad got wind of it, and now everyone knows me as Sam Buckshot. I usually don't tell the truth to everyone, to be perfectly honest with you. I usually make up a story of some heroic proportions to explain my name, but you're a friend, and I couldn't lie to you. Besides, Frank would probably end up telling you the truth eventually anyway." Sam forced a goofy smile.

Cassie looked at Sam with the same innocent look, but then she shook her head and said, "Sam, Sam, I don't know about you." She followed up with a cute grin that slowly slid off her face. "That has got to be the most painful and humiliating way to get a nickname. Couldn't you have done something easier?"

Relieved Sam smiled. "You know it! I couldn't ride a horse for almost two weeks," Sam said, laughing.

Cassie laughed. "Now I know why you keep squirming around in your seat. You can't sit still for more than two minutes."

"Yeah." Sam slapped his leg.

Cassie interjected serious all of the sudden, "Sam!" In a scolding tone she said, "I certainly hope you have learned your lesson." She scowled and pointed a finger sternly in his face. Sam's eyes got big, and he sat up straight. She said, "There will be no sleeping with married women, right?"

Sam swallowed and said soberly, "Yes, ma'am."

Cassie smiled her approval. "Okay."

Nate had the team pointed down a straightaway, and ahead of them lay a shallow turn to the right. The turn was about a quarter of a mile up the road. The sun was at its highest point in the sky. Brad squinted. Up ahead of them was a small figure turning the corner into their direction. Then the figure stopped.

Brad said, "You see that?"

"I do," Nate replied. He narrowed his eyes and cupped his hand over his forehead to block the sun. The figure looked to be a man next to a horse standing at the corner of the turn.

Nate slowed the pace just a tad. Brad waved back to Frank and Toby and pointed up the road at the man with the horse at his side. Toby whistled loudly and held his hand up with a clenched fist, which told Nate to stop his team. Frank grabbed his Winchester and threw a small pack over his shoulder. He jumped from the stagecoach as Toby set the brake. He moved so quickly Toby didn't see him clear out.

Al barked aggressively out the cabin window, "Here, here! What seems to be the problem? Why would we be stopping when we just took a break?" He was eyeing his pocket watch.

Frank glowered at him and snapped back, "I'm not in the mood for your attitude."

Al huffed and moved for the door. "We're going to be la--"

Frank beat him to the door and held it shut, he caught Al off guard. "Stay right where you are," Frank ordered. "If there was enough room in there, Maggie would be in your seat, and you would be tied to the back end of this rig."

Maggie snorted and stomped and shook her head.

Frank tipped his hat to Cathy and said calmly, "No need for alarm, folks. Just going to clear the road up ahead. We won't be but a moment."

Al sat back in his seat mumbling all sorts of obscenities.

Cathy scowled and said, "If you're not careful, he's going to kick your ass someday."

Al glared back. "We'll see about that."

Cathy mumbled, "If he doesn't, I will." She sat back in her seat and crossed her arms.

Frank went to the back of the stagecoach where Maggie and her new partner patiently waited. He untied Corduroy, who was always kept saddled for situations such as this. He slipped his rifle into its scabbard and leapt into the saddle. Maggie whinnied to show her disapproval. Frank patted and reassured her. "We'll be back, Maggie, don't you fret." He heeled Corduroy past Toby and trotted up alongside Nate and Brad.

Frank said, "I'm not sure what's going on." He paused, focused up the road. "It might be a distraction, watch my back."

Frank took his Winchester and handed it to Brad. "That scattergun won't do us much good from this distance, so take this."

Frank then took his binoculars from his bag that hung across his shoulders. He looked up the trail, but he couldn't see who was waiting ahead.

Frank said, "He's kinda behind a bush, and at this angle I can't see him. I'll check it out."

Frank and Corduroy cantered ahead to see if the man and his four-legged companion were a threat. At about half the distance to his point of interest, he started to see the figure, but the man was still well shadowed by the trees. At that moment a rustling came from his right. Corduroy became spooked and stepped back.

"Whoa, boy, it's just a raccoon," Frank said. He urged the Steeldust ahead.

As Frank approached the man he could tell right off that there was no immediate threat. He was an elderly gentleman who was more than likely a harmless nomad. Frank figured he was just a wanderer who came out west in search of gold, but only found enough to stay alive. *I bet he stayed because of a girl, or maybe he continued to search for the big find that was never going to come.*

"Hello, old-timer," Frank said with a friendly smile. He dismounted.

A plump man, all bundled up wearing buckskin and furs from six different animals, stood by a pack mule. He looked up from the ground slowly. Frank rested his hand on his gun and looked around in case the old man was a planned distraction. Maybe the plan was to catch them all off guard. Brad had Frank's back covered with his rifle. Behind the gray-colored beard Frank could see friendly eyes.

The man said, "Howdy, young man. It's nice to see a kind face when one travels these lonely dusty trails. Not really trails anymore they've been so heavily traveled."

Frank waved back that everything was okay. He said, "Where you coming from?"

"Oh my, I've been all over everywhere, I imagine. My last stop was Sawmill. It's a nice little community, real friendly place." He looked up at Frank. "That where you headed?" He looked around Frank's broad frame up the road to get a glimpse of the stages and its travelers.

"Yes, it is. We started off in North Fork, and we aim to be in Sawmill by tomorrow night."

The friendly old man held Frank's arm tightly with his fragile hand as he looked back for a second time toward the stages. He acted curious.

"North Fork, yes, that's another nice town. Well, it shouldn't be a problem for you. Hey, mind if we mosey up the road? I would love to meet the folks, it's so lonely out here, you know."

Frank said, "Sure, I'll wave them up to us, though. We'll let them do the work while we rest here and wait." He waved the teams forward, and Nathan snapped the reins on his Bays thus advancing them.

"Sounds good, son. My dogs are howling. I've been walking for quite a spell now."

Frank looked at the older man and wondered why he was walking and not riding. He asked, "Why don't you get yourself another mule so you can ride? That way, if one does go lame, you won't have to leave behind your supplies."

"I did. I did have a wonderful mule but she passed. I would like to say that I haven't replaced her because of my finances, but that wouldn't be the truth. I guess maybe I grew somewhat attached to her, and I ain't had the heart to replace her yet." He stood looking down, quiet for a moment. "I reckon it's time. Maybe I'll get a mule in Lasso or maybe North Fork."

Frank said, "That you should. Hey, what's your name old-timer? I can't really introduce you to my friends without knowing who you are."

"Custis is my name, and you?"

"My name is Frank Savage, and it's nice to meet you, Custis."

Frank shook his hand as Custis looked at him with recognition. He didn't recognize his face, but he recognized the name.

"It's an honor, sir. Thanks for your service."

"Thank you," Frank said with appreciation.

They all took another break to keep Custis company for a few moments before moving on. All to Al's disapproval, but they didn't care.

Frank said, "Why are you so nervous?"

Al acted as if he didn't hear the question.

Custis smiled ear to ear as Frank introduced him to everyone. He was especially giddy when he met Cassandra and Cathy. He even talked to Maggie and Corduroy for a while.

Custis said to Maggie, "I used to have a Quarter Horse just like your friend here. He was my best friend in the world. I can tell he's yours, too, ain't he?"

Maggie nodded as the kindly gentleman smiled and fed her and Corduroy chunks of apple. Cathy and Jesse stood arm in arm and watched Custis as Frank and Brad tried to get the show on the road.

"I'm sorry to cut this short, but we need to hit the road," said Frank.

Custis said, "Gentlemen, thank you for the beans and flour and everything. Oh, I do want to mention as I rode up this way from Sawmill, I did see some riders milling about along the way."

Toby asked, "Who was it? Do you know if they were up to no-good?"

"Not sure. They looked just like regular cowboys, but they didn't seem to be goin anywhere in particular. I know there are some ranches and some cattle in these parts. There were three of them, and, that's about all I know."

"Thanks for the heads up, Custis. We should be on our way," Frank said.

Brad nodded his agreement and added, "Custis, we should be back in North Fork in about three days. When you get to town, go to Frank's store, and we'll get you a good deal on supplies and a new mule." He shook Custis' hand and leaped up onto the stage.

Everyone said goodbye to their warm and friendly newfound friend and took their seats.

The road was rough. Everyone bounced to the uncomfortable ride.

The new stage had a sturdy frame and a built in spring system designed to absorb shocks from the rocky ground. But it didn't seem to matter.

Brad assured Nate that the rough ride would be short lived and that it would eventually smooth out. While they were on it, though, bouncing every which way, it felt like forever.

Frank was lost in his thoughts. He wasn't totally cognizant of the ride conditions. It didn't register to him that a divot almost knocked him from his seat. His thoughts went to memories, searching for an answer to the question that plagued him. Who is George Cummings? Frank was so close but there were too many people from so many missions. He knew it was when he was in Montana on his way to the Nebraska territory. It was a time period he recalled often, but at the same time, it was the period he so much wished to forget.

George Cummings, he thought, *I don't know that name, but I do know those eyes. His name must be an alias, and he has changed his image, too. He doesn't look or act the same. The man has completely turned his life upside-down for some reason or another.*

Frank gripped Toby's arm. Toby about jumped out of his seat and turned to him. Frank stared intently straight ahead. He looked into the sun that was low in the western sky.

"What is it?"

"We need to stop."

"Again? We're not even close to moving as fast as we should," Toby opined.

"I know, I know, but something doesn't feel right. You see that small clearing on the right?" Frank let go of his arm and pointed to an open area not far ahead.

"Yeah."

"Whistle up to Nate," Frank ordered.

Toby did as he was told. Nate heard the alarm and turned to look back to see what was the matter. He understood Frank's directions and followed his request. He guided the Bays to the clearing.

Setting the brake, Toby listened to Frank. He said, "I'm not sure, but we might make camp here. We'll not be early into Sawmill, but we should still be on time. I want to make sure we're doing the right thing."

"Okay, what do you want exactly?" asked Toby.

"Keep everyone together and . . . well, I'm going for a walk."

"A walk?"

Al hit his leg with a fist and was about to bust out the door when Cathy held it shut. She shook her head back and forth and eyed him sternly. He slowly sat back in his seat.

Frank leapt to the ground. He stood at the stage and faced Toby. He noticed how soft the earth felt at his feet.

"The ground is soft," Frank said.

"Yeah, point being?" Toby inquired quite confused.

"You ever try running in these damn boots? It's really difficult."

"Okay, I guess I never gave it much thought, to be honest," Toby replied putting his hand to his face to rub his stubble.

"Try it sometime. It's uncomfortable. The whole time you keep thinking that you're going to sprain an ankle. You'd think we could make something just as durable as boots, but more flexible," Frank said, bordering on rambling.

"Frank, what the heck is going on?" Toby shifted in his seat and looked down at their leader who was concentrating on his boots.

"I have to think. I'm going for a walk," Frank said.

Frank turned to leave, and only one person had stepped out of the cab. Cathy stood in front of him and her eyes were sympathetic. Frank tipped his hat and moved away from the stage. He split the trees in the direction of the sound of flowing water. The leaves clipped his hat as he walked through the narrow muddy path that lay in front of him. He walked for a time before he took stock of how late it was. The sun was about to set.

He said, "It's going to be a full moon tonight and a cloudless sky."

Finally, Frank came upon the river whose sound he'd been following. It was a narrow and shallow river, more of a stream. It flowed quickly through the tapering bend.

Frank stared at the water as it flowed by. Standing at the edge, he could feel the pull of the liquid trying to draw him into the cold, wet creek. He noticed his boots were muddy. He set them lightly into the water, and watched the river grab the mud and carry it away. Frank wished his stress were the mud. If stress could somehow be tangible, he would throw it into the water so that it could be whisked away downstream never to be seen again. There was always worry and stress, especially in war.

The military had beaten him down. The burden just always seemed to be unending. He had hoped that if he left the service, that his heart would be allowed to roam free. That didn't happen. Even as a civilian, he had concern on his mind. He would worry about his store, his home, and women. Frank then attempted to relax. It was always a conscientious decision to relax. No matter how hard he tried, the burdens of life would creep into his muscles and keep his back in a constant state of rigidity.

He looked at the bubbles and waves of the flow at his feet. His eyes moved left to right, picking a wave and following it as far as it would go.

"Now, what the hell?" he whispered. "What's going on?"

His discomfort was obviously triggered by his fight in Lasso City, then exasperated by Mr. Cummings. That wasn't all. He felt his future closing in on him. Approaching rapidly was his destiny that could not be changed or altered. Frank would have to kill again.

Frank was a weapon. This was something his previous employers felt he was good at, and they exploited him. Savage carried the burden of ending other people's lives, but he also carried with him the knowledge that he was just mostly lucky. He tried to tell them that, but they disregarded it. How could a man be in so many unfortunate situations and come out on top every time?

The first man Frank killed was during his first year in the war. He had found himself separated from his squad. While working his way back to his unit, he came face to face with a confederate soldier. Both men had been caught by surprise. Frank saw fear in the other man's face.

They went at each other in a desperate attempt to catch the other unaware. They were too close for rifles, so a hand to hand struggle ensued. His face was right there, almost touching him. They could smell each other. They moved almost as one, countering each other's moves. When the soldier went for his knife Frank knocked it away. When Frank went for his, the soldier kicked it loose. Desperately swinging and kicking, each man fought for their lives.

In a moment that took less than a second, Frank looked into his adversary's eyes and saw the desperation they were both feeling. He heard a whimper in the struggle that sounded of despair. At that instant, Frank wanted to say to him, 'let's stop, we don't have to do this.' He didn't, and they both slipped and slid down a steep incline. At the base, Frank had fallen into soft ground. Jumping up, he hollered "wait," but the man with whom he fought lay there motionless. Frank walked cautiously over to his fallen enemy. He kicked his leg, but the man didn't move.

Where the base of the ravine had provided Frank with a forgiving spot to land, it had offered his opponent a stony rock on which to rest. Frank stood for a moment as he watched the blood flow from his head down the rock left to right. He dropped to his knees and tried to resuscitate the dead man. Frank franticly tried to bring back a man with whom he'd been combating with only moments before.

Frank's unit found him standing over their enemy's dead body. Everyone slapped him on the back and said, 'good job man' and 'you are a savage.' He held back his angst to accept the commendations that came from his peers.

When his division officer Captain Conrad Bovis heard the story of how Frank had killed a man with his bare hands, he took him under his wing and worked with him one on one. That event made him the man he turned into. He accepted it at first, but eventually Frank ran from his life of death. But it always seemed to find him again.

Frank suddenly felt a presence as he stood contemplating his past and staring at the river that flowed below him. He turned, pulled his gun and squatted. Through the brush he saw George Cummings working his way through the trees.

CHAPTER 9

Nate paced the field with a sick stomach. He mumbled, "What the hell is going on?"

The others milled about equally concerned. Toby mentioned that Nate's godfather had been despondent.

Nathan also felt that Frank seemed especially distressed as of late. It was noticeable because he had originally started the trip in such high spirits. He was always a bit moody, but this was different. Nate was empathic and was able to sense these things. He could also tell that everyone else was worried, too. The group sat about sulking, wondering what was going on. Nate decided to lighten the mood a bit.

Nathan approached Cassie and said, "Was that you who was snoring so loudly last night?"

Cassie was looking down at the ground, so when she heard Nate's question she snapped her head upward. Her hair flared up and over her head, and she glared at Nate. "What?"

"I think you're turning red, Cassie," Nate said with a grin. A few of the others were eavesdropping.

"What did you say?" she asked.

"I said, I think your face is turning a mite red."

"No, before that," Cassie said, agitated.

"Was that you snoring last night? I mean, I reckon it was you. The sound was coming from the girls' side of the camp. I know you can't hear yourself when you sleep, but you must have woken yourself up with all that racket," Nate said. He stood with his hands clasped casually in his front. His frame leaned back on his heels. He knew he was poking an agitated snake with a stick, and he awaited the strike.

"Nathan Hansen, you tell everyone here that you're kidding and that you didn't hear me snoring," Cassie stammered with her hands on her hips. Sam was trying not to snicker. She was adorable when she was angry.

"Well, Sweetie, I can't rightly lie now, can I? I mean, it was coming from the girls' side of the camp, and Cathy was up with us drinking coffee at the time. It's nothing to be ashamed of, sweetness of my desires." Nate trailed off with a smile as he attempted to add a little charm to his demeanor.

"You, I can't believe you, and in front of everybody!" *She is adorable.* "Whatever." She grumbled as she stomped off with Nate casually following. He was stepping with long strides. Brad grinned, appreciative of the comic relief. Al Turner scowled with a patronizing flare.

"Where's Mr. Cummings?" Toby remarked, looking about.

"What?" Brad said confused. "He was right here a minute ago." Brad turned his head all around the area. "What's up with all that horseshit?"

Al began to scan the area. His head swiveled about dramatically. He began to fidget and move around the small field with short quick steps. He then stopped, ran his fingers through his thinning hair and stared at the ground.

"He followed Frank into the trees," Cathy remarked.

"Why didn't you say anything?" Al snapped.

Jesse looked at Al, he only moved his eyes, and then they narrowed.

"Shut up, Al," Brad ordered.

"Why would he follow Frank?" Cassie asked. She warmed up to Nate. He held her tight against his body.

"Something's about to happen. I can feel it," Brad said.

"It's already started," said Cathy. It was only loud enough for Jesse to hear.

Frank ordered, "Hold it right there, Mister." Crouched down, he held a gun in his right hand that was resting on his left forearm leveled over his knee. George threw up his hands. He waited as he tried to focus his eyes to see through the brush.

"Frank?" George said, choking on his name. "Please tell me that's you." His arms shook.

"It's me," Frank said, pausing, then, "What do you want?"

"I came to talk." George's voice pitched high. He held tightly to his right arm to stop it from shaking.

"Go on," Frank said suspiciously.

"I'm here to tell you who I am."

Frank stood as he slowly holstered his gun, and he stepped out into the open. He stood with his back to the small river. He said, "I remember you, George. I know that's not your real name, though. I recall seeing you. You were in the process of being interviewed up in Montana about a case. But for the life of me, I cannot make out what case. I think it's because I'm afraid of what the answer might be." Frank lifted his hat off his head and wiped his brow with his forearm.

George said, "Frank, my real name is Jim Dancer."

"What?" Frank barked. He looked up and left as he tried to recall the name.

"It's not George Cummings, he was just some kid I knew growing up and I used his name. My name is Jim Dancer, and I'm not a gambler. This hat, this mustache, these clothes, it's all a ruse." Jim shivered. "I'm . . . I've been overwhelmed for so long, and I can no longer hold it in." He held the back of his hand to his mouth.

Jim Dancer stuttered as he spoke with wet shiny eyes. "I'm a damn farmer, Frank. I'm so tired of running. I had to change my whole life because of the information I gave you and those damn rangers, or whatever the hell they were. Damn them forever." Jim scanned the sky above, and then he looked back at Frank with helplessness in his eyes.

Frank was quiet.

"I gave them information that they obviously gave to you. You took it, and damn you, Frank, damn you. You used my knowledge to kill a man. I never thought you would have found him, never in a million years. I'm so fucking tired and scared. I'm beside myself as what to do. My life is closing in on me. You used my words to kill Danvil. Frank, you used my words to kill Victor Danvil, and now his psychopathic brother--"

Frank's world halted at that moment in time. His head was swimming, his brain floated in his skull. His body felt like it was being enveloped with quicksand. The clouds spun violently above the trees. He had put it together. But it would be too late. "Damn it all to hell."

Calmly and coldly Frank turned it all on. He had to. He alerted that area of his mind that got things done. One way or another, he always got things done.

Frank looked straight, and then said, "Run."

"Where? I have nowhere else to run to. I am so, so tired."

"Run." Frank promptly moved past Jim Dancer. He hit the trail running, running in boots. They sprinted up the trail back to camp.

Frank swiftly ran over the same soft earth he had just traveled over moments earlier. He hated running in boots. The trees smacked him in the face. He didn't even try to avoid them. They fueled him. The sting made his blood move, and the chemicals in that blood gave him energy.

Flashes in his mind showed him the past. It was a reminder of a distinct memory of death in Nebraska. The pictures in his thoughts were of the shooting of two men from their horses. One was a known felon who was a murderer and a rapist. When Frank was a spy, he had hunted down a man by the name of Victor Danvil. Danvil was a killer he had chased for over a year. He was glad he was dead, but Frank had killed an innocent person in the process. Killing Danvil's hostage was a tragedy he could not forgive himself for, and it was one he would not allow himself to forget.

Frank heard Jim struggling to stay close, but Jim managed to find the energy. Jim's life was at stake, and he wanted to live. Even if his life had been torture, he still had a strong will to continue.

Both men were sweating excessively. Beads of sweat covered Frank's face. His shirt was soaked. He could smell his own body odor.

As Frank recalled the past, he tried to solve the dilemma that he now faced. He had to answer the question of how to get everyone out alive. Trying to play catch up with the enemy was not where he wanted to be.

Jim Dancer mentioned that Danvil had a brother, but that was just hearsay. Frank had been on Victor's trail for so long that he should have been able to confirm the rumors of a brother. *Was there a brother? Was there a brother or was it just an alias? Is there really a Shane Danvil?*

Frank came busting into the small open yard where everybody stood in two lines as they waited, except Al Turner, who stood off to the side.

"Brad, Toby, Nate," Frank said, pulling the three off to the side. "We're in a shitload of trouble."

"Talk to me. What's the problem?" Brad interjected.

Frank spoke hurriedly. "George is not George Cummings. His real name is Jim Dancer. He was the man who spilled the beans on Victor Danvil, a murderer I shot and killed over two years ago. The deal is that I think he has a brother by the name of Shane Danvil who is looking for revenge, maybe."

"What?" Nate questioned nervously. He looked over at Cassie who was looking at him from the stagecoach.

Frank said, "And guys, I got no idea what is going on. All I know is, is that I got a bad feeling, and I think those asses in Lasso City are just a part of the gang who may be hunting us."

"Holy-shit," Toby said. He took his hat off and rested his hand on his head. He circled in place.

"We've got to decide, do we want to continue? Do we go back? Or do we abandon the stages and get into the wilderness?" Frank was looking for any suggestions. He looked each man in the eye, and then glanced over at the others. Jesse was approaching.

"Excuse me, Frank?" Jesse said politely.

"What's up?" Frank answered.

"Cathy wants to know if you guys know that someone is following us. And if you do know someone is following us, who is it?"

Frank's face drooped, his mouth opened, and the color faded from his skin. He ran to his stage, then pulled his bag and Winchester from the coach baggage. Running as fast as he could he moved into the trees once again and worked his way into the brush. He yelled over his shoulder, "Get ready to roll. Arm yourselves. Back in fifteen."

Frank had seen a slope to high ground when he had gone for his walk. It was a ways away, but it would allow for a view that might show him if they were being followed. Finding a path, he hustled up a steep hill leaving behind soft ground and introducing a harder and rockier surface. He found a large boulder, climbed to the top and laid down on it. Grabbing the binoculars from his bag, he looked back up the road. In the direction from where they had already been, he could see the trail that would lead them back to Lasso City. On that road in the distance he saw a dust fog.

"Figures."

Maybe three riders at best, that's all he could see. Frank pivoted around on the big rock and looked down the hill into the clearing where his friends and Al waited. He could see someone mounting Corduroy.

Frank whispered, "Oh, no." He sprang from his perch and almost fell in his mad rush to get back. *Okay, calm down. It's not Nate. He would have ridden Maggie.*

Frank flew down the side of the ridge allowing gravity to assist. He lost his footing at the base of the rocks, but as he fell, he held onto his Winchester and rolled with the fall. Rolling over twice down the hill, he bolted upright. In air he managed to get his feet under him and kept his legs moving.

Completely out of breath, Frank arrived at the camp. He looked about and said, "Where'd Sam go?" Frank sounded spent and confused.

"Frank, we got to head back to Lasso. There is something out in front of us," Brad blurted as Frank was catching his breath.

Frank replied, "We can't go back. We're being followed. Did you see someone up the road?"

"No, I didn't see anyone. Sam volunteered to take Corduroy and take off up ahead and see what was there," Brad answered.

"Well, how in the hell do you know someone is up there?" Frank said.

Toby answered, "Because Cathy said there was someone up the road waiting for us."

"How does she know? And how did she know we were being followed?" Frank said as he looked over at Jesse and Cathy.

"I don't know," Brad said, "but I believe her."

"Me, too," Frank added. "Mount up. I'm not about to leave Sam behind, and I don't have any better ideas."

In haste everyone loaded up into his or her respective stages. Nate helped Cassie into her seat and buckled her belt. He closed the door and hollered back to Frank, "Make everyone strap themselves in, you hear? This is not going to be a nice ride through the country. Sam's got about a fifteen minute head start on us!"

Frank ran his hand over his head. He stuffed his hat into his bag and checked his gun. He loaded a round into the sixth and only empty chamber. Toby snapped the reins as soon as he saw Nate do the same.

"I made a promise to get you back to your folks," Frank said.

For Savage this wasn't all about him this time. There were many others along whom he cared a great deal for and who were now in danger. It worried him that it might be his fault. Danvil would most surely be after him. He also wondered how he ended up on a stagecoach that also carried Jim Dancer. It didn't make any sense.

The roll of the wheels on the ground was loud to Cathy. Every sense she had was on high alert. She had hoped she and Jesse could start a new life out west. But it seemed that their past was riding up on them as well. Death rode a horse and was armed to the teeth.

The wind rushed by Nate's ears making him holler even louder, "Yee-ah!" Nate worked hard to keep the speed up, but manageable. He yelled to Brad, "Bradley, you know this road better than anyone. Is there anything I need to watch out for?"

"Keep the pace you got," Brad answered calmly as he held the rail at his right side, with Nate to his left. "A ways up, though, there are some major sharp turns. The road will run along a ridgeline on the right. There will be a ditch running alongside to the left. You don't want to run into either. Understood?"

"Understood," Nate answered.

The moon was large and low in the sky. It was helpful that it was full. The sun was long gone and the night's sky lit the pathway marginally at best.

Sam had slowed his pace. He looked into the lowly lit area around him. Corduroy moved nervously, but steady. Sam felt the hairs stand on the back of his neck. He didn't know what he was riding into. He didn't want to let his friends down. He'd do whatever it took to ensure their safety.

Sam pulled Corduroy to a stop and spun him around to look back to see if the stages might be approaching. He had just decided to turn back when he heard a shuffle of hooves. Sam turned and pulled his six-shooter as quick as he could. It was too late.

A loud discharge exploded in front of him. Corduroy received the lead in his chest and the blow knocked him back to his hind legs. A stream of blood shot out of Corduroy's chest and sprayed the gravely road. Sam lost his balance and fell to the ground, losing his weapon. The injured Steeldust almost fell to his side but managed to get his bearings and bolted into the trees up an incline and out of sight.

Sam had moved to steady himself on all fours when he felt the burn of a rope around his neck. It pulled taut on him and knocked him back to the ground.

"Whoa, stay there." A man wearing a black hat and black vest came into view. He was riding a black horse. Two other men on horses rode up behind him. Sam could only see the outlines of his tormentors. They were shadow ghosts that rode horses.

"J.D.," the man on the black said bitterly.

J.D. turned his horse to face his boss, Conrad Bovis. His gun was still smoking.

"I would ask you why you shot that horse. But I know an idiotic moron such as you probably has no God-dang idea why he would do something so dad blasted stupid." Bovis lowered his head and was barely keeping his eyes open. His distaste for J.D. dripped from his voice.

Sam cautiously worked to loosen the rope on his neck.

J.D. glared back at his boss, Bovis couldn't see his expression. The third rider was about to say something, but Bovis stopped him. "Shut up, Styles."

Conrad Bovis loosened his grip on the rope so Sam could stand and said, "Well, partner." He stopped for a moment, his head dropped and he put his fingers to his forehead. "This just isn't your day."

"Tell me about it. It's been a bad year," Sam said. "Got headaches do ya?"

"Maybe."

"Me, too."

"What's your name?"

"Go screw your horse, jackass!" Sam snapped.

"Styles," Bovis said under his breath.

Styles moved up close. "Yeah, boss?"

"There's not much light left, and that stage is getting close."

"I'm on it," Styles said.

"Just don't let it get too close. Don't kill anyone, okay? Alive, remember?" Bovis added.

Styles nodded and said, "I'll aim for the horses."

He touched his Dun with his spurs, and spun off into the darkness.

Bovis threw his end of the rope up over a tree limb that hung perpendicular over the road. He grasped the end and pulled Sam up to his feet. Sam grasped at the rope, desperate to find the knot. He wanted to get lose, but it wasn't to save his own life. He had to help his friends. He could see Cassie's face and how she looked at Nathan. His friend Frank, he must warn him. He had to stop these murdering bastards. *I can't believe I got caught*, he thought. *Please help my new family, God.*

Bovis said, "J.D., I do apologize. My head--" He stopped abruptly, then he continued, "Take the rope please."

J.D. trotted over and took the rope from Bovis. J.D. then said to Sam, as Bovis stepped back to let his henchman do the dirty work, "What's your name?"

J.D. pulled back on his horse's reins, making him step back. Sam was on his toes now, mumbling something inaudible. He twitched about, dangling.

J.D. loosened his end, which allowed Sam to rest on his heels. Sam was breathing heavy. J.D. repeated, "What is your name?"

Sam squinted, and through clenched teeth he said, "Mister Jones."

J.D. pulled tight then relaxed his grip then said, "Wrong answer. What's your name?"

Sam glared and spit out, "Oh, I'm sorry, it's Mister 'I'm gonna fuck you up' Jones."

Nathan slowed his team. The road was somewhat lit for it being nighttime, but was still too dark to take it too fast. As they rode, Nate continued to slow the pace.

Nate said, "What the?"

"Nathan," Brad said with a heavy heart, "isn't that Corduroy?"

Nate pulled abruptly on the reins bringing the stage and his team to a dramatic halt. The moon was fat and low, and just under it, on a hill with no trees, there was the outline of a horse.

"That's a Steeldust, and I don't see Sam," Brad said.

Corduroy stumbled and fell back on his hind legs with his front legs straight. His front legs worked to pull him back up again, unsuccessfully.

There was nothing they could do. They were so close, but just too far away to help him.

A loud boom echoed through the still air. It was so piercing Nathan turned to see what it was.

Frank jumped up startled. Maggie pulled on the rope that held her to the stage. Frank looked down on Nate's horse and watched her in disbelief. Maggie had charged forward alongside the stage. She attempted to move toward the hill and yanked on her harness. Her force was so hard that she broke the wood panel she was tied to. She whinnied and stomped. She pulled and pulled on the rope that was still tied to a bar on the stagecoach.

Maggie struggled abeam the stagecoach horses of Frank's stage. The lead horses started to get nervous and stomped about. Maggie was about to break loose. The strain she put on the bar caused it to bend. The force made a screeching sound of bending metal.

The stage jumped with each effort she threw into it in her desperate attempt to get loose. She had to get up that hill. Maggie started to go wild then she began kicking like an unbroken bronco.

She turned with her back to the hill and got low as she pulled on the rope. The harness that Nate had rigged for her put all the pressure on her frame. Maggie pulled and pulled as she tried to move backward. She urgently tugged to break free from the stage. Her legs were strong. The stage slid in the dirt, sliding an inch with each pull.

She turned to face the hill again and watched Corduroy, unnervingly silent. Maggie stood motionless as Corduroy's front legs gave, and he fell to his side. Maggie screamed. A scream that shattered the black sky and breached the heavens.

Nate was upon Maggie now. He leapt to her back and untied the rope from her harness. Maggie went, and he let her. There was no slowing her down. The only thing for Nate to do was to hang on.

Maggie took Nate up the hill at a speed he had never known possible. Riding fast, he could hear his favorite horse breathe and moan. Each breath sounded like she was saying, no.

At the top Maggie slid to a stop, and Nate jumped from her back and moved out of the way. He watched her with his fists clenched.

He whispered, "I'm so sorry, Maggie."

Maggie walked to Corduroy's still body and stomped the ground. Trying to wake him she snorted and huffed and stomped. He did not move. Nathan stepped over to Corduroy to make sure. Nate put his ear to his chest. There was no breathing and no heartbeat to be heard. He stood and looked up at Maggie who looked into his eyes.

"I'm sorry, Maggie." He choked.

She groaned.

Nathan noticed that Maggie's eyes had changed color. He stepped up close and saw two eyes that were now the same color. Both of her eyes were gray.

"You'll never be the same, will you, Sweetheart?" He hugged her neck.

Nate then pulled the saddle from Corduroy, threw it on top of Maggie, and bolted back down the hill to the awaiting members of his party.

"Shot in the chest, looks like," Nate said to Frank.

"Okay, tie Maggie up. Mount up, and let's roll. We have no place to go. Sam may still be alive, and I'm not leaving him behind. Sound like a plan?"

"Yes, sir," Brad and Nate answered simultaneously.

"Shoot to kill," Savage added.

As Nate went to tie up Maggie to the back of the stage, Frank grabbed his arm. "Remember what you've been taught, and we'll get home alive."

"I will, Uncle Frank." Nathan tied his heart-broken horse to the back of Frank's stage. As he walked by, Toby hollered, "Give those Bays hell, Nate! We got a friend lost up ahead." Nate nodded and ran to his post.

The pace was quick, too quick, but someone's life was on the line. It was so dark, Nate's abilities with a team were unmatched, but this speed was insane. The ride was rough, too. Nate was barely able to keep his seat.

"Where are those turns that are next to the ridgeline? You know, the ones you spoke of." Nate screamed.

"Not positive, but it's up a ways. I'll give you a warning when I think they're coming," Brad answered. He grunted when they hit a bump.

Nate used his whip. He never used a whip on a horse. Cassie was on board, and Nate had to get her home to her family. There was a whistling sound. It was immediately accompanied with a loud discharge. It echoed off the rocks. The bullet sailed down their right side.

"You hear that? Someone is shooting at us. Kick it, no holds barred, Nathan. Go!" Brad hollered.

Frank never heard the bullet that struck his riding partner. He heard Toby cry out. Toby slipped in his seat. The bucking of the ride almost knocked him forward under the stage. Frank grabbed Toby with his left hand as he took the reins with his right just as they were slipping away. If he had moved one second later, they would have been out of control.

"Toby!" Frank screamed.

"My leg. The sons-of-bitches shot my leg." Toby started to wail, "It's bad, man. It's way bad."

Inside the cabin of Frank's stage, Jim Dancer, the farmer on the run, squatted at the door. He looked like he was about to jump.

"What are you doing?" Al asked.

"I'm going to go. I can't stay here. They're after me. I can't live with myself if they kill everyone because they're after me." Jim panted.

Al snapped, "They ain't after just you, you idiot."

In the blink of an eye Jim threw himself from the stage. He lucked out. He hit the ground rolling and bounced off the road into the brush.

Frank was as strong physically as he was strong willed. He held Toby with one tired hand as he guided the reins with the other. Frank then laid the reins across the foot rail. He put his boot down on the leather to hold them in place.

The stage jolted, causing him to almost lose his balance and fall from the rampaging stage. He continued to look ahead as he worked. While holding Toby up with his left, he grabbed the rope from his bag and ran it through the side rail on his right. After he looped it through the side rail he ran it under himself and around Toby and tied him down. He looked at Toby's eyes, and they were big. Frank recognized that Toby was going into shock. He examined the leg as best he could. In the moonlight Toby's entire leg was covered with dark black blood. *Oh, shit.*

"You hold on, Toby! Don't you let go, man. Don't you let go," Frank wailed as he took the reins again.

He grabbed Toby's leg. He could feel the warm thick fluid flow from between his fingers. His hand slipped around as he felt for the wound. Finding the wound on the inside of his thigh, Frank gripped the flesh like a clamp. He squeezed as hard as he could in an effort to stop the bleeding. It wasn't just a hole. It was a tear all along the artery.

Frank then heard whooping and hollering from behind. He said, "No way is this happening." He could always get out of any situation. That was not going to be the case this time. He had lost one friend and another was about to die.

"Maggie!" Frank looked back to check on her. They were going so fast, and it was way too dangerous for her to be pulled along.

While working a stagecoach that was moving too rapidly, he held Toby's leg. Frank then eyed the oncoming force that was gaining on them. He put the reins in his mouth and bit down. Frank pulled a knife from his boot and cut the rope. It freed Maggie. He buried the tip of the blade in the top of the stage.

"Get the hell out of here, Maggie," Frank bellowed.

Al was still strapped in his seat, but he held onto the door handle.

"Don't do it, Al. It's much too risky," Jesse said.

"We are going to get killed if we stay on this runaway hell ride." Al paused, then nodded. "Screw this malarkey," Al hollered as he jumped from the stage. Jesse and Cathy held on to each other.

Frank glanced back at three riders. There may have been more, somewhere in the dark. He turned to Toby and looked into his eyes. Toby's grip on his arm was weakening. His eyes had rolled back into his head.

"Nooo!" Frank cried out. He gripped the wound tighter.

Once again they hit a divot, and he almost lost control of the reins. At the last second he saw Nathan's stage turn left. Frank responded, and he narrowly missed a steep incline that shot up from the ground on the right side straight up.

Off his left was a ditch and on his right was a wall. A rider, who was on the right, had to back off and step to the rear of the stage, or he'd have run into the rocky ledge face-first.

Frank's hand was tired, but he wouldn't let go. He screamed at his riding partner, "Toby, don't you die on me."

Frank studied the path ahead. His eyes darted back and forth in a spasm of desperation.

There was a slight opening on the right, and the closest rider took a chance and came up along his side. Frank saw the glimmer of a gun barrel. He stepped on the reins with his boot once more and reached over his shoulder with his right hand. While holding Toby's leg as tight as he could, he grabbed the shotgun. He cocked back both hammers. Just as the rider was side by side with the stage, Savage threw lead at his adversary with a thunderous blast. The gunman was shot off his horse with flesh flying out. He spun twice before he hit the ground with his head snapping his neck.

Savage caught a glimpse of a second rider through the corner of his eye. The pursuer was gaining on the stage, fast. With both barrels spent, Frank flung the scattergun at the man, nailing him in the stomach. The rider lost his balance and hit the ground with a heavy thud.

The third rider made a wise decision to back off. Frank shifted his attention back to guiding the stage around the harrowing turns. The ridge on the right was building again, and the ditch on the left was deeper now.

"Toby, you will not die on me, do you understand? You can't die. You can't die on me. It wasn't supposed to be you. Damn it!" Frank screamed. Toby's eyes were closed now. His body was lifeless. Frank still held tight to his partner's leg. He gripped harder than ever, even though no blood exited his torn artery any longer. Frank knew it. He always knew.

The ride was worse than ever. The enemy gunman from the rear was gone, but they were still hearing shots from the top of the ridgeline.

Nate was one with his team, but nobody could handle what came next. From the right side and moving straight at them was a large fast moving object. If it had not been a full moon, he may never have seen it. A wagon came barreling down on them on a collision course. Nathan did all he could. He pulled hard. Nate used his experience as best he could, but they were going too fast.

A sharp snap shot up from below. Something had given out. The stress of the ride had caused the frame to break somewhere below. The front right corner started to droop to the ground.

In an attempt to keep the stage from turning into the oncoming wagon, Nathan let loose of the right reins. He then pulled with both hands on the left reins, hard. Both of the lead Bay's heads snapped to the side. The forceful pull caused them to move, and the other horses blindly followed. But the pull was so drastic and aggressive that Nate caused the neck of a lead horse to break. It didn't matter. The momentum of the horses sent them into the ditch. The two front horses fell into the crevice. The middle two horses ran uncontrolled over the top of them. The last two horses tried to stay up, but the stage was bearing down on them.

The runaway unmanned wagon just nipped the right side of the stage on its way by. Nate's stage then overran the body of horses in the ravine, thus upending itself. The weight of the stage came crashing down on the last two Bays, killing them instantly. Brad and Nate flew forward and landed in the brush that ran along the ditch, rolling with their falls.

Frank saw a flash of the runaway wagon as it rolled harmlessly in front of his team into the ditch. When Frank pulled the reins right to avoid the wagon, his stage took a sharp turn. Frank and his team of horses whizzed by Nate's fallen stage that rested in the ditch.

Frank's team of horses broke loose. The left wheel buckled. He let go of the reins, and the Cleveland Bays ran off into the darkness. Frank's stage was now rolling with no team of horses. The left wheel had faltered such that the stage collapsed and tipped over onto its left side. It slid in the dirt for ten feet on its side before stopping.

Frank lay on top of his dead friend. The only sound he could hear was the crying of the horses that rested at the bottom of a heap in the ditch.

This is hell.

CHAPTER 10

Jim Dancer, also known as George Cummings, felt like he was waking up from a bad dream. Not only was the memory of his nightmare fuzzy, but so was his eyesight. Slowly, he moved to his feet and looked around. He then lay back down in the weeds.

When he had jumped from the stage, he managed to hit the road in such a way that he rolled and bounced into some bushes among some trees. He looked in the direction they had been headed. He couldn't see around the many corners. He felt the thumping in his head along with the clumping of horse hooves in his ears. They sounded as if they were on top of him. He remained still and quiet.

Jim wondered if he should try to move ahead to his companions. He then thought that maybe he should stay and keep the danger away from them. *Should I give myself up?* He wanted to turn himself in so that he might protect the others, but something inside wouldn't let him physically do it.

Jim felt sick to his stomach that he was so weak, that he couldn't save the others because of his selfish desire to live at all costs.

He had always had the ability to control his heart rate during a poker game, but in life or death situations, forget it. Anxiety streamed through him, and it caused his hands to shake. It got worse when he remembered why he was on the run.

His heart about exploded when he heard a shotgun blast off in the distance. *What to do*, he thought. He entertained running ahead in the hope of finding Frank and everyone else waiting for him. Frank didn't know he was gone. They could still be riding hard to Sawmill. He didn't want them to turn back for him. Al would never let them turn back. He would lie and say, 'Oh, Jim is dead.' *Does Al even know my real name?*

He whispered, running his hand down his face, "Damn, why did I jump?"

Jim knew deep down he wasn't going to find the others. He knew damn good and well he was going to run. He would run as fast as he could for as long as possible. Panic was starting to take him over, like it always did. He *was* worried for the others. His self-preservation was stronger, though. He didn't even know what he was doing anymore. He was no longer Jim Dancer. He was some strange fellow named George Cummings who was a gambler. He'd been on the run from Shane Danvil for so long that every corner was a possible trap. Every new acquaintance was a probable spy. His nerves were shot so badly that trembling was a common occurrence.

Jim was so unsettled that he didn't realize how much time had passed since he had jumped from the cabin of the stagecoach. Nor did he realize he was talking to himself. Because he was mumbling, he didn't notice that two riders had ridden upon him.

He heard a horse snort, followed by the strike of a match. Then a voice said, "We know you're in there."

Jim slowly sat up and turned. He could see in the darkness two of the riders who had caused the Southwest Stagecoach line to take flight. Jim stood cautiously and noticed a big bald ugly man rubbing his back and stretching as he sat atop a huge Roan. He looked like he was over six feet tall and heavy. He didn't have a hat on.

A double-barreled derringer slipped quietly from Jim's shirtsleeve into the palm of his hand. The two gunmen didn't notice.

With the moonlight behind him, Jim could see into the eyes of the large man on the Roan, and he couldn't feel the presence of a soul. This man felt nothing, Jim was sure of that. He did not love nor hate. Hector only did what he was told, and he did it well.

"Hec." The man on a horse behind the bald man spoke. Kelton Brass sat on his sorrel in the shadow of Hector smoking his cigarette. Hector's roan was most likely one of a few horses that could carry his oversized body.

The large bald man turned in his saddle sideways with his hand on his lower back. He kept an eye on Jim. Hector may not feel emotion, but he was polite.

"Yes, sir," Hector replied. He brushed dust off the front of his shirt.

"Hec, I need you to ask the man a question," the mysterious man said between pulls on his smoke. His hat sat low over his eyes, one of which was covered with a black patch. He acted casual and was hunched forward while resting his arms on his saddle horn.

"Sir?" Hec said.

"Ask him his name," his boss Kelton said.

Hector had kept his eyes on Jim the entire time. He said, "What is your name?" Hector's voice was serious and slow.

"Wh-what? Why?" Jim said. His fear controlled his legs. He could not run even if his brain ordered him to. He noticed the tingling sensation on the back of his head that he had felt before. It was of a thousand tiny needles that would start at the back of his skull in a small pinpoint and spread out in a circular pattern over his whole skull. It felt like ants spreading out over the back of his head. The only time he had felt this sensation before today was when he would awake from a nightmare in which he had been shot in the back of the head.

The bald gunman pulled his gun from his hip and let it hang straight down casually at his side. He then cocked the hammer back. Jim heard it.

"Okay, okay, my name is George Cummings," Jim lied.

"Sir, his name is George Cummings," Hector said. His delivery was deep and monotone.

His strange partner lit another match and pulled a piece of paper from his pocket. He read the paper with his good eye. He blew out the match with smoke flowing from his pursed lips. The strange man may have been known by many names, but he was known for doing only one thing.

"Kill him," he said calmly, and as if annoyed, "Kill him now."

Jim overheard the order, and he drew his weapon in self-defense. It went off harmlessly. The explosion from Jim's hand caught Hector slightly off guard, but Hector had pulled his gun up in line with Jim too fast. Hector shot him. The back of Jim's head split open and he fell onto his left leg with his right leg stretched out in front of him. He landed sitting upright. Jim breathed two quick breaths. He wet himself as his right leg jerked three times, then stopped. He died sitting up and slightly hunched over. A tear rolled down his right cheek.

"Yes, sir," said Hector.

Nate was conscious, but for a few minutes he couldn't move. Once he got his bearings, he sat up and looked around. He could hear some of his horses kicking about, breathing heavy and crying. He could see Brad on all fours with his head hung down. Fluid flowed from his face to the ground.

It was quite dark. The clouds overhead had thickened and covered the night sky. Everything looked blue. As the clouds floated by, it caused shadows to creep over the ground.

Nate's nerve endings were still firing and he startled himself. The stage was starting to come into focus for him. It was upside-down in the ditch on top of the twisted and mangled Cleveland Bays. He covered his mouth with his hand. The ring in his ears started to morph from an annoying high-pitched squeal to the sound of a girl crying. He tried to stand. It happened slowly, and he patted around to make sure he was okay. No blood could be found except for what he could taste in his mouth.

"Brad?" Nate said.

Brad was quiet. He swayed slightly as he rested on his hands and knees facing the ground. Nate stepped forward slowly. He was working his way to his partner. Brad's head moved to the side. He said, "I'll be okay. Find Cassie, she might be hurt." He was beginning to breathe heavy for he had had the wind knocked out of him from the impact.

"What is up with all this horseshit?" Brad whispered. He spit saliva and blood to the ground.

Nathan continued to the stage. He picked up his pace and called out, "Cassie?"

The sound of the horses jerking to free themselves from the mass of bodies that lay in the ditch chilled Nate to his core.

Nathan said, "Babe? You okay?"

From the stage Cassie responded, "I . . . I don't know. The blood is rushing to my head." She cried out, "Get me out of here." She sniffled.

Nate searched for a way to the door, which hung only from one hinge now.

"Nathan!" Nate heard Frank's voice bellow from the darkness.

Nate responded, "Over here, Uncle Frank. We're over here."

"You okay?" Frank asked.

"Yeah, but I don't know about Cassie. Wait one."

"Toby's dead," Frank cried out.

Nathan noticed that Frank was on the edge of despair from the tone of his voice. Nate stopped in his tracks and bent over. He rested with his arms straight and his hands on his knees to take in what he had just heard. He threw up. He stared at the ground. Nate swallowed hard and went back to work. He had to step on a dead horse to get to the door. It almost made him sick again. Nate peeked into the stage door. He had to stand on his toes to reach the top of the door jamb of the upside-down stagecoach. Cassie hung in her seat in the dark cabin. Her hair hung with the ends just skimming the ceiling.

"Are you hanging from the belt?" Nate said.

"Yes, get me down please," Cassie answered.

Nathan pulled himself up into the cabin using only his arms. He pushed his way into the stage and under Cassie. He held her as he worked her belt loose. Once she was free, she grabbed and hugged him. He looked through the cabin and noticed that the cabin itself didn't break or bend much in the crash.

"I'll get you home safe," Nate said. "I promise."

They were hugging when Nate heard a gunshot a little less than a mile off. It was behind them up the road from which they came. Brad and Frank arrived at the same time and helped the two to the ground.

Frank gathered everyone together and led the group into the woods about a hundred yards away from the crash site. He inspected everyone for injuries. Nate had lost a tooth, and Brad had a bloody nose and some bruised ribs. Cassie had some pretty ugly bruises, but Frank said, "She'll live." Cathy and Jesse were in pretty good condition considering what had happened. They had bumped heads giving them both a headache. Jesse had a large lump on the right side of his head, and Cathy conversely had a massive bump on the left side of her head. Jesse told everyone how Jim and Al jumped from the stage.

"Who do you think that gunshot was meant for?" Jesse asked. He spoke quietly and calmly while holding his wife's hand.

"I know who I hope it was for," Brad interjected.

Cathy looked at Frank and shook her head.

Frank whispered, "Jim." He put his hands on his face to hide his emotions from everyone. After a moment of silence, he looked up at the group with just his eyes. He breathed into his cupped hand that rested over his mouth. Everyone sat quietly and waited for some direction, some reassurance. Frank's head abruptly snapped right, and his gun was in his hand without anyone seeing him draw it. He whispered, "Stay here."

Brad and Nate pulled their weapons and circled the group. Brad moved to one side, and Nate went to the other. Frank set out into the dark wilderness pursuing the hint of a sound.

Cathy said under her breath, "There's something out there."

Cassie whimpered. Cathy grabbed her arm firmly. "It's time to grow up, right now." She looked gravely into Cassie's face and continued, "Dig deep into your heart for that strength that you know is there."

Cassie halted her crying, pulled herself together, and nodded.

Frank moved quickly and stealthily through the trees. He heard a brush of a leaf. He stopped and crouched next to a stout oak tree. Peering around the tree, he gripped the bark with his left hand. He squinted as he looked into the darkness and strained his ears. He heard a horse's breath blow and the rattle of reins. He leveled his six-shooter in the direction of the sound.

Sweat popped from his forehead and dripped down his face. He could hear his own breath, so he held it. The sound seemed to be slowly moving in his direction. Frank heard hooves step softly on the dirt floor. He saw some motion. He lifted the barrel to where the rider would be sitting.

Frank noticed the flash of the horse's head, then he could make out the backside, but the saddle was empty. *Oh, crap.* Straightaway Frank shifted around as he frantically looked all over. *How could I be so stupid? I should have brought Brad to watch my six.* He got as low to the ground as he could, but stayed on his feet. He saw nothing. Slowly Frank moved along to the side of the tree again. He could see the hindquarters of the horse. *Spots! It's an Appaloosa, it's Maggie.*

Frank quietly worked his way over to his godson's horse and escorted her back to the camp where Nate was ecstatic to see that Maggie was okay.

Frank said, "Okay, Brad and I are going back and take care of the Bays. We can't leave them like that. We have to bury Toby, too."

Nate asked, "Won't they hear the gunshots?"

Frank's eyes were barely slits, and solemnly he shook his head. Frank pulled his knife.

"Nate, stay vigilant, okay?" Frank said.

"Absolutely, Uncle Frank."

"Hey," Frank said with a slight smile, "you can just call me Frank." He turned and disappeared into the trees. Brad followed close behind.

After a few cautious moments, Frank and Brad reached the tree line next to the ditch. They could hear three suffering horses.

"Aren't you afraid they're out there?" Brad asked. "You know, the bad-guys."

Frank glanced over to him and smiled. He said, "Afraid?"

Frank looked out, "No." Then he said, "Scared out of my mind?"

Looking back again at Brad, he replied, "Yes."

Brad said, "Then what the hell are we doing?"

Thoughtfully Frank answered, "It's dark. More than likely they'll wait till first light. The odds are in our favor at night. Before it gets too light, I'm going to have Nate split out of here to get help. He can ride Maggie, and as long as he has a head start, no person could catch him."

Frank moved into the mass of bloody animals and ended their cries. Afterward, Frank made the decision to wait until just before daybreak to rummage for supplies. They buried Toby and marked the grave so they could come back for him when they could.

Once they were back at their campsite, they huddled for warmth and replenished their liquids. Frank and Nate stood the first watch. Brad and Jesse stood the second.

Jesse got everyone up as Frank had instructed. Their eyes were adjusted to the darkness. The sun had not started to come up yet, but the sky was brightening.

"I'm not going," Nate said defensively.

"Nate, we all need you to do this. You're the only one who can get by these guys and get help. Maggie will ride hard for you," Frank said sternly, but with a hushed tone.

"I am not leaving you here alone, and I am not leaving Cassie behind," Nate said adamantly.

Frank was about to get angry, but stopped as he looked at Cassie. An understanding enveloped his face.

"Frank," Brad interjected, "he's right. I think I should go."

"Okay," Frank said reluctantly. "We don't have any time to waste. I bet they're about to make a move."

Brad patted Maggie's neck as Frank spoke, "Head north through the valley, move fast. They'll probably send someone after you, unless you get lucky and they don't see you. Once you get to a shallow river, follow it to the right. After about five miles, it will start to parallel the train tracks. At that point shoot straight north again, and you'll find a road that will lead you to an abandoned town. Take your hat off as you enter the city. If anyone gives you any grief, tell him my name and that it's an emergency. You want to talk to Derek Wright. You got that?"

Brad nodded. "Yeah, Derek Wright, okay." He sat on the ground and started to put on his spurs. As he was buckling his right spur, Nate stood over the top of him and asked, "And what do you think you're doing?"

Brad waved his hand and said, "I'm putting on my spurs. Why?"

Nate said, "I don't think so."

"Nate, I need to move as fast as possible. I know Maggie is--"

Nate interrupted, "I had a talk with her, and you won't need them."

Brad hesitated, then said, "Okay." He unbuckled his spur and mounted Maggie. He spun and heeled her to the north as Frank had advised.

Bovis, the determined gunman in black, had positioned himself on top of a tall hill. He sat on his muscular black horse as he looked down in the direction of the fallen coaches. A shred of light began to capture the sky. He pulled his looking glass and stared through the tube with the hope that he might be able to see something.

As he glared through the magnifying lens, he noticed an object sprint over the road and into the trees. Bovis continued his search. Looking for his prey, he listened to how loud the wind was, but he could still hear the two riders who accompanied him talking.

Bovis felt his hand begin to shake meagerly, and thinking about it made it worse. He whispered, "Shut the hell up." Anger began to boil up in him without much reason. The pain in his head intensified. As he lowered the eyepiece, the pain shot from the back of his head to his forehead. He couldn't keep his eyes open.

The riders noticed the quivering in their leader's back. They also noted that his left arm shook almost uncontrollably. His periods of calm were becoming shorter and shorter. At this rate he would have to kill someone soon - maybe that would ease the pain. Rubbing his eyes, he was able to get his right lid partially open.

Bovis urged his horse to the side and spoke to J.D. "Did you bury Sherm?"

J.D. replied, "Yep."

Bovis nodded. His tone was deliberate. "There is a man getting away on a horse. Bring me that man." His head pounded in agony. "Alive, if possible . . . wait . . . Savage."

J.D. glared. "Yeah, I know him."

"Bring back Savage, alive. That is, if you think you can."

"I can handle Savage," J.D. blared. He carried a large bone-handled

Bowie knife. He stroked it gently with his hand as he spoke. "He'll be bleeding, but he'll be alive."

J.D. turned his horse, but before he got going, Bovis spoke up, "Come back with a body over your saddle. If it ain't his, then it had better be yours." He eyed J.D. as he spoke.

Bovis stopped shaking, the pain in his head was still strong, but it was becoming bearable. J.D. rode off. With one eye open Bovis said to himself, "Pray it's not Savage, you dumb-shit."

After J.D. was gone, Kelt said, "You know he can't get Savage."

Bovis nodded, "I know, that's why I sent him alone. But it ain't Savage, he would send someone else to get help. He would send the best rider. Savage has training and abilities that lie elsewhere. He won't leave the group."

Brad and Maggie busted through the brush like a bullet through a leaf. Brad yelled, "Yeah, ride, Maggie!"

The ferocity with which Maggie rode stunned him. It was as though she knew life and death depended on her. She rode harder and faster as they progressed. The wind whistled in his ears as the tree limbs flew by. Brad knew the pace was too much, but he focused on the ground in front of him and let Maggie set the stride. There was a good chance that they would be followed. Everything was a blur as they galloped for help. Brad was going through his head what Frank had told him when he happened to look over his shoulder. There was movement on a hill to his right.

"Uh-oh," Brad mumbled. "We're being followed, Maggie."

Brad's mind was moving fast. He had to keep up with his swift horse while attempting to come up with a plan. His pursuer was too close to try and outrun. "Think, what's it gonna be, Bradley?" He subtly pulled back Maggie's reins and felt the back of his saddle for his rope. Finding the leather tie-down, he pulled it loose and snatched up the rope. Brad couldn't see his stalker, but he was sure the man wasn't far behind.

Brad and Maggie bolted down a shallow hill into a narrow section of a valley that was a dried up streambed. Brad could see a sharp turn approaching on the left. They slowed down for the turn. On the opposite side of the corner he pulled Maggie to a quick halt. On the right Brad spotted what he needed, a tree with a thick sturdy limb. He lassoed the limb with the rope and pulled it tight. As he jumped from his saddle he said, "Go, Maggie!" After slapping her hindquarters, Maggie trotted off down the streambed.

Brad swung into action. He began by laying the rope along the ground as he moved to the opposite side of the path. Hiding behind a tree, he held the rope that was tied to a tree on the other side. The rope lay flat on the ground and was loped over a tree limb on his side.

A clomping of hooves quickly approached. The pursuer was moving fast. Looking through the bushes, Brad timed his trap perfectly. Just as the rider whipped around the corner, Brad pulled the rope rigid across the man's path. The attacker never knew what happened to cause his fall. The barrier struck him across the chest, level with his shoulders. A couple inches higher, and it would have cut along his neck. The rider with the bone-handled knife tumbled off the back of his horse. Flipping in the air, he came to rest flat on his back with a thwack. The air in his lungs spewed out of his body with the blow.

Instantly J.D. sat up and attempted to breathe. He sucked in a little air. Still reacting, he moved with the knowledge that his life was in danger. He stood up and yanked his gun out and up. He was shooting as he lifted the barrel in Brad's direction, and the first shot was wasted when it struck the ground.

Brad moved fast as he ran around the corner of the tree. He shot back at J.D who had decided to run up the dried creek bed. Both men missed with every shot. Each explosion came after little pause. Dirt splashed up, and bush leaves blossomed out in shreds with the impacts of the slugs.

J.D. ran with his hand tightly gripping his piece that had only one bullet left. Just as he was getting the angle right for his kill he pulled in his first full breath. Taking in the air he turned just enough to see Maggie. She was standing with her four feet square, staring at him with her black-gray eyes. Her head lowered, and she snorted as she moved to charge him.

"What the?" J.D. said with his first full exhale of air.

Surprised, and petrified of the Appaloosa, J.D. never even heard the shot that sent lead into his brain.

Brad walked over to Maggie and patted her on the neck. He said, "That's one down. The rest are yours, Frank."

Brad bounced into his saddle as Maggie split out. And they moved with purpose.

CHAPTER 11

Frank stepped over a dead bay's head. Blood had soaked into the dirt from the six horses, and it was causing his shoes to feel squelchy as he walked. A chill ran through his back as he looked over the carnage. He wondered if his own team of horses would be okay. He prayed, hoping they didn't get too far away. There was the possibility that maybe they could be used to get home. Frank was doubtful. He knew they were in a rough spot, and someone was waiting in the woods. If Frank's hunch was right, it was Victor Danvil's brother and his men. After considering their odds, he concluded they were at best, not good.

Jesse and Cathy waited at the campsite while Nate and his girlfriend Cassie sat in the trees under the cover of brush by the road just as Frank had ordered. Cassie's face was buried in the crook of Nathan's neck. His arm was wrapped around her, and he held her wrist. Cassie breathed heavily.

Nate whispered, "Cassie?"

She snapped her head up. "What?"

"Baby, I need you to stay calm," he said.

"How in the hell--"

Nate interrupted her by putting his palm over her mouth. His eyes narrowed, and his forehead wrinkled. He said sternly, "Cassie, I love you, but you have to understand the situation we're in. Also, you're our weakest member. Cathy has warned you once to step up."

Cassie looked and listened intently.

Nate continued, "You will be calm. You will listen to me. You will do as I say. Understand?"

Cassie's eyes were round. He removed his hand and Cassie said quietly, "Yes, dear."

Nate said, "There are evil men coming soon, and we all need each other if we're to get through this alive."

"I understand."

"If you need to, you know how to use a gun. Remember what I talked to you about. Be confidant and aim, okay?"

Cassie nodded.

A shuffle sound slowly scrapped across some pebbles and small rocks on the road. They sat silent, listening. Nate put his hand on his gun and unhooked the leather loop from the hammer for a quick draw if needed.

The sky was a light blue, and peering through the trees Nathan was now able to make out the road. Up the path he could see a man lying on his belly. The man was attempting to pull himself forward with one arm. Nate noticed he wore a gray torn and bloody shirt, and a matching gray hat.

"Oh, my God, it's Sam," Nate said.

Nate moved quickly for the road. He wanted to help Sam. He stopped and looked around the area. Cassie followed while gripping his shirt. He turned and said, "You need to stay here."

Cassie frowned and said, "I will do as you say, but you must be out of your freaking mind if you think you can leave me here by myself."

Nate grinned.

Hugging the trees as they moved through the woods, they inched their way forward while paralleling the road. A few yards from their injured friend, Nate hesitated. He sat and pulled Cassie down, too. They watched him as he rested his face on the dirt and rocks. His hand feebly reached out in an attempt to move forward. He was only able to pull pebbles and dirt back.

"Okay," Nate whispered, "I'm going to have to move quickly. Once we get him, you get under his other arm, and we'll get him back to the campsite."

Cassie asked, "Shouldn't we get Frank, first?"

"Yes, probably," Nate said sincerely, "but I don't think we have time."

Nate glanced over the road to the other side in an attempt to see any movement. He paused, being careful to scan the entire area around him.

"Sam might be the bait, so keep an eye out and scream if you see something," Nate directed.

"Okay."

Nate carefully moved to the edge of the road with his head swiveling side to side. He said with a hushed voice, “Sam, it’s Nathan. Hold still, I’m coming out there.”

Nate looked all around one last time to ensure the area was clear. He moved rapidly to his friend and pulled him up from his lying position. After he had wrapped Sam’s right arm over his shoulders, he noticed he was looking down the barrel of a gun.

“Shhhh.” Conrad Bovis in Sam Buckshot’s hat lifted his head and looked into Nate’s eyes.

With a sneer, Bovis said, “Now be a good boy and follow my instructions. If you do that, I promise not to blow your head clean off in front of your girlfriend.”

Nate nodded.

Bovis said, “Trust me?”

“No, not really.”

Immediately after the initial shock of all that had happened during the night, Frank’s eyesight had sharpened. All of his senses were on high alert. He did feel better that Brad was on his way to get help, but he hated to separate the group.

Frank’s head jerked in response to a rustling sound that was creeping up on him, he stood up quickly and turned. He was shocked to see someone approaching him from behind. He pulled his gun from his hip and cocked back the hammer. At that moment he saw a face come slowly into view from behind some thicket. It was Al Turner.

“Holy hell, Al. I almost shot you,” Frank said. He relaxed with relief.

“Sorry. I’m a little out of it myself. I think I hit my head,” replied Al.

“Jesus, where you been?”

Frank holstered his weapon and turned. He moved to continue his search through the debris. As he rotated away from Al, a brilliant bright flash of orangish light filled his vision. Along with the flash came a mass of pain that dispersed through his head and down his spine. He could then feel the cold blood-soaked ground under his right cheek. This didn’t make any sense for it felt like he was still standing. The bright orange field of view soon closed in upon itself into tunnel vision. That tunnel continued to narrow. It closed up with blackness and engulfed his awareness as well as his consciousness.

Al Turner stood over him and talked to himself. He said, "It's Allan."

It was an extremely uncomfortable position to be lying in. Frank, still in a muddy haze, tried to move, but he couldn't. The road they traveled was rough. Each bounce caused a torrent of pain to flow through his head. More than likely, they were no longer on a road. Barely holding onto consciousness, he could hear the wheels rolling along the ground. He felt the potato sack that covered his head and the rope that bound his wrists and ankles. He attempted to stay awake. Maybe he was only dreaming. Frank began to feel warm, and his body felt engulfed. He never knew when he fell back asleep. All he knew was that at one moment he was on a wagon, then the next moment, he was somewhere else, and his head didn't hurt.

Cathy sat quietly with a group of people. They were blurry, and she couldn't recognize them. She sat with two men and one girl. The girl was crying and she said, "Nathan?" She said it twice and her voice trailed off as she spoke. It was cool out. There was a nice breeze and a pretty purple sky.

Cathy looked up and smiled. She smelled the sea air. She noticed she was sitting in a small rowboat. One man was lying on the bottom of the boat. The girl and Nathan were sitting across from her. *Oh, it's Cassie*, she thought, *and why is she crying?*

The boat rolled up and down in the water effortlessly and deliberately. Everything seemed to move slowly. The sky drastically changed color. It became dark out, and the breeze turned hot. The fresh sea smell went foul.

Cathy said, "Where am I?"

The new odor made her want to vomit. The sea became unsteady. The boat rocked with water in the bottom, soaking into her shoes. She looked down at her feet. She could see that the water was blood. The sky was black, and the sea went from blue to a cloudy red. Cathy hung her hand over the side. She lifted her arm up to look at it. Blood streamed down her hand and continued over her forearm. She watched it flow till it dripped off her elbow.

Blood gushed from her head down the side of her face now. She looked toward the front of the boat. There sat another man with a dark head, a head of tar and no arms. The black guck swirled around his face. He said, "I want you dead. I will see you dead." He floated in the air, and he slowly started to move closer to her. She went for the gun on her hip, but her hands were tied.

Off the back of the boat, over the dark water, was another man. He was walking on the sea. He was talking, too. Cathy strained her ears, but she couldn't understand what he was saying, even though she could hear him perfectly. He walked closer, then she could hear him whisper, "Cathy." She turned her head to an angle and looked at him quizzically. He said again, "Cathy." Over and over he said the same thing. The man with a tar head and no arms was closer now, too. The man on the water spoke again, forcefully, "**Cindy!**"

Cathy snapped her head up from her unconscious state. She looked at the wooden planks at her feet. She glanced all around, and on her right sat Cassie and Nate. They were tied to chairs that sat at a forty-five degree angle forward. Frank was bound and lying on his stomach on the floor next to her. She looked to her left and saw her husband tied up. He looked at her with concern.

"I'm okay, Darling," she said.

"I love you, Cindy."

Drip, drip, drip was all Frank could hear as he came to. He couldn't see yet, but he could hear the dripping of water. The pain in his head was massive. The feeling of wetness was starting to come to mind. He tried to open his eyes, and it took some effort. *Wake up,* he thought. The pain was disorienting, and he felt queasy.

Frank couldn't remember what had happened to him. His last memory was of sending Brad off to get help. Slowly his eyes opened to darkness. There was not much light, and he realized he was lying on the ground on his front. The right side of his face was on a cold wet hard floor. He couldn't feel his arms or legs. *Am I paralyzed?* He could tell he was tied up, somehow. He couldn't move his limbs, but he was beginning to feel the bindings. *Thank God.*

Frank wondered why he felt all wet. He ascertained that he was lying in a half inch of water. His body shivered from the coldness of the floor. Trying to hold his body still and quiet, he attempted to assess his surroundings.

Looking up from the floor was difficult. His right eye was immersed in a pool of water. He got some in his mouth, and it tasted of rust. The room had an odor of metal and dead animal carcass. Frank had no idea where he was.

There was a slight whimper. He figured that it was coming from a small room off to the left. There was an open door to another space where the light seemed to be coming from. His vision was too hazy to see what or who was in the other room. He heard a footstep in the water that came from behind his head. He didn't lift his head to turn and look for fear that he'd be seen. He figured it best to play asleep. Not that he could move his head far even if he had wanted to.

Immediately next to him he saw two figures who sat in chairs. Straining just a bit to look up at the faces, he recognized Jesse and Cathy. They appeared to be awake, but their eyes were down. They were bound at the wrists behind their chairs, and their feet were tied up as well. Cathy was the closest, only a few feet away, with Jesse seated next to her. Frank was seeing double. He relaxed his neck and lowered his face back down into the cold dirty water and listened. He could hear two men. They stood behind him mumbling to each other.

Frank felt tottery as he lay motionless. Creaking sounds cracked from the floorboards with his ear to the ground. With his dry ear he strained to make out the whimpering he thought he could hear. It was definitely coming from the other room. It was a man's whimper. Anxiety started to creep into Frank's brain with the thought that it might be Nathan in trouble. *Stay calm. You're no good to anybody incapacitated with fear.* Concentrating on the far room, his vision improved and the contents of the room were coming into focus. He heard a clanking sound. It sounded like metal on metal. Then he heard metal on wood.

A cry from the room burst out and sliced through his nerves like a blunt and rusty blade. "No."

Frank's insides began to cramp up. He now knew that evil was having its way with an innocent person in that room.

Shifting his head slightly to get a better look, he could see a set of shoeless feet barely touching the ground. They were legs of a man and his toes were just barely skimming the floor. Blood and water slid down his legs, and rolled off his toes. The feet looked as if they were reaching out for the floor, but unsuccessfully. Then Frank watched as a giant of a man stepped into view. He almost completely filled the doorframe with his mammoth body. The man was shirtless and covered in scars and sweat. Wearing rubber boots and black pants, the large man shuffled around the room as he circled his helpless victim.

The man moved around as if taunting his prey. He was trying to make a decision. The demon then approached the poor soul hanging from the ceiling. Frank heard metal on bone. The voice said, "No," breathing hard and fast, then, "Stop it." Then the man was silent.

Except for the continuous dripping of water, Frank could only hear his heart beat. It thumped in his ear and made his bruised skull throb. Cathy just stared at the floor. Frank pondered what was going through her mind. He was fascinated with her. The look on her face was not fear. It was something else - maybe it was strength. It was unusual, not because she was a woman. Anyone in their right mind would be terrified. Jesse drew off her stability and was calm as well. They strengthened each other. Cathy seemed reassured with Jesse around.

A crunch erupted from the small torture room, and it was answered with a snap. Frank peeked into the room, and he watched as the abominable man pulled on something. His victim recoiled as the object came free. A grapefruit sized ball of blood splattered onto the floor like a raindrop. The victim's feet no longer searched for the floor below. The lifeless legs dangled with no motion except for a slow turn as the torturer released him. He was done playing. He would need a new play toy now.

Cassie was crying quietly, trying to stay strong, but this was too much. It was overwhelming for everyone, even Frank. He couldn't help question how Cathy could stay so strong in the face of certain death. Her expression suggested she knew something.

Frank was listening to Cassie cry when he heard the sound of Nathan vomit. It was followed by the discharge hitting the water that coated the floor. Nate's agony tore at Frank's soul. Frank had had this emotion only one other time in his life. It was a situation in which he had absolutely no control. And someone would die.

"Cripes man, did you see that?" a man spoke, then chuckled.

"Yeah, I saw it," said the second man. Frank recognized his voice.

"That's what I like to see. Did you see it diffuse into the water? Keep up the good work, boy. What the . . . it looks like you need to eat more, son. Your godfather should be ashamed of himself."

The man moved about. His feet sloshed around in the pool in which he stood. Then there was a squeaking sound as if a rusty screw was being screwed into a metal nut.

The first man said, "I need to put some oil on this thing." He paused, then said, "This is your damn fault."

Frank noticed that Jesse and Cathy both eyed the man he could only hear.

"Yeah, you," he blared, "and I will see you dead." Under his breath he said, "Bitch." Cathy never flinched.

"What in the world was I saying?" The man stopped pacing.

The second man said, "You were going to invite everyone to supper."

"Right, right, Bovis, what would I do without you? Anyways, Nathan, I'm going to be a better friend to you than your godfather has been by making sure you all get fed."

He laughed and continued, "There's no reason to die on an empty stomach, now, is there?"

The psychopath stopped his tirade. It was strangely quiet, as if the man was waiting for a response. "Well, Bovis, please arrange for our guests to be moved in time for dinner."

"Understood," Bovis said, unintimidated.

"Savage isn't asleep. He's faking. Bring him to my office."

Two men untied Frank's legs. As they lifted his body, the pounding on the back of his head intensified. He was overcome with pain and couldn't walk without assistance. Frank attempted to look around the room as best he could. It was exactly as he had pictured it, dark wood paneling and dimly lit. It was not a big room, and the floor had a layer of water covering the entire surface. He could see Nate and Cassie tied to chairs that sat forward, their heads hung. He wanted to say everything was going to be okay. He wasn't so sure it would be. He wasn't even sure if Nate was conscious or not.

"Remember, stay calm," Frank said quickly. He felt a jab to his rib cage.

The two men held Frank tightly. Even though his hands were tied behind his back, they each pointed a six-shooter at him, just in case. He noticed a man hiding in the corner as he exited the room. The door slammed shut behind him.

The man in the corner stepped out of the shadow with a long barreled gun in his holster. Cassie was crying loudly now.

She whispered, "Nathan?"

Nate's head hung with his chin in his chest. A man with a black patch over one eye stepped from the shadow. Cassie sobbed desperately.

Cathy and Jesse were silent. Cathy remained calm, and she did not draw attention to herself. But she knew Cassie didn't understand that her crying was only agitating them. It was going to get someone killed. Just as Cathy was about to speak, the man walked slowly over to Nathan. He lifted his gun from his holster. Pointing the barrel at Nate, he rested the muzzle on the top of his head and cocked the hammer. All the while, the one eyed stranger never stopped sneering at Cassie. Cassie screamed. The sound pinged off the wood walls and the ceiling. It was deafening.

She slowly halted her crying and hid her anguish in her whimpers. Kelton Brass put his left forefinger to his lips. "Shhhh." His sneer shifted instantly to a look of hatred. His jaw tightened, showing the muscles pop from under the skin on his face.

He whispered through clenched teeth, "You see, it ain't all about you, sweet-thing. Neither of you is of much use in the matter, you understand? So, unless you want this man's brains all over your cute little dress, well, then I suggest you shut the hell up."

Kelton Brass looked Cassie up and down and glared down her top. He smirked, then said, "I'll be seeing more of you, later."

CHAPTER 12

The room Frank had just exited was dark, but the staircase they entered was almost pitch-black. There was not enough light to navigate visually. His captors, using the knowledge that came with having been there before, led Frank up the staircase.

He contemplated making his escape, but he had absolutely no idea where he was. Now was not the time. Besides, he couldn't even keep his balance, not yet.

Frank counted the steps, mapping the dungeon out in his mind. He counted about three flights of stairs before they came to a heavy wooden door. Just as they reached the door, Frank felt himself move. *Whoa.* He wasn't sure if the floor had moved or if maybe the blow he took to his head was causing him to feel unsteady. He could have sworn his two captors swayed, too.

The door was open and there was no lock. When closed, it made a tight seal where no light could slip through. The floor was dry as they stepped into the hallway. The light seemed bright, but it was still dimly lit. Frank's bruised skull made things seem brighter than it was. Only one gas lantern hung from the ceiling. Being sensitive to the glare, he squinted.

Walking down the hall, they walked by a door that had a window with bars, a jail cell most likely. His eyes slowly adjusted to light. There were no other doors and no other people. A muffled animal growl permeated from one on the walls. Then the sound of a violent barking came from the same room.

"We're taking you to Danvil's office, and I suggest you behave," Bovis said.

Frank turned to look at his old mentor and said sarcastically, "Gee, thanks, buddy. It's good to see you've done something with your life."

"Very funny," replied Bovis.

Frank was familiar with what Conrad Bovis was capable of. Bovis did teach him what he knew about killing. Frank had taken in what he'd been taught, but over time he grew to despise Bovis. Bovis' techniques as a spy, torturer, and killer were not what Frank wanted to stand for. Bovis slowly drifted away from what he knew was right. Frank had not seen him since.

Frank had expected to see a certain look from Bovis, but he saw something else. It startled him, and he didn't know what to make of it.

Frank said, "Behave? Maybe, for now."

Bovis grinned and said, "I wouldn't expect anything else."

There was a hint of respect in what he said, but Frank was cautious. Bovis would not blink if he had to pull the trigger. Life meant very little to him. He was a killer, but he would follow certain rules of combat.

Frank was forcefully positioned in front of a chair that faced an empty desk. The two guards exited the door from which they had entered and took their posts. The office looked like a lawyer's office with books and a lantern on the desk. The room was obviously used for paper work, but for what? The paintings were anything but normal. They were paintings of dead animals such as butchered buffalo. One was of a beheaded man standing on a ship with his head on the deck at his feet and a sword in his hand penetrating his own temple like a skewer.

A door behind the desk opened, and Frank could see into the next room. It was a large white room with two rows of seats that wrapped around the wall balcony-style. About a dozen men sat in their seats staring at the center of the room as if waiting for a show. They were all busy among themselves with money in their hands.

A dark haired man just under six feet and slightly heavyset walked into the room and shut the door behind as he entered. He entered not looking at his guest and moved around the room as if alone.

After a moment he said, "Sit, your head must be killing you."

Frank recognized the voice from the cell. He was the man who had taunted Nate. Frank sat in a leather bound chair. The man carried two navy pistols with marble grips, butts forward.

"My name is Shane Danvil," Shane said. Shane lowered his head, then looked up at Frank to see if he was going to respond. Frank provided him with no indication that he knew him.

"Congratulations," Frank said.

Shane continued to stare with his right brow raised. He obviously wanted to make Frank feel uncomfortable, but Frank showed no signs that he was, except for maybe a headache. Shane pulled a black glove from his left hand with his teeth. It was only then that Frank caught a glimpse of Danvil's right appendage. A black wooden fist existed where a hand used to be.

"Nice. Do you really want to fuck around with me? Especially knowing who I am, and the fact that I have your friends wrapped up tight down below? It is quite the precarious situation, is it not?"

Shane spoke sternly, but his face showed that he did find some humor in his hostage's plight. At least humorous from where he sat.

"You're gonna do what you're gonna do. There is not one damn thing I can do about it," Frank said, quiet but confident. He had been trained on how to get through an interrogation, as well as torture.

"See, that's where you're wrong, but we'll get to that in a moment," Shane said while looking at his pocket watch. He then glared at his prisoner, and his head twitched to the side.

Frank could hear dogs barking from the other room. The door was solid, so the sounds of barking and cheering were muffled. It was clear enough what was going on next door. He had to stop his mind from wondering what Shane was going to do with him. Frank did not want to let his imagination make things worse. He would have to deal with things as they came.

"You've got a nice little house of horrors here. You should be very proud," Frank said. He was ignoring what he had been taught, but he couldn't help himself.

Shane said, "You like it? Well, you'll get to enjoy it for a little while longer. That is, before you become a permanent addition to my humble home away from home." Again he glanced at his watch and continued, "As a matter of fact, in about ten or so minutes, you'll get to see the next room on your tour here. But first, I have something to discuss with you."

Shane handled a cigarette with his good hand and asked, "Smoke?"

"No, trying to quit," Frank said, then, "May I please have some water?"

"Oh, I beg your pardon." Shane stood and poured a glass of water from the beverage cart by the desk. Frank looked over the room. He was looking for something, anything. Shane then moved behind Frank's chair and untied his hands.

Shane said, "Before you get any ideas about getting slap happy, please understand that your godson will not live long if you do decide to try something."

Shane stepped behind his desk, pulling on his smoke. "Even if you take me out, Nathan will be killed, that I can assure you. You see, that monster down below only knows one thing." Shane sat and paused, then said, "I think you know what that is, and he could care less what happens to me. So, your thoughts of using me as your hostage, well, let's just say Nate's death might be quick. But my employee has a way of making it extremely painful."

They stared across the desk at each other. Frank drank his water, and Shane smoked. He smoked casually, like a man without a care in the world, not like someone seeking retribution for the death of his brother.

"Frank?" Shane spoke slow and pausing often. "Tell me about the activities of Sabotage."

Frank looked past Shane's face, a tactic he had learned from the military. He sat straight and finished the water. He knew never to turn down water. It was one of the many necessities required for survival, and for escape.

"I would like to get everyone else some water, too, and some food. We're all dehydrated," Frank said.

Shane's eye twitched once and he nodded right. He sat a bit, then said, "Okay, okay, Frank Savage."

Shane stepped around the desk to the door where his two men waited. He opened it and ordered some water and bread to be served to the prisoners. Walking back to his seat, he spoke again. "You see, I'm an okay guy. Alright, I know about your operations in the town of Sabotage. What are you attempting to sabotage now?" Shane spoke faster now as he strained to stay calm. He looked again at the time as he tapped the floor with his foot. Restlessly he put his cigarette out and lighted another. Shane then leafed through some papers that lay on his desk.

Frank said, "Sabotage is not a town that I know of--"

Shane interrupted, voice strained, "Abandoned?" His upper lip lifted to a sneer on the left side of his face. It began to quiver.

Forcing a smile, he said, "I know, I'm just like my brother. We both have a short temper. You should have been there when I found out you had shot him dead." Shane laughed. "Whoa, Nellie! I shot my God-dang horse." He pointed to Frank. "Speaking of that, you owe me a horse. A good one, not some old hag jackass, mind you. Maybe I'll take Maggie. She'll do well in the fields. Or maybe I'll just cut her up and eat her. You know the Italians eat horse? I hear it's quite good."

Frank said, "I'm feeling a bit discombobulated right now."

"What the hell are you talking about?" asked Shane.

"I'm feeling, unnerved."

"Uh?" Shane hit the top of his desk with his wooden hand. He blurted, "Did I fail to mention I have Nate? I will tell my lovely friend downstairs to rip pieces of skin off his body if I fail to get what I want."

Frank didn't allow any emotion to show what ran through his head. He said, "I don't feel well. Can I get something to eat, and I want to see the others?"

Shane's face went red and he said, "I know about your partner Derek Wright and about your operations in Sabotage. So, why don't you just let me know a tidbit of information that might be useful to me? Maybe some information on the current case that is being worked on. Then I might be inclined to make sure your godson gets out alive."

Frank said, "I'm not in the military anymore. You know that I own a store."

"God-dangit!" Shane screamed as he abruptly jumped to his feet. Before he could continue, he was cut short by a knock on the door behind him. "Shit." He rubbed his eyes with his fingers and wrapped the desktop with his fist. "Bovis told me that this would be a waste of time."

Shane bellowed towards the back door, "Bovis."

The door opened, and Shane made a sweeping motion with his hand. Instantly Frank was blindfolded, and his hands were retied behind his back.

"Savage, you try me, but I have a job for you." Shane spoke as his two minions led Frank to the adjoining room. When Frank got to the door, he could smell the sweat and anger from the dogs.

Shane Danvil said, "You will do what comes naturally, because if you fail, everyone you brought along with you, will die. I might even go into town, no, scratch that, I will go into your darling little town and kill that nice elderly couple you work with. How does that sit with you?" Shane whispered into his ear, "Frankie."

Shane stood silent and stared at his prisoner, who couldn't see him through the blindfold. It was as if he once again awaited a response that never came.

"Avanti," Shane blared as he waved to the center of the other room. He pushed Frank forward with his black wood fist.

Frank was shoved to the edge of the white room along the lowest level of the arena. The seats were filled with patrons that Frank could only hear.

The barking of dogs was loud now. A new fight had started. The audience was safe from the combatants who fought in the ring. Frank, pushed to a crouch, was guided along the inside of the wall while Shane and Bovis walked along the second level that was elevated about two feet above the arena. Bovis guided Frank by his shoulder. He then pushed him to a sitting position against the wall.

Two pit bulls circled each other as the patrons cheered their approval. Frank was the only human in the ring. As he sat, he began to sweat profusely. His head pounded, and his heartbeat accelerated. The sound of the vicious animals was quite close. It sounded like they were in his ear. He could feel their motions as they moved towards each other. The barks made his heart palpitate.

A black pit bull latched onto the shoulder of the other dog just missing the neck. He clamped down tight and didn't let go. The two dogs began to turn as the other tried to latch his jowls onto the black. With each effort forward, the black moved in the opposite direction. The muscles in their legs were working to topple the other.

As the dogs fought, they moved closer and closer to Frank who could feel their presence. It felt like they were on top of him. Frank sat with his legs outstretched forward, with knees slightly bent, into the ring. The sweat and mucus that covered the dogs flew about the arena as they clashed. Blood and saliva that was flung from the fight hit Frank in the face. He could feel the animals wrestle at his feet. He couldn't see them, and they didn't know he was there, yet.

Shane laughed to himself as Frank pulled his knees to his chest and pushed his back as tight as he could against the wall. As tight as he was, the fight still ended up on top of his feet. The black still held strong, then the other pit felt Frank was there and turned to him. Savage could feel the breath of the bark that was directed at him. The dog was stretching to bite at Frank's face. He pulled his boots up and kicked both dogs with his soles as hard as he could. Both dogs went tumbling to the center of the ring. The black lost his grip on the other. Shane bellowed with laughter. Half of the audience cheered when the smaller pit latched onto the neck of the black. The other half booed knowing that it was all over. The black was tired, and the smaller pit took his life in a matter of minutes.

Frank whispered, "Where in hell is this place?" He panted heavily trying to dig up courage. His hands tingled as they went to sleep in the tight bindings.

A couple of men began to protest the fight's outcome due to Frank's interjection into the arena. Shane reminded everyone of where they were and reluctantly their complaining subsided.

Breathe, relax. You're no good to anyone incapacitated with fear, Frank thought, as he attempted to calm himself.

Shane swung over the ledge to the floor level and took the blindfold off and said, "There, how are things? Is the adrenaline pumping to your heart? I hope so, because I think you're going to need some."

Frank hoped for something, anything as he surveyed the small coliseum.

Shane said, "I really need you to give 100 percent on this, and so does Nathan, and Cassie and, oh, hell, no reason to stress you out anymore. I hope for your sake that Bovis is right about you. You killed my brother, so make me some money, and all will be forgiven."

The floor was a dry splintering wood. A large man with a shaved head stepped into the far corner about eight paces away. As he walked into the arena, the crowd grew louder. They were bantering and exchanging monies with a man who carried a black book.

Shane said, "That ugly bald fellow is Hector." Shane kneeled as he spoke.

A man from the audience wearing a large hat and a big silver buckle hollered, "Danvil, you already interfered with one fight. You better not be manipulating this one, too."

Shane snapped to his feet and barked back, "Well, hello to you, too, Charlie, you crazy bastard. I've got a headline for you," Shane moved his hand across the sky as he spoke. "Charlie Johansen's Head Found Floating in Kimball Lake Late Last Night." Shane cocked his head. He continued, "Wouldn't that just be swell? Maybe we could plan for your son to find it while fishing."

Charlie stammered, "Now come on, Shane, there's no need for threats."

Shane contorted his face with a quizzical tilt. "Wait a sec, you angry Charlie? Your rants all night long, they've been directed in this direction?"

Charlie glanced at Bovis. Conrad Bovis stood still with one-eye open, and he looked perturbed. The look was not anger, but it was severe. He was resting his hand on the butt of his gun. Charlie sat down without saying another word.

Shane shook his head and said, "What the hell?" He waved his hand. "Who even invited you?"

Shane kneeled and spoke only to Frank, "If your own life isn't motivation enough for you, I have a little incentive. Besides the fact that your friends are in danger, I do have a piece of information you might find intriguing. That man Hector . . ." Shane paused as Frank looked over to Hector. Frank noticed he had vacuous eyes. "He shot and killed Jim Dancer. Now, you may know him as George Cummings, but his real name was Dancer, the man who led you to my brother. I tell you something you probably already know, but I just wanted you to understand that Hector here shot Jim in the face. I really, really had hoped to catch Mr. Dancer alive, but my men screwed the pooch and shot the poor son-of-a-bitch."

Frank remained quiet.

Shane rubbed his chin with his black wooden fist. He then tightened his appendage with a curt squeak. "I was quite angry. I was so looking forward to watching him bleed to death, but," Shane continued with a smile, "when I heard that he pissed himself, well, that visual will keep me smiling for awhile, I suppose."

He stopped, waited again, and acted curious as to why he didn't get a response.

Shane continued, "Anyway, I guess I'll leave you two alone. I wouldn't want to be accused of tampering with the fight because I got my money riding on you."

Shane stood, looked at the ground and angrily said, "God-dang that bump on your head, if you lose I think I'll skin Al. Not that he'd feel anything." He rubbed the thick stubble on his chin as he walked away. He turned back and whispered, "Oh, by the way, it's to the death. So, I wouldn't mess around if I were you. Good luck, champ."

Hector stood only a few feet away. He was shirtless, and he looked pale, almost dead, but lethal just the same. Frank was hoisted to his feet, and his bindings were cut. Frank visualized Jim getting shot, and Nathan and Cassie along with Cathy and Jesse being captured and tied up. He imagined the entire group thrown into a wagon and forced into this living hell, all within a split second. The room rotated slowly in Frank's mind as he analyzed every detail he could absorb.

When Hector's first swing came, Frank knew it was coming before Hector even thought it. As Hector swung his arm back to a cocked position, Savage gave him a left to his bottom rib. Frank's fist hit impacted solidly. He broke Hector's bottom rib clean with a loud crack. He didn't stop there. Savage was moving quickly as he delivered a right uppercut straight up under the big man's jaw. Hector's knees buckled, but his pain was mostly in his rib. On his way down, Frank came fast again with a left that landed on his nose. Blood exploded into Hector's eyes. Hector fell on his knees, and he swung wildly, barely catching Frank, but it was all he needed. It struck his groin.

"Ugh," could be heard from both men as they sprawled to the floor.

The audience flinched and said, "Oh!" when they saw Frank take one in the crotch.

Frank rolled away just as Hector was moving downward with a fist. He missed his target, hitting the floor. The crowd cheered and yelled.

Frank was on all fours next to the wall where he had previously been sitting. Hector's adrenaline was moving as he charged head-first. In an instant Frank sprung forward, rolling with his fall out of the charging bull's way. Hector's huge bald head impacted the wall. His hard skull hit a wood board. The crash caused the wood to break in the middle and splinter out on the ends.

Savage was on his back. He tightened his legs and kicked with his right heel, striking a blow to Hector's broken rib. The impact sent the tip of the bone into his lung. Hector leaned backward on his knees with his head up and screamed into the ceiling in agony. He silenced the crowd.

Shane sneered as Bovis watched his back. But every so often Bovis would look down on Frank and Hector.

Hector grabbed the white sliver of bone with his forefinger and thumb, and slowly pulled it from his abdomen. As the boney shard gradually left his body, he screamed again.

Frank rolled to his feet. He was surprised at how quickly Hector got to his. Hector's breathing sounded shallow and wet as he charged again with his arms outstretched. Frank moved out of the way but Hector readjusted to grab Frank in a bear hug. When Hector squeezed on his adversary, he sent more blood into his own lung and pain to his brain. He let go abruptly and stumbled back, wheezing. His soulless eyes were pools of red with rage.

Frank's world slowed down as his attacker moved in. Savage took his elbow and sharply smashed it into Hector's back as he flew by, but Hector snapped up, swung around and caught Frank in the back of the head. Stars filled his vision, and the bright orange-colored glare overcame his sight once again. Frank was beginning to lose consciousness. He fell to his knees and tried to duck, but his movement wasn't quick enough. Hector hit him on his cheekbone, causing his face to swell up. Frank rolled away with the punch, careful not to hit his head on the hard wood floor. Frank stood quickly but didn't see the fist coming that caused him to spray blood on the violence-thirsty crowd.

Frank paused lying on his stomach. Slowly he forced his way to all fours but then a fist hit his back. It brought him straight up with the pain. He rolled forward again just as Hector tried to kick him in the back of the head. Hector slipped on the slick body fluids that coated the floor and fell with a bloody expulsion of breath. Red liquid shot from his throat into the air in the shape of a mushroom and fell back to his face.

Frank was in awe at the man's resilience and surprised by his own. Hector slowly got to his feet. Frank stood next to the wall, facing it. He waited with his arms forward on the wall and his back to Hector. Hector walked confidently over to Frank. He planned for his final blow to impact the massive bloody knot on the back of Frank's head. With fist cocked back, Hector was going to give it everything he had. Savage turned around and completed a massive wallop to Hector's left eye. The large bald man screamed with a high pitched pain-induced squeal. His hands unclenched, framed his face as he cried out, dropping to the wood floor. A nail was sticking straight out of his eyeball. A rusty metal nail, with a small thorn of wood still attached, protruded from his eye.

Hector yelled, "I give up, I give up! Oh, God!"

Hector was promptly silenced with a bullet to his head. His brains splattered out the back of his head in a line that extended five feet from where he lay dead. Frank watched Shane spin his Navy pistol as he holstered the weapon.

Shane looked around with a questioning look and a smile as the crowd stared. He said, "What? It's supposed to be to the death, give me a break."

"That was beautifully executed Mr. Savage. Exquisite, what savagery!" Shane said. He then waved to his gunmen to set bindings to Frank.

CHAPTER 13

Frank sat quietly in the new surroundings of his perpetually dark world. He could only hear some panicky breathing that loomed all around him. The panting bounced around the walls of his skull. Why he had to be blindfolded, he did not know. It didn't make any sense. He'd been moved only twenty paces or so to a different room. Frank continued to maintain his composure. He was able to do this by keeping his mind busy by constantly updating his mental map of his prison. The wound on the back of his head was beginning to clot up again, stopping the bleeding.

Where he sat now was not as damp as the original cell and it was not as overwhelming as the arena. Frank heard a swivel door swing open and flutter shut. An intense aroma of food engaged his sense of smell. It was elk or maybe deer, but he couldn't tell for sure. His hands were free to move, but his ankles and knees were tied tightly to his chair.

The smell of food was a welcome change to the stench of death he previously had to endure. He heard a tray clunk down as it was placed upon a wooden structure. He just assumed it was in front of him by the tone of the sound. Frank also noticed a slight whimper from a young woman. Maybe it was Cassie, but he could not be certain. The sound of a match being lit in front of his face startled him. He could make out the flame through the cloth of his blindfold. Then silence followed for almost ten minutes with only the occasional interruption of a voice off in the distance.

Frank woozily and unsteadily sat still. He dared not move. More people were ushered in and placed at the table near him.

Frank slowed and deepened his breathing in an effort to stay calm. He ever so slightly moved his fingers and reached forward with his hands away from the arms of his chair. This was the smallest of movements, but it still caused his blood pressure to rise. He slowly slid his arms forward until the tips of his outstretched fingers touched an object that he presumed was a table. Not sure if he was being watched, he slid his hands carefully under the wood object with his palms up. Digitally he felt around until he found what he had hoped for, a nail. He worked the nail gingerly with his fingertips, but he couldn't get his fingers around it. With his fingernails, he began to gently pick at the wood around the slender metal spike.

Without warning there was a tug on the tied knot at the back of his head that loosened his blinders. Frank's heart rate jumped so much that he could feel the thump of his pulse in the arteries of his neck. He immediately halted what he was doing, at least for the moment.

Frank sat at a rectangular table lit with candles interspersed among some food. There were all sorts of food stuffs crowding the board which included more than one plate of a red undercooked, unknown meat. There was also hen, vegetables, and wine in glasses scattered about, and no silverware.

Eight chairs surrounded the cuisine. Three seats sat on each of the long sides of the rectangle, and the ends had a chair each. Across from Frank was an empty seat with Jesse and Cathy in the other two. Next to Frank sat Cassandra with an empty spot next to her. On one end, the side that looked to be for the head of the table, stood a large empty throne. The chintzy seat was made of red velvet, and it had emeralds imbedded into the wood around the frame. On the other side, the seat just left of Frank, sat a large chair covered with a long black cape. Frank scanned the seat with suspicion and noticed it looked as if there was something or someone under the black cloak. With his heart quickening, he looked down and saw blood drip from the arm of the chair. Frank squeezed his fists until the muscles in his hands ached. He held them firm for a few moments and then relaxed.

The entrance to the dining hall opened. Shortly thereafter Shane Danvil entered with his head held obnoxiously high, and he was screwing his black wooden fist onto his arm. It made a shiver-inducing squeak. Shane stared up at the ceiling. It was as if it would pain him to even look at his own deformity.

All eyes were now transfixed upon Shane. Everyone could feel his nefarious intentions as they sat motionless. Nothing could describe the intense feelings that everyone experienced.

Frank noticed the wine that sat on the table seemed to move inside the glasses. It was as though the wine was a liquid metal, and as Shane passed by he attracted the wine like a magnet, pulling the ore in his direction.

Shane sauntered through the room in an arrogant and effeminate manner. He moved slowly with each step. His head twitched as hc took a position behind the chair draped with a cape. He paused behind the chair and lifted his chin as he proudly showcased his oily grin that was glued to his face. Shane was extremely confident, and his demeanor came across as eccentric. *He is an odd man*, Frank thought. It was a given, Shane Danvil was an insane and dangerous foe.

Shane rested his hands on the shoulders of the figure that sat deathly still under a black cover. He looked about the table and said, “I wonder who this is.” He continued to hold his never moving grin as his eyes darted around the room.

He stopped his gaze upon Frank, Shane asked, “Worried?” His smile didn’t move when he spoke.

Frank thought that if he jumped hard enough he could take the chair with him and strangle Shane to death. *If that’s Nathan, Shane will die where he stands.*

“Have you all met,” Shane said. He paused a moment and then, “Mr. Turner?” He snapped off the black cover to reveal a shirtless, bloody, and dead Al Turner. Both his ears were missing.

Cassandra gasped and turned away, but she abruptly stopped when she looked up and across the table at Cathy. Cathy sat perfectly still with a serious look on her face, and she had narrow slits for eyes. With intensity, she stared at Cassandra. Once Cathy got her full attention, she slowly shook her head side to side as if saying, no, you don’t, keep it together.

Cassie nodded slightly and bit her lip hard. She sat up straight, and didn’t blink. If she blinked, her eyelids would force out the tears that had welled up in her eyes and send them traveling down her cheeks.

Cassie stuttered, but said forcefully, “Where’s Nathan?”

Shane ignored the young girl.

Jesse’s muscles pulled taut as he squirmed in his seat. He looked over to Al Turner’s corpse which had a gruesome cut from ear to ear deep in his throat.

Shane said, “You see, people.” Shane spoke as if he was a king addressing a crowd of loyal servants. “Al was . . . how should I put it? An imbecile. The deal is, or was, that he would help me round you all up in one place. Some of you already know why you are here, I am sure of that, but others will be asking, ‘what do you want with me?’ I assure you all, you’ll know soon enough. Although, it will, unfortunately for you, be closely followed by a distasteful event. Anyway, I digress. Al had a job to do, and I have to give credit where credit is due."

Shane stopped and grasped the cape with his good hand. Without hesitation he swung it around his shoulders. He then moved his wooden appendage to his chin. It seemed that he had forgotten about his disfigurement and still had a good arm. When he realized that he couldn't use his right hand to attach the cape around his shoulders, something snapped in his head. His demeanor changed as his eyes grew, and his face puffed up.

Shane caught Frank looking at him. Moving briskly, Shane brought his wooden club of an arm around in a full back handed round house blow to Frank's face. Frank saw the impact coming and saved his nose by turning his cheek to the side. Just as Frank turned his head, he grabbed tightly to the piece of wood he had been picking at. The punch landed hard on the side of his face. The blow was so great it knocked Frank onto his back. He almost hit his head on the floor. He had kept hold of the large splinter, causing it to rip clean from the table when he fell back.

"It can be quite useful, can't it?" Shane said.

Shane turned his back to the table. After a moment he swiveled around to face his helpless audience. His cape was now fastened beneath his chin, and he acted as if nothing had happened. He then nodded to the back of the room. Out of the darkness walked a man wearing a long dark black overcoat and a holstered gun about his waist. Conrad Bovis. The ominous gunman walked over to Frank and bent over to lift his chair.

Frank said as he looked up at Bovis, upside-down, "Conrad, you don't look so good. Sickly even. Is this line of work not treating you well?"

Bovis said, as he lifted Frank back to a sitting position at the table, "It pays well enough." He then returned to his post in the shadow at the back of the room. As he stepped into the shade, his head snapped forward. His hand shook and fluttered over his gun.

"Where was I?" Shane asked. "Please don't interrupt me again. Oh, okay, credit, yes, yes that's where I was. You see, he did do a spectacular job of getting you all together." Danvil pointed around the table as he spoke. "There is the famous lawman Frank Savage, the beautiful Cassandra Jones, and the lovely and charming couple known to me as Cindy McManus and Jacob Sanders. I hear you two got married, congratulations. Short-lived as it will be, though."

Frank knew them as Cathy and Jesse. There had to be an explanation.

Cindy and Jacob? Does anyone go by their real name anymore?

Frank did not show his surprise. He had already made one mistake tonight, and he wasn't going to do it again. His eyes still watered from the last one.

"Anyway," Shane continued, "Al was marvelous, but he thought he deserved more." Rage spilling over in his tone, he said, "We had a deal." Shane grew redder in the face and more agitated. "He would get paid 'X' amount of money once he accomplished his duties. And I was prepared to do that, but he felt that because he clocked the 'deadly Frank Savage' in the back of his noggin, that he deserved more." At a scream now he turned to Al's body and hollered. "Well, you got some more Al. How does it feel?"

Cassandra jumped in her seat and it attracted Shane's attention. In response to the interruption he said, "Oh, don't you fret, little lassie, at least not now. I tell you what." He walked over behind Jacob and Cindy. "I promise I won't kill you. I have plans for you. You won't like them, but you'll be alive. That's got to count for something."

Jacob squeezed tightly the handles of his wooden chair.

"Mr. Sanders, relax. You're holding that chair so tight that I believe you're going to hurt yourself," Shane said, laughing out loud. He then took a seat at the end of the table in the plush gaudy chair. A harmless looking cook went to and fro from the kitchen. Shane's only bodyguard was Bovis, who still stood in the shadows. Shane sat as if deep in thought, then said, "I hear voices." He looked expressionless at Frank with lazy eyes.

Frank said, "Well, I didn't say anything."

Shane smiled. "No, I hear a voice in my head." He tapped his index finger to the side of his head as he spoke.

"Why am I not surprised?" Frank said.

"Ha," Shane said, genuinely humored. "I know a lot of people hear voices, but my voice is different. First of all it's a woman, which is quite disconcerting to say the least." Shane drank some wine, then continued, "The other difference is that most people's voices, if they are telling them what to do, are telling them to do bad, hurtful things. My voice is always telling me to do good things. She tries to make me do what most would consider as honorable."

Shane pulled on his cigarette, blew the smoke forcibly across the dining room, and said, "I don't pay her much mind." He grinned slyly as he leaned forward against the table.

Frank felt the sturdy splinter of wood in his hands. He was tempted to look at it, but refrained from doing so. Savage hoped that Bovis was at an angle such that he couldn't see what he was doing.

Frank asked, "Does your voice ever tell you to kill yourself?"

The humor just melted from Shane's expression for a moment. "No."

Frank said, "Too bad for us."

As Frank spoke he attempted to reach forward for the nail again, but when Bovis repositioned his chair he was now too far from the table. It would be too risky to reach out again. Frank did not want to be caught in the act, so he kept the wood in the palm of his hand. *It's better than nothing*, he thought.

Shane blurted, "Cassie first. To be honest, she's sitting here because Bovis is somewhat of a softy. He just can't find it in himself to kill a defenseless woman." Shane looked at Cassie and added, "That's a problem I don't have." Cassie broke her eye contact with Shane.

Frank asked, "Where's Nathan?"

Shane said, "Don't worry, he's already been fed and watered. I thought it prudent to keep him in a cell as insurance. I don't want you to get any crazy ideas while we sit and enjoy each other's company."

"Name me one person who can say they ever actually enjoyed your company," Frank scoffed.

"Mr. Savage, it seems Hector hasn't taken all the fight out of you. I can't say that I'm surprised. I did put my money on you."

"I still wouldn't bet against me," Frank said, leering at Danvil. The throbbing in the back of his head was continuing to subside.

"I am wise to your capabilities. You will be secured in your cuffs and shackles soon enough. Oh, if you were curious about your friend on the Appaloosa, I'm sorry to inform you, but he ran into a bit of trouble. The meat on the table is evidence of that," Shane said. He cut a piece of meat and clumsily jammed it into his mouth. Shane licked his fingers and said, "Appaloosa, mmm, who would have known? I must be part Italian, eh Frankie?"

Frank glanced over at Cindy for an answer to the question, 'was Danvil telling the truth?' Cindy looked at Frank confidently and without any sign of distress.

Shane put his black fist on Cindy's hand, gently stroking it he said, "Well, how you been?" He waited again for his response, or he was listening to the voice in his head. Shane always seemed a bit thrown off and confused when he didn't get a reaction. Or he didn't like what his voice was telling him.

Shane said to Cassandra and Frank, "Jacob and Cindy, or maybe you two know them as Jesse and Cathy. Jacob, Jesse . . . Cindy, Cathy." He stopped to ponder what he had just said and looked up, then, "That's cute. You stayed with the same initials. Anyway, I had a bit of a run-in with these two a few years back. It honestly took me this long to find them."

Shane said as he stared at Cindy, "Nice shot, kid. Whoa!" Shane laughed. His smile looked pasted but sincere. "I've learned to live with my loss quite well, don't you think? You, however, will not. After I take your husband from you, you will surely die soon after."

He stood and said, "You recognize these?" Shane whipped back his cape to showcase his two guns strapped to his body. They rested on his belt with the butts forward. Standing proudly, he reached down slowly and pulled one from his left holster. Holding it to the side with the butt forward to Cindy and Jacob, they could see it. Frank's eyes narrowed as he tried to see what they were looking at. Cindy's eyes became shiny, and Jacob's enlarged with sadness that quickly turned to a blaze.

Shane leaned back on his heels. "Frank, you look confused. It seems they recognize the marble grips. It is quite rare. But what is most upsetting, I imagine, is the S-S carved into the marble."

Jacob sat still with an expression laced with wrath.

Cindy said, "You're going to die today." Her tone meant business.

Frank breathed in quick and paused in order to hide his shock. When she said something, for some reason or another, it happened.

Shane said, "Good luck, Sugar." He sat back down and nonchalantly filled his plate. "Eat, people." Nobody moved, not even to breathe.

Frank said, "Is it poisoned, Bovis?" He didn't even look at his ex-mentor.

Bovis said, "It's safe."

"Guys, we must eat. It's okay," Frank said. He took a leg from the hen at the edge of the table in front of him.

Shane asked Cassie, "Aren't you hungry, dear?"

Cassie replied contemptuously, "I could eat."

Shane said, "You all might want to stick to the fowl. If you're sentimental that way." Shane continued with his story, "S-S is the initials for, or was for, Scott Sanders. By the way, he was an excellent tracker. His posse had apparently all gone home after a couple of days of looking for me. They never knew how close they got, except Scott He was on fire."

Excitedly he said, "I really thought they were going to find me. I guess when everyone quit, it leveled the odds for me. I knew I had him. He was working on too much emotion."

Shane continued mostly speaking to Frank. "I had recently slaughtered a family, and Sheriff Sanders just happened to be the man to find the bodies."

Frank sat still.

Shane paused and looked down. "I reckon he took it personally. He was on a mission, but one thing he didn't consider, I don't fight fair. I shot him in the back. So there would be no evidence, I burned the body of the Sheriff, but I had to have those two beautiful Navy Pistols he carried."

He grinned as he spoke to Jacob now. "So, I belted my own guns onto your dad first before I set him aflame. I didn't know it, but he wasn't dead yet." Jacob's eyes were red and bulging. "I thought he was dead, but once the fire caught, he started kicking around and he came to screaming."

The table was painfully quiet. Cassie's head dangled and her shoulders slouched.

Shane said, "Afterwards, I had no plans to head back to town, so I headed south. I should have gone north. I ran into some Texas Rangers about two weeks later who just happened to be coming north to help in the case of a missing sheriff. I am quite the actor, I must say, but like an idiot, I was prancing around with my two new Navy pistols, each with S-S carved into the side. Lucky for me they didn't know Scott Sanders. If they had known the man, I might be dead, hung from a tree most likely. My mind was racing, and when they asked me my name, I just said Shane Shayne."

Danvil smiled like he was the cat who had just caught the canary. "You wouldn't believe how that changed my life. I now had a group of Texas Rangers who could vouch for me, and they did. Those sons-of-bitches did! I offered to help them to town since I knew the area, but once I got to town, I hid my lovely new man-killers. I knew someone would recognize them. Those poor bastards were so appreciative of my help and guidance, I ended up taking Sander's job as sheriff. Can you believe the irony of this? Can you appreciate it in the least?" Shane leaned back in self-satisfaction. "I loved that job. The power, and the mayhem and waste I caused while hiding in that town, behind that tin-star."

As Shane spoke, Frank worked his splinter of wood with his fingers, he was using a slow side to side motion. He worked the narrowest end of the small piece of timber sideways against the grain of his chair's arm. It was becoming flatter and sharper with each swipe against the rough grain of his chair. The three-inch piece was blunt on one end and flat on the other. Frank wasn't sure how it would work, but it was worth a try.

Shane pointed to Frank. "You even came into the neighborhood when you were looking for my brother, but I wasn't on your mind. Besides, the Texas Rangers vouched for me. I was untouchable until, long story short, she did this." He held up his black fist. "And, I couldn't let the only two eyewitnesses to a double homicide get away. Why, their testimony would put me away for life, or more than likely it would send me straight to hell. But, they got away, so I had to leave before Mr. Savage came looking for me. That is why you are here, Mr. Savage."

Frank listened as he worked his wooden key.

"Sure, I'm pissed about Vic, but Victor was an asshole. Now, I know you have orders to kill me. You have orders to kill, on sight, Shane Danvil. Whether you work for the U.S. government or not, I knew you'd eventually find me. I mustn't let you live."

Shane sat quiet in thought, he looked around the table at each person. He started with Frank, then Cassandra, then Cindy and Jacob. He said, "Anyway, I have plans for all of you, whether it be a contest, or maybe use you in a whorehouse in Mexico, or just to torture for a bit."

Shane stood and walked to the door. On his way out he said, "Bovis, give our guests a few minutes, then lock them up with their friend."

Jacob stared with a cutting glare as Shane exited the dining room.

Cindy whispered, "Darling?"

Jacob said nothing and swallowed hard.

Frank said, "Everyone, listen up. Eat what you can." Bovis watched from the shadow of the room. There was no need hiding what he was thinking from Bovis because he already knew. While eyeing Bovis' dimly lit wooden face, he said, "We need the nourishment. Killing people tends to take it out of you."

Bovis stepped from the shadow suddenly and walked to the back door. He opened it and said, "Kelt."

Kelton replied, "Is it time?"

The two escorted their prisoners one by one to a new cell only ten paces away from the dining room. Frank, blindfolded once again, counted the steps. With the map etched out in his mind, it continued to take shape. If need be, he would be able to get from their new cell to any other room he had seen or been to, but he had no idea how to get out.

Frank had been unconscious when they had first arrived. He didn't manage to wake until after he had already been secured in the torture chamber. The room that existed in the bowels of their hell was one he desperately hoped he would never see again.

CHAPTER 14

Kelton removed the blindfolds one by one. He moved slowly from his left to his right. First was Cassie. She sighed with relief when she saw Nate was next to her, unharmed. He was awake and locked up in a chair as well. Next Kelton removed Frank's blindfold, then Cindy's, and finally Jacob's.

Once Kelton exited and had closed the cell door, Frank whispered, "You okay, Nathan?"

"Yes. I'm so relieved to see you guys. I had no idea where they had taken you all. That one eyed freak was spinning all kinds of shit," Nate said.

"Nate, were you awake when we all got here?" asked Frank.

"I was, and I think Cassie was, too, but they had us blindfolded. I couldn't see a damn thing," Nate replied.

Frank, looking left at Cindy, said, "Do you know where we are?"

Jacob said, "Cindy was unconscious because of some sort of drug."

"You were drugged?" Frank asked.

"I think so," Cindy interjected. "Somebody charged into the campsite and put a wet cloth over my face. The next thing I remember was waking up and looking at that wet dirty floor as that man was being tortured to death."

Frank interrupted, "I think that was Al."

Cindy nodded.

Jacob said, "They snuck up onto the campsite somehow. Cindy was aware of them, but it was too late and there were too many. I got a whack on the head, but I was able to stay conscious. I was blindfolded, too, but I do know we were put on a wagon."

Frank asked, "How long was the wagon ride?"

"Few hours. A half-a-day's ride at most. I did hear a splashing of water as we got here."

Frank said, “Anyone else have the feeling that we’re on a boat?”

“I do,” Nate interrupted. “That would explain why I got sick.”

“You’re right,” Cindy added. “I was having a dream before I woke about floating on a lake in a boat.”

“I can feel the motion,” Frank said. “I thought at first I was just unsteady because of the blow I took to the back of my head, but--” Frank stopped abruptly. Cindy thrust her attention towards the door.

No one moved.

A narrow sliding window opened. Kelt’s one eye peered through the opening. Then he abruptly slammed the small window shut.

“Cindy?” Frank said. “Can you see my cuffs?”

Cindy cocked her head back. Everyone was sitting in chairs with their ankles shackled to the wooden legs and with their hands cuffed behind their backs.

Cindy said, “Barely, but yes.”

“Describe them for me, please. Color and everything.”

“They’re silver, with metal links connecting the two hoops around your wrists.”

“Are there teeth in the hoops?”

“Yes.”

“I thought so. I’m going to need your guidance,” Frank said quietly. He paused and looked at the door. The door stood about six feet in front of him.

“Okay.”

Frank manipulated the flat narrow three-inch piece of wood in his right hand.

Frank said, “The teeth, if I’m not mistaken, are on the male section of the lock.”

Cindy replied, “Yes, you’re right, and they run along the top side only, looks like.”

“Perfect,” Frank whispered enthusiastically. He began to feel around the left hoop of his cuffs. He tried to work the wood into the opening. “If I can get the splinter of wood into the female end on the top side, I might be able to push the lock mechanism up and wedge the wood in so that the teeth will slip open without catching on the lock. Make sense?”

“Yes, you’re close. It looks like it should pop any second,” Cindy said as she strained her head back. She looked down peering over the top of Frank’s hands.

"I'll need to . . . shh," Frank whispered, interrupting himself. "I hear something."

A busy rumbling of footsteps reverberated through the walls from the ceiling down to the floor. Then there was a loud thump as if someone had fallen.

"Something's going on up there," Jacob said.

"The guard is coming," commented Cindy.

"How do you know?" Nate asked.

"Oh, trust me," Jacob replied with a crooked forced smile. "She knows, and she probably already knows what's going to happen to us. She just won't say."

A whack at the door and a jingle of keys penetrated through the wooden entry. A dead bolt on the door clanked open. With an audible crack from the door jam, the jail entrance slowly opened inward, allowing more light to invade the space. The tall one-eyed guard stood in the doorway. Light slithered around his body leaving an apocalyptic adumbration on the floor.

In a gravelly voice he said, "What's all the racket?" Kelton stomped heavy-footed into the cell. "Trust me, you'll all be making plenty of noise soon enough."

Frank caught a glimpse of the guard's cragged face. Under Kelton's eye patch existed three nasty looking scars that ran parallel to each other at an angle across his face. It looked as though a tiger claw had swiped a gash across his mug. The brute walked over to him. He stepped heavily and cumbrously as he moved.

"Ah, hell, not again," Frank whispered.

"Pretty, ain't it?" the guard said as he lifted his eye patch to show he had an eye socket minus an eyeball. The cavity was deep, and it was dark red displaying purple lines spread out like a spider web on the concave surface. It had dried blood and puss pockets along with a rotten odor. Cassie let out a short screech and turned her head.

Frank said, staring into his empty crater, "You know, if you don't stop picking at that, it's never gonna heal."

The guard backhanded Frank across the mouth. Frank, slightly stunned and shaking off the sting, said, "Well, at least you have a sense of humor about it."

Kelton replied, "I know what's funny." He walked over to Cassie, reached over and tried to give her a kiss. She turned her head in disgust. Kelton pulled her head back by her hair and licked her neck.

Cassie held back her cries into a snivel. Nathan bucked against his bindings as he yelled, "Get your hands off her!"

Nate's plea only egged Kelton on.

After a moment Kelton stopped as if something had grabbed a hold of him and physically yanked him back. He turned. Cindy stared him down. It sent a shiver up his spine and through his shoulders. Kelton moved his mouth to speak, but his tongue tied up. Nothing would come out of his mouth. He stood frozen in his tracks. Kelton Brass, in a quiet fit of fury, pulled his keys out, unlocked Cassie, and yanked her to the ground. Nate continued to pull on his wrists to no avail.

Frank calmly worked his cuffs.

Kelton began to drag Cassie out of the cell by her arm.

Nate hollered, "Where you taking her?"

Holding tightly to Cassie's arms, Kelt turned and said with a hushed tone, "I've got a friend in the belly of the ship that's been looking forward to meeting you all. And if you listen careful enough, you should be able to hear her scream." He sneered and locked the cell door behind him as he marched Cassie to the lower level.

Nathan went into a panic. "Holy shit, holy shit, holy shit, holy shit."

Nate hyperventilated as he yanked on his cuffs and leaned hard on the chair. He pulled desperately with his legs to free the shackles on his ankles that were bolted to the floor. "Uncle Frank, Uncle Frank! What, I got to help her, what the?" His chains rattled loudly announcing Nate's desperation in volumes.

Frank worked persistently at his cuffs, but he could not get the lock to release. Cindy continued to watch the positioning of his hands in an attempt to help.

Jacob said, "Nate."

Nathan's head jerked violently forward and aft. He arched his back. He pulled up on his feet with all he had. The metal shackles bolted to the floor were sturdy.

Jacob tried to get Nate's attention and said, "Nate, look at me. Look at me, Nathan."

Nathan pulled frantically on his hands. Blood began to stream from his self-inflicted wounds on his wrists. The metal dug into his skin. He was beginning to separate his skin from the muscles on his hands. He cried, "If I can break my thumb, I can get my hand out." The energy was seeping out of him.

Frank said quietly, "Are you done, Nate?"

Nathan screamed, "You bastards, I'll kill every damn one of you!"

Nate then stopped.

"I asked you a question, Nathan," Frank said. Frank's tone was calm but direct.

Nate sat still. Blood dripped from his fingers to the floor. His head hung low and he tightened his jaw.

Frank said, "Nathan, if you are done, we shall proceed. Are you okay?"

"Yes," Nate answered as he caught his breath.

"Good, because we cannot get out of this without you."

Cindy said, "He's coming back."

Frank continued to work on his lock. His hands were sweaty, and the wood was slippery now. His right palm began to ache. Frank feared it would cramp up. He heard men hollering to each other off in the distance.

"What the hell is going on out there?" asked Frank.

A loud clash boomed through the cell and it almost caused Frank to drop his man-made key. Kelton stormed into the hold with disgust on his mind.

Kelton yelled, "That skanky little bitch bit me! I bet you're a real bitch, too, ain't you?"

Cindy said smoothly, "More than you can handle."

Kelton walked over to Cindy and slapped her. Frank worked furiously. He could not understand why the lock would not come loose.

Kelton grew more agitated as he slapped Cindy again. His face shown with frustration. He said, "Scared bitch?"

She never showed it.

Jacob hollered, "It doesn't make you a man cause you can beat a handcuffed woman. Why don't you try me?"

Kelton backhanded Cindy again and said, "I got a better idea. How about I show you that I am a man, right now and in front of you with your wife?"

Frank pushed hard on the wood. It didn't budge the lock. Sweat poured off his face as Kelton moved behind Cindy. Kelton then forcibly kicked the back of her chair. The impact caused her to spill forward onto the floor. She turned her frame to the right and landed hard on her side.

Kelton surveyed Cindy. His breathing was forced and choppy. He wrung his hands about with nervous energy. He yelled, "Screw Shane Danvil's orders, you are all gonna die right now!"

At that moment multiple gunshots resounded from outside. A few bullets impacted the boat, and there were some muffled orders being barked in the distance.

Are those Winchesters? It's got to be Brad, Frank thought. The sounds of a possible rescue gave him newfound energy.

Kelton continued his rampage by back handing Jacob with a left across his ear.

Frank's desperation almost got the best of him, until he switched hands. He moved the wood from his right hand to his left. In less than a second his left hand had undone the lock that was attached to his right wrist.

Frank clutched his hand into a dense fist.

Kelton said, "Screw it." He pulled his gun from his hip.

Nate caught a glimpse of Frank coming loose from his cuffs and yelled out, "Hey, you one eyed freak show!"

Kelt turned and uttered, "Wha--"

Savage snapped around and socked Kelton in the guts. Kelt dropped the gun to the floor. They both went for the six-shooter, but on his way down Frank changed his mind. His instincts took over his body. With his feet still bolted to the floor, and his left hand still attached to the cuff that was locked to the chair, he went for Kelton's throat with his free hand.

Frank savagely gripped his enemy by the neck. The muscles in his hand were stiff from working the cuffs and his palm ached. He dug a thumb into Kelton's neck just left of his voice box. Frank's four fingers drove into the other side of his neck. Pushing forward and using every muscle in his body, Savage was able to push Kelton into the back wall. He couldn't let him go free. Frank's body stood at an odd and twisted angle. If he were to let go, he wouldn't be able to reach Kelton again, for his ankles were bolted to the chair.

Kelton began to slide down the wall as he fought to release the strong grip. He punched Frank in the nose. Savage didn't even feel the impact. Kelton tried to pull back Frank's fingers from his own neck, but it was too tight. Frank's hand cramped up around Kelton's Adam's apple along with his windpipe. The tightening grip was wrapped around all the muscles and veins in the soon to be dead man's neck.

Kelton's gurgling stopped as Savage squeezed tighter and tighter. He eventually stopped the flow of air. Frank's arm vibrated with a violent fury. His face said one thing, kill. His eyes blazed with fever, and the muscles in his arm bulged.

"Aaah!" Savage screamed. His face turned red as he furiously squeezed the life out of his victim. With his enemy dead, Frank still pushed and crunched simultaneously until a loud pop sound came from Kelton's head. Kelt's good eye rolled forward in the socket. The strain was such that the muscles holding his eye in place snapped. As it rolled forward, it exposed all the veins from the back of his eye.

Savage was panting hard as he finally let go of his victim's lifeless corpse. Without wasting any time, he began to search for the keys.

Frank attempted to relax his muscles and catch his breath, there would be no chance of getting any rest. He said, "We don't have much time, so listen up." With the keys in hand Frank quickly worked his cuffs and shackles, he then moved to the others.

Frank ordered, "Jacob, you and Cindy need to get off this boat."

"No, not a chance," Jacob said.

"What?" Frank snapped.

"We have a job to do, too," Jacob said as he looked at Cindy.

Cindy said, "I'm sorry, but we're not leaving this hell-hole until Shane is dead."

Frank continued to work the locks until Nathan was free of his bindings. He picked up the gun. He checked the chamber and handed it to Jacob. Jacob checked the chamber as well, pulled the gun belt from their dead cell guard, and strapped it around his waist.

Frank said, "Fine, but when you're finished, get the hell out of here. Nate and I will get Cassie and set this boat on fire. I'm guessing the gunfire outside is Brad's doing. I'm hoping he got some help. Once you smell the smoke or see fire, get off the ship. Most everyone left onboard will be more interested in saving their hides than to worry about us, except for one."

"Do you know which way to go to get out of here?" Jacob asked.

"Up," Frank said with a half smile. "Good luck you two." He shook their hands. Jacob and Cindy moved quickly out of the cell.

"You ready?" asked Frank.

"Let's go," Nate answered.

Frank led the way down a dark and narrow staircase creeping closer to the innards of the ship. The heat intensified as they proceeded towards the torture chamber. It just happened to be next to the engine room, and they could hear the motor chugging along.

Sweat continued to bead up on their faces, and their shirts soaked up all the perspiration they could hold. Moving as one, they continued down, step by step, neither sure what lay ahead of them.

Anxiety was welling up from deep inside their hearts as they moved farther into what best could be described as a descent into Satan's lair. The walls seemed to narrow as they got deeper. It progressively grew darker. The enclosure that surrounded them was wet, and they found it difficult to walk on the slippery steps. Holding each other up, a beam of light shone in through the bottom crack of the door at the base of the staircase about fifteen steps away.

A scream from Cassie pierced through the small crack at the base of the door. Nathan burst past Frank in an effort to get to the entrance, to open it, and to rescue Cassandra. Frank grabbed Nathan by the arm and whispered, "No, abide with me. Please, trust me." Frank's eyes pleaded as Nathan looked back at his godfather. He was barely able to see him, and he was right in front of him. Nate's face cried desperation.

There was another painful cry, "No, stop. Help me, Nathan!" It was Cassie, and she was in physical pain. Nathan bolted down the stairs, unable to hear Frank say, "Wait." Nate was only focused on the agony that surged from his bones. Her cry was shattering the silence and filling him with urgency. Frank fell on his back when Nathan broke his grip. Time began to slow down as Nate sprinted down the stairs to the lowest level of the boat. The darkness surrounded Nathan's frame as he disappeared into it.

Nathan frantically kicked the door with such force that he almost knocked it off its hinges. He could see the torture room now and sprinted forward. He hit the door with his body. The door exploded open, impacting the backside of the beast that was torturing Cassandra. Cassie was hanging in the middle of the room from the ceiling by her hands. She was only wearing her undergarments. Tears were rolling down her face, and blood was flowing down her body. The torturer, alarmed, stumbled and grunted in irritation.

"Nathan. Help me," she cried out.

He was a massive man. Nate noticed he had no nose, and that he could see into the abyss of his face. There was no humanity in this monstrosity. The hulking man charged as Nathan got to him. The torturer had hands twice Nathan's size, and he grasped him by the neck with his left and lifted him off the ground.

"No!" Cassie's cry split through Nathan's brain, and he could feel her pain.

In the attack Cassie had been bumped, and she was spinning from the rope that was attached to a large rusty hook in the ceiling.

Nathan was almost two hundred pounds, but the mutant lifted him up as if he were a small bag of potatoes. Nathan clocked him with a left, and then a right, but the blows were just minor inconvenient distractions.

The demon held a four-inch blade in his right hand and thrust it forward, aiming for Nate's heart. As he pushed forward with the knife, Frank came in low out of nowhere and impacted the side of its legs. He was aiming for the knees. Frank threw everything he had into his attack. The creature's blade missed Nathan's heart and landed in his shoulder. A loud crack resounded as the large man's right knee shattered with the sideways motion, and Nathan went flying and fell at Cassandra's feet.

Nate looked up just as she looked down, and they locked eyes. Torment and suffering was all they saw in each other. Only desperation and angst flowed between their souls.

The beast bellowed out in pain. It sounded not like a man, but like an ogre who had just been speared by a knight.

Blood seeped from Nathan's wound as he slowly pulled at the blade in an effort to free it from his arm. "Aaaah."

Frank fought to untangle himself from his adversary, and he urgently attempted to right himself. But the monster was angry now and he took a hold of Frank's leg. Pulling with all his might, Frank was still not able to free himself from the vice-like grip. Savage punched the beast in the mouth with three quick blows, breaking the lip open and causing blood to splatter all over his knuckles.

It bellowed as Nathan reached the scene and buried the four-inch lance deep into its neck. The pain caused it to swing its arm, knocking Nathan to the ground, but in the process it freed Frank. Without hesitation Frank moved quickly to a four-foot long piece of lead pipe covered with dried blood that hung from the wall.

Cassie pulled both her legs up to her chest and kicked the beast in the head as it tried to stand. It fell to its busted knee and cried out. Full of rage and out of control anger, Savage furiously and deliberately brought the lead club to bear on the skull of the man who had wrought so much pain on so many people. He clubbed him again and again, even after it had stopped moving.

Savage stood over the dead beast. He looked down upon him like a triumphant warrior. He was animalistic and primeval with weapon still in hand. Savage watched his adversary slowly pass to the beyond. He observed the dying man's eyes as they looked up at him in frustrated hatred. The animal's eyelids and fingers started to twitch as it relinquished its life.

Savage hung over his dying assailant and said, "You are a total and utter asshole." Then he whispered, "Tell Satan to expect more company, cause we're not done yet."

Frank watched over his enemy to make sure it died while Nathan lifted a knife from the table of torture and cut Cassie free. She looked as if she would cry, but for some reason she didn't. She quickly massaged her wrists as Nate put on her shoes.

Frank said, "I am past the point of no return."

Nate asked, "What?"

"Anger, power, more than anything I've ever felt before." Frank paused a moment. "Identifying the need to keep moving with the plan . . . wait a sec."

Frank walked to the table that had knives, hooks, pinchers and every cutting tool imaginable. His head followed his eyes to the counter top that rested against the wall. His gun belt rested on the table.

"Watch the door, watch my back," Frank dictated. He picked up his belongings and inspected the gun. It seemed to be in good working order. He opened the cylinder and pulled a bullet from the belt. He then filled the last remaining charge and snapped it shut. He placed the gun back into the holster and removed the knife sheath.

"Nathan," Frank said sternly to get his attention. He then tossed the gun and belt to him. "You'll need that. Take Cassie and get the hell out of here."

Nathan pleaded, "I'm not leaving you to fight this alone."

"I told your folks I would make sure you got home okay. Now, get up top and get her someplace safe. Which is anywhere but here. Got that?"

"But--" Nathan tried to explain, but Frank interrupted, "Your job is to get her out alive, and my job is to get you out alive. Don't let her down, because if you fail, so do I. Oh, and I'm going to want that back." Frank pointed at the gun. "So don't lose it."

Frank pulled his hunting blade from the sheath. Looking it over, he flipped it around in the palm of his hand and placed it back into its housing all in one smooth motion.

Cassie quietly walked over to the table and lifted Cindy's single shot derringer from the top. She opened it, inspected the bullet, and replaced it. She closed the chamber and said, "Okay, I'm ready now."

Frank's eyes seared with determination. "Remember, my plan is to burn this ship till it sinks. If you see or smell smoke, well, hopefully you'll be gone by then."

Nathan nodded and held Cassie's arm.

The three moved fast up the staircase uninterrupted. Frank then pointed in the direction he felt was the exit. And with some trepidation, he allowed Nate and Cassie to head out alone.

CHAPTER 15

Jacob escorted Cindy by the hand as they drifted through the narrow corridor. The gunshots from outside were growing louder with each step, but there were fewer of them. There was some loud scuffling and foot-stomps from the top most deck. Ducking into an empty room, they just missed being discovered. Two armed men hurriedly scrambled by to get topside to fight off their intruders, or possibly to jump ship. Jacob and Cindy then noticed that someone had seen them. It was the feeble cook.

The cook said, "Psst, over here." He waved to them from the dining room. "I must leave, but please help the horses. They are in the back. I cannot stay to help. I know too much. Mr. Danvil will shoot me."

The kindly chef waved the two into the dining room where they had had dinner only an hour earlier. He opened a secret door using a hidden handle that was built into the wood paneling of the wall. The cook pointed down a long hallway. "Please help them. I must go." The cook scrambled up a circular staircase and was gone.

Jacob asked, "Why does he care about the horses?"

Cindy said, "Not sure, but this is what we need to do."

"Is this a secret passage?"

"Yep, looks like."

"Where in the world are we?"

Cindy said, "It doesn't make much sense, does it? But then again, we're talking about Shane Shayne."

Jacob smiled briefly, then turned down a hallway. He said, "We can't leave the horses to burn to death or to drown on a sinking boat."

Cindy agreed. "Yeah and besides, if Nate found out, he'd kill us."

Jacob hesitated. He said, "This is important, too. If he gets away, he gets away."

Cindy said, gripping her husband's shoulder, "It is important and

Shane will wait."

Nate's vision was beginning to either adapt to the darkness of the ship or more light was working its way in, but it was still difficult to see.

Cassie said, "How do you know where to go? It's so dark."

"I'm just working my way up. This whole place is a maze. It's driving me insane. At least it's starting to smell better, I guess."

Manipulating his way through the dark hallway with his hands, Nate led the two up, he hoped. The sounds of gunfire were reassuring to him. The sound of men fighting gave him a sense of relief that maybe Maggie and Brad had broken through to get help.

Cassie whispered, "I'm sure Maggie's fine."

Nathan nodded. "Here, I feel some air. Do you feel that?" He said excitedly.

A small stream of air blew into Nate's face, ruffling his hair.

"Yeah, yeah," Cassie replied. "It smells fresh."

Nathan felt the wall, running his fingers over the surface. "I think there is a hidden door here." Gliding his fingertips along the edge of a cut in the wood, he followed it around. "It feels like a door frame. There's no damn handle anywhere."

Cassie said, "Wait . . . do you hear something?"

Nate looked up and said, "I think so." Nate put his ear to the wall. "I hear some moving around on the other side."

Cassie felt a hot flash, and her hands started to shake. She said nervously, "Maybe we should find another way out. There might be someone in there." She griped Nate's arm digging in her nails.

Nate pulled away from the door and turned to Cassie. He whispered, "We can't go back. That would lead us back to where we came from."

"Well, if you think so," Cassie replied. Her eyes were round and swollen.

As Nathan turned back toward the wall, he found himself face to face with a man who had opened the entrance and stumbled upon the two. He seemed just as surprised as they were, but he was quicker. He punched Nate in the chest, and with a whoof of air exiting his throat, he fell to his rump. With a burst of speed the man swung his gun upward and knocked

Cassie down to the ground next to Nate. As the gunman drew to aim his weapon, Cassie shot the man straight through the heart with Cindy's single shot derringer. The gunman, with a befuddled gaze, fell where he stood.

"Nice," Nate said, "nice." He turned to Cassie. "You okay?"

Cassie, surprised, said, "Yeah, I am. I really am."

"Let's go." Nate grabbed Cassie and pulled her up by the arm, but they only got as far as the entrance to the secret chamber. They abruptly stopped their movement and stood motionless. They stared into the room.

Nate said, "Maybe you were right." They stood in place as they looked into the face of four growling pit bulls.

Cassie said, perturbed, "A little late to start agreeing with me, don't ya think?"

The dog's eyes glowed in the dark. They looked like four angry demons floating in the black space of the room.

"Step back slowly," Nate whispered. "No fast movements."

The dog's jowls showed they weren't going to let them get away that easy. The lead alpha dog started first. He bounded over its dead master in the blink of an eye focused on his targets. Nate and Cassie started running backwards as all four dogs began barking viciously and pursuing them with purpose.

Nate's gun leapt into his hand, and with what little vision he had, he unloaded his rounds into the direction of the rushing dogs. Each time he pulled the trigger, an outburst of light emanated from the barrel, lighting the hallway. As he spent his last shot, he tripped and fell backwards, pulling Cassie down with him. Nathan immediately covered Cassie to protect her from the oncoming charge, a cover from an attack that never came.

"Where'd they go?" Cassie said, straining her eyes. The two lay still for a moment. They listened intently for the dreadful barking that they had been subjected to only seconds earlier.

They slowly stood to their feet, and Nathan emptied his spent shells to the floor for a reload. He said, "I think I got 'em."

Nate stepped forward and kicked with the toe of his boot as he felt for their bodies. He bumped into the lead dog. It was shot through the head.

"I got 'em." Nate said. "One, two, three, four, I got every damn one of them."

"Nice," Cassie said.

"Remind me to thank Uncle Frank. Let's move."

Nate pulled his girlfriend through the secret room in the direction from which the air flowed. Once they reached the back of the dogs' holding cell, they found a window and opened it. Carefully glancing outside Nate could feel the breeze off the water. It was refreshing. It was much more pleasant than the horrible smell of death they had been forced to endure. Nathan worked the back door latch and opened it. He exposed a set of stairs that led to the surface of the boat.

Nate said, "We're almost home. Don't worry. We'll be okay, I promise."

Slowly they moved up the stairs. It was only a few steps. At the top, Nathan opened a door that was only half the size of a normal door. It creaked on its hinges as he pushed forward. He looked around. Some men ran by heavy footed. Just as they came into view, they jumped over the edge of the ship hitting the water with a splash.

Nate said, "Okay, it looks all clear."

He took Cassie's hand, and they moved cautiously outside.

Nate whispered, "Stay low." He could see some structures, including the boat's air-stacks that might provide some cover.

"Let's move over there. That looks like a safe spot, at least until we can find the others."

Cassie said, "Okay."

As they started to move forward, they heard a gun discharge from behind them. Nate turned sharply with his gun drawn. A man with a pistol in his hand fell to his knees. Nate cocked back the hammer. The man looked at Nate and then to the sky. He fell over sideways and was dead before his head smacked the deck.

Cassie held tight to Nate's arm and said, "Who killed him? Was it Frank?"

"I got no idea."

Nathan, with sharp movements, guided the two into the midsection of the ship among the stacks. They watched for the others as they hid. Nate held Cassie with one hand and held his gun with the other. His hand was sweaty, and he could barely keep the gun from slipping out of his tight grip.

Frank rummaged through the dining room as he looked for a match. He managed to find some whiskey and a bit of kerosene in the kitchen. The boat, for the most part, was deserted. He figured it was due to the fighting that had been going on outside. More than likely most of the crew had bailed already except for Shane's most devoted. Once the fire was started, his most faithful would give up and abandon ship. That is, except for Bovis.

Frank lifted a container full of lamp oil and immediately proceeded to spread it around the dining room. He then emptied the moonshine whiskey onto the dining room table. The flammable liquid flowed over the top of the table and off the edges and onto the floor.

Frank stopped and pulled a whiskey bottle towards his lips and stopped. He paused, then said, "No, that would be too cliché." He tossed the bottle to the floor with a crash.

Frank hustled over to Danvil's office in his search for a match or a lighter. He rifled through Shane's desk. In one of the drawers, Frank came across some paperwork on Danvil's plans. It included orders and some interesting information on two other operations of the same type. Upon Frank's first glance of the writings, Shane Danvil and his cronies looked to be just a small faction of a larger operation. He folded the papers and slipped them into his pants pocket.

"Think, think," Frank whispered to himself. "He lit his cigarette with a lighter that was built into the desk," Frank spoke as he moved through the room as if remembering more with each step, "a bookend!" Frank grabbed the bookend and pulled down on the lever, igniting the flint. He ran to the dining room while lighting some pages he had torn from a book. Once the pages had caught fire, he threw the flame to the floor, and in a matter of seconds the dining table was aflame. Frank exited upward using the spiral staircase, accelerating as he moved, with his knife drawn.

The smell of horses, hay, and manure permeated the air. Jacob and Cindy were close to the corral of horses. The mission to save the horses was a welcome diversion for Jacob because it took his mind off Shane Danvil. It stopped him from focusing on the images of Danvil burning his father.

The boat was well lit on the upper levels. Jacob and Cindy continued to work their way to the aft end of the ship. They continued to be vigilant, even though it looked like no one was onboard. There were no more shots being fired outside. It seemed that the fighting had subsided.

The wood paneled walls were painted white, and pictures lined the hallway.

Jacob said, "There must be some sort of corral built into the backend of the boat. Whad'ya think?"

"Makes sense, I reckon," answered Cindy.

Jacob had his gun drawn as they approached a large door at the end of the hallway. Jacob positioned himself on the left of the entrance, and Cindy hugged the opposite wall to the right. Jacob waited and watched his wife patiently. They sat still for a moment.

Cindy winked and said, "Yeah, there's someone in there."

With a raised brow Jacob said, "Ah, great. You know, if I didn't know any better, I would think you were enjoying this."

"Well, like you said, I know how this all works out. I just ain't say'n."

Jacob said, "It's now or never. I'll lead the charge. Any idea where he is?"

"Nope, can't help ya."

Jacob took a deep breath and slowly opened the door. He peeked into the corral, he looked left and right, then straight, then up. He opened it farther and snuck in; he positioned himself behind a square of hay with his back to it. Cindy moved in as well, but off to the side. She slid towards the back of the ship. She hid herself by lying on her face as flat as she could.

Jacob counted the horses. He counted six of them. No Maggie.

An image penetrated Cindy's mind, it was accompanied by the spread of goose bumps up her arm and across her shoulders and then down her other arm. With the image imprinted on her brain like a photograph, she became physically ill, and she had to hold her stomach contents down with force.

"Hey," Cindy said quietly to get his attention.

Jacob snapped his head as he looked back.

Cindy said, "This guy killed Toby." She paused, then, "With a long gun, and he knew what he was doing."

Jacob became sullen and said, "Okay."

Cindy said, "He's goin down."

"Right."

"No mercy?"

"None," Jacob said. "Not today. Not from us."

"Right."

Jacob rose up and looked over the top of the hay that blocked his view and protected his body. Everything was quiet except for the shuffling of hooves. He shook his head back and forth. Cindy made a sweeping motion with her hand, indicating that she was going to move around to the right. Jacob pointed with two fingers at his eyes and then he pointed a finger at her. She gave him a thumbs up.

A slack slick click divulged a presence on the other side of the corral. It was from the hammer of a gun being delicately pulled back.

Jacob observed a dark shadow that moved sluggishly along the wall in front of him. He scanned the room with his eyes. He watched the shadow ascertaining where their enemy was by noting its movement and the angle of the dim light as it entered the room.

The horses began to get restless and they moved away from the nefarious figure, thus allowing Jacob to triangulate Toby's killer. He moved with the shadow.

Jacob got a bead on the general position in which his target lay, sluggishly he stood. He moved smoothly farther into the room with his gun leveled. Abruptly Jacob began to fire. Styles stumbled and hesitated, taken off guard by the forceful attack that Jacob laid upon him. Explosion after explosion from Jacob's gun rumbled through the boat's corral.

Splinters of wood showered Styles' face as the bullets impacted the beams around his head. He covered his eyes with his hand to block the flying debris. Slivers imbedded themselves into his cheek. Styles shot back, but his bullets went into the floor.

Jacob used five shells, then sat to reload. He kept the sixth shell inside and ready, just in case. Jacob expertly reloaded his weapon. He stood again, hidden behind a wooden beam. Firing quickly, his eyes flinched as Styles, moving aggressively, shot back. The two exchanged shots back and forth. The distance between them was only a few feet, but each hid behind a thick wood beam.

Jacob had fired his fifth shot and was about to turn to reload when there was a clomping of horse steps. Cindy, on a horse bareback, charged Styles. She pulled the mane, causing the horse to rear up with its front hooves, then coming down on Styles. He fell away from the beam, but quickly got his footing and fired at Cindy. The shot would have hit its target, but Cindy was long gone from the back of the horse. It allowed the bullet to cut through thin air.

Jacob's sixth bullet was aimed carefully, but Styles stumbled, and he missed. Styles worked to remain upright. Jacob didn't have time to reload. He quickly pulled a shovel that hung from the beam on a hook. The scoop was coated with manure. Jacob swung the shovel ferociously right to left across Styles' body, just under his chin. The blade cut a one-inch deep ditch across Styles' neck. Styles began to bleed from the cut. He couldn't talk.

The duo had forever silenced the man who had killed their friend. Blood gushed down the front of his shirt as he fell to his knees. He sat himself slowly up against a wood beam.

Jacob said, "You're dying because you killed my friend." He paused, then said, "Just so you know."

Cindy said, "I smell smoke."

"Me too. Look for a lever for the back door," Jacob said. He scrambled to the back of the boat.

The scent of smoke was agitating the restlessness of the horses. The smell of fire told their instincts to take over and run.

Cindy found a rope tied to the back wall. She said, "I think this is what holds it shut. There's another rope over on the other side."

Jacob found and untied the knot. He said, "On three, lower it slow. One, two, three."

Working together, they released the ropes, and through a series of pulleys and weights, a large door opened in the back of the boat.

Jacob yelled, "Take it out all the way."

They stepped to the edge and looked down at the lake on which they floated. They stood about two stories up from the water. Not far off in the distance they could see land with the sun creeping up over the horizon.

Cindy said looking down, "That's quite a drop."

"We don't have any other choice."

Jacob reloaded his six-shooter as Cindy attempted to gather the already spooked horses together. She seemed to have a calming effect on them, and they followed her instructions.

Jacob said, "Get them as close to the edge as you can, ready?"

"Ready."

Jacob fired his gun and hollered as Cindy snapped a whip. They both charged the horses. It caused them to panic and run out the back end and into the lake. The horses all landed safely in the deep waters below.

Jacob looked over the edge and said, "Just one more thing left to do."

"Dang-blast it, bloody hell! Dammit, dammit, dammit!" Shane hollered. He began slamming his wooden hand down on the boat's control panel with every syllable of his swearing rant. His head twitched side to side uncontrollably.

The smell of the burning vessel was strong in his nose as he sneered at a billow of patchy black smoke that wafted up from the growing dark hole on the surface of the deck. An aperture began to appear in the center of the foreboding circle that existed between the bow of the ship and the control deck where he stood. It wouldn't be long now.

"Don't leave yet, you sons of bitches." Shane had lost his authority as the last of his crew and passengers jumped ship. He watched helplessly as bodies threw themselves into the water and swam to shore. The shoreline was only a few hundred yards away, and nobody was going to wait and see if the ship could make land when it wasn't a long swim.

The loss of control he felt was infuriating him more and more as he swore to himself while pacing his small bridge. Shane stopped, pulled a gun with his good hand, and discharged the bullets out a side window. The lead soared over the side, landing in the water causing no damage except for the broken pane of glass.

"To hell with it all. To hell with you all, you bastards," Shane barked at his deserters.

Realizing his predicament, he whispered, "Bloody hell. I can't swim."

The cracking from the burning wood popped loudly as the first flames finally breached the topmost deck. The blaze itself was feeling invigorated with this new breath of fresh air. The oxygen fed the flare as the arms of the fire reached out to the morning sky.

Shane was so overtaken with anger and frustration that it caused his thoughts to become random at best. He didn't know what to do, let alone keep his thoughts straight.

"I'm going to kill every damn person left on this ship. I am not very happy right now. I need a drink," Shane yelled in desperation.

Shane then decided to leave his bridge and begin his trip to the deck below. What he would do once he got there was contingent upon what bizarre thought was most prevalent in his mind. Voices were whirling about in his head, telling him to jump ship, but then they told him to get a drink. Then he said, "Kill Savage." He wasn't too sure that he could go below and find Frank Savage, kill him, and get out alive. But his rage was so great that he went with it. "Kill them all."

Danvil turned his back to the fire and hurried to the door. He braced his hand on the door's frame to get into a position to move quickly down the ladder to the lower deck. Just as he was about to swing through the doorframe on his way down, something stopped him. The heavy wooden door to the bridge abruptly slammed shut on his good hand.

"Aaaugh!" Shane screamed out when an explosion of pain ran up his arm like a fuse on a stick of dynamite. The pain he felt was familiar. Looking up, he saw a figure that was too dark to recognize. The fire was at the man's back, and the flames were sprouting up from the surface of the ship. They reached as high as the bridge, and they were growing. The position of the light from the dancing flames cast a shadow over the man's face.

Shane went berserk and thrashed at the door, but his wooden appendage was useless. He was unsuccessful. The outline of the man moved closer, and Shane was slowly picking up the features of his assailant as the shade covering him lightened. It was Jacob.

"What the?" Shane whispered, stunned.

"Need a hand?" Jacob slyly commented just as his uppercut caught Shane in the ribs with a crack.

Shane wheezed and fell to his knees. His fall caused the skin to tear off his fingers, thus dislodging his hand from the door. Jacob aggressively threw Shane head-first toward the bow of the bridge house. Shane could feel the heat with the fire looming large and close. The ship was cracking, and it would soon be taking on water. The sounds of the dying boat where growing louder.

As Shane stood to face his opponent, the windows began to shatter as the blaze licked the surface of the glass. He stood hunched over with two marble-handled guns on his waist. He looked down on them. They might as well have been bars of lead because he had one hand that could not hold them, and he had useless fingers on the other that couldn't pull a trigger. Screaming and moving with everything that he had, Shane rushed at Jacob. With every ounce of hatred he could muster, he lashed out with his club.

Jacob faced a wicked man, an atrocious man who had killed his father. Jacob's eyes announced that he was going to kill him.

Jacob moved smoothly and quickly as he ducked and stepped to the side as Danvil's punch swung wild, causing him to stumble. All his momentum sent him flying to the back wall. The punch he threw stopped suddenly in a crevice of metal that was part of the frame of the bridge. The fist had penetrated deep into the open crack, thus lodging itself in a cleft of steel. Two parallel pieces of framework had trapped his weapon like a vice.

Bleeding from one hand, he tugged desperately at the other with tears of hatred and frustration filling his eyes. Shane was hyperventilating when he screamed, "No bloody way. What the hell, man?"

"Having a bad day, are we?" Jacob taunted his enemy with a roguish grin.

Disbelief, confusion, and contempt gleamed through the water in Shane's eyes. Shane began swinging wildly with his free arm with blood flying everywhere. It was a last ditch effort. As he swung back and forth, an audible snapping sound emanated from his steel and wooden entrapment.

Jacob got in close and smashed into Shane's face with a massive blow using the top of his forehead. Shane's nose burst with blood spreading out over his face.

Jacob stepped back, and Shane noticed his adversary was holding the marble-handled guns. Jacob slowly put both guns into his belt.

Shane screamed, "Well, just shoot me already."

Jacob said, "You'll be dead shortly."

Jacob got down low. He was reaching as low as possible, then using the muscles in his legs he uppercut Shane into his chin. The blow was so solid the screw that held Shane's hand to his arm stripped. He departed the wall and stumbled, then fell to the floor. His body was free, but his wooden hand was still jammed into the wall's frame. Jacob grabbed the screw that exited the base of the appendage with both hands and wiggled it up and down until the wood splintered enough to allow the fist to come free.

Shane staggered to his feet with his back to the bright hot flames that were eating his ship alive. Jacob held the black and splintered fist. A fist that was Cindy's doing only two years earlier with her pocket derringer. Walking forward towards Shane, Jacob backed him up to the broken windows.

Jacob looked at the face of the murderer who had shot his dad in the back. While looking deep into his soulless insane eyes, he said calmly, "It's time."

With a brutal and swift full-bodied swing, Jacob smashed Shane across the face with his own wooden extremity. The impact sent Shane backward through the pilothouse window to the burning decks below. His body was engulfed within the blaze. He was burnt alive, screaming.

Jacob looked into the fire, stared hard a moment, and tossed the fist in and whispered, “I feel much better now.”

As he turned to leave, Cindy stood by the ladder with gun in hand. She had watched over him the entire time. They ran to each other and embraced.

“It’s getting a little warm for me,” Cindy admitted.

“Really? I thought it was never too warm for you,” Jacob said with a smile. “Let’s get the hell out of here.”

CHAPTER 16

Frank waited. Hiding, he surveyed the area for one man. He watched the last remainder of Shane's crew jump ship abandoning their leader to fend for himself.

Frank caught himself staring at the wooden planks of the deck. As he focused, the corner of his eyesight caught a flash of movement off to the side. The cook was readying himself to jump overboard. The short slender man held a bag under his left arm and plugged his nose with his right. Frank smiled as he noticed the cook count to three before jumping. Frank looked over the edge to make sure the fragile man resurfaced. He came up dog paddling as he worked his way towards the shoreline. The cook did that for about a minute before he rolled over onto his back and kicked the rest of the way.

The last couple of escaping men seemed to be disinterested in their boss' fate, to say the least. They leapt over the side and never looked back.

Bovis was the only man with whom Frank was truly concerned. He looked carefully as he searched for him. Frank would need to see him first.

The deck showed no movement through the thickening smoky haze, and he didn't worry himself with Danvil. He was confident that Jacob and Cindy would take care of him. Frank's purpose in life right now was to get his friends off safely, and he would need to find Bovis to do that. Conrad Bovis was dangerous and apparently on a mission. For some reason unknown to Savage, Bovis wanted him dead. And he had yet to fail on any mission that he had been assigned.

Conrad Bovis had been on many assignments, but a large portion of those had been given to him by the military during the war. But the mission that Frank remembered most was not one assigned during combat or by anyone from the government, for that matter. Bovis had assigned himself a task. It was something he did because he felt he should out of friendship. Due to some sick adherence to a distorted code of conduct, he made a decision that would send him down a path of which he would not return. Secretly, he enjoyed the challenge.

After the war Frank found out his wife had been having an affair, and he was completely devastated. Bovis saw Frank's hatred for the man his wife had been sleeping with. He misread it as a wish to see the man dead. Bovis hunted the man down and shot him in his apartment in New York.

Bovis had hoped Frank would never find out who did the execution, but he also thought he would be glad to hear of the man's demise. He was wrong on both counts. Frank knew and was furious. Bovis' mental state would not allow him to understand why his friend didn't approve of what he had done. They never spoke to each other again.

Moving slowly over the top of the floating vessel, Frank caught a glimpse of Nate and Cassie in the dark cover of the stacks. They were holding out and waiting. Nate wouldn't leave without the others, even if Frank had ordered him to.

Frank decided to stay put for the moment. Then his heart skipped a beat as he saw Bovis step from one shadow and disappear into another. He was moving in the direction of Nate and Cassie, but he didn't seem to know they were there. But Frank assumed the worst.

Brad sat upon Maggie overlooking the lake. Both had an equal interest in what had happened to their friends. Waiting in a small clearing, they watched the gambling boat burn. Anxiety swept through Brad as he sat helplessly. He wanted to swim out to help, but what good would that do?

Derek rode up on his sorrel and said with a smirk, "Ten to one that's Frank's doings."

Brad said, "That's the biggest damn gambling boat I've ever seen."

"It's made for more than gambling," replied Derek.

Brad analyzed the swimmers who swam clumsily to dry land. He studied each man, looking for a familiar face.

Brad replied, "I hope you're right, Mr. Wright. If that is Frank's doing, then he's running the show now."

"Oh, he's steering that ship alright. But it never seems to be smooth sailing when Frank's at the helm. He'll get the job done, though. He always does. No matter how rough the swells are."

Maggie stomped her front hooves restlessly and blew out.

"I know, I know, I'm worried, too," Brad said, patting her neck. "If they're not here in fifteen minutes, I will swim out there."

"Sir," a voice bellowed from the tree line.

Derek responded to the call, "Yo."

The voice answered, "Jeremy noticed that there is still some movement on the deck. It's hard to tell who is who with all the smoke."

"Thanks. Tell him to hold his fire unless he is 100 percent sure it's not a friendly."

"Aye, aye."

Jeremy, the group's sharpshooter, rested on his front on a rock by the water's edge. He concentrated intently as he looked though his eyepiece that rested on top of his rifle. Jeremy watched diligently, but he couldn't make out any faces.

Derek said, "We're probably too far out for our sharpshooter to get a clean kill from here."

Brad responded, "So, it's up to them then. I feel so damn worthless." Maggie snorted her concurrence.

Derek's men gathered and arrested the last remaining swimmers as the rest of Danvil's crew and guests slowly walked ashore. Most seemed happy to just be alive.

Brad asked, "What'll happen to them?"

Derek replied, "My guess is that most of them are just gamblers and thrill seekers. They may have partaken in some illegal activities, which are mostly just misdemeanors. If they supply us with the information we need, most will be let go shortly. The man we want probably won't make it to shore, knowing Frank."

Brad said, "You mean the man everyone keeps mentioning, Danvil?"

Derek continued, "No, the man we're keeping an eye out for is someone else. Sure, we'll take Danvil if we can. He'll hang sure enough. The fellow we want has information on the whole outfit. He was hired by someone we didn't even know existed, not until recently anyway. But with the history this gunman has, and his relationship with Frank, well, only one of them is getting off that boat alive."

Frank stalked quickly over to the last place he had seen Bovis. He wasn't there.

"Damn," Frank whispered to himself. "He's probably looking at me right now."

Frank ducked and dropped to all fours and crawled over to Nate's position. Out of sight, but within earshot, Frank said, "Nathan, it's Frank."

Nate said, "Jesus, I was getting worried. Have you seen Jacob or Cindy?"

Frank slid up next to Cassie.

"They'll be along shortly. Keep an eye out for the man in black."

Hiding tight and low against an exhaust-stack, Frank, Nathan and Cassandra sat arm in arm. They quietly watched until they saw Jacob and Cindy across the back of the deck.

Frank said, "Let's go."

Moving quickly, the three met up with their friends at the rail that overlooked the water. As the five stood preparing for the final step of their escape, a powerful bang vibrated from the decks below their feet.

Frank said, "I think the keel just broke."

Jacob added, "The ship's taking on water now."

The boat was slowly tilting at the middle into a 'V'. They all grasped the rail that faced the lake. Frank could see men and horses scattered along the beach line.

Frank was in the middle of the group with Nathan to his immediate right. Cassie was tight up against her boyfriend. Jacob and Cindy gripped the rail on Frank's left.

Nathan was helping Cassie up the two-rung rail barrier when he noticed Frank was not next to him anymore. He turned and looked across the back of the ship. It looked like he was looking into a mirror. Jacob and Cindy were on the other side looking at him. Nathan slowly turned his head until he found Frank. His godfather was standing still facing the front of the boat.

Nate said, "What's the matter?"

Frank didn't say anything.

The ship was still moving, tilting toward the center. Nate recognized the concern pasted on Frank's face. He turned all the way around to see what was going on. Everyone stood still, staring at the fire. Nathan recognized the man who had been wearing Sam's clothes. The man in black was the man who had captured him and Cassie.

Bovis could only keep one eye open. He leaned against the pull of the tilting boat. The smoke was thick, and it swirled around his ghastly body as he stood hauntingly still. The ship was collapsing in on itself only a few feet behind him. Flames devoured everything that slid its way, like a black hole sucking in the worlds that got too close.

Bovis said, "I'm sorry, Frank, but I have to kill Nathan first. It's nothing personnel, bu--"

Nathan heard an explosive discharge so loud it caused him to jump. He was watching when the man in black pulled the trigger. The ball of lead splintered the wooden deck only a few feet in front of him. Nate watched with astonishment as black fluid began to seep from Conrad's slightly open mouth. It was thick and moved creepingly down his chin. Nate was unaware of what was happening. He was completely at a loss.

Nate knew Frank wasn't armed because *he* had his gun. Nathan looked up at him. He stared at Frank who had his left arm outstretched in front of him gripping his own six-shooter. He glanced down at his own hip. Standing in awe, he glared at his empty holster.

Frank watched his dying victim. He said, "Thanks for keeping it loaded." He never took his eyes off Conrad.

Nate's mouth hung open as he caught up with real time. Frank spun the gun into Nathan's holster.

Nate said, confused, "I didn't know you were left handed."

"I'm not," Frank said as he stepped forward. "Watch my back."

The flames were hot and sparking closer. Frank's eyes tightened as he worked his way forward. He approached the dying man dressed in a black vest. Conrad had dropped to his knees. He looked like he was on fire. He still held his gun in his right hand. He exhaled air with blood out his nose, and then calmness settled on his face.

Conrad let go of his weapon, and it clunked to the deck and slid into the center of the ship. Both of his eyes were open, and his face relaxed with relief. Frank kneeled, and they locked eyes. Conrad was shot in the chest. The lead ball had just missed his heart. Blood oozed out the wound and continued to flow out his nose and mouth. He then reached his right hand out to Frank.

Everyone watched still and quiet. They all held the rail with questioning looks on their faces. Frank took his hand. Conrad started to settle backwards into the fire. Frank helped him lie down and kept him from sliding to the flames. He stayed low and held a plank in the deck with his fingers.

Conrad said, "I'm sorry."

Frank said, "Why did you make me do it?" He stuttered when he spoke.

"I am sorry, my old comrade." He coughed blood as he spoke.

Frank squeezed his hand, but still almost lost his grip.

"Why me? I can't kill anymore. It's tearing me up inside." Frank cringed from a blast of heat that floated into his face with a puff of black smoke. Sparks and ashes bombarded his face.

"You were the only one who could. I took the job not knowing it was you." He breathed in hard. "I stayed on the job because it was you. I can't go on. It's just that simple. I didn't have the courage to put the bullet in my brain myself."

Frank said, "Now I have to carry your pain. I can't carry anymore."

"I'm sorry that I took a path that I knew I shouldn't have, but . . . I did. You were the only one who could free me," Conrad said.

Conrad began to slip with the gravity, and he released his grip on Frank's hand. Conrad's body spun with his feet pointing to the fire. His boots almost touched the flames as Frank began to slide with him. Frank then felt a hand take a hold of his belt. Through teary and puffy eyes he looked back. Nate was holding him with Cassie behind him. Behind Cassie was Jacob, and Cindy was anchoring them all to the rail of the ship. Frank was looking straight up at the heavens into the brightening sky. Large white fluffy clouds floated slowly behind Cindy's face. He still held tight to Conrad who had already passed.

Nate yelled, "Let him go, Uncle Frank. He's dead."

Cindy nodded. It was only then that he released his grip on his old lost friend. Conrad's body slipped into the fire and into the center of the chasm of the dying vessel. Nathan leveraged himself and Frank on the wooden planks of the deck with his boots, and pulled with his entire body. Cassie struggled, but held true, and Jacob clung tight. He always worked best under pressure. Frank had saved his friends, and they returned the favor by doing the same.

Once again, they were all focused on the ripples that floated across the water. They hit the wet waves at the same time. It was cold and alarming to the senses. It let them know they were free.

Cindy called an image to her mind. It wasn't disturbing. Even though it did give her goose bumps, she didn't feel sick. She felt enlightened.

"Frank?" Cindy said. She stood behind him as he tightened the belt on his horse. It was a horse that Jacob and Cindy had saved. He had a bandage on the back of his head and a hat on top of that.

"What's on your mind?" asked Frank.

"Well, when we were on the trail out of Lasso City, I was the one who mentioned that someone was waiting up ahead on the road for us. You know, when you went off alone?"

"Yeah," Frank said. He looked down at his boots.

"So, it was me, you know, who caused Sam to volunteer to ride up ahead to take a look, alone."

Reassuringly, Frank said, "It's not your fault."

"I do feel for Maggie, losing Corduroy. But, that's the thing, if I had somehow caused Sam to go and get himself killed, I would normally be devastated. With that knowledge, I would not be able to live with myself."

Frank cocked his head to the side and said, "What are you saying?"

"I'm saying . . . what I'm saying is, is that I feel," Cindy said, then, "I feel fine. I feel good."

Frank's eyes grew round and large as he thought over everything Cindy had said. His mouth smiled. He said, "Thanks."

Frank jumped into his saddle and yelled, "Derek!"

Everyone stopped talking and looked up. Nate and Cassie were helping each other get dry, and Jacob was readying some horses. They all halted their activities to see what the fuss was about.

Derek answered, "Yo, what's up?"

Frank spun his horse to face north, back in the direction of the road. He now pointed to the same road where they had all started their nightmare together.

Frank said, "I'm going back for Sam."

Nate perked up and said, "What? Why, for his body?"

"Nope," Frank said, smiling and looking everyone in the eyes one by one. "He's probably pretty thirsty, a tad hungry, but he isn't dead."

Instantly, Nate mounted Maggie. Brad leapt into his saddle as well.

Brad said, "What, don't you think we want to go? What's up with all that horseshit? We're coming with you."

"So are we," Jacob said as he and Cindy trotted up next to Frank.

"I'm coming, too," Cassie bellowed, "and I need a horse!"

Nathan said, "Now, Sweetheart, I don't think--"

Cassie interrupted, "Nathan Hansen, I'll do what you say, but if you think I'm not going with you to look for my friend Sam, you are out of your mind!" She stood with her hands on her hips.

Derek walked a saddled horse over to Cassie and said, "Here you go, young lady. You seem pretty determined, and I'm not one to get in the way of a woman who has her mind made up. And if Nate has any sense at all, he won't either." Only his eyes moved as he looked over at Nathan.

Nate stepped down to help her get onto her horse.

Cassie said curtly, "I can do it myself." She swung into the saddle in one confident fluid motion.

"Well, I'll be damned," Nate said.

Cassie's right brow popped up.

Nathan asked, "Did I teach you that?"

Cassie looked down on her boyfriend. She smiled and winked at him. "You worry too much. I know how to ride a horse, and I can take care of myself, thank you."

Nate followed Cassie's lead and joined the rest of the group by leaping onto Maggie, once again.

"Nathan," Cindy said. "Did you notice Maggie's eyes?"

"No," Nate said, as he careened forward to look at his horse's eyes. "Why?"

"They're both a lovely dark green."

"Well, I'll be. What do you think caused that?"

Cindy said, trotting away, "Ride her easy. She's pregnant."

Nate, beaming, said, "Congratulations, Maggie." Maggie stomped her hooves and nodded her head.

Frank trotted to the front of the group. He spun his horse. He said, "Let's go find our friend. Knowing Sam, he's getting mighty ornery about now."

Frank Savage pulled his pistol with a flash and opened the housing with a snap and inspected the chamber with a glance and holstered the gun with a spin and led the group with a turn into the trees.

The End

A SAVAGE DARKNESS

AKA THE BIG HATE

★ ★ ★ ★ ★

CHAPTER 1

Is that me?

He was hunched over. He stared at the ground. A reflection in the sand. So he thought.

The wind felt rough on his face. He stood next to a horse with a six-chambered rod tight in his fist. His horse was a strong sorrel that he cared nothing for. He had just recently acquired the animal. Not to say that he cared for anything or anyone.

Sand and dirt kicked up from the desert landscape and scraped against his face as he ran his fingers over his pockmarked skin. Small sticks and fluffy tumbleweeds swirled in and out of the brown dust that floated around the wood-paneled store resting at the edge of town.

There was the front door, blinking at him. Wanting to rush in, he fought hard against his urges and remained still in his blood-splattered boots. The sorrel announced its displeasure with a whinny and that it was time to get out of the wind with a restless tug. But the horse's new partner held firm. What was needed waited inside for the taking, and he wasn't about to leave. Not quite yet.

As he held tightly to the reins, the mud- and blood-covered visitor focused on his hands. While watching his fingers twitch he recalled vividly the first drop of blood as it had sploshed onto his boots. It had satisfied an urge, for the moment, but now he realized, it had only whet his appetite. He craved more.

At the time of the killing it had aroused a feeling inside that he had only touched on as a child while torturing animals he had caught in the woods behind his father's barn. Halfway into his new conquest, he had become so excited that he shook his dying victim, forcing the expelled blood to spill and splatter out onto his clothes. He quivered thinking about the rush it had given him. Smiling as he revisited what he had done, his mind ran wild. It made this killer want to, no, *need* to do it again. He planned to do it many, many more times.

He waited on the outskirts of Angon Town with gritted teeth. The vile wretch surveyed the storefront as his feet shuffled about restlessly. He growled as customers entered the storefront one after the other. Every time the buyers left with their newly purchased goods another would enter to replace them. As the moments stacked upon themselves he could feel his frustration radiating from his skin.

The sun would be gone soon. Maybe that was best. No reason to attract too much attention. He did want to get away to kill again. And again.

Turning his head to the side and down he ranted through his teeth. "I know what I'm doin'. Don't you know who I am? I'm the Kingston Killer, and don't you forget it." Nobody was there to hear him, except his horse.

The Kingston Killer's horse watched his new master with round eyes. His legs lightly rippled as they ached to run, but he had learned not to test this man. The sorrel stood still and quiet, but waited for an opportunity.

The Kingston Killer stared hard into the pupils of his new slave. The killer could feel the sorrel's thoughts as visions of its loved ones being cut to pieces ran through its brain.

The killer blazed his glare into the horizon and upon the setting sun. He gnashed his chew down to nothing. He turned toward the unsuspecting town and watched a carriage ride up to the front of the store.

A middle-aged man and a young woman stepped off the buckboard and immediately entered through the front door.

Without averting his eyes, the stranger spit his chew onto the ground without aiming. The chewed-up tobacco hit his horse's leg and dripped down to its hooves.

He chuckled, then said, "They best not be long, or I'm gonna have to carve up Daddy." Then with childlike mocking and a feigned tear, he said, "And make his little girl cry."

Gilbert had only been a shop owner for a few months. He liked it okay. He never talked about his past or his personal disappointments. He'd do anything for his wife. Everything would be fine, just as long as he could keep it hidden.

Gilbert said, "Well hello, Jared, and how are you, Betsy?"

Gilbert was a serious but always friendly person. He was only forty years old, but he had an old soul. It was a soul that was well aware of the evils that roamed the dim spots of his world.

"I'm good, Gil, thanks for asking. Where's Tami?" Betsy responded with a smile and a look about the room.

Gil's head turned side to side. He looked around the store from his short five-feet and seven-inch frame. He had dirty blonde hair that was perfectly and purposely split down the middle with pomade. He stood proud with squared shoulders to everyone he spoke to. Gil began to beam as he heard his wife approach from the backroom.

"Right here." Tami jumped from the back room with the robust energy of a schoolgirl. She smiled. She always smiled.

"Now weren't you two in here yesterday?" Gil said. "Do I have my days all askew again?"

"Oh, Gil, what do you care?" his wife inquired.

Gilbert's eyes swelled. "Well, I was only making conversation, that's all." His voice cracked high.

Jared interrupted. "We forgot some things the misses had asked us to get. I guess we both plum forgot."

Betsy added, "Yeah, we just got to talking, kinda like what we're doin now. You know, Dad, we might forget again if we keep going on like this."

"That would not be good."

"Nope, not good at all, I reckon," Betsy said. "Hey, Gil? How long has it been now? How long have you two been married?"

It was quiet as Gilbert covered his mouth. His eyes still smiled. He spoke through his fingers. "Oh, let me see, about a lifetime, maybe more."

"Gil," said Tami.

Laughter filled the store.

"Oh, Tami, we know he's teasing. Everyone in town knows how smitten your husband is with you," said Betsy.

"Yeah, I suppose," Tami said suspiciously as she stared at her husband with narrow eyes and a slight grin.

Gilbert said, "Absolutely, there are no two ways about it, I'm done, well done. Take me off the fire."

"Sure, I bet," added his wife.

Gilbert continued, "Oh, it's been three years, five months, sixteen days and—" He stopped to pull out and check his watch. "Six hours." He closed his watch, visibly proud of himself. The corners of his mouth reached out to each ear.

"Nicely done, my strong-handed man. Nicely done." Tami's face was pink with puffy cheeks.

Gilbert said, "Well, you two need anything from the back room?" Turning to his wife he continued, "Sweetheart, would you put the closed sign up? It's past that time."

Tami moved casually to the front window. "Anything for you . . ." She turned, leaned back, and with a flirtatious smile she said, "Darling."

Jared and Betsy worked their way through the aisles. Jared looked up at the ceiling in thought. He said, "You know, it's not on the list, but while we're here, let's get some sugar and some flour. What do you think, Betsy?"

"Sounds good, Dad."

"Coming right up. Some sugar and some flour. Speaking of sugar," Gil moved towards the back room and continued, "Tami, don't let me forget to swing by the stable on our way home."

His wife grinned and winked. Betsy giggled at the storeowner's flirty behavior as her dad walked through the spices that lined the wall. Jared popped the top back on a plastic container and took a sniff from the opening. His face contorted and he sneezed spilling some of the spice to the ground.

"You okay, Dad? What're you sniffing over there?" asked Betsy.

"I don't rightly know." He sneezed again and said, "But I don't think I like it."

Tami chuckled and said, "You don't smell it. You put it on your food and eat it, goofy."

The short hardworking storeowner could hear his friend Jared talking as he stepped into the back room. "Gil, we need to have you two over for din—"

With large hands, his work came easily to him. Gil picked up a bag of sugar with his left hand and a large bag of flour with his right.

When Gilbert had started his trek to the back room he had felt genuine joy in his heart. That happiness was short lived. It had completely evaporated from his insides as he stood straight. Standing as still as possible he focused. He could smell something. He didn't know what it was, but he could feel his blood flow through his veins, and his nerves spring awake.

Concentrating, he steadied his movements and slowed his heart rate back to normal. He then heard something that caused his head to snap towards the storefront.

The sound of a vicious whack vibrated through the air, and it ripped through his body. It was followed by a dull thud. Gil stared at the curtain that separated the two rooms. His face drooped. The smile he had carried was gone.

There was a sharp gasp, and then a "shh" from the store's front. Gil's eyes turned to steel as he stared through the crack made by the two pieces of cloth that divided him from the others. He could see the register and the drawer that rested under it. In that drawer was a compartment that housed his Webley .455, a top-break revolver. Kept there just in case.

Eyeing the drawer, Gil slowly walked to the storeroom. He had forgotten that he still carried a bag of flour and a bag of sugar. His slight figure stepped into his small but well-stocked store to see a man in dirty brown buckskins and a tattered brown hat. It was a grotesque vision of evil and hatred. Tami and Betsy stood mute.

As Gilbert scanned his intruder, his eyes stopped on the shiny lead knobs that rested in the cylinder of a gun. A gun that was pointed directly at him with the hammer pulled taut. Gil glared at the finger. The finger that desperately wanted to send a slug into his chest. It was twitching inside the trigger guard.

The stranger smirked. The sloppy grin allowed his tobacco-stained teeth to show between narrow lips. He had eyes that sat way too far apart, and his mouth curled.

The Kingston Killer glowered, fully aware of his effect on others.

No one knew what would happen next. Betsy moaned loudly and swayed slightly. At her feet was her dad. He was on the floor leaning against the spice rack, unconscious. Sitting with his back to the wall, Betsy's dad breathed shallow and fast. His nose was broken. A dark black bruise bulged from between his eyes. Even if he was awake, he would be unable to open his eyes, for they were puffy and swollen shut. Blood trickled from his nostrils and from a cut that ran across the bridge of his nose. Gil could feel the bruise throbbing as if he were the one who had taken the blow.

Gil's strong hands slowly released their grip on the bags and allowed them to fall to the floor. Gil then jerked forward but stopped abruptly—he was too far away from her to stop it. Betsy swayed somewhat and then fainted. On her way down she hit her head solidly on the corner of a table. She fell across her father's legs and remained motionless. The strange man stood over father and daughter. He shrugged his pointy shoulders. "Well, I guess that takes care of them. They won't be bothering us anytime soon."

The gunman snickered as he took stock of his handiwork. He sneered and peered around the room. He appeared rough and mean—son-of-a-bitch mean. He waited, striking a pose as if he had an audience. Death and malice radiated from black eyes that subsided in his static shell. He soaked up the fear that floated through the room like a sponge, and it energized his callous heart. He smelled of blood.

Tami felt sick and desperate. She tried not to smell his foul odor by breathing through her mouth. The presence of danger made the color drop from her face.

Fear ran up and smacked Gil across his face—a hard slap of fear for the lives of everyone in the room. It was obvious what the man's intentions were.

The night sky had expanded—the sun's flames had all but extinguished.

The intruder grumbled, "Let's go." He barked, "Slow, to the back room." He paused and then said, "Now." He looked over his right shoulder and said something that only he understood. Then his head snapped forward. "Didn't I say now?" Chunky brown saliva flew out of his mouth when he spoke.

Eyeing Tami and then Gil, the infiltrator followed the husband and wife team. He watched Gil, short, pint-sized Gil. Gil's large hands appeared strong but they shook. He didn't sweat, and his skin was dry.

Did this wretched man of death know? Gil had always hoped to keep it from his wife. He had been successful in hiding it from her. Could he hide it from him? Gil's wife didn't know; was now going to be that dreadful time?

"Move slow," said the man clad in buckskins and animal excrement. He pushed some yellow mucus through his gritted teeth. "I didn't say stop."

His top lip curled up farther until it touched his nose. He turned to the side and whispered to himself, "Shut the hell up. I ain't going there." Then louder he barked, "I don't care how nice a hotel they got, I ain't going there. Palmer's house my asshole." He barked loudly multiple obscenities and reined himself back in.

Gil stumbled backward over his own feet. He moved awkwardly. Tami followed him and lowered her hands from her mouth to help her husband maintain his balance. She shivered from a chill that ran through her body as the icy hard muzzle poked her in the small of her back. It was a cold chill that moved harsh and fast, but the shiver stopped at her hands. The frost that shot through her nerves impacted her hands that were now touching her husband. She held his body, a body that was hot to the touch. A body that was almost *too* hot to touch.

"Take a seat—no." The gunman put forward the barrel of his gun at Tami but spoke to Gil. "Do as I say, Pops, or the dame gets it in the mug. Got that?"

Gil's eyes were drippy and his hands shook. His skin was very dry. Heat bubbled out from deep inside his body. "Yeah, yeah, please, please don't—"

"Shut your blitherin' yapper, Pops. I ain't gots the time, and it won't matter a whole hell of a lot." He scrutinized Gil with quizzical eyes. Analyzing his prey he sniffed at the air.

"You," the gunman blurted as he pointed the gun at Tami. "You are about to shit yourself. But you—" He paused to glare at Gil, and then said, "Woman, get that rope, and you, get that chair."

"Yes, sir," Gil said. He moved quickly and then stumbled to his knees, got up and did as he was told with a slight whimper that emanated from his throat.

"Hey," the stranger snapped, "get your-no." He stopped. "Damn, it's dark. I can't barely see nothing. Light that lantern, woman."

Tami moved carefully and quietly as she lit the lantern that sat atop a desk.

"Grab the rope and get over there," he dictated as he waved his pistol. "You, Pops, sit down. You—" He turned to spit; it landed with a splat. "Tie his hands and feet. I'm watching, so make it good or I'll, well, you know. Unless you're some sort of nitwit or something."

Gil looked at his wife then out the window, then back at his wife. "It's okay, Sweetheart, make it tight, just like he said." His voice cracked and his lip trembled. His mouth was wet.

"Yeah, okay, good," the Kingston Killer added. His hot breath filled the back room with a horrid stench.

He pulled the curtains closed as he observed Tami. He stared hard at her womanly figure.

The perpetrator's clothes were covered with blood. His hands were crusted over with dried blood, too.

The blood-stained killer yelled, "Okay, okay, now, now, get in the corner, bitch." He glared at his fresh victim. "Get."

The dim light of the lantern shined across Tami's face and cast a shadow on the wall. Tami covered her mouth tight with a quivering hand and stepped into the corner using short fragile steps. Tears rolled over her knuckles.

"Sit down—no." The killer held tight to his weapon as he grabbed a bottle from the shelf. After removing the stopper with his teeth, he sucked from the top as if the liquid were water. It splattered to the floor as he lapped at the rye whiskey like a bloodthirsty dog. He never took his gaze off Tami.

Looking over at Gil, he said, "You get to watch." With a cocked head he continued, "Wish I got to watch. I'll be sure to give her plenty of warming-up time. I know women like that." He growled as he smiled. "You ain't ever gonna wanna touch your bitch again after you see what I do to her. Not that I'm gonna let you li—"

Tami screamed as she charged with arms flailing. "No!"

She was met with a closed fist upon her jaw that sent her flying two feet to her back.

The animal snarled. "Psycho whore, now don't be doin' that. I'd hates for you to be dead when I do this here thing. I like a woman who gives a little when she's gettin'." He turned to Gil and winked. "You know what I mean, don't ya, Pops?"

Gil stared out the window and cried. He wept as his heart remained steady. Gil's heart rhythm plodded along in his chest as if he were sleeping.

The Kingston Killer hung over Tami. He spit whiskey on her face. He said, "God-dang that whore."

Gil whimpered, "What, what?"

"She's asleep. That's just not what I had planned. I'm just gonna have to wait till she wakes up. I don't want her to miss anything, I reckon." He stood and scowled at Tami as he drank.

Gil watched and waited. His eyes shifted to the window. *In a couple more minutes*, he thought. T*hen he'll know*.

After a while, the intruder, agitated, kicked Tami's legs. Tami moved and rolled to her side and then to her back. The killer, who had been sent to earth by the devil himself, took a swig and set the bottle on the floor. "I'll leave the light on for ya." He held tight to his gun as he used his other hand to tear open Tami's top.

She moaned, "No. Gil, help." Tami fought back the tears as best she could, and she blacked out for a second. Her body could barely move as she struggled.

The rapist's hands moved violently over her body. He laughed and snorted as he buried his face into her bosom. Tami had nothing left inside to fight with as she bounced back and forth from unconsciousness. She snapped awake as he reached under her dress and ripped the undergarments from her body. He tilted his head back and drool fell from disgusting lips and dripped onto her chin. He laughed loudly. He released a laugh that came from a place that lay deep inside his black guts.

Abruptly he halted his cackle when the light went out.

"What the?" He pulled the trigger on his gun. No discharge, not even a click. "Where's my gun? Where's my—"

In the black air of his surroundings, he attempted to see his enemy. He sniffed. What he smelled sent a shiver through his bones.

"Who are you?" he wailed as he reached out to grab Tami. He was met with a blow to the chin. He then felt an enormous hand lift him up by his hair and then toss him across the room. The killer landed on the whiskey bottle breaking it and sending shards of glass into his back. "Ahhh, who are you?"

Fear flowed through the room like never before—a new kind of fear. The Kingston Killer rolled around desperately as he stared into the night, blind, searching frantically for his dangerous adversary. There was nothing. He stood and swung recklessly, striking only air. Then he swung again, this time impacting the wall and breaking his hand and wrist with a crunch. Lurching about in pain he let out a cowardly scream.

Gil moved deliberately and with purpose. He could see perfectly in the darkness where his enemy was blind. His view was shades of blue and dark shadows. But he could see. He watched as fear draped itself over his perpetuator's face. But no one could see Gil. *He knows now*, Gil thought. *He knows now*.

A bullet shattered the brute's shoulder blade as it exited his body. "Agh." He fell to his knees. "Who the hell are you? You son of a bitch," he cried out.

Gil said with a steady, confident, and stern voice, "You may not know who I am. But now you know, don't you."

"What the hell are you talking about, you bastard?"

Gil answered with disgust, "I'm the man who's going to send you straight to Hell."

The desperate criminal groaned, "What? But I'm the Kingston Killer."

Gil paused, then said, "Correction." He cocked the hammer. "You were."

"Noo—"

The lead entered the top of the killer's head sending a thick stream of blood into the air. A stream of blood that only Gil could see.

The body foundered to the floor. It shuddered. Gil swallowed hard. He breathed in through his nose and out his mouth.

In his own blood-splattered boots, Gil declared, "Now you know. Now you know. I kill too."

CHAPTER 2

Walking solidly through the hotel lobby he kept his hat low on the top of his brow. With slow-moving steps in his dark leather boots, the broad-shouldered cowboy worked himself smoothly and measuredly across the maple wooden planks. The cowboy's eyes were aware of everything—watching and analyzing as he moved.

The hotel clerk was stoic. He rested his hands on the check-in desk. A pencil was laced through the fingers of his right hand with the lead point resting as if in the middle of a sentence. He moved to speak but stopped as if he had decided not to. Maybe he decided he shouldn't trifle with the man about the busty redhead who had just left the hotel in an embarrassed haste only ten minutes ago.

Inside the cowboy's gun-belt was an identification slip. Between the two pieces of leather that wrapped his gun solidly but loosely to his waist was a well-worn and important piece of paper.

AGENT FRANK SAVAGE
MEMBER OF THE ARMED UNIT
LAW ENFORCEMENT DIVISION
UNITED STATES OF AMERICA

Frank's hat was a dark tan, and it matched his shirt that was tailored to fit his V-shaped frame. The brim of his hat was bent up and inward on the sides from years of wear, and it shaded his eyes from the clerk.

"Morning, sir," the clerk welcomed.

"Morn," Frank said indifferently. He removed a slip of rolling paper from his front shirt pocket. He poured tobacco into the fold, and he had his cigarette rolled and lit in a matter of seconds.

"Is everything okay, Mr. Savage?"

Frank drew smoke into his lungs and exhaled. He answered, "You know, a woman can and will drive a man to drink, to smoke, and to gamble his life away."

The hotel man allowed a self-conscious grin to sprout on his face. Frank glowed deviously from under the brim of his hat and said, "A small price to pay."

The sun was shining in from a window behind the clerk's desk. The light moved along the floorboards too slowly for the eye to detect. Frank turned and stepped shy of the front door and stopped. Hands steady. The tips of his boots rested even with the inside edge of the doorframe. He regarded the bright day.

The street was sprawled out in waiting with wind whisking up small pockets of dust that would float a moment and then settle. The hotel structure cast a shadow over the road barely touching the opposite side of the street. Frank tilted his head down then up, left then right, checking every angle. With his back to the clerk he asked with a deep voice, "Any visitors this morning?"

"No, sir. None that came in, that is."

Frank took one long pull on his cigarette. He then put the smoke out on the bottom of his left boot heel with his thumb and forefinger in a twisting motion. A cool breeze streamed in between his body and the doorframe. He smelled the clean air.

"Got any plans today, Mr. Savage?"

"Frank."

"Uh?"

"Call me Frank," the government agent said. "I'm just cooling my heels today, that's all. Gonna do whatever I decide at that moment in time."

The clerk stated, "We got your Appaloosa saddled and ready, Frank."

The sound of small feet impacting the street's dirt approached from a distance. It grew louder as a young boy came running up to the hotel. Then the boy's voice blurted as he stepped up to the open door. "Mr. Savage?"

"Yes, Son, you're looking at him."

"I have a message for you from the telegrapher's office," said the eager messenger. He beamed as he added, "It's marked as urgent."

Frank looked down at the message and said, "Isn't it always."

He didn't move. His demeanor screamed disappointment at the paper. Over his shoulder he said, "Oh well, so much for taking the day off."

Frank took the note and handed the boy a coin. "Thanks, good work." Frank analyzed the words on the note. Without reading the orders he was aware that he had to do what he had to do. But it didn't mean he had to be happy about it, and that was for damn sure.

Start, Urgent message for Frank Savage, stop
Johansen's ranch two miles west, stop
Murder, stop
Culprit unknown, stop
Presence required ASAP, stop
Targets wanted dead or alive, end.

Feelings of despair laced in emotional hatred swirled around Frank's chest and dropped heavily into his stomach. Atrocities of past cases flickered through his brain. He flinched abruptly and then whispered, "God, if you are listening, I've about had enough. As a good friend of mine would say, *what's up with this horseshit?*"

Slowly-moving fingers neatly folded the telegraph message and slipped it into a pocket. It was then that Frank noticed that the messenger was still standing in front of him.

The boy didn't have eager eyes anymore. He seemed deflated. At attention, like a sergeant listening for orders, he patiently waited.

Frank asked grimly, "Where's the sheriff?"

"Sheriff Smith is at the courthouse. He's sitting in on a trial, sir."

Frank stepped around the boy into the street. He drew up his horse's reins from the hitching rail. With a jump step he leapt into his saddle. Frank spun his young Appaloosa and edged him up the street with the sun at his back. The sun was hot on his wide shoulders and would only get warmer over the next two miles. As he moved towards Johansen's ranch, he realized that he had forgotten to eat. No matter, his appetite was lost in a folded-up telegraph message in his pocket.

Agent Frank Savage stopped about a hundred feet from the front porch of a two-story white house. Off to his right, not far from the home, was a brown wood barn with its doors wide open.

In between the house and the barn, protruding up from the soil, was a stocky bald man fiercely chopping wood. The wide individual was not cutting wood for the winter. He hacked away for another reason all together.

Frank dismounted and slowly led his horse toward the front yard. By the porch was another man who was wearing thick glasses. He had a dark brown hat with a black band and a neatly trimmed beard across his chin.

The bearded man looked up and said, "Before I go off all halfcocked and ready to shoot wondering what in tarnation you're doing here, I'm going to assume you got a damn good reason to be walking towards me."

Frank stopped and forced a smile. "Thanks for giving me the benefit of the doubt. I'd hate to get my head blown off before I got to introduce myself."

"Well, get to it."

"I'm Frank Savage."

The man with the beard could hide a lot of emotions with all the hair on his face, but he could not hide the recognition of Frank's name.

Frank continued, "I'm from the Law Enforcement Division of the US Government."

The man furrowed his brow. "So, am I supposed to be impressed? I never even heard of that unit, or whatever you call it."

Frank's smile immediately turned sour. "But you have heard of me."

The man in thick glasses stepped back with a slight upturn in the corner of his mouth. "Yeah, I've heard of you. You assigned to this case, I bet."

"Yes."

"I thought you worked undercover."

"Not anymore. Too many people know who I am."

"Didn't you retire?"

Frank said with a true smile, "It didn't take." He paused. "And you are?"

The two men shook hands. "Well, I'm Texas Ranger Coleman, but my friends, and enemies for that matter, call me Cole."

"Hi, Cole. And who's the angry woodsman?"

Their attention shifted. Cole turned his head to look over his shoulder. "That is one tough son of a bitch, I'll tell you what. But . . ."

"Yeah?"

"That's Alfred Kincaid. His daughter was killed here." Cole looked down, took off his glasses, and rubbed his eyes. "Sorry, you'll know what's going on soon enough."

"Take your time."

Cole rested his thick glasses back on his nose and ears. They slipped down slightly. "Not killed, brutally slaughtered or executed might be a more appropriate description. Alfred lost his daughter here, along with his son-in-law and their three children, we think."

Dirt and broken blades of grass flew up and out as Frank kicked the ground surveying the broad man off in the distance, the father—and grandfather—who attacked wood with a red-handled axe.

Frank asked, "You think?"

"Well, we're missing the youngest, a girl."

Frank pulled a bag from his horse and threw it over his shoulder with a flick of a wrist. He tied the Appaloosa to a tree limb about twenty feet from the front porch.

The axe never slowed its attack. Alfred stopped once to wipe the sweat from his forehead. Every tissue in his body cinched up as he swung the blade down splitting some timber down its middle.

"He found his family late last night," Cole said. "His son-in-law was supposed to have been in town yesterday morning. So, when he didn't show, Alfred came out to check on them. When he got here, well, he gets in close and sees Gary, his son-in-law, and Gary Jr. dead on the front porch there."

Frank walked to the front porch for a closer look. He pulled a notepad and a pencil from his bag and started jotting down notes while Cole continued to talk.

"As you can see, the boy was cut up with a knife and maybe an axe. It was an axe Alfred had given the boy when he had turned sixteen."

"Why is it red?" asked Frank.

"Not real sure. My hunch is that it was covered in blood. I think sometime last night Alfred painted it."

A chill ran up Frank's back as he realized why Alfred had painted the axe. He glanced back and forth between the two bodies and Alfred. He said, "I wonder when the sheriff is getting here. He does know, right?"

"He knows, but he ain't on this case."

"And why not?"

"Alfred was the sheriff for nearly twenty years. He only recently retired, so he had his old deputy, the current sheriff, deputize him."

"Is that wise?" asked Frank.

Cole paused, adjusted his glasses, and said, "Look at him."

The whack of the axe hacking at logs grew louder. Splinters of wood shot out from under the sharp heavy blade and showered outward.

Cole continued, "Whose gonna stop him?"

After pondering the question, Frank said, "Nobody, I reckon."

"Nope, not me."

Frank said, "Besides, you won't find a more dedicated man when it comes down to hunting the people who did this."

"I'm dedicated to the fight, Frank."

"Glad to have you, but why so far north?"

"I was hot on a trail. I was following a man who killed an old man and his mule down in Fort Worth. Ever hear of the Kingston Killer?"

"Not sure if I have, can't recall the name."

Cole shook his head. "He is absolutely one hundred percent pure evil. His trail led me to a town about ten miles south of here. I was on my way to Canton when I came across some folks who knew of what had happened here. So I came over first thing."

"You think he did this? The Kingston Killer?"

"Well, he may have been here, but he wasn't alone." Cole's voice was tight.

Frank examined the area for footsteps in the soil.

Cole added, "Oh, and another thing about Alfred."

"Go on."

"When Alfred found his daughter . . ." Cole's voice cracked.

"Go on."

"Alfred only spoke to me briefly, but he said he blacked out. When he awoke and found his daughter dead, he let out a scream. It was a scream from the guts of his insides. A yell that sprang out from so deep in his soul that it broke his Adam's apple."

"Huh?"

"Yep, when he talks now, it's all scratchy and deep, almost grating, like the sound of running a large hoe over rocks."

"We'll get these bastards."

Cole nodded.

Looking over the bodies that were splayed out on the bloody porch Frank pulled the folded piece of paper from his shirt pocket. He read it all the way through, twice. He then read aloud, "Dead or alive." He sighed as he refolded the note and slipped it back into his pocket.

"You talking to me?" inquired Cole.

Frank looked at the dead teenager. "No, but—"

"I'm listening."

"My orders are . . . let's get to work." He snagged his pencil from the top of his ear and began to scribble again as he spoke. "Looks to me like father Gary here took two to the chest and one to the leg. Then he bled out."

Cole curiously followed along without speaking.

"It seems that the three shots hit him at the same time while he was still standing. None look to have hit him after the fall. The boy was cut up with a knife, possibly tortured for a few moments, I'm guessing." Frank rubbed his chin. "But he was not armed. Maybe Gary Sr. was armed, but where's the gun?"

The porch had been well taken care of. Frank knelt. He then looked around the floorboards. He shifted his eyes to the yard.

"Look," he said as he pointed to the yard next to the porch. "A shotgun blast, wide berth, and lots of shot, both barrels. I'm thinking he took his hits and as he pulled the trigger the gun was pointed downward. He had the gun resting." Frank stood as if holding an imaginary shotgun in his arms. "He held it in a resting but ready position."

Frank looked at the dead father's face and said to the unresponsive corpse, "You were ready to protect your family, but they were too fast." He paused. "You were too trusting, my friend."

"Maybe he knew 'em." Cole said

"Maybe."

"So far everything makes sense," Cole said.

"I bet the boy was holding the axe. How did they get him to drop it?"

The young man was lying on his side. The muscles in his face still read anger—defiance. Frank squared his shoulders on the entrance to the house. The skin on his face relaxed as he said, "They had a hostage. They threatened to kill someone he cared about and he gave up his only defense."

Cole interjected, "It don't matter much. An axe against a gun? He was stuck in a no-win situation once his pa was shot down."

The two detectives paused to listen to Alfred Kincaid who continued to let out his pain. Frank rubbed his jaw with the pencil passed through his fingers.

Squinting, Frank said, "Gary Sr. may have still been alive when they killed his son. I see three sets of footprints. I assume one set is Kincaid's?"

"Yes, sir, the pair here." Cole pointed out a set of boot prints that traversed through the blood and into the front door.

"Yep, the blood was somewhat dry by the time he got here. If Kincaid was on the scene last night, my guess is that the attack happened maybe that morning. I don't see any animal tracks so it couldn't have been that long ago. The night before at the earliest."

Cole added, "They do have some moth balls scattered about the outside rim of the house. I know those things will keep about any animal with a sense of smell away, at least for a bit."

Savage looked up from his kneeling position and agreed. "You're right, so, maybe sundown the night before. We're lucky it didn't rain very hard."

"It rained?" asked Cole.

"Yep."

"Then the shower was only in town, I reckon. There wasn't a drop out here. Near as I can tell."

"How can you tell?" asked Frank.

"I can tell by the footprints left behind by the culprits who were here. I'm an expert on prints in the ground. My father was a tracker."

Frank nodded and moved across the porch to the side of the house. "It looks like two riders came straight up the center of the property to the front of the house. How did they have a hostage?"

"Maybe they didn't. Maybe Gary Jr. was afraid and gave up the hatchet."

"If that boy is any relation to that man—" Frank pointed at Alfred— "then he isn't afraid of a damn thing. No, this boy held his ground until they threatened someone he cared about."

"You're right. Then there was someone else."

"Exactly. Let's work the inside. Wait—" Frank said.

Gary Sr. had passed with his eyes open. Frank bent over, and resting his own head in his left hand, he closed Mr. Johansen's eyes with his right. After a silent prayer, Frank straightened himself and turned toward the boy. "He played a hand with a group of men who dealt from the bottom. He didn't have a chance. Let's make sure these bastards cash out."

Spinning on his heels, Frank turned and slowly entered the front door. After a curt step he halted his forward motion.

The front room was once a living room for a loving family. It had been built with care to be a gathering place for a happy and sharing family that was no longer alive. This family room now ceased to exist and it had been repainted. It was not a sanctuary for God-fearing people anymore. It had been transformed into something that showed evil's true face.

Cole peeped over Frank's shoulder only to fall backward in disgust. He whispered as he looked away to the sky, "What was here? No way they're human."

The thick stain of death was ferocious but Frank didn't avert his gaze. Dried blood was caked to the mantle. A trail of red forced his attention to the middle of the room. In the center was a large circle of blood droplets, stars from Hell that stared up at the two men. In the center was a large blot; it was as if the eye of Satan was looking up at them. Streaks of dark red smears and prints—almost black—walked their way to the couch where a young woman had been murdered and left like a dead animal.

Blood splatters shouted out from all four walls and the ceiling.

Cole said, "It looks like they took part of her. Is she all there?"

"Cole, I'm deathly afraid that this isn't the worst of what we'll see today."

Disgust echoed from his caustic tone.

Cole said, "I've never seen anything worse than this, and I've seen some shit."

"We're still missing a daughter, and a granddaughter."

Frank slowly lifted his right arm and extended his finger. Cole's eyes followed the end of Frank's finger, across the blood-red face of Kincaid's oldest granddaughter, then across the dark-soaked carpet to a small chest. In the side wall of the chest was a scattering of holes.

"No," Cole blurted sternly. "I refuse, no." He shook his head and bit his tongue. The pain was more bearable than his reality. Fighting hard not to tear up, he asked, "Why, why?"

Frank moved cautiously over to the chest. His legs were weak. When it came to children, he was in trouble. The death of small children was the most challenging to him as a man. He attempted to prepare himself for what might be inside that dark wood chest in the corner of the room.

As Frank lifted back the lid, their worst fear was realized.

Cole said quietly, "Alfred has not seen her yet. He thinks maybe she is still alive somewhere, waiting for her granddaddy to come find her."

"I know."

Frank squinched his eyelids together, and, with everything he had, he made a wish to travel back in time. Maybe if he really believed it, he could go back to two days earlier and stop the slaughter. He rubbed his head as he worked around inside his skull. He desperately prayed as he forced his body into the past. Frank hollered out to God with his brain to allow him this one gift.

When Frank opened his eyes he was staring into the wooden box in the corner of the room. Everything was blurry, but nothing had changed.

Frank whispered, "Cole?"

"Yeah."

"Our orders."

"Yes?"

"Our orders are to destroy the scum that did this."

What they had just seen was horrific, but it would provide the fuel for the fire to do what they had to do. They turned and looked out the front door.

"Understood?" asked Frank.

With his fingers rolled up tight in two firm fists, Cole said, "Understood."

CHAPTER 3

A snapping creak sounded from the boards of the first stair. It reminded Frank of the house where he had grown up. He noticed that there was no blood on the steps except a smudge that Kincaid had left behind on his way to find his daughter. Even the handrail leading up to the second story was clean. *How can that be?* The entire living room was masked with a red sad countenance. The kitchen and the washroom had been contaminated as well.

A set of footprints led out the back door and two walked out the front. W*as she killed first?* That might explain things. There was even a bloody boot print on the door to the cellar that someone had left behind trying to get to the basement.

Frank studied the living room from his perch in order to view the area from a different angle. Maybe he could find something he hadn't seen when he was at eye level. Eyeing the couch, Frank caught a flash of something. There was a flickering of material. A flutter caused by the breeze that worked its way through the house. It was a tear in the couch.

In order to get a better look he walked down the steps and into the living room. He leaned over to pick up a tiny screw that rested on the floor below the tear. Frank twisted it around between his forefinger and thumb before putting it into a pocket on the inside lining of his bag. He pulled a knife from his bag and cut off some of the loose threads dangling from the couch. The material was brown with a soft yellow intertwined in a crisscross pattern with some green. He put the threads and his knife into his bag.

Swinging his pack up over his shoulder, Frank turned back to the staircase. He had hope that Cole would be able to let Alfred down as easy as a man possibly could. The two felt it best to let Alfred know his granddaughter hadn't made it. Alfred was a grandpa who would not survive the ordeal if he ever saw her that way.

Once upstairs, Frank looked down the hall and saw nothing out of the norm. Moving steadily, he hunted for clues. The floor, the walls, and the ceiling were immaculate. It was how he imagined the rest of the house had once been only a day or two before.

A sharp beam of light entered the hallway from the master bedroom. Frank looked into the berthing area where Alfred had found his daughter. It was here where Alfred Kincaid broke his voice box.

Crown molding framed the ceiling. A dark-gray divan with a large square pillow for back support extended out from a corner. A picture of the family quietly spoke to Frank from the top of a dresser snug against the back wall. The bed sat in the middle of the room. The soles of Rosemary's feet lightly touched the cold steel of the bed frame. Frank slipped into the room careful and slow. At this cautious pace he could analyze the place where Alfred's daughter was murdered.

The purpose was to capture as much information from the scene as possible. But there was nothing but Rosemary with her arms straight and tight at her sides. She was in her clothes. Her throat had been cut and there was very little blood.

Frank stepped to the open window off to the right of the bed and next to a nightstand. Nothing seemed to be disturbed except for Kincaid's daughter, Rose. He studied her face and light brown hair. She was a beautiful woman who had lost a lovely family and her own life in the same day.

He shoveled his foot as he moved and heard a vibration come from under his boot. He lifted his toe to expose some splinters of wood. The curtain from the window blew in his face as he knelt down to pick up the debris. He perked his jaw out and up as he studied the ceiling. There was a bullet hole spying down on him. "Well, hello there."

He turned to Rose and said, "You were gonna fight back, weren't you?"

To the right lay two spent shells from a Winchester rifle.

Then from behind him came a low deep grating voice. "One shot went out the window."

Frank's hand was halfway to his Colt when he realized he was looking at Alfred Kincaid.

Kincaid had a very stocky and visibly strong frame. The rugged body looked almost off kilter resting under such a kind and open face. The corners of his eyes drooped on the sides giving him the look of a basset hound.

"One shot?" asked Frank.

"My Rose, she was an excellent shot. So, I know she hit whatever she was aiming at. Sorry about the voice," Kincaid said.

"No, it's fine." Frank stepped in with his hand extended. "I'm Frank Savage and I am sincerely sorry."

"I'm Alfred Kincaid." Alfred extended his arm and the two men shook hands. "We will get the men that did this," Alfred added with a steely gaze.

"Yes, sir, we will," Frank said. "You get everything worked out, out there?" He nodded his head to the window.

Alfred stood expressionless except for the sad droop in the corners of his eyes.

Frank continued, "I mean, you got all your frustrations out? Is all your hatred lying in a pile of splinters out there by the barn?" Frank pointed out the window.

The red-handled axe squeaked under the pressure of Alfred's firm grip—it hung as if it were growing out the palm of his hand.

Cole stepped into the room from the hallway and peeked in around Alfred's head.

Alfred said, "Hell, no."

Frank pondered the slight thorn of anger that cracked off Alfred's voice. He said, "Good, cause we're gonna need it."

Frank slid over to Rose, knelt, rested his hand on her forearm. At her bed he said, "These bastards are going to die and I need your help to make sure they suffer."

Alfred's wet eyes stared back as he nodded.

Frank stood and said, "You're gonna have to trust me and do as I say. You must be patient."

Alfred listened intently.

"You have to work with your head as well as your heart. If you do that, we will catch them. And we will kill every one of them—without hesitation. We're not herding cattle and driving them to Kansas City. This mission will be to take them to the slaughter house."

The agent, the ranger, and the deputy sheriff stood in a circle. They were in the middle of the open field that looked up to the front of the two-story white house. Frank tilted his hat to the top of his forehead.

Cole stood with the sun on the back of his neck. His hands were resting on his belt. "I'll be a son of a gun."

A black hat now shielded Alfred's bald head from the sun. A smile slipped into the corner of his mouth. His eyes were still sad.

Alfred said, with pride, "I told you she hits what she aims at."

"That's something," Cole said.

"Tell me you've never seen a scalp before," added Frank.

"I seen a scalp, but not one attached to an ear," Cole said.

Alfred interjected, "I taught her how to shoot."

The three hunters analyzed the ear. It had a piece of scalp with blonde hair and connected to it was a bloody flap of skin.

Frank said, "Okay, we're looking for a blonde man, with part of his scalp . . . missing. More than likely it was separated from its owner by a bullet that exited Rose's Winchester."

"And no right ear either," Cole said.

"Right. And no right ear," Frank allowed.

"We'll have to sneak up on his right side then," Cole said.

They stood silent a moment while Frank removed a handkerchief from his bag. He wrapped the ear inside with some string to hold it tight.

"That explains the two shells. Someone was up there to stop her," Frank said. "That second shot went into the ceiling. Maybe due to a struggle, or maybe she was startled."

Alfred Kincaid said, "Frank." His voice shuddered from the broken chords in his voice box. "I'll let you two talk. I will start . . . I am going to lay to rest my—" Alfred lowered his head and walked away and clenched his red-handled axe.

"Okay, Kincaid, we'll be there shortly," Frank said.

Cole waited until Alfred was out of earshot. "Think he'll be alright?"

"Yep, he's tough. Once we get his family buried, he'll only have one thing on his mind." Frank said.

"When we rolling out?" Cole asked.

"Tonight. We'll follow the tracks that leave out the front entrance. It looks like they left as a group." Frank said.

"There was no blood from Rose's wound," Cole said.

"She was dead before he cut her."

"Why would he lay her dead body out just so he could cut her?" Cole asked.

Frank kicked the dirt, shook his head, said, "That's part of the puzzle. We may never know what motivates this person. The others are easy to figure. They were looking for money, maybe a thrill, or they just had evil, short tempers maybe. You know, criminals we're used to seeing. But the man who doesn't leave a trace that he was even here except for a dead body that he cut after she was dead. I don't have a clue. It is worrisome. That's why he needs to be destroyed."

"He strangled her didn't he?" Cole asked.

"There was a bump on her head, but I think that was to subdue her or she got it in a fight for her life. There were these bruises on her neck in the shape of fingers. He definitely strangled her. Both hands were upside down, looks like. So, she was lying down when he did it."

A grumble reverberated in their eardrums. They turned. Alfred was trying to hail them by waving his arms. He yelled, "Look here."

The two men ran up to the hitching rail. Alfred said, "My grandson's horse was here. The rein is still attached to the rail. He snapped it. That took some force."

A narrow band of leather hung loosely on the wood.

"Moonbeam," Alfred said. "Her name is Moonbeam. My granddaughter named her. Moonbeam is feisty. You can see her prints in the dirt. She was watching something that she didn't like." He pointed at the ground. "We have to find her. If they stole her—she's got sand and she will fight. She will cooperate for only her family and no one else. Moonbeam has always been that way. They may get fed up and put her down."

"You recognize her track?" asked Frank.

"You bet," Alfred said. "She's got spunk, but not Ruby. Ruby is gentle. Too gentle."

"Ruby?" questioned Frank. "Who's Ruby?'

The ground was hard. It hurt to lie on after a while. It was cold to stand on let alone to sleep on. It was dark. The smell in the room was musky. There had been others here before her.

It didn't matter how much Ruby whined; she knew her family was not alive to rescue her. She had watched them die. Nosing around the bowl she hunted for some food and water. She shivered as she sat back on her hind legs and sniffed the air. Strands of her red hair covered the floor.

A dusty flow transfused into her cell from under the door and around its frame. He was coming. Ruby backed into the corner as a scent hit her memory center. The smell was familiar for two reasons. And it was getting closer. She lay on her belly. She nuzzled her cold and wet and bruised nose into the crook that her paws made against the floor. That smell was like the bottles that her Rose used to keep in a cupboard in the kitchen. Sometimes her Rose would spread the smelly liquid around the house. If she got too close Ruby could feel a burning sensation in her nostrils.

The second reason the smell was familiar was because of the man who came to their home. He smelled like that same foul nose-burning liquid. She knew it was him. He was coming again.

The door snapped open and light exposed her cell. She could see her cage. The hinges on the door creaked as it moved open. Ruby whimpered. She looked away and then down when she saw that the man was carrying a stick. The rattling meant she was going to get whacked. She spun around. Nowhere to run. She wished for her loved ones to save her. Even though she knew she would never see them again. *Maybe Grandpa will come.*

The man hollered out as he unlocked the cage door. Ruby didn't know what he was saying but she understood the intent by his tone. She cried out as the end of the stick struck her nose. She squinched as far into the corner as she could get and kept her snout low.

The door slammed shut. Slowly Ruby inched her way over to her newly-filled bowl of water and lapped up a swallow. The beautiful but tired Irish Setter sniffed the food that was slopped down by her captor. It didn't smell good. But she ate it.

Alfred allowed a short prayer over his family's graves. The three men mounted up, spun their horses, and followed the tracks that had been left behind by the killers' horses and Moonbeam.

Frank said, "Okay, Kincaid. One of these prints is a dog. Ruby?"

Alfred said, "Yep, an Irish Setter."

Frank said, "Not sure why they took her. So, they took a horse and the dog. Maybe that's in our favor. Every track helps. And every clue gets us closer."

After a half hour of riding they came to the train tracks that flowed in a north-south direction.

One set of horse tracks went west. Two riders. Another set of tracks went east. One rider.

"Damn," Cole said. "We're missing a rider."

Frank nodded and removed his hat. Alfred jumped from his horse to analyze the tracks. He said, "I think we're missing two riders. I thought maybe one of these horses was light, no rider. It looks like one went west with a horse in trail. Maybe carrying supplies. This horse print going east is Moonbeam."

Frank turned his Appaloosa to point east. He trotted up to come to a rest on the train's tracks.

"Train stopped here for some reason, and two got on," Frank said.

"Where's it heading to?" asked Cole.

"Eventually Chicago."

Alfred's head snapped up with recognition. He said, "Off to the west is Deviltry."

"Crap," Cole blurted. "I knew it."

Frank shook his head.

Cole said, "Well, then what's off to the east? Hell?"

Alfred answered, "Angon Town. I suggest we go east to start. We're only about an hour's ride. We can make it there by nightfall."

"I agree, that's where Moonbeam is and it's a nicer town," Frank said.

"That's the understatement of the year. You ever been to Deviltry?" asked Cole.

"Yep, was hoping not to go back."

"I've been there once and the stories are true. There is nothing good there. It's a town of murderers and thieves. And once you get in, you have to blast your way out," Cole said. He was so excited his horse started to become restless.

"Hold onto your chaps there, chief," Frank said. "We knew this wasn't going to be easy. One thing about that town is that there is no loyalty. I've found that with some money, a bit of tact, and a bunch of whiskey, we can get the information we need."

Cole sighed and nodded.

"How far is Chicago from here? Along the tracks, by train?" asked Alfred.

"Less than a day," Frank said.

"So that means the two men and Ruby are already in Chicago. Right?" Alfred said.

"Yep."

Cole asked, "How many people live in that damn town?"

"Oh, just shy of a million I reckon," Frank said. He rested his arm across his saddle horn and leaned forward.

Alfred lowered his head.

"Is there something you want to tell us, Kincaid?" asked Frank. "Is there someone in Chicago who may have business with your son-in-law?"

"Nope. My son-in-law was a kind man with not an enemy in the world."

"Is there someone who might want to do you harm?"

"I was a lawman for many years. I had all kinds of threats thrown at me. I even had someone take a shot at me years after I had killed his father in a bank robbery."

Frank and Cole listened.

"I received so many threats I couldn't count them, but I had to disregard them. It would have driven any man insane if he took even one seriously." Alfred's voice rumbled from his throat. "But, there was one I never could let go of. I testified in a case that sent a young man to the gallows. The letter arrived shortly after the trial, and it contained a threat to get even. I remember that one because he knew everything about me. He knew things about my family that I didn't even know until years later."

"What can you tell me about this man?" asked Frank.

"All I know is that I saw a thirteen-year-old boy run away from the scene of a murder. It was a woman who had been strangled. I got a letter shortly after from the kid's father. He promised to take from me what I'd taken from him." Alfred wiped the sweat from his forehead with his arm. "I threw the letter out, but I do remember that it had been put in the mail in Chicago."

Frank nodded. "I thought it looked too planned out. It's personal, I reckon."

Alfred sat silent, then said, "Let's move."

The sheriff of Angon Town knocked on the front door of the store. Alfred was already in the barn with Moonbeam. Gilbert, the storeowner, opened the front door. He had his Webley pistol in a shoulder holster under his arm.

The sheriff looked at the gun. He said, "Carry a gun now, Gil?"

Gil looked sternly but not offensively at the sheriff.

Frank stepped up and extended his hand. "I'm Frank Savage."

The two men shook hands. Frank noticed the strong grip Gil had. But he could tell Gil wasn't trying to be aggressive. He just had large strong hands.

"Name's Gil, nice to meet you. Reckon you're here to talk about the killing." Gil opened the door for his visitors to enter.

Cole introduced himself and said, "Congrats on getting the Kingston Killer. There's a reward waiting for you in Texas."

"Have it sent to my wife and me here if you would."

Cole nodded. "I'll telegraph the information today."

"Thanks, kindly."

"Can we see the room it happened in?" asked Frank.

They stepped into the storage room in the back of the store. Alfred was standing at the back door. "That's my horse in your barn, mister," he said in a guttural voice.

Gil nodded. Unfazed he said, "And she's a fine animal."

In the middle of the floor was a large oval-shaped bloodstain.

"Head shot. He died rather instantly," Gil said. "He knew he was gonna die, though."

"Is there anything you can tell me about him? Anything at all?" Frank asked. "Maybe there was something about him, something he said."

Gil thought sincerely for a moment. "He was covered in blood. It was like he never tried to clean himself after what he had done. He was proud of his name. Kept saying he was the Kingston Killer. I didn't really give a shit, so I shot him in the brain-pan."

Frank jotted notes on his pad as he listened.

"But," Gil said, "he did mention something as he spoke to himself."

"To himself?"

"Yep. He actually was mad at some voice that came from his brain or somewhere about some hotel. Then he said something about Palmer's house."

Frank scribbled some notes. "Did he say anything about Chicago or

Deviltry?"

"I don't recall him saying that. That doesn't mean he didn't though. I did have other things on my mind."

"Thanks, Gil." Frank turned. "Sheriff, may we look at the body and his belongings?"

"Sure, let's go. We want to put his worthless carcass in the earth before it gets too offensive," said the sheriff.

The Kingston Killer lay pale over a rectangular wooden table in the middle of the room. Cole analyzed the bottom sole of the killer's boots while rubbing his chin. He said, "I got a weird memory. Once I see something, it stays there. Like an imprint. This boot was all around Junior's body on the front porch. And I bet that's the knife he used to cut him up with."

The blade was initially stuck as Frank tried to pull the knife from the dead man's belt. The knife was so bloody that he couldn't see any glimmer of the metal. The Kingston Killer's clothes stunk and were a crusty dark red. Frank analyzed the blade. With taped lips he shook his head.

"Was this boot ever in the house?" asked Frank.

Cole looked back to the scene in his mind. He said, "It was. He had walked through the living room, but he didn't kill the oldest girl, I don't think. That was someone else. And it was not the earless killer. The two girls were killed by a gunman who came in the back door."

Frank asked, "Could you recognize the boot print of the little girl's killer?"

"I think so. Yes."

Frank said, "One down, thanks to Gil. He prevented a lot of future murders by killing that one. The Kingston Killer was insane. There are no ifs, ands or buts about it, he was certifiable." He stared at the dead killer. "His type only breeds filth."

Alfred stood by the door. Once again he held firm and stern to his red axe.

Frank said, "Sheriff, this scum's all yours. Do with him as you wish. We'll need some room and board. If you could recommend some place for us to stay, we would appreciate it. Something affordable and that doesn't . . . smell bad."

"Not a problem, but don't you boys have to do some paperwork or something on Gil killing this man?"

Frank caught some motion in the corner of his eye. It was Alfred as he stepped away from the door and went out. Frank answered the sheriff's question. "No."

The sheriff nodded. "Okay." Confused, he shook his head and stepped outside and turned back to Frank. He opened his mouth to speak but just shook his head again instead and walked away.

Cole said, "I've been on many murder cases and I always look for an answer as to why, each and every time. Every murder leads to questions. These questions are always the same."

Frank said, "And so are the answers—they're always the same."

CHAPTER 4

The ground was unforgiving. Moonbeam sounded off against the lack of rest with a huff. Alfred Kincaid patted her neck. His voice grumbled but he said nothing. His shoulders lay relaxed as they trotted. His head bounced along with a side-to-side motion. Even though he was distraught, he did find comfort in riding Moonbeam again. She was a part of the family. *I hope we can find Ruby. Alive. He thought.*

Cole watched his new partner and smiled. Alfred was a big man, and Moonbeam was not a big horse, but she was strong with thick legs and clomped along determinedly.

As they approached the train tracks they slowed their pace.

"What do you reckon caused the train to stop?" asked Frank.

"These conductors are trained to stop for nothing," Cole said.

"I agree," Alfred said. His words resonated off the iron rails and wooden beams of the tracks. "They're not allowed to stop unless it's an emergency. Maybe these sons-a-bitches we're after were able to fake some kind of injury."

Frank rubbed his chin and gently guided his young Appaloosa to a stop. He looked down the track to the north and rested back into his saddle. He said, "That's a good guess, but I don't think they would stop for a group like that. I wouldn't."

Cole nodded. Alfred rubbed his eyes and sighed.

"It seems to me that this was all planned out well in advance," Frank said. "And this may have been planned as well. This train stop might have been set up. You know, ahead of time."

"We'll get 'em, girl. You and me, we'll hunt down every damn one of them," whispered Alfred. He thought back to that day when his testimony had hung a young man. His mind wandered. What if his words had hung an innocent person? Maybe his testimony had initiated a chain of events that caused the death of his daughter and her family.

Alfred let the reins drop from his hands. He barked, "Damn it all to hell. Help me God—" He jumped from his saddle and walked away.

Cole leapt down from his horse and followed.

"Alfred," Cole said. "I, uh, it ain't your fault."

"I know. I know it isn't, but I can't help but feel it is."

Alfred lifted his gun and pulled the trigger. He sent five shells into the air. He stood for a moment, dumped the spent casings to the ground, reloaded, and said, "Okay, I feel better now. Let's move."

"I think," Frank said, "it's best we don't do any more of that. We are chasing someone."

"My apologies."

"I think we should head to Deviltry."

"I knew you were going to say that," Cole said.

"Every chamber full," added Alfred, as he pulled himself into his saddle.

"Yep, that's best," Frank said. He filled the sixth and only empty chamber of his colt. "We'll carry rifles and shotguns—and an axe—in with us."

"Sounds fine by me," Cole said, then to himself, "I knew he was gonna say that, dadblastit. Damn that God-forsaken town."

A few hours silently rolled by as they came to the edge of the all-but-abandoned town. There was not much daylight left as they made their plan of attack. With resolve, and their heads on a swivel, they moved into Deviltry. Alfred fell back behind the other two as they had planned.

The only structures that looked lived in were the hotel and the saloon. They approached the saloon. Frank and Cole tied their mounts to a hitching rail and removed their firearms from their housings.

Frank stepped into the smoky bar a step ahead of his partner. The door was slimy, and he fought the urge to wipe his hands clean as he and Cole entered. The room was full of drinkers that had forgotten to stop. There was a bar top on the left and a potbellied stove on the right. The stove hadn't been used in a long while, and the bar looked as though it had never taken a break.

Immediately a voice bellowed out from one of the tables by the bar. It had an annoying twang to it. "I recognize that Goddang son of a bitch."

Frank pulled the stock to his shoulder, loaded a round into the breech with a downward flick of his hand, and pointed the barrel all within the flash of a second it took the man to take to his feet.

"Hold onto your hat, Mister Man," Frank ordered. "I've got no qualms about splashing you right here, right now."

Cole, with a disbelieving sigh, perked up.

Frank whispered, "I can't go out in public anymore. Too many assholes know who I am."

The sloppy-looking gunman was dirtier than an outhouse. He had a belly that hung over his belt. His front teeth exposed his tongue through the gap in the middle, and he spit when he talked. He said, "I know you, lawdog. I seen you, Savage. I seen—"

"I don't give a good Goddang what you've seen," Frank said. He aimed his rifle. "But I guarantee you this, if you so much as shiver from a cold breeze, I'll make sure you don't *see* anyone or anything ever again."

"Wait," Cole said from the front door. Two strangers approached the entrance to the saloon. "We won't be but a few minutes," Cole told the two men. "And if you don't like my tone, take it up with my convincer." He lifted his ten-gauge double-barreled shotgun. The pair looked at it, then at each other. One scoffed as the other grunted. But they were convinced and departed to find another place to drink.

A coin rolled across a table and tumbled to the floor. Frank surveyed the room. It was a one-level saloon and not a woman in sight. Less than a dozen cowboys sat and stood about the room holding lukewarm beers. Half of the bunch looked ready for a fight—the others looked ready for a nap.

"I ain't here for you, Harvey," Frank said to the man. "I got much bigger fish to fry than to screw around trying to drag your ugly ass into jail. Besides the fact that I'd rather not dirty up my clothes with your filth."

A splash of tobacco fused with spit sounded off from the back of the saloon. Harvey pulled a face. His legs were scarcely bent at the knees. He stood between his table and the bar with his hand hanging loosely over his gun. His shoulders were shrugged up tight to his neck and his forearm swayed at the elbow, rocking back and forth slowly. The tips of his fingers stroked the butt of his gun as his hand swung to and fro.

Frank recognized the look in the man's eyes. Harvey, more than likely, was the top gun in Deviltry. And if he could take Frank Savage out, it would solidify his reputation.

Frank's voice was deep, clear, and loud. "Whoever don't want a piece of this, leave now, and leave slow." He kept his eyes on Harvey. "And don't come back."

Seven men moved slowly but assuredly out the front door. Harvey stayed where he stood, steady except, that is, for his swinging arm. As the seventh gunman was walking out the front door he abruptly turned and grabbed Cole's shotgun by the barrel. The gun shot flames as the two stumbled into Frank with force enough to knock him off balance. The blast sent down a shower of dust and wood splinters from the ceiling.

Harvey saw his window of opportunity and drew his six-shooter. But Frank's hold on his rifle was solid. Frank's trigger pulled tight against the stop. The bullet hit Harvey in the shoulder, causing him to drop his gun with a puff.

Two men at the bar swarmed toward Frank as he attempted to regain his footing. He caught his fall as the two left-handed gunmen whipped out their pistols. Frank adjusted his grip on the stock of his rifle and swung his weapon right to left as hard as he could. With two smart whacks, in one fell swoop, the steel barrel of Frank's gun sent their two Colts flying out the front window with a crash.

Frank's motion was so fast they didn't have time to get their guns cocked. The two men glanced down at their empty palms. They paused a tick and then hollered out from the pain that ran up their arms. One let loose a high-pitched shriek.

Cole, still in a struggle over his shotgun, bumped into Frank a second time. This time it was solid enough to cause Frank to go face first into his two adversaries. The rifle was loosened from Frank's hands. It flew up and forward in an arc and bounced sharply off the top of the bar and into the back wall of the liquor shelf breaking a row of whisky bottles. The rifle came to rest on a pile of broken glass on the ledge.

Frank said, "Jesus Christ, Cole, who's side you on?"

"I'm doin' the best I can," barked Cole as he struggled to get hold of his weapon.

Harvey screamed as he held his shoulder. "Piss, this hurts." Blood squeezed out between his fingers.

The bartender moved abruptly. Harvey looked around and then frowned at him. "Get that gun and shoot—" He was cut off as the bartender fell into a trap door behind the bar. Harvey looked around desperately for his own gun. It rested on the ground under the shuffling feet of Frank and his two attackers as they fought in a circle on top of it.

Cole's glasses started to slip from his face as his attacker attempted to twist the shotgun from his grip. He pointed his face upward to the ceiling, wrestling for control. He squinched his nose. The effort was barely enough to keep the glasses from falling off his face. He'd be useless without them.

The man Cole struggled with reached for the pistol at his waist. As the gun came up Cole clutched the muzzle. He twisted his body, and the abrupt motion dislodged his glasses from the bridge of his nose.

The two men stumbled out the front door and down the steps and into the dusty street. A group of men were lined up along the side of the boardwalk with their guns at their feet. Cole squinted in an effort to see the gunman who held everyone at bay. The gunman was a bald and broad man with a six-shooter in one hand and a red-handled axe in the other.

Inside the saloon, Frank had his hands full. One of his hands held onto a little guy. But the guy was fast, annoyingly fast. His other hand held tightly to a large man, freakishly large. Frank did not want to have to tangle with him for much longer.

The little guy sent a quick jab into Frank's cheekbone. It was not much, so Frank pulled the little guy down by kicking his feet out from under him.

Harvey was on his face trying to reach into the mass of moving legs to get his pistol. He yelped out as he got his fingers stomped. "Piss, piss, piss." He put his fingers in his mouth.

The large man lost his grip. Frank clamped onto his ear as tightly as he could and pulled firmly downward. "Aaw," screeched the large man.

The little guy was back on his feet and running toward Frank in a fury. Frank laughed inside as he watched the little legs taking such short and quick steps. Frank picked up a chair with his hand that didn't have an ear in it and held it up in front of his short-legged enemy. The leg of the chair nailed the little gunman in the Adam's apple. The angry little man's eyes blew open to the size of silver dollars, and he gulped out like a frog. He held his throat as he tried to breathe. He wheeled around in a full circle and fell to his knees.

Frank adjusted his attention and pulled down on the large man's ear as he accepted a blow to his stomach. He had seen it coming and had firmed up in anticipation. The large man cried out in pain from his ear. Frank then kneed him in the chin with considerable force. The big man's knees buckled and he was knocked out cold before his huge head bounced off the ground—hard.

Alfred's raspy voice barked, "Drop it." He pointed his gun at Harvey who stood behind the bar with Frank's rifle in his hand.

Frank slowly walked to the bar and reclaimed his weapon. "Thanks," he said. Then with a roundhouse right he belted Harvey. Harvey fell, whacked his head on the bar top, and moaned himself to oblivion.

Frank tucked in his shirt and rubbed his face with his sleeve.

Alfred said, "Well, that was easier than I thought."

Frank looked up with a puzzled smirk and shook his head. "I've got a bad back, you know. Damn, that little guy is punchy." He rubbed his neck.

Frank leaned over to pick up Cole's glasses and jerked back up with the pain as his muscles pulled on his spine. He held his lower back as he reached again for Cole's glasses. He used his legs this time. "I really do need to think these things out more," he mumbled.

"I got the impression that you like to do things off the cuff."

"Who's watching the others?" asked Frank.

"Cole, of course," Alfred said.

"You are aware that he is as blind as a bat without his glasses, right?"

"I know," Alfred said. "But they don't."

Frank allowed the corner of his mouth to turn up and he shook his head again. "Easy, my ass."

Two men sat and ate. They had stopped at a somewhat small and slightly uncomfortable spot for a campsite. Goth Furse had decided it best to not build a fire. Just in case. All they had was some light from the night sky to help guide them as they ate cold beans with some ham and a biscuit, along with a pint of whiskey to wash it down.

"I ain't one to complain, Goth, but I really think you're being paranoid," said Rocco.

A long pale face made Goth Furse appear ghostly. He sat with his left hand balled up in a tight fist that he couldn't release—ever. His food rested on a plate carefully balanced on his knees. He'd had lots of practice. Goth said, pausing often between syllables, "Just because I am paranoid does not mean someone is not trying to kill me." He glared at his companion.

Rocco nodded. "Point taken." He continued to eat.

Goth sat, radiating irritation.

"Some coffee would be nice, though," Rocco said under his breath.

Rocco was stout with frizzy hair and four days' worth of stubble on his face. His physical appearance was messy, and his hat looked like he slept with it on, like he never took it off. Rocco was aware of his untidiness and was also aware of the fact that he had bad breath. He learned to keep his distance from others when speaking. If he liked you.

"You know that I do know what you did," said Rocco, "and I really don't give a damn. I'll follow you anywhere cause you're my brother. But what has got you so spooked you can't even sit still for a moment? Not too many lawmen will trek through that shit-hole to find some piss-ant criminals like us."

Unmoving, Goth frowned into the fire. "I got no idea, man, I got no idea. I had me a dream. It was not good. But I liked it." Goth dramatically stalled in between his words, he always did. "I done some awful, evil, dark things. And I feel nothing. I feel nothing about what I've done. No guilt, no remorse, no regret, nothing." He looked seriously at his brother with round eyes. "But Rocco, I had a vision after I met someone. They got me to do evil. I have to go to Chicago—that is where I must go. My dreams tell me to go there and find this person." He paused to take a bite then said, "I liked it."

Rocco listened and shrugged and chewed.

Goth purposely stoked his anger. He knew of no other way. His anger was wound tight, and he carried it all inside his chest and clenched fist. Rocco knew not to look at it. Sometimes Goth would get cramps in his left arm. Sometimes it was so intense that he would have to rub it to loosen its painful pull. The muscles at times could get so tight that he could feel it in his neck and down his back.

"How do you expect to find this person?" Rocco asked.

"We have to go to Palmer's house." He glared at his brother. "That's all I know."

Rocco avoided eye contact. "Whoever the heck Palmer is." He then tried to change the subject and said, "So, what's it like in Chicago? I bet there are some lovely dames up there."

"Dames is dames, they're no different wherever you go. They all get what they deserve."

Goth's holster housed two guns, the left gun was seated for a cross draw and both were easily accessible to his right hand. He could beat anyone who challenged him to a draw by using either. He never knew which gun he would go for until after the battle was done.

"Okay. I, myself, am looking forward to the ladies. There wasn't nothing in Deviltry," said Rocco.

"Rocco, stop flapping at the gums, will ya?" snapped Goth.

His eyes bounced up and down.

Moving slowly, Rocco stood with his food and walked away. He mumbled, "Man, you're bug'n me out. You're such a downer. I have no idea who you are anymore."

Goth Furse stabbed his ham with a fork and ripped a piece off with his teeth. His left arm slowly tightened. Attempting to fight it didn't help. Goth had once owned a meat cleaver, and on more than one occasion, he had gotten drunk and attempted to chop his hand off. The doctors couldn't help him either. Drugs did nothing to release the tension in his palm and fingers. He could be passed out drunk and still have a cinched-up left hand. The real stinker of the whole thing—he was left handed.

Through a feathery haze of distorted light, Harvey slowly came to. At that moment a door shut. It was too dark to see, and all he could hear was the sound of his own breathing. The wood chair creaked as he tried to move. His wrists and ankles were tied to the chair. He squinted in an effort to focus.

There was the scratch of a match followed by a flash of a flame. The now-lit lantern on the table in front of him illuminated a very broad and visibly angry man.

Alfred Kincaid grumbled as he picked up his axe. The metal end drug along the wooden floor with a clonk as it hit the leg of the table. It then thudded as he pulled it over the floorboards.

A cold stark frost streamed through Harvey Watson as the axe blade caught the light just enough to flicker. Kincaid slowly removed his hat to show his closely shaved head. He moved behind Harvey's chair. He pulled the axe along behind him.

"What the hell?" Harvey stuttered disdainfully. "What you gonna do?" Fear fell off his words like the sweat off his forehead. He twisted his head as far around as he could, but he didn't see Alfred Kincaid kick his chair.

With a thump, Harvey's seat shot forward closer to the table. Kincaid sharply kicked it again. Now Harvey's hands rested on the splintered tabletop.

It was quiet a moment, then Kincaid said, "Pick a finger."

Harvey's brain processed the where, the what, and the why. He felt sick to his stomach. "What? What? What do you—no way, no, no way." Harvey dug deep for courage and spoke forcefully. "No."

Kincaid spoke again. "I hear you're the information man in this town."

Straining against his bindings, Harvey glanced around the room. All he could make out was the door, a lantern, and a table with two chairs.

Kincaid said, "No one comes or goes without you knowing. We know that." He shifted to the side.

Harvey stared at the axe. Mesmerized and without looking up, he said, "I, I don't know what you mean."

Kincaid lifted the axe, only slightly but deliberately.

Harvey blurted, "Okay, okay, yes, yes, yes nobody comes or goes without me knowin'. It's true, so what?"

Harvey's bullet from Frank's gun had been a through-and-through. The wound had been tended to, cleaned, and stitched, but he didn't notice. Something else was occupying his mind.

Kincaid's damaged voice vibrated throughout the room. "I'd be willing to bet that you already know who we're lookin' for." He lifted the axe.

Harvey's breathing quickened as the axe rested on top of the table.

Alfred continued, "Stick out the finger you want me to cut off."

"Want you? Want you to cut off? You got to be shitting me. I don't *want* you to cut off anything." Harvey pulled on his bindings and squirmed in his chair.

Kincaid's face pointed downward as he looked through the tops of his eyes. His expression was silently eerie. He said, "I mean to show you we aren't screwing around here. I'm going to hack off a finger, or your whole hand. Then, then I'm gonna ask you a question. I figure you'll answer all I need to know."

Sweat-drenched hair fell into Harvey's face. He jerked his head around the room. He tried to scream but choked on his tongue that had swollen up to twice its normal size. He said hoarsely, "Help me. Please somebody, help me. Savage, I'm in here, please help me." He coughed up phlegm. "I'm sorry, I'm sorry." Then with a touch of anger he said, "I am so damn sorry."

Alfred Kincaid, a man looking for his daughter's killer, hovered and swayed with a heartless air.

Grinding his teeth, Harvey again looked for courage. The rope was cutting the circulation off to his hands and feet. Abruptly Kincaid raised his red-handled axe to the ceiling and said, "The hand it is then."

Spit flew off Harvey's lips as he swore out in horror to his captor as the keen blade of the red-handled axe swiftly sliced through the air. With a whoosh followed by a penetrating whack the blade easily buried itself into the wood table—barely missing Harvey's knuckles—just by a hair.

Harvey released his bowels.

"Oh, crap," Kincaid said. "I missed. I guess you get a free one." He pulled his weapon from the wood. "Now, a man came through town in the last thirty-six to forty-eight hours. We are hunting this man. And as you can see, we have no time to waste."

It was silent. Harvey looked up at Kincaid.

Alfred said, "Don't kid yourself. You're not out of the woods yet. You tell me what I need to know, and you can keep all your limbs." Alfred pivoted around the table to face his prisoner. "This man was one of four who brutally killed a family. One was the Kingston Killer. He's dead, so he isn't providing much information. Two others hopped a train, and the third came here." He pointed his forefinger into the top of the table. "You're our only lead."

"Why are you doin' this to me? I don't understand."

The ire vanished from Alfred's face as he snapped straight. He looked at the light and slowly he sat down. The room was so, so quiet. The axe lay on its side on the table. His face hung loose off his bones. Alfred quietly whispered his daughter's name. He swallowed the bulging knot of emotion in his throat.

Angrily, Harvey barked, "I know who you're looking for, you bastard. You deranged lunatic, you, you, insane son of a bitch. I got word of what he had done and I had him removed from town." He paused. "You hear me? I had him booted because I don't allow violence towards children or women. Look at me."

Alfred indulged his prisoner and looked into his eyes.

"You have shot me, hit me, tied me up, and worse off, you have humiliated me. You took my manhood from me. I soiled my God-dang britches."

Alfred said nothing.

"All for information I would have given for nothing."

Alfred's eyes glazed over.

"I'll tell you what you want to know. And not because of your damn axe, but because I loathe the man who kills children, that's why."

Alfred listened and didn't move.

Harvey continued, "The man you seek is Goth Furse. He is a whack job almost as screwed up as you." He laughed. "You two would get along."

Alfred waited.

"Goth, he split north no more than twelve hours ago with his partner Rocco."

Alfred nodded. His skin was pale.

"Rocco is loyal, but not too bright. Rocco's the one who spilt the beans on Goth. I think they might be brothers. Goth is not one to be messed with. That's all I know."

Alfred swallowed.

"Now, would you please get me out of this chair, get me a bucket of water, and get me some clean britches?"

Alfred sighed and shelved his chin on his chest.

CHAPTER 5

The sun shone through a side window. Ruby cowered in the far right corner of the office. Her shiny auburn hair was beginning to dry but she was still cold and shivering. She wore a shiny black leather collar.

With the threat of vicious attack, another dog barked. It never rested, throwing its frustrated anger in her direction. This room was a different place. She was not in her cell. The food was getting better. But that other dog had been terrorizing her off and on for over a day now. Ruby couldn't sleep much, even when it was quiet. She was scared.

Curtains slowly parted. No one was in the room to open them. They just opened. There was another set of curtains on Ruby's end of the room. They hung to the floor between her and the other dog that was held secure with a leash around its thick neck. The curtains were red and they were the only objects in the room with color. Saliva flew as the bully continued to growl and bark. He had bloodshot eyes.

A door opened inward on the other side of Ruby's prison. The big black Doberman was distracted and turned its aggression toward the two that had entered.

A medium-sized man in a black round bowler hat and a handlebar mustache walked in first. A slender, tall woman with curly blonde hair that rested on her shoulders followed him. Immediately after they stepped into the center of the room the door swung shut with a muted clack.

Both strange characters stood without speaking and faced the unopened curtain. The lady with curly blonde hair leered at the barking Doberman and sneered. Her teeth were bright white with sharp pointy incisors. The dog backed up and moaned and sat in its corner. The lady laughed quietly to herself. The man in the bowler hat allowed no change to his facial expression. Ruby watched. It was quiet for a brief moment.

"Jesus." A man's voice jumped out from a tubular wood horn attached to the wall next to the curtains. The curtains opened exposing a large shiny mirror.

The voice hidden behind the mirror said, "I'm gonna have to change his name. Killer, in my opinion, isn't working for him. It's just a thought."

It was quiet again.

The voice spoke in a hoarse whisper. "Lake."

The man in the bowler came to attention with a slight lift of his chin and said, "Yes, sir."

"I have good news. You have been promoted to my lead assassin."

The lady stepped back. With contempt she let out, "You louse."

Their boss, safe behind the mirror, said, "Your first job is to remove the previous lead. Immediately."

Lake Lagoon drew an extended barrel peacemaker out of the pocket of his long black coat. His coat flapped out with the motion. As he leveled the gun, he attempted to arm the weapon. Hauling back the trigger it clicked.

At the same moment, his own brains exploded out the back of his skull, spraying the wall and sending his hat into the air. It tumbled to the ground as his body fell.

Ruby winced and backed into the corner, and Killer began barking at the dead man who lay motionless.

The smell of gunpowder filled the room as the lady casually emptied the chamber of her shotgun-pistol. She sniffed the used and smoky shell and then slipped it into her pocket. Her weapon of choice was messy, but it worked. She shivered.

The voice laughed as he said, "He botched that one nicely. Or, maybe, Plenty, you are too good."

Plenty Sky said, "I warned him. He knew if he crossed me, he'd only end up breathing dirt for the rest of eternity."

"You know you'll always be my favorite." He paused, "Don't you?"

Plenty Sky holstered her handheld shotgun as blood rushed to her head filling her cheeks with a rosy red. Her eyes teared up, and she smiled. She said, "I have my doubts sometimes." Goosebumps spread out over her arms.

Her boss said, "Mr. Lake Lagoon was sloppy. Not that your way is particularly . . . hygienic." He laughed. "But he is hired to be neat and to cover his tracks; or rather, was hired. I really don't want to have to do *all* these things myself."

There was a dampened ruffle of papers then her boss said, "I want you to keep a lookout for his possible replacement. So, you'll be working solo from now on."

"That's the way I like it, Boss. You know that."

Boss said, "Clean up this mess. I can't stand the sight of blood. You know that."

All summed up, there were some sixty years of experience as lawmen between the three trackers. Today they worked with a singular mind and purpose as they pursued their prey. Everything was going well until they lost the trail. Frank wasn't worried—it didn't matter much. They were following them in the direction he had anticipated. Before they knew it, they found themselves on the outskirts of Chicago.

Dark gray smoke floated over the city like a lazy raft on the water. It blocked the sun as the bright yellow orb moved slowly off to the west.

The three cowboys, on their horses, came across a major road that paralleled the train tracks on its way into the bustling mass of people at the center of town.

Too many prints in the road camouflaged the tracks of the two killers they hunted. It was going to be harder now with very little to go on, but Frank managed to stay positive. There were some things he knew that his partners did not. He debated on whether or not he should share his information with them.

As they came to a circle of trees still untouched by the city, Frank called for a halt. They decided to take a rest before finishing the journey. Frank advanced his Appaloosa up to a white oak that had a broad trunk and plenty of cover. Cole and Alfred quietly found a spot nearby to have some jerky and rest their horses. Moonbeam pulled on the reins as Alfred tried to tie her to a tree limb. She continued to stomp about restlessly as Alfred smoothly coaxed her down and she slowly gave in.

"We'll move on soon enough, but it's time to take a break. We have a tough job ahead of us and we all need our strength," Alfred said.

"The wind is picking up. We best not be too long. I see a storm in our future," Cole said.

Frank kicked some twigs away from a spot he'd picked out for himself. He made sure to find a seat downwind. With the wide tree at his back it would block the breeze that was picking up.

Sitting with legs folded under and in front of him, Frank pulled a thick notebook from his pack and laid it across his knees. Lifting the hat from his head, he rested his forehead on his fist with his elbow on his knee. He sighed. Frank turned the pages one by one looking until he found what he sought. It was notes from a previously unsolved case:

Jan 17, 1871 - Ogallala

Victim, female, found unclothed in a lying position on kitchen floor. All doors inspected and found locked. No sign of forced entry. Doors and windows all locked from the inside only. No tracks were found in nearby vicinity of home. One set of horse tracks found by Deputy Sheriff that proceeded to the south. Deputy lost trail after 2 or 3 miles. A search to pick up tracks farther down the road was unsuccessful. Victim was lying on a buckskin rug with her arms tucked in close to her body. Only visible marks; bruises on neck and 4 cuts, each about a foot long, and an inch deep. 2 ran along the insides of each leg, along the artery. 2 on insides of both arms. Little blood splatter, but victim did not bleed out. Victim had been dead for hours before being cut. Inspection of backside showed two burn marks on the back of the knees (some sort of branding). Object used looked to be a double bladed knife of some kind. Possibly a throwing knife. From the burn - looks like same knife used to make the cuts on the arms and legs. In the burn was an emblem of a circle and a cross overlapping on the right side of the circle. The left leg had the same but inverted. Emblem does not match any branding iron registered in Nebraska or any nearby region. Sheriff of Ogallala, lead investigator.

Frank looked up from his notebook. Cole and Alfred sat under a tree. Cole tapped his pocket watch and shrugged his arms. Frank motioned with a finger for another minute. He turned in his seat to pull his personal notepad from his bag. Swiftly he found a page that was in his own handwriting:

Kincaid - upstairs - bedroom-

When I turned the body I noticed a branding mark on the back of both knees. It looks like the burn was made with the blade of a knife. Inside the burn was a mark left behind, an emblem of some sorts that was carved into the knife's blade. It's a circle with a cross. The cross is laid on top of the right side of the circle. I've read of this from a previous case.

Frank covered his mouth with a firm fist. He sat quiet and then maneuvered up to his horse. Cole and Alfred followed his lead.

Frank loaded his pack to his saddle and pulled his canteen from the saddle horn. He poured some water into his hat and let his Appaloosa drink from it.

"Hey, watch the backwash, I gotta wear this."

Cole trotted up slowly and asked, "What's the plan?"

"We'll find the train's hump yard. I think if we nose around we can find the train they were on," Frank said.

Frank always felt wonder and respect whenever he came to Chicago. There were rows of large stone and iron- and steel-framed structures. The massive buildings were separated by wide brick streets that spread a web through the entire metropolis.

After the Civil War, Frank had worked as a spy in the city, so he had memories of the first Chicago, the city before the fire. When he'd caught news of the destruction, he had returned to the city to work and to help rebuild. That was over five years ago, the last time he had walked the streets. There was more sophistication and fewer horses now, but overall it felt the same as it always had.

"Kind sir, may I ask you a question?" Frank said to a debonair man on a one-horse carriage.

The man tipped his hat and smiled. "Certainly."

Frank asked, "Can you tell me if you know of a business called Palmer's House? I think it's a hotel, but I thought it was destroyed in the fire."

The gentleman answered, "Why, yes it was, but old man Palmer had it rebuilt, and it's grander than ever."

"Can you tell me how to find it?"

"Yes, it is in the heart of the city. When you get to State Street you must look for Monroe Street. Monroe is south of the river, and that is where she'll be," said the gentleman. Then he was quickly on his way.

"Thought so," Frank said to himself.

Cole smiled and nodded at Alfred.

Cole found himself counting the rail spikes as they followed the two parallel steel rails. When he couldn't keep up, he'd just start over. It gave his mind the distraction it needed.

More tracks came into their path as they got closer to the station. Steel and cross ties and spikes and dirt washed under their hooves as they trotted into the hump yard. Black smoke filled the air and the metallic sounds of trains with intense whistles and engines chugging along filled their senses. Some makeshift wooden signs led the way. Frank slowed their approach as they got within sight of the half-brick half-wood office. Two men stood out front.

A tall man chomping a cigar and wearing an engineer's hat scowled as he stood next to his shorter assistant. His assistant wore a white shirt and sported a bow tie.

"Look at that," said the man in the bow tie. He couldn't take his eyes off Alfred. "That man is huge. He looks like a barn riding a pony."

The man smoking the cigar chuckled deeply and crossed his arms.

Frank leapt from his saddle and said, "Hello, gentlemen. I was hoping you could answer some questions for me."

Cole and Alfred followed close behind on foot.

Gruffly the cigar smoker said, "And why would I want to do that?"

Frank had his notebook and pencil in his hands. He said, "You the boss? The foreman?"

The man squinted and said, "The foreman?"

"Yeah, the man in charge, the boss."

With a patronizing grunt, the railroad man laughed.

Frank said, "Look, I don't know your title. I just need to know if you're the right person to talk to. That's all." His tone tensed. "And you know exactly what I'm talking about. I'm Frank Savage and—"

The gruff man interrupted. "And is that supposed to mean something to me?"

Frank looked at Cole and said, "Where have I heard that before?" He turned to the two guards of the train station and said out the corner of his mouth, "Cole, could you say something before I do something I might regret." He disguised his frown with a fake smile.

Cole stepped up. "Gentleman, I'm Texas Ranger Cole." He flashed his Ranger identification. "And—"

The cigar smoker interrupted again. "What the hell you doin' way up here?"

"What do you mean?"

"Shouldn't you be in Texas? You're way out of your jurisdiction, ain't ya?" the man quipped.

"You guys got any Illinois Rangers?" Cole paused for a response, then said, "Huh?"

"Nope."

"Didn't think so, and that's why we're here, you know, to clean up your mess. Now if you don't mind, I would appreciate some cooperation, okay?"

They all stood silent. Alfred, ready and waiting, remained close to his friends. He turned and lifted his red-handled axe from its sheath attached to Moonbeam's saddle. Moonbeam stomped her front hoof and snorted and shook her head. The man in the bow tie nudged his boss in the ribs with his elbow.

The cigar-smoking man said, "I reckon."

"Yeah, you reckon alright," Frank said. He shook his head and stepped forward. "You've got a train track that runs southbound between the towns of Deviltry and Angon. Did you have a train run through there," Frank looked at his notes and continued, "on Wednesday?"

"Which Wednesday?"

"What?" Frank said.

"Which Wednesday? The one on the third or the one on the tenth?" asked the man with the cigar. Spit stretched between his lips like string as he spoke.

"The tenth," answered Frank.

"Last Wednesday?"

"Yeah, yeah, last Wednesday. Did a train run through there anytime on that day? Last Wednesday."

With crossed arms and a bowed chest, the man said, "I reckon."

"Is there someone I can talk to that was on that train? Maybe the engineer or the conductor?"

The man chomped on his smoke and said, "I reckon."

Frank turned to Cole and shook his head and tossed up his hands. Cole shrugged his shoulders.

Frank said, "Do you have a log book I can look at that has dates and times and names?"

The man's mouth began to open when Frank said, "You reckon."

The man paused before saying, "I suppose."

"You suppose. Suppose you get me that book because it's obvious you're not going to be much help in catching the murderers who killed a whole family. The killers of children."

The man's expression rounded out and he dropped his arms. He said, "My apologies." He turned into the house and came out quickly with the logbook.

Frank looked at Cole and turned to Alfred who was replacing his axe in its sheath.

The man explained, "There are two men responsible for the train that sign for it. But one doesn't speak much English. He's a German and still learning. He's off today, so you need to talk to . . ." He looked at the book and said, "Mister Crowley."

Frank moved quickly, leaping into his saddle. "Where can we find this Mister Crowley?"

The trains flew by in a blur as Frank pushed his Appaloosa forward through the maze. He kept his eyes forward before glancing quickly over to the man he followed. Mister Crowley moved ahead and to Frank's right.

A scrawny Crowley had seen his problems approaching before they caught sight of him. He took off on foot. And he knew the hump yard well.

Frank would have to stay close if he was going to catch him.

"Cole," yelled Frank, "you and Alfred swing around from the other end." He motioned with his hand.

Cole and Alfred Kincaid broke off the chase and darted between two locomotives, one of which was moving.

"Hey," hollered a train engineer as the two scooted by. "Get yer dang horses outta here before you all get killed."

Black-smoking metal chugged quickly by as Frank dodged the heavy locomotives. He attempted to keep his pace quick. The spry Mister Crowley was moving sideways perpendicular to the tracks. He rolled under one slow-moving train only to leap on top of another and exit out the other side.

From train to train he moved. As quickly as he jumped onto one, he was off the opposite side, running as he landed.

Frank reacted swiftly and took a sharp right turn. He barely missed colliding with a parked caboose. He found himself riding head-on toward a train that was chugging along right at him. His horse turned acutely out of the way and saved his life. On a full sprint they moved into a mass of tracks and cars without much room to maneuver to say the least.

Frank said out loud, “I didn’t plan this out too well.”

Frank was about boxed in and running out of options. He abruptly reined to a halt. With hooves sliding on gravel Frank was propelled right out of his saddle. He took no more than two steps before he realized that he was being followed.

“Whoa, boy,” Frank said as he turned back around. He motioned his palms down to the ground. “You stay here.”

The confused Appaloosa snorted his disapproval and stomped his hoof, emphatically stating that he was going too. He nudged forward as Frank was stepping backwards a step at a time.

“Now, you’re going to have to learn to trust me. Stay here. I don’t want you to get hurt,” Frank spoke as he continued to walk backwards. In the corner of his eye he saw Cole and Alfred—they were on foot as well and about six tracks over from where he anxiously stood. Moonbeam was following Alfred, unbeknownst to him.

Frank smiled at his Appaloosa. “You’re exactly like your mother.” He turned and ran. “She would kick me all the way to Kansas if she knew I left you alone.”

Cole ran briskly over the tracks with Alfred not far behind and Moonbeam in close pursuit.

“Halt, halt, I said,” Cole said. He tried to catch some air. “Tell me again, why did I choose a profession that involved running?”

The noises of metal clanging and steam hissing and wind whistling sounded off as they entered deeper into the train station’s busy yard. Alfred slowly fell behind. Cole pushed his sliding glasses back up to his eyes. With each step they drifted down the ledge of his sweaty nose.

“Halt, gawldangit. Oh crappie—” Cole trailed off as he cut across a track and noticed at the last second that a train was bearing down on him. He dove clear of its nose.

Kincaid's raspy voice shouted out, "Whoa." But he wasn't yelling at Cole. Alfred's warning was directed at Moonbeam who was in chase and not watching where she was going.

The train's engineer hit the brakes and pulled the whistle. The screech was painfully loud as the locomotive slid on its rails. Alfred yanked Moonbeam's reins to the side just in the nick of time.

Cole lay face down and tried to focus as he looked for his target. He caught a glimpse of a boot boarding a moving passenger car.

"Man, that guy's wily," Cole said. He slipped his glasses back into position with a forefinger. "Agile little shit," he grunted as he got to his feet. "I lost him."

An engine rolled by, and then the fuel car and a passenger car followed it. As the car passed, Cole watched through the windows. The man they were chasing was running toward the back of the train. "Damn." As the next car whipped by, Cole noticed Frank inside running in the opposite direction. There was going to be a head-on collision.

Cole whispered, "Where in the hell did he come from?"

Mister Crowley was about to be introduced to Frank Savage, and he didn't know it, yet. He propelled himself out the back of the car just as Frank flew out the front of his. With a whack, Mister Crowley's head shattered the glass on the door. Frank grabbed Crowley by the straps of his overalls and flung their two bodies off the train. Crowley landed flat on his back with Frank landing on top of him. Crowley wheezed as he hit and blacked out. Cole ran up with Alfred close behind.

Frank slowly stood holding his lower back with one hand and his head with the other. "I've got a headache." He swayed.

"You are way rough on our leads. You do know that, don't you?" Cole said.

"He'll live," mumbled Frank. He dusted off his pants with his hat.

"No thanks to you," Cole said. "Well?"

"Cole, help me get him into this here drinking car." Frank blinked hard as he rubbed his head. "The one that isn't moving, I think." He turned to Alfred. "Kincaid, go and collect our horses, if you will."

Alfred glowered, shrugged and with a terse turn moved off.

"It's not like that," Frank said.

Alfred turned to face him.

Frank said, "You did a good job in Deviltry. It's just *that*." He pointed at Alfred's chest. "That stuff, that anger you got holed up inside. We're gonna need that and I don't want to use it here. Not now, it's not the time." Frank looked sincere. "Not today. The time will come. It always does."

CHAPTER 6

With a cold slap of water to the face, Mister Crowley rushed to consciousness. His hands came up to his head as he awoke leaning back in a tall chair.

"What the hell?" he said. He shook off his induced slumber as he wiped the water from his eyes.

It was a corner mahogany bar in the back of the passenger cabin. Crowley sat behind it. He pushed himself straight in his chair. His eyes bugged out as he opened them.

Frank sat with Cole standing behind him. Cole pushed up his glasses.

Frank whispered over his shoulder, "Remind me to get you some new glasses."

Frank lit a cigarette. He smoked as Crowley collected himself.

The trains' passenger cabin was first class. Dark blue velvet curtains blended into the navy blue wallpaper and into the light blue davenport and matching chairs. A glass decanter full of brown liquor sat on top of the bar.

"There was no need for that," Crowley squawked.

"No need for what?" asked Frank. "The water in the face or me knocking you on your bony ass?"

"Both," Crowley blurted with water still dribbling from his lips.

"Why, that was just an artifice to initiate some conversation."

Crowley frowned.

Frank poured a drink of whiskey and then two more. He gave one to Cole over his shoulder and set one on a small round table in front of him. Frank looked stern. The look on his face seemed to say I am going to kill you if you don't do as I say.

Frank tossed off his drink. For a moment it appeared that he was going to grin, maybe even smile. But at the very last moment he changed his mind.

"We'll start off with something easy, like, what is your name?"

Cole sipped his whiskey and rested his hand on his gun.

"None of your damn business."

It was quiet. Then there was the sound of Cole snapping back the hammer of his pistol.

"It's Mister Crowley," he blurted.

Frank said, "Your full name." He poured another drink. The other glass still rested untouched on the table.

"Mister Crowley." The note of his words and aspect of his face didn't understand how it could be different.

"There are two ways to get information," Frank said.

Cole lifted his eyes and dropped them. It was difficult to see his expression through his beard but his eyes showed a scheming grin through his thick lenses.

With wet floppy hair and big bug eyes and lips that barely moved when he spoke, Crowley said, "What do you want?"

"We know that your train made an unscheduled stop on your route earlier this week. Why? And who did you stop for?"

"Are you a copper?" Crowley swallowed hard.

"Something like that."

"Go home, copper. You'll live longer. You're in way over your head on this one."

"I don't mind being in over my head. It's a place I'm comfortable with. How'd you like to be buried up to yours?"

"I've heard of worse things."

"You had better be sure of that."

"You dumb lug," said Crowley. He spoke with an arrogance that he could only be born with.

Cole blurted though gritted teeth, "Let me paste him. Right here on this train. Right where he sits. This is rubbish. If he was in on it, he deserves to die anyway."

Frank stood and carried the whiskey to Crowley. He set the shot of hard liquor on the bar and maneuvered back a step.

Crowley gawked at the beverage that he so desired.

"Go ahead," Frank said.

In a slow move, Crowley tipped back the drink. Frank followed up quickly with a new pour. As Crowley downed the second, Frank lifted his pistol. Crowley spit up the whiskey and coughed. He watched from the corners of his eyes as he faked finishing the beverage. His eyes watered from the booze leaking into his sinuses. He cleared the moisture from his chin with the sleeve of his shirt. He held tight to a cough that burst its way out of his throat anyway.

"Careful," added Frank.

The chamber of Frank's gun spun and snapped closed in his competent hands. It was part of the show. After snapping it shut, Frank lightly placed the pistol on the bar within reach of their prisoner's right hand. Crowley kept his gaze on the weapon that called to him. That is, until he saw Cole square up on him with a hand hanging loose by his own six-shooter. Cole pushed his glasses up with his free hand.

Frank interrupted the silence. He was losing patience. "Yep, there are worse things than dying." He stood quiet. "You a gunfighter, Mister Crowley?"

Crowley didn't say a word. Sweat oozing out of every pore of his body.

Frank continued, "This gentleman here, is." He pointed at his partner. "And he's good at what he does. He probably could kill you with one shot. You wouldn't even feel the back of your head hit the wall behind you." Frank stopped as if he had had an epiphany.

The only sound came from the nearby trains. Cole held steady.

"Yeah." Frank picked up his gun and placed it back in his holster. He grinned. "Okay, Mister Crowley, you win."

Cole and Crowley both said, "What?"

"You can go," Frank said.

Crowley's hands shook and he said, "Just like that?"

"Yeah," Frank said. He stepped away from the bar and said, "Just like that."

Crowley sat. Cole stood. Frank grinned.

"You're gonna shoot me in the back ain't ya?" said Crowley.

Frank, with his back to Crowley, said, "No, Mister Crowley, we won't. You're a shyster. You always have been and always will be. And everyone knows it." He turned to his captive and with a circular gesture of his hand he said, "Once we let it known on the street that you spilled the beans on your little, *event* outside Deviltry, I imagine someone *will* shoot you in the back. Or, like you said, do something to you that is much worse than death."

Crowley's eyes vibrated in his head as his brain worked too fast.

Frank said, "Don't hurt yourself."

Crowley looked at the bar top with eyes that floated in liquid fear. His nerves woke up. "Okay, okay, what? Okay, yeah, okay."

Frank smiled at Cole as he poured another drink.

Crowley said, "It was like this, see, I, I'm just a man. They gave me money, lots of it, no questions. That's all. I was to stop the train at a marking in the middle of bloody nowhere, man. It was a mark outside Deviltry, and I was to have a door open in the back. The way back, you know, close to the caboose. It was a place to ride, an empty car to ride in. They wanted a lift without having to get on the train in a town. That's all, see, that's it, understand?"

"No guff, who?" asked Frank.

Mister Crowley anxiously bit his lip. As he looked at his drink on the bar he said, "Some guy named Uncle." Then loudly, "Some guy named Uncle, that's all I know, I swear to God. That's all I know. Some bastard named Uncle." His face was flustered but his tone told the truth.

"Who got on the train? Just this Uncle?"

"Two, two men. One was Uncle, I think, and some other man."

"What'd they look like?"

"Well," Crowley said as his voice cracked. "The man, the other man, I couldn't see, I never spoke to him. He was behind a tree by the tracks, behind, too far back. I couldn't see him."

"What about Uncle? Describe him."

"He—" Crowley stopped as he tried to remember. "His hat was pulled wide. I believe it was cut to fit his head. Like his head was swollen or something . . . like, it was as if his hat was cut to fit his fat head. His hat was maybe too small. Yeah, he bought a hat that was way too small. And, his, the side of his head had bandages with blood kinda, coming through it by his ear." Crowley glanced up and tapped his ear. "See?"

Frank knew the man was telling the truth. He felt sick to his core. Guilt didn't hit all men, and those who felt the useless emotion didn't carry it with them. Frank did, and would. Just like Alfred would. But Frank should be used to it by now. This guilt would lie on top of all the other shame and remorse he had collected through the years. Even though there was no more room for it. But, his tactics, they worked. They always did.

"Anything else?" asked Cole.

"No, sir," Crowley mumbled with his head hung to his chest. "You ain't gonna spread around what I told you, right?"

Frank mumbled, "You have our word." But it wouldn't matter.

Mister Crowley was scared. Not of Cole or Frank, his fear existed somewhere else—as it should.

The two detectives stepped from the car. Cole was walking out backwards with his eyes on Crowley.

Heavy deep-blooming clouds released their weight. The rain splattered with a wave moving across the ground. Somber and slow, the two men walked a few feet to where Alfred patiently held their horses.

Simultaneously the hunters moved to their respective saddles and opened up their bedrolls that were tied to the backs of the saddles. All at once, their long dark gray slicker coats unfurled. Casually they put them on. The coats hung off their broad shoulders down to below the knees.

Frank buttoned up his coat without saying a word. He paused and sighed and mounted his Appaloosa. They trotted through the mud unhurriedly as the sky cracked loudly from above.

Side by side they worked their way through the train yard. Behind them was Crowley as he emerged from the passenger car. He stumbled to the ground and screamed at his muddy hands and shook his fist in the air. Frank and his partners couldn't hear his cry. The storm was speaking louder.

Crowley lowered his head and clumsily stood up and stepped away from the train with his face in his filthy hands. Slow and unsteady, he walked.

The drops plummeted onto the brims of their hats. On its trek downward the rain had collected the dark smoke that was hanging above the industrial city staining the water that would crudely darken their clothes.

Frank was fixated on the pommel of his saddle. He counted on Cole and Alfred to watch the road. Another explosion from the sky burst into the moody and grim scene with a flash that lit the wicked and desolate street.

The brick and iron buildings came into Frank's peripheral vision. The black iron and dark gray buildings flowed and moved as the water gushed over them and down their walls and into the street. A shallow stream washed over the horses' hooves.

The Chicago alleys and thoroughfares were bare. There wasn't a soul in sight. That is, until they reached a long street that sprouted up and away and into a building. It was a multistory building with tall narrow windows and a foyer entrance. A sign read Palmer House Hotel.

As they approached, they came upon a figure with an umbrella standing on the corner in the middle of the downpour. They trotted closer to the man. He didn't move. Frank could see that on his jacket was a tag with a name and it also read the hotel's name in bold letters across the top.

Frank dismounted and slipped the man a silver dollar. The three men walked into the hotel leaving their three soaked and tired horses. Moonbeam was too exhausted to complain.

Dripping wet, they stepped into the elaborately decorated lobby of the hotel. Water rolled off the back of Frank's hat as he looked up to the high ceiling. The timbered room exposed crystal light fixtures that lined the walls and chandeliers that hung down from a thick wood beam that crossed the vaulted ceiling. Red carpet showed a path to the polished check-in desk. They followed the trail. They passed by furniture cushioned with red velvet that hollered out to the three cowboys to take a seat. They approached the desk. Water dripped off their coats only to be quickly soaked up by the thick carpet.

A young man smiled at them. Frank tilted his hat to the top of his head and waited.

"Yes, sir, I'm Jonathan," said the affable desk clerk. "Can I help you?"

Frank said, "Three rooms, please."

The tired travelers showed some wear. And the day wasn't over—not even close.

A red light saturated the outdoor corridor. The glow bounced off the red brick and off the wet street. Dirty grimy water coated the ground in splotchy shallow pools. Frank Savage and Alfred Kincaid stood at the end of a narrow alley. They had decided earlier to venture out and allow Cole to monitor the Palmer House Hotel.

Frank didn't take but two steps before his boots entered a basin of water that wet the bottoms of his pants and slicker.

Frank led the way toward his contacts. Contacts he was not sure he could trust, but contacts nonetheless.

Alfred's axe was a part of him now, and it was hidden under his long rain-soaked coat. He put his hand on it to make sure it was secure.

The two cowboys stopped at a door that had a red lantern hanging above the frame and a sign that said Sam's.

Alfred looked up the tall brick building at a middle-aged woman smoking on the balcony. She smiled and flashed her wares from under her dress. His droopy eyes didn't wince.

Frank lifted his hat and shook off the rain. He pulled the handle on the door and it easily swung open.

Inside the bar the red glow continued.

Alfred asked, "This is it?"

"Yep."

"I'll hang close."

"Okay."

The floor creaked as Alfred stepped to a corner and took a seat in a chair in front of a small round table. He immediately began to roll a cigarette and sparked a match to life off his boot.

Frank casually walked to the bar and took a seat on a stool. He conceded a small smile.

Frank spoke first. "Hey there, Handsome Sam."

"Hi, Frank."

The two moved slowly to shake hands.

"Scotch?"

"Nope."

Sam was a roughly handsome man with deep cracks of work and living that somehow had only added more charm to his face. He could still date women much younger than himself.

"Bourbon."

"Okay," said Sam.

"It's American made."

"Sounds like you," Sam said. He grinned.

Sam poured Frank a glass of bourbon and a side of water and leaned across the bar.

"I'm guessing that Detective Vance Stranger still frequents this glam-dive," Frank said.

"Yep."

"Running late is he?"

"Yep." Sam paused. His eyes were soft and kind. "We missed you."

"Me, too, Sam, me too." He took a sip of his bourbon and followed it with a swallow of water.

"We think about you often in this place."

"Thanks. I think of this place often."

Frank pulled at his tobacco bag, rolled a fresh cigarette, made a once-over of the hazy bar, and touched a flame to his smoke.

"Who's your friend?" asked Sam.

"Oh, you noticed him?"

"How could I not? He almost brought the door frame in with him."

"He's broad alright."

"I bet he stepped sideways down that narrow alley just to get here."

Frank lured some smoke into his lungs. With smoke slipping out of his mouth, he said, "You know I have some questions."

The door sounded as someone entered the bar. A short kinky-haired brunette stumbled in alone.

"Well, I'll be," she blurted. She staggered.

Frank didn't move fast with his response. "Hello, Roxy." Frank turned to Sam and whispered, "You take the good with the bad."

"She's a nut of the first water," said Sam.

Frank nodded.

"Where in the—" said Roxy. She stopped, grinned, dragged on a cigarette, tossed it to the floor, and lit another.

Roxy Desire had been cute once, but she was past her prime. She had perky breasts and a rugged face. One that looked walked on. Not with a boot, but as a boot.

"Long time no damn see, Frankie." She worked hard on her cigarette as the door slammed shut behind her.

"Yep, been long, Roxy." Frank whispered, "Not long enough, I reckon."

"Aren't you supposed to stand for a lady when she walks in the room?"

Frank said, "Well, show me a lady—"

"Yeah, yeah, and you'll stand. That's not funny anymore."

Sam interjected, "Roxy?"

Roxy said, "Whiskey, same old, same old."

"Yeah, I reckon, nothing changes around here, does it, Roxy?" Frank said.

"One thing does. You ain't bedding me down anymore."

Frank looked down at his drink. "Well, we all have to spend a night in the sewer at least once."

Alfred smoked, unaffected.

She blurted, "Ha."

"Sam, when you reckon Detective Stranger will be in?" asked Frank.

Sam splashed a shot of whiskey in a glass and slid it down the bar to Roxy. She scooped it up and downed it in a flash like a man. She slid the glass back to Sam, and said, “How ’bout a beverage a lady can suck on for a while, huh?”

Sam smirked, put away the glass, and said, “Yeah, no problem, Roxy. Not a problem, Sweetie.”

He grasped a tall highball glass. He dropped in two cubes of ice and filled it within an inch of the top and then tossed a spot of water into it. He slid the glass down the bar as effortlessly as before.

Roxy swooped up the glass and said, “Where you been, Frankie?”

“I’ve been around.”

“Not around here you haven’t.” She drank and swallowed with a loud gulp. “Yeah, that’s about right, Sammie, thanks.” She stumbled and swayed as she walked closer to Frank.

Frank’s foot vibrated nervously on his bar stool.

“What’s the matter, Frankie?” asked Roxy.

“What do you want from me?”

Roxy pulled on her stocking. “I want you to show me what you used to show me. You know.”

Frank’s foot stopped shaking. “You know damn good and well I’m not showing you shit,” barked Frank.

Roxy couldn’t help herself. “I bet you’ll show Becca-fucking-Devlin a thing or two.” She smiled and looked down at Frank’s waist. “Nice rod. Care if I touch it? Or are you afraid it might . . . go off?”

Frank scoffed. Roxy pitched a drink. Sam wiped the bar. Alfred kept breathing on his cigarette.

Roxy said, “Come on, Frankie, we had some good times. Didn’t we?” She moved closer along the bar.

“I don’t care to go down those rapids again.”

“Oh my God, you’ve got nothing to complain about.”

“I’m done with you. I no longer desire you, Roxy Desire.”

Roxy drew on her beverage and smiled with a mocking air.

“You’re such a bitch,” Frank said. He chuckled as he spoke.

Sarcastically she shot back. “Oh, that hurts.”

“Roxy, fuck right off.”

Roxy walked closer to Frank. “You know and I know you want to do me, right here and right now.”

Frank slowed down and relaxed his face. He stood and turned. His mood had shifted. They surveyed each other a moment as Frank softly stroked her arm. Abruptly he grabbed her arms and turned her to the bar.

"Look at that, Miss Desire," Frank blurted, crazy eyed.

The mirror shot back a reflection of Roxy, exposing deep cracks from years of smoking and dark circles from any number of late nights. The image screamed a complete lack of self-respect.

Frank said, "Would you sleep with that?" He pushed her away with force and sat back down.

Roxy stammered. She threw her drink down. The glass shattered and spread along the wooden floor. She said, "You always did know how to turn a girl on. But you already knew that."

Frank shook his head.

Roxy allowed a disgusting grin and walked away.

Sam charged another drink for Frank and said, "Vance is here same time every—"

The door sharply swung open and a man in a gray fedora and matching trench coat stepped into the bar.

"Vance," Sam said. "No tables tonight. Take a seat at the bar."

Detective Vance Stranger tipped his hat to the back of his head and eyed Frank. A slight grin slid onto his stubble-covered jaw. He had a strong tan mug with a wide chin and a dimple in the middle.

Detective Stranger walked in with a confident force. He was followed in by another man who was similarly dressed but taller and thinner.

Vance sat next to Frank.

"How goes it, friend?" Frank said.

Vance said, "Been too long, way too long."

The two old friends shook hands. Vance whispered, "Do *not* trust my partner." Then, so everyone could hear him, he said, "This is my partner, Detective Fulsome."

Frank shook Detective Fulsome's hand. The detective's grip was limp and wasted in the effort.

Frank whispered, "I see what you mean."

Two more drinks were poured and set carefully on the bar as the men spoke.

"Have you seen Becca yet?" asked Stranger.

"That's not why I'm here." Frank's posture was rigid.

"Yeah, but—"

"I said that is not why I'm here." Frank spoke between sips.

"You sure?"

Frank turned in his seat to face the detective.

"You might . . . wait," Vance said. He stopped short. He analyzed Frank's expression. His head angled funny. "Frank, you talk to her when you left? Mail? Anything?"

Frank turned and pulled his drink close. It was about empty. He said, "Another, pour it in thick."

Sam obliged.

Vance continued, "Frank, I'm serious."

"No, nothing."

"I think you two need to talk."

Frank rotated towards the detective. "Out with it."

Vance and Sam locked eyes, then Vance said, "Becca, she should have told you."

Frank stared hard. He gritted his teeth.

Vance said, "Becca, she was . . . she lost a baby, Frank."

Frank blinked twice and his head fell back. "A baby?"

"Yes, she—when you left she was pregnant with a baby and lost it. After carrying for about five months. I think but I'm not sure. I hate to be the one to tell you but you should be taking care of a four-year-old little girl right now."

Frank let his drink tip and slip from his fingers. The glass bounced off its rim on the bar top. The liquid spread out onto the bar. His foot dropped from the rung of his stool. He sat sullen for a moment.

"I, I thought about writing, but—" stammered Frank.

"Frank," Vance added. "I'm sorry."

Alfred put his cigarette out. He was too far to hear but he stood up straight and quickly sat back down. He lowered his head.

Frank sat for a moment and with grit he said, "That's not why I'm here." He choked down the emotion of what he had just been told.

"Oh?"

"I'm on the trail of a group of men who slaughtered an entire family. The trail has led me here."

Vance took a sip of his drink.

"They used a train to get back to Chicago and the only clue I can share with you is that the Palmer House Hotel is some kinda meeting place for whoever did this."

Detective Fulsome was eavesdropping on the conversation and butted in. "Isn't Chicago out of your jurisdiction? You should report this to—"

Vance interrupted. "Everywhere is Frank's jurisdiction. Now sit back before he knocks your jaw so it hangs at a crazy angle."

Fulsome went to speak but didn't. He scowled and scooped up his hat and stormed out the door, slamming it behind him.

Vance ignored the tantrum and said, "I have a feeling there is one man who can help you. Dr. Lore Ethos is rumored to have his pulse on the city, and not in a good way."

"What makes you think he can help?"

"Dr. Ethos used to work for the police station as a doctor of psychology. He was fired due to connections with a mob out of some Eastern European country."

Frank listened.

"We've seen some pretty messed up shit—like the killing of families, even torture. It seemed to start about the time these guys got to town. It's a revenge sickness and they've all come down with it. And it's bloody contagious."

Frank straightened his glass and set it on the bar and said, "Thanks."

"Not that I need to tell you this, but watch yourself with this guy. Things don't go well and he'll go after the people closest to you."

"Thanks for the warning."

Frank tapped his fingers on the bar top.

Sam asked, "Another for the road?"

Frank nodded. "I'm not leaving. I'm just getting started."

CHAPTER 7

Cole stepped one foot into the hallway. He moved casually. He was naked except for a towel wrapped around his waist. He carried his toiletries in his hand. Before leaving he blew out the light. He walked down the long corridor from the washroom toward his room. He had showered and shaved. He'd even patted powder under his arms. He exited the washroom without looking.

The hall was lit by one gaslight, then, poof. It was pitch black.

Cole said, "Who's there?"

There was a crack from above followed by a creak from down the hall.

Cole moved slowly. He felt the wallpaper as he walked with his hand sliding along the wall. It was quiet as he shuffled his feet over the floor. His eyes strained to view the space around him. There was nothing. "Is anyone there?"

There was no answer as he reluctantly pressed forward. His toes looked for something as he walked.

"Hello?" Cole asked into the darkness.

He stepped again with his toiletries in hand. His heart skipped a beat.

"Frank?" He paused a moment and stood. "Alfred?"

Nothing spoke back.

"Crappie," Cole said, but he knew.

A blade slipped up against his skin.

"Shit."

He felt a pang in his back. His lower spine felt a snip of some kind. He couldn't guess what was happening to him. It was too sick to believe.

Cole fell to the shag carpet and he moaned. A hand had kept him from smacking hard as he settled.

Cole grunted, "What?"

"Relax," said the voice. It was in a whisper floating in a hot breath.

"No," Cole said. "Please."

Cole's muscles relaxed, and he released his weight slowly. It was black except for a gloom-laden shine that polished the curtains draping the far window at the end of the hall. He blinked hard as he tried to focus.

"No, stop it," Cole pleaded.

"Yes. Just relax," said the voice.

Cole's muscles stopped working. He released his grip on the toiletry bag and then squeezed his hand into a loose fist. His nerves fought against his orders.

"Yes," said the voice.

Cole cringed as the warm wet fumes nuzzled the back of his neck. He strained to see what was in front of his face. Nothing came to view. "No," he said again. He didn't dare struggle. The blade was in him, and it was close, too close. It was touching the bony part of his lower spine. He could feel the vibration of the blade scraping against the rough surface of the bone. The wave of the ripples went through his skull. It made his eyelids quiver.

"Yes," said the voice. "I don't think you'll feel a thing, not that I know from experience. Maybe if you lie still, it will go away. But I doubt it."

Cole could not help but relinquish himself to his captor; he lay still as panic hijacked his mind. His face rested on the carpet. Spit collected at the corner of his mouth. He couldn't feel the blade itself anymore.

The keen point silently ascended into a dull spasm. A tingle spread out over his skin.

"Listen. My blade?"

"Crap," Cole said.

"Yeah, it's in your backbone. Can you feel it?"

Cole blinked hard, breathed in heavy, then said, "Screw you."

"I thought as much. This is the reckoning, and it's all by happenstance. It's nothing personal. Just need to stop things from going any further. Can't let you get too close," said the coarse whisper.

Cole could feel a click in the small of his back as if something had been cut.

"I did what I did, why? Cause I like it. It's sort of a hobby. Like you here now. If it wasn't you it would be someone else. Maybe someone I know, even."

Cole breathed.

"By the way, did I fail to mention? The blade is touching your spine. Can you feel it? I know you can. I can feel your goose flesh."

Cole whimpered.

"With one move it'll all be over. You see, the blade is touching the nerve here. This is it. All I got to do is move or even twitch. Get it? I move, and you never walk, ever again. That is, if you don't die. Either way, you will never walk again." The voice continued with a perverse satisfaction. "Mmm."

Cole spit out, "You don't scare me."

"Oh?"

There was a loud whack and then an expulsion of air. Cole was free of his perpetrator, but he couldn't move.

"Son of a—" the voice cracked with a high-pitched huff.

A smack reverberated down the hallway as a large hand slapped the voice up against the wall. Cole felt relief except for the knife in his back.

"Who—" said the voice.

The voice was abruptly quieted and a loud bang echoed as a body slammed into the wall.

"Who the hell are you?" said the voice.

Then it was silent.

Cole lay still.

A large hand grabbed the perpetrator and a loud boom resounded through the hallway.

"What—" squeaked the voice.

Cole snapped his head up and noticed a shadow of a man toss another up against the wall. The two fought. But only one was in control.

The one in control was short and strong. A blade appeared out of nowhere. The stab was blocked and the strong one tossed out the other who flew out of the hallway window with a crash into the alley below. Then it was quiet.

Cole lay silent as he felt his back with his hand. There was a knife sticking out of his lower body. His legs tingled.

"Don't move."

A match was struck to life and a face came into view.

"Who are you?" asked Cole. Looking up with his eyes he recognized the face.

"It's Gil. It's me, Gil."

Cole sighed and said, "Gil?" Then he passed out.

Gil knelt down and rested his large hand on Cole's head.

Gilbert said, "I've had to trot through my own filth to get to where

I am. Just a rat moving from one sewer to another. This tears it. This is when I take all the bad I've done and use it for what I'm supposed to."

It was early. A thin slice of light cast itself across the bed. Charlotte's eyes snapped open. She stared at the ceiling a moment.

"Henry?"

She lay quiet, just for a moment, then said, "Henry, are you up already? What time is it?"

She rolled to her side and focused her sleepy eyes until she could see the beam of light that came in through the window. Her feathery silver hair tickled the wrinkled corners of her eyes.

Slowly she swung her fragile feet over the edge of the bed. She gripped the floor with her toes, an activity she had done every morning for the last eighty years. Ever since she was a young girl she had done the same routine. She started the exercise a year before her family moved to America from England.

She looked at her toes while slowly positioning herself to stand. She moved carefully as she balanced her weight on her tender puffy soles.

Gradually, Mrs. Charlotte Sturgus slipped on a light blue robe over her cotton and lace nightgown. Walking barefoot, with slippers by the bed, she floated to the door and stepped into the hallway.

A cold breeze flowed through her hair. She shivered.

"Henry, it's cold in here."

There was no answer. Charlotte stood in her bedroom doorway. Behind her was a bed. Half was messed up. The other half was still tidy, never slept in, except for the top quilt that had been pulled over in the middle of the cold night.

Mrs. Sturgus followed the cool air to the washroom. At the far end of the washroom was a window. The window was half open. The opening formed a triangle where one edge fell to shut but the other end was stuck in its frame.

She attempted to lift the window in order to straighten it. Her effort was strong, but her weak arms couldn't budge the window that was stubbornly wedged in its frame.

"Oh, Henry." She rolled her eyes.

She wheeled around and reentered the hallway.

"Grandma?" a voice said.

Mrs. Sturgus turned to the voice that called her.

She said, "Stage, have you seen your grandpa?"

Stage was nineteen years old with light hair and round blue eyes and a long nose. He sat on the edge of his bed with his back to his grandma and the doorway she stood in.

Stage paused in the middle of a full Windsor knot in his brand new black tie. Resting his hands on his knees he sighed and said, "No, Grandma, I haven't seen Grandpa." He rubbed his red eyes.

Charlotte didn't say anything.

"Grandma?"

Charlotte perked up and said, "Yes?"

"Nothing."

"Your grandpa left the window open in the washroom."

Stage was quiet. He finished his knot and turned his body to meet her gaze.

Charlotte said, "Can you close it, please?"

"Yes, I can."

She turned around. "Thank you, dear. Now, where is Henry?"

Mrs. Sturgus walked across the house to the living room. The room was square with a modest fireplace and a broad walnut mantle cluttered with pictures. Photos big and small lined the wooden shelf.

Mrs. Sturgus, with small steps, worked her way to the mantle.

"Henry, you left the window open in the washroom. You know I'm not strong enough to close it myself."

She stared at the mantle and then said, "Would you like some coffee?"

Charlotte nodded and kissed her husband, leaving a lip smudge of moisture on the glass. She went to the kitchen and moved some pots and pans around. She stood in the middle of the room with a befuddled turn of the head as she tried to remember what she was looking for.

The creaking of floorboards announced that her grandson was moving about. She stepped back into the living room.

"Henry, what was it that you wanted me to make?"

Surprised, she stepped back and said, "Gretchen, what are you doing here? I didn't know you were coming over, otherwise I would have made some cookies for you. Hello, Jerry, you are getting so big." Charlotte smiled from ear to ear. "But I love these kinds of surprises."

A picture of her sister Gretchen, and Gretchen's grandson Jerry, stared back.

Stage walked up slowly and put his arm around his grandmother and said quietly, "Grandma, Gretchen isn't here, that's her picture. That's a picture of my Great-aunt Gretchen and my cousin Jerry. Remember that fourth of July?"

Charlotte looked up and frowned. "Stage, you're embarrassing me in front of the family."

Stage looked down. "I'm sorry, Grandma."

Charlotte said to the picture, "Now, Jerry, would you like some banana bread? I think I have some left over from the other night."

Stage said, "I have to get to work now. Mrs. Travis will be over in a little while to check up on you."

Charlotte looked at Stage with addled eyes. She rested her trembling fingers on her lower lip as she attempted to arrange her thoughts.

Stage said, "You know Mrs. Travis, you play cards with her. She'll be over in no time at all. She'll be here to keep you company. I have to get to work at the hardware store now."

Charlotte's eyes lifted with relief as she remembered her neighbor that she plays cards with. Played cards with.

"Yes, yes, that's fine. Henry and I will get the house cleaned up so we can play cards. Is Tony coming over too, I hope? It's hard to play with only three people. It's much more fun with four, you know."

Stage hugged his grandma and said, "Yes, maybe. You just stay inside until she gets here. You wouldn't want her to come over to an empty house and not be able to find you."

"Oh, you worry too much." She stopped, confused again. "Did you say work? Don't you have school today?"

Stage held her tighter. "Yes, that's what I meant. Afterwards, I'll go to work."

Charlotte hugged Stage with feeble arms and patted his back.

"I normally would stay until she got here but I'm gonna be late. Bye now. I love you."

"I love you too, Sweetheart. You be good and listen to your teachers."

"Okay, I will."

Stage threw on a long coat and a similarly colored gray newsboy hat and walked out the front door.

Charlotte turned toward the picture of her late husband.

She said, "Henry, Mrs. Travis is coming over to play cards."

Henry said, "Yes, I heard. Maybe you could get some coffee and cookies together, that is, so we can be hospitable."

"Yes, I will."

Charlotte held her hands clasped in front of her. Her head bobbed up and down in small nods.

"We did good with Stage. Didn't we?

"Yes, dear. We did good."

Charlotte smiled as her head slowly wobbled in little circles. It was quiet and then she said, "I wish his folks could be here. They'd be so very proud."

Henry said, "Hey, what's in the trunk?"

Charlotte thought a moment as she eyed a large black trunk that rested against the wall. It had a lamp on the top with a short stack of books.

"Well, I'm not real sure," she said. Her mind tried to assemble the pieces, but she couldn't recall what was in the box.

Henry's voice said, "Open it up and take a look."

Charlotte didn't move for a moment but then she said, "Okay."

She was able to move the books easily, but the lamp was slow. She almost tipped herself over, not because of the weight, but because the lamp was cumbersome to move.

Henry laughed a terse laugh.

"That's not very nice, Henry," said Charlotte. "That hurts my feelings when people laugh at me." Charlotte's eyes shined with sincerity as she looked at her husband's picture.

"I'm sorry. Now open it already."

Charlotte lifted the latches and pulled open the lid.

"Oh, it's the blanket I made for Stage, for when he goes off to college."

"Take it out. Let's take a look." Henry's voice was coarser and louder now.

Charlotte's fingers trembled as she lifted the quilt from the box.

"It sure is pretty, ain't it little brother?" the coarse voice said.

"This isn't fun anymore, Goth. Let's go," said another voice.

Charlotte, puzzled, said, "Who was that, Henry?"

The voice ordered, "Get in the box."

It was quiet as Charlotte looked at the curtains.

"Get into the box, old woman."

Charlotte tried to focus on the long navy blue curtains. Slowly the curtain stepped into the living room. She put her hand over her mouth. A sullen but smirking Goth Furse emerged from the dark spot.

"Who are you? Henry, Henry?"

Henry was quiet.

Goth put his finger to his mouth. "Shh."

Goth's brother stayed behind, hidden by the curtain with one eye looking out.

Rocco said, "Goth, let's go. You told me we were just gonna rob 'em."

Goth shifted toward his brother and grunted. He slipped the trigger guard off his gun as he rotated back to a startled and scared Charlotte. His face went red as his eyelids moved up and his demeanor turned sour.

Charlotte whimpered, "Henry, why won't you do something?" She tried to breathe in but the air got caught in the back of her mouth as her throat tightened.

Again, Henry's picture said nothing.

Goth's left hand, as always, was still tight in a fist and it hung at his side. He turned his head down to bite his aching tendons. He held his fist in the grip of his teeth. His black eyes peered out from the center of his slightly shut lids.

Charlotte pleaded, "Help me, Henry." Her lip vibrated.

Goth said, "Oh, Charlotte, you know Henry is just as scared as you are if not more so. He ain't gonna lift one finger to help you. Seeing as how you're talking to a damn picture."

Goth spit out the side of his mouth. He slowly loosed his pistol and stepped towards Charlotte. Charlotte stepped back.

"Now. Get in the box."

Frank stood in front of a large brick building with Chicago Hospital painted across its awning. The rain had subsided and a brisk wind ruffled his slicker. He was talking to Alfred when Detective Stranger and his partner Fulsome walked up.

Frank noticed Detective Fulsome's scowl and the dandruff that covered his shoulders like a light coating of snow. His collar was popped up and his hat was pulled low over his forehead.

Vance asked, "How is he?"

Frank said, "He's gonna be fine. He's got some tingling in his legs, but he's moving them without too much pain. He should be able to walk out in a few days."

Vance nodded. "Don't worry about your friend. We'll keep an eye on him. I've called in some men trained as defensive guards. Nobody is getting in."

Gil stepped out of the front entrance of the hospital and took post next to Alfred.

Vance asked, "Did you get any sort of look at his face?"

Gil answered, "Nope, he had a mask on of some kind. I tried to remove it, but it stuck in place."

Vance asked, "And what were you doing there?"

Frank interrupted, "No."

Vance knew the tone and backed off.

"I may have something for you," said Vance.

"Yeah?" Frank said.

"I think you should check it out."

Fulsome glared at Gil and said, "And how do we know *he* didn't try to kill your friend?"

Gil stepped forward and Frank stuck out his arm to stop his motion.

Frank said, "You're an idiot for even thinking that, and a total and utter moron for allowing it out of your stinkhole."

Fulsome huffed and stalked away, shaking his head.

Frank said, "I know that was rough. There's just something about him I don't like."

Vance continued, ignoring the disruption as if it were expected. "Afterwards, you can hunt down Lore Ethos. I may have been wrong about him."

"Alright, what's the scoop?"

"First off, after the inspection of the hotel we found a dead body."

Frank said, "What?"

Vance pulled a pad of paper from the inside of his overcoat and he read aloud: "After a thorough search of the hotel in the a.m., a man was found dead in a storage room by the name of Crowley, first name Mister. Estimated time of death was around five a.m. The man was tortured. Burns and cuts and abrasions covered his legs, arms, and abdomen. Death due to heart seizure."

Frank frowned. "That was *after* we took Cole to the hospital."

"Does the name sound familiar?"

"Yeah," Frank said. "He helped us put two and two together. Eventually the numbers will add up. He attached our unknown killer with the Palmer House and to a guy by the name of Uncle."

Vance's eyes rounded as he blurted, "Did you say Uncle?"

"Yes."

"There's an Uncle Baldwin with the Irish mob."

"I'm listening."

"Check out the street market at Maxwell Street. Ask around there. He's a two-bit hood who hires out for odd jobs."

"What are we waiting for?" Alfred said. His voice was still rough, and rippled through the air as he spoke.

Vance said, "No, not yet. We got a pretty grisly murder of an elderly sick woman, and I want you to check it out."

Frank asked, "What makes you think it's related to our case?"

Vance tipped his hat to the back of his head and said, "Well, the woman was forced into a trunk, and the trunk was shot to pieces with her in it."

Alfred's face fell to his boots and his eyes read rage.

Frank nodded. "These are the men we're looking for."

"Well, there's definitely more than one person at work here," said Vance. "This shooting took place around six a.m. I believe the killings are too close together to be done by the same man."

Frank said, "We need to keep moving then if we're gonna catch 'em."

Vance said, "That's what I figured. I'll lead the way."

Frank, Gil, and Alfred and Moonbeam rode up to the small modest white house nestled in the cozy Chicago neighborhood. A young man in a newsboy cap with tears in his eyes and a determined stance watched as the three men rode up.

As they dismounted, Stage said, "You're the men I've been waiting for."

Frank flung him a confused glance.

Stage looked through his bloated eyes up the street and said, "Those others, those cops, they're weak. They aren't gonna find the bastards who killed my grandmother."

Frank pulled his pad and pencil and said, "I'm Frank Savage, this is Alfred and Gil. We're searching for the men who did this. And you're right, we will get them."

"I'm Stagecoach Sturgus, but you can call me Stage."

With sympathetic eyes Frank asked, "Can you tell me what happened?"

"I left her alone. I never should have left her alone. She's not . . . she wasn't well. She was losing her memory. The doctors aren't sure what it was. I guess it happens to old people if they live long enough."

Frank took notes as Gil and Alfred inspected the inside of the house.

Stage said, "I usually wait for Mrs. Travis to come over before I go to work, but she was running late." He paused then blurted, "But she always shows up." Stage's voice split high, and he held his hand to his lip. "Mrs. Travis wasn't feeling well. I didn't know she was sick. I should have walked over to check. But she always shows, always." Stage looked up.

"It wouldn't have mattered. From what I understand she just would have been killed as well. Who found her?"

Stage removed his hat and wrung it in his hands as he collected his thoughts. He said, "Mr. Jenkins across the road saw two men beat feet up the road there." Stage pointed. "He got suspicious and came over to check on us. That's when he saw the blood by the trunk." He pointed at the house as Alfred and Gil walked out.

Alfred nodded, his axe hidden under his overcoat.

"We'll get them, no doubt about it. And they aren't walking away from the fight either."

Stage squeezed his hat as tears trickled down his face. He walked slowly toward the house. He glanced back and said, "I want to help."

Frank said, "It's best if you stay here. If we need you, I promise, I'll call for you. Okay?"

Stage walked away. "Okay."

Frank gripped his pistol and whispered, "Maybe I should get an axe."

CHAPTER 8

The crowd thickened, indicating that they were approaching Maxwell Street. The three cowboys dismounted as the area became too busy to navigate on a horse.

A man hollered, “Hey, you have to clean up after your horse here.”

Frank gave a curt nod.

Alfred looked up at a building and then at the people scattered about the debris-covered street. “I swear there are more people living here than all of Texas.”

Alfred led the group as he tugged on Moonbeam’s reins. The horses were handling the crowd well until Moonbeam became restless and swiveled about.

Alfred said, “Whoa, come on, I’m hungry. You must be starving.”

Frank glanced around. “We have got to settle these horses somewhere. There just isn’t room here for these animals.”

Alfred barked, “Uh oh.”

Gil asked, “What?”

“Here comes a police officer. He don’t look none too happy about us.”

The officer in dark blue carrying a black bludgeon and a red frown walked up to Alfred. He was rising up until he saw Alfred’s black piercing eyes—then he slowed himself down. He said with a forced and twitching smile, “Gentlemen, you have to turn back.”

Gil asked, “Why?” His .455 bulged from under his jacket. Even an inexperienced lawman would notice it as plainly as a third appendage.

“Why? It’s your horses. You can’t be walking through the market with your animals. Not now. This isn’t Denver for Christ’s sake. We have city ordinances that don’t allow hosses in the marketplaces.”

Gil said, “Sir, why don’t you go have a drink? You’ll feel better.”

The officer said, “I can’t feel better. I’m married.”

Alfred stammered, “Well, I never heard of no such thing. Look here.”

He flashed his deputy's badge. "I'm in town on a case this—"

"I don't care if you're the city's chief of police, now get."

Moonbeam sniffed and then snorted. Her eyes circled around in their sockets once and then rolled back into her head as she swiftly picked up her nose, yanking on the leather straps Alfred tightly held.

Alfred held firm and said, "Whoa, girl."

Moonbeam pulled her head up. Using the strength she possessed in her back, she stepped away and stared right.

Frank moved up closer. "She senses something that she doesn't like. I've seen this before."

"Yeah, what is it?" asked Alfred. His horse stomped as a group of people walked by.

Frank said, "It's not a what. It's a who."

The officer said huffily, "Now, I told you boys. Stop beating your gums and turn your horses around before they hurt someone. There's a stable about—"

Moonbeam whinnied and pulled even harder on Alfred's grip. Her muscles twitched violently under her shiny coat.

"Hold her head lower so that I can see," ordered Frank.

Alfred used his weight to pull Moonbeam's head down.

Frank looked directly into her eyes. She wouldn't look at him. She sniffed as she looked to the right.

Frank straightened as he said, "Holy shit."

"What?"

"Turn her head to the side."

Moonbeam cried out and stomped forcefully.

Frank followed her gaze. He shoved his own horse's reins into the officer's chest. "Hold this."

The officer tossed a glare of disbelief and said, "Yes, sir."

Frank caught a glimpse of a blonde-haired man about twenty feet away imbedded in a clan of shoppers.

Alfred and Moonbeam fought against each other.

Frank yelled, "Uncle Baldy."

The blonde man turned sharply, exposing a bandage on the side of his head.

Frank said, "It's on."

Uncle began a frantic attempt to escape his pursuers.

Gil yelled, "Go, go, go."

People floated everywhere as Frank leapt forward, pushing his way into the crowd.

Frank said out loud to himself, “You better not lose him.”

Uncle Baldwin was quickly plodding along through the bodies when he slammed into an unsuspecting woman. The blow put her up and off her feet into the air. She landed solidly on her rump.

Frank pushed and shoved and hollered as he cleared the way. He was intently focused on his target as it ran away up the busy street.

Frank whispered, “I do hate running in these boots.”

People flew by one after the other in a blur. Frank didn’t see faces. Only the flash of their shock as he forcefully pushed his way up the street with his eyes locked on a killer.

As he approached a corner, Uncle Baldwin took a turn. As Frank saw the move, he pulled his gun, but when he leveled the weapon he noticed the faces of the crowd. A woman screamed.

Frank re-holstered his pistol and took off again. He was angry for having stopped. As he turned the corner he hit the true heart of the market. A sea of people’s heads bobbed like a pulsating wave against the backdrop of a great wall of tents and buildings.

“Damn it all to Hell.”

Frank, slipping through the mob, started asking everyone who could hear him, “Anyone see a one-eared blonde man come running through here? No? He seems to be in a hurry.” No positive response followed his query.

Frenzied, Frank slowed as he noticed a light post. He stepped up on the base and scanned the herd. Desperately he looked around. Just as he was about to step down, he saw a disturbance across the street.

A man in the middle of the confusion blared, “Hey, what’s the idea?”

Frank launched himself from his perch, and his legs carried him smoothly through his jump into a run. He glided through the pack of bodies and was flowing into a rhythm. It was getting easier.

Another scream called out in front of him. He was closer. Frank altered his course. He stepped into an open and unpopulated area. He caught a glimpse of Uncle a block up as he was clumsily taking a turn to the left. Frank took his immediate left and accelerated.

A salesman’s voice hollered, “Hey, that’s two dollars.” as Frank snatched up some rope from his table.

Frank yelled, “I’m only borrowing it.”

The market was clearing out as Frank bolted up the street faster than before. As his boots clomped briskly down the grimy street, he said, "It's in the timing." At the corner he took a fast and sharp right with the rope unfurled in his hand.

Frank's boots sounded out against the brick buildings that guided his path. With the rope draped over his fingers, he eyed the oncoming corner.

Uncle came running out in front of him, and he was looking in the opposite direction. He just happened to be smiling.

With strong shoulders, and perfect timing, Frank launched his weapon. The lassoed rope floated above Uncle's head. It settled around his body coming tight at his knees with a powerful tug.

Before Uncle could even respond, Frank yanked on the rope with an angry jolt. The violent contraction pulled the loop tight around his legs. Uncle Baldwin never saw the rope or the ground that smashed into his face with a splat.

Out of breath, Frank stopped and rested his hands on his knees as he hunched over. He stared at his boots.

After he caught some air he walked gingerly to the fallen man. Uncle didn't move even as Frank disarmed him of his pistol. Blood had pooled around his head. In the pool floated two teeth.

"Ground's hard, ain't it?" mumbled Frank.

Frank patted his victim down and found an identification card that showed he was Uncle Baldwin. He whispered, "At least I killed the right man." He sighed.

Gil stepped up from a run and asked, "You okay, Frank?"

"Yes . . . and no."

Gil looked down at Uncle.

Frank's stare dripped with a confused air. Confused as to why he felt no regret. "He's dead."

"That's what we came here to do." Gil, with his face to the ground, looked up at Frank.

"I know—it's just that he's a lead, and I blew it." He wasn't going to admit that it was his anger that pulled on the rope that sent Uncle to his grave. He said, "I knew what I was doing."

Gil knew the gaze.

Alfred and Moonbeam trotted up through a group of people that had circled the scene. He stepped down and turned Uncle's body over.

Gil said, "Where in the hell is his nose?"

Alfred grumbled, "It's in his brain, I reckon."

The officer worked his way into the scene. He said, "Frank Savage." Then he saw Uncle's motionless figure. "Christ."

Frank said, "I'm Savage."

The officer couldn't pull his eyes away from the pool of blood. "It's been explained to me who you are. But I need you to come down to the station and verify it."

"I understand. Detective Stranger can vouch for me."

"If it hadn't been for Moonbeam's nose," added Gil, "we never would have found him in this crowd. How did you catch that shifty bastard?"

Frank said, "He didn't have the makings. That's all."

The room was small and square. It had a shiny lacquered wood desk that was kept fastidiously straightened. A few pictures and a police academy diploma were lined perfectly along the back wall. On the desk was a nameplate for Detective Stranger. It didn't say "Stranger"; it said "Strainger". An inside joke.

"And what God-forsaken planet are you from?" Vance Stranger screamed.

Frank and Vance stood next to a water pipe that shot up along the wall into the ceiling.

Vance held a piece of paper that he'd scribbled on: *Just go along. It's my job I'm worried about.*

Frank said, "Yeah, but—"

Vance spoke with a clear, firm annunciation. "But, my ass. You ain't got the God-given sense of, of . . . a goose."

Frank whispered, "Wha?"

Vance shrugged, then said, "I ought to knock you into pulp and then pour your ass into a jail cell right now, but I don't want to have to explain it to the president." He pointed at the ceiling as if he were the lead in a play reciting Shakespeare on a stage. "But, I could drag your partners in so quick it would make your head spin."

"Yes, sir," Frank said. Then he whispered, "Be careful now."

"I want you and your partners to keep your guns in their holsters from now on."

Frank's head jerked up with a quizzical glare. "But—"

"No buts about it, mister. You keep your asses out of my office, and we'll get along just fine. Understood?"

Frank said into the pipe, "Yes, sir. Understood."

Vance whispered, "Thanks, Frank. I'll be asked to keep an eye on you. Not that I'll do it."

"No—thank *you.*" Frank patted his friend's arm with a smile.

"Oh, before I forget." Vance went to the top drawer of his desk and removed a piece of paper and handed it to Frank. He spoke quickly while pushing his friend out of his office. "Here's Rebecca Devlin's address with directions. She's only a twenty-minute walk from here. You could be there by," Vance looked at his pocket watch, "oh, let's say, noonish."

"I've got things to do."

"Yeah, and this is one of them. You need to take a break for a bit anyway. Now this is an order. You'll go and talk to her. You can't think straight anyway. I know you, and until you can get some closure or whatever with her, you're not worth anything to anyone."

"I'll go talk to her."

"You ruddy-well better, mister." Vance grinned and extended his hand.

Frank accepted his hand. "You're a good friend. Thanks."

"Yeah, yeah. I just think she's a swell dish, that's all."

Frank nodded and smiled and walked down the hall with his face buried in the note he held.

During his walk, Frank scripted words to say over and over in his mind. Just when he had something down he would change his mind. The twenty minutes went by in a flash. It didn't register with him that it had started to drizzle.

Vance's directions took Frank past the water tower on Michigan Avenue. The building was very familiar to him because he had helped rebuild the area surrounding the castle-like structure. It felt like a lifetime ago even though it had only been a few years.

Frank found himself outside the apothecary. His long brown slicker protected him from the light sprinkle that descended from above. He looked at the directions he held in his hands. His hat, with the front brim drooping due to so much rain pounding on it over the last couple days, pointed to the paper. The bell of the door jingled as customers moved in and out of the drugstore.

Frank's pants had been freshly pressed and his shirt had been cleaned by the hotel launderer the night before, but you couldn't tell. He knew he was at the right place, but he hesitated. He stalled as he pretended to read.

The bell faintly jingled as Frank stepped in without thinking or looking. He was turning his head and removing his hat when he felt the hot coffee hit the skin on the back of his hands. He yelped, "Holy moly, that's hot."

Frank stepped back abruptly as the cup slipped from slender fingers. Frank dropped his hat as he attempted to catch the porcelain coffee cup before it hit the floor. It shattered to pieces as it hit.

A woman's voice quipped, "Holy moly?" She leaned over and picked up Frank's hat and put it on her head. "It doesn't fit me so well, clumsy," she said softly.

"Hey that was ho—" Frank stuttered.

The young woman tried to look up at her intruder, but the hat slipped forward covering her eyes. Only her lips were visible under the brim of Frank's wet hat. Perfect full lips stared back at him. Her mouth was slightly parted with the bottom half of her top teeth showing. Her skin was smooth with rose-colored checks. Frank knew those lips. To not kiss them, well, took some concentration.

She said, "My, you have a big head."

Frank knew the voice, and it melted over his ears.

With an index finger, she tipped the hat back so that it rested on the top of her forehead. Frank swallowed as he looked into two large round blue eyes enveloped in long eyelashes. He was well aware that he had been caught off guard. In more ways than one. Her face was soft and round. He stared at her mouth and mumbled, "Hot . . . that heat was . . . um, hot."

The light-brown-haired beauty did not look shocked. Frank was aware that Rebecca Devlin had never thought she would ever see him again. Not after how he'd left things.

"Hello, Cowboy."

Frank breathed out quick with a grin and blushed. They stood silent. "Um."

Her oval eyes narrowed. She forced herself to breath. For that moment they looked at each other. Longingly they took in the presence of each other.

A middle-aged woman with two small children excused herself between the two to exit the store. The smallest boy said, "Mommy, why are they just staring at each other?"

His mom answered, "It's been too long for me, Sweetie. I forget."

"Here's your hat, sir," Becca said sternly. "Yes, now, if you'd excuse me, I have work to do."

Becca tried to step past Frank. He moved to block her exit. He gripped her arms. She gasped. Frank held her up as she shivered and her legs relaxed.

Frank said, "Becca, I need to talk to you."

Becca regained her bearings and pulled back, to no avail.

She said, "Talk?"

"Yes, there are some—"

"Listen, Cowboy, there is nothing I have to say to—"

Frank interrupted with his mouth full on Rebecca's. She whimpered, but she didn't fight it. Her hands came up to his chest. After a long kiss, Frank slowly loosened his grip with his hands and leaned away from those full lips.

"That's not fair," Becca said.

"Let's go for a walk."

Rebecca thought for a second. She opened her mouth to speak but didn't. Then she took a long breath and said, "Okay."

Walking in the light drizzle, Frank pulled up his collar and said, "I spoke to Vance Stranger."

Becca looked straight as she said, "Yeah?"

"He told me about the baby."

Becca was quiet.

They strolled for a bit then Frank continued, "I'm sorry."

Becca said, "I never blamed you."

"I know, but I should have written or something. I wish you would have sent word."

"I should have. I was angry with you. You never really said goodbye."

"I was on the move then, I was following—"

"Like you said," Becca said. "You should have written."

It was quiet. Frank rubbed his eyes. He said, "It's wet and cold."

"We can go to my place."

After a short walk, Frank and Becca entered a three-story brick building. On the third floor Frank followed Becca into her apartment. Becca stepped in and stopped. He stood behind her and swung the door shut with his boot. He rested his hands on top of her shoulders and slid her jacket off her body over her arms to a crumpled heap on the floor. Her keys fell from her hand and landed quietly on her coat.

Becca wore a white dress with straps. The dress was fitted around her breasts, and it clung tightly to her hips.

Frank said, “I missed you,” into her ear.

He put his hands on her shoulders again; they were still wet from the rain, and a shiver shot through her body. Goose bumps spread over her soft skin. Water glistened off her shoulder as Frank kissed the nape of her neck. He reached up and pulled his hat and dropped it to the ground. His lips kissed their way to the crook of her neck as he tilted her head back with his hand cupped under her chin.

Frank wrapped his arms around her as she tried to breathe.

Becca said, “I missed you, too.”

Frank abruptly turned her to face him and kissed her with an open mouth. Becca draped her arms over his shoulders and pulled him down as he pulled their hips together.

Becca bit lightly on his lower lip as Frank tightened the embrace. She whispered into his ear, “I guess you did miss me.”

“More than you know.”

“Maybe you need to show me.”

“I intend to.”

Frank grabbed the back of her head, and their lips came together. His hands ran up and down her body. Becca pulled Frank’s overcoat off and began unbuttoning his shirt. He pushed forward and Becca stepped backwards until she found herself on her back on the bed. She didn’t feel herself fall.

CHAPTER 9

Frank rested with his hands behind his head as Becca slipped back into bed. She moved close to him and sighed.

Frank's thoughts wandered; they were questioning and doubting. He felt anxious.

Becca said, "I missed you."

Frank was silent.

"Frank?"

"Oh, yeah, me too."

"Thanks for nothing." She buried her head in her pillow and pouted.

Frank grinned and quietly chuckled.

"Want a smoke?" Frank asked.

"No." Becca blurted. She didn't move her face. She kept it buried deep in the pillow with the sides pulled up over her ears with her hands.

"Are you pouting?"

"Yes," Becca snapped, muffled by the down.

"Oh, baby," Frank said teasingly. "How bout some love, huh?"

"No."

"Please."

"No, you're mean."

"I know, but you love me just the same."

"Not anymore, I don't."

Frank turned to her and rested his face in the crook formed by her shoulder and her neck. She wiggled around. Her skin felt warm and smooth.

"You sure are cute when you're angry," Frank said.

"Go away."

Frank busted up in laughter and tickled her sides.

"Aaah," bellowed Becca, laughing. "Stop it." She twisted and turned about, never releasing the pillow from her face.

"Okay," Frank said. He rolled on top of her back with his full weight.

"You're heavy."

"Mmm, this is comfy." His face was in her hair. "You smell nice."

"I can't breathe."

"Well, take your face out of that pillow."

"No," she said with muffled defiance.

"I'm not moving till you give me a kiss."

"No." She was louder this time.

"Okay, I can stay here a long time."

"You're fat," she blurted.

Frank let loose a cackle that transitioned to a loud cough. He rolled off Becca's back. She turned her head and said, "Are you okay?"

Frank coughed louder, grinning with his back to her.

She said, "Babe, you okay?"

She moved up close, and Frank spun around. "I got you."

Becca screamed, "Aaah."

Frank jumped on top of her and gripped her sides.

"Stop it. That tickles." They howled with laughter and fell to the bed, side by side, with their faces to the ceiling.

It was quiet as they caught their breath.

Becca turned her head towards Frank. She said, "What's on your mind?" Her light brown hair intertwined with her long lashes.

"My case, that's all. I'm used to it. There's always something."

"Oh? You have to catch somebody?"

Frank turned to Becca. "They don't call me in if they want someone captured. Not this time."

Becca swallowed. "Oh."

It was quiet.

"That's my interpretation of my orders anyway."

"Do you ever feel bad about people you've killed?" asked Becca.

"I killed someone the other day who I didn't mean to. But in a way I did want it to happen. In our minds he deserved it, but . . . I don't know. Maybe he did deserve to die or maybe he was only there to hold the horses. I don't think he ever killed anyone. Just a fool following orders. We'll never know because I killed him."

"I'm sorry I brought it up."

Frank said matter of factly, "You can say no." His mind had quickly shifted to something else.

"Say no to what?"

"I need your help. Will you help us?"

The soft feminine features of Becca's face contorted to form a fiery and fuming displeasure.

Frank said, "Uh, oh."

Becca sat up on her knees. "Frank Savage, did you only come here because you needed my help?"

"Nooo." Frank laughed nervously.

Becca's eyes filled her face, and she pointed at him. "You did. You only came here to kill some bastards and you want my help."

Frank jumped up. "No, no, no, that's not true. I came to Chicago to catch someone, but I am *here* because I wanted to see you. I swear."

"You, you—what was I thinking?" Becca said as she shuffled to get off the bed. "I should've traded you in for a good horse when I had the chance. I can't believe it. I can't believe I fell for your, your—"

"My what?"

"Your bullcrap."

Frank grabbed her by the arm and pulled her back to the bed as she wriggled to free herself.

Frank said, "Wait."

"No, let me go."

"Becca, I swear to you." Frank held her arm firmly as they held a gaze, face to face. Becca was beyond angry. Frank slowly released his grip and let her go. She stood up and went straight to the washroom and slammed the door and locked it.

"Oh, the nerve. I should have my head examined."

Frank sat on the bed rubbing his chin. He stood and walked over to his clothes and put his pants on. He pulled up his pack and withdrew a book of his notes. Page by page he looked through the papers. Frank then collected the pages he had been looking for and walked over to the washroom door. He rested his forehead on the doorcase and said, "Rebecca, I, I honestly came to you, to see you. It came to me today that you might be able to help me. That's all."

No sound came from the washroom.

Frank said, "Can you at least let me know that you're still in there so I know you didn't sneak out the window."

It was quiet a second then Becca said, "I'm still here."

Frank said, "I don't know what's going to happen with us. That's the honest truth, but I do know that I do still love you, and I missed you very, very much."

Frank fanned the pages with his index finger and thumb. He said, "I'm going to put some of my notes under the door, and I want you to read them. It's not easy reading. It's about the men we're chasing and what they did to my friend's family. So," Frank carefully slid the papers under the door, "please read them, and then make your decision."

Becca pulled the papers from under the door. Frank sat on the bed and waited. After a few minutes the door opened and Becca stepped out wearing a nightgown on her body and a row of tears on her checks.

Becca leaned on the door as they locked eyes. She nodded and said, "I'll help you."

"Thank you." Frank stood and pulled her into his arms.

Becca sighed and hugged and said, "I'm sorry."

A white foamy film floated and oscillated with the waves, but it never reached the shoreline, no matter how close it got. The bloated body with no face bobbed up and down in the shallow waters amongst the foam. A boot stepped down, sinking into the mud with the water level just above the ankles.

"Watch where you step," said Detective Stranger. "Don't want to muck up the crime scene."

Fulsome wore a look of scorn. He hung over a dead body that was smartly dressed and had no face.

"Male," said Detective Fulsome.

Vance lit a cigarette. The match threw a yellow blaze across his face and cast a shadow over his eyes that rested under the brim of his hat. A few stars twinkled between the slow-moving clouds behind his head.

Fulsome knelt down and rummaged through the pockets. He withdrew a wallet.

"It's empty, no cash." Fulsome found an identification card. "Lake Lagoon of New York, it says."

"Lake Lagoon, New York, or Lake Lagoon *of* New York," asked Vance.

"Lake Lagoon of New York."

"Never heard of him," said Vance. He blew smoke as he spoke.

A group of blue-uniformed police officers formed a semi-circle around the detective. One of whom carried a lit lantern.

Vance ordered, "When the detective's done, I want you boys to carefully load our corpse into the wagon and escort it back to base. And don't lose it."

"Aye, sir," answered a voice from the crowd.

Fulsome pulled away from the body and said, "Ouch." He sucked on his finger. "I think I cut myself on something." He hauled his leg back, as if he were going to kick the dead body of Mr. Lagoon and then stopped in mid-swing.

Vance said, "Let me have a look-see."

Fulsome slowly retrieved a blade from the boot of the dead Mr. Lagoon. He said, "Looks like a letter opener."

Fulsome stepped from the edge of Lake Michigan and handed the blade to Vance who quickly slipped on a pair of black gloves before handling the evidence.

Vance lit another match to get a better look. He inspected the knife using the match flame. "It *is* a letter opener and it's damn sharp. It's too sharp to just be used to open a letter. Might have some blood here in the handle."

Vance squinted as his match went out. He ignited three matches at once and squinted again to confirm blood caked into an emblem embedded in the side of the letter opener. A letter opener that for some reason had been turned into a knife.

Fulsome watched with a raised brow.

Vance said, "Okay, men, you can take the body now." He turned to his partner. "You done?"

Fulsome said, "I'm done."

Vance pointed his troops to the floating corpse with a flick of the wrist.

The group of officers lifted Lake Lagoon from the water.

Fulsome said, "His head was blown open by a shotgun blast, and he saw it coming." He made the shape of a gun with his hand and pointed it at his own face.

Vance puffed on his dying cigarette as he listened and examined the blade. He motioned his head and directed his eyes to get Fulsome away from the others. Once they were out of earshot of eavesdroppers, Vance said, "Look."

Fulsome got in close.

"What do you see?" asked Vance.

"It looks like an engraving."

"That's what I thought. Of what, though?"

"The blood is covering it, but it looks like a cross maybe."

Vance flipped his depleted smoke to the wet muddy ground and said, "Don't tell anyone."

Fulsome nodded.

Vance slipped the letter opener into a bag and walked into the night.

The red-colored wallpaper and the red glow from the lamp was disconcerting to the senses. After a while it would make anyone agitated and angry.

Alfred grumbled, "I can't believe we're still staying here."

Alfred cleaned his gun at the edge of one of two beds as Gil smoked. Gil was seated in a chair eyeing the door of the hotel room.

Gil said, "They won't try anything here again."

"What makes you so sure?"

Gil grinned. "I ain't so sure. I was just trying to make you feel better."

"Maybe they should try again. Maybe being here and in the open can draw someone out."

"Maybe . . . maybe."

Alfred gripped his axe that was sheathed to his belt. "I'm gonna cut all their heads off." Alfred coughed hoarsely and held his throat. "My voice is getting worse and worse." He took out a sharpening stone from his bag and got to work honing the axe blade.

Gil said, "Maybe it'll get bad enough so as I don't have to listen to you blabber on all day and all night."

"Very funny." Alfred said.

The room was quiet as Alfred worked the stone and Gil slipped shells into his sidearm. They both remained cognizant of the door and what was behind it.

"I have something I need to get off my chest," Gil said. "Maybe you're the one to talk to. Not rightly sure. I usually have a feeling about such things. Just not sure about this."

Alfred paused in thought, nodded, and went back to work.

Gil continued, "Or, maybe you're the one I shouldn't mention this to—because of your loss and how it happened. How it happened because of men not very much unlike myself."

Alfred rubbed his throat with the back of his hand, waved his axe for Gil to continue.

"I've done some killing. I've done some, done some things on the wrong side of the law. I'm not proud of it. It was when I was stupid and young, quite violent. I thought I was the best with a gun. You know how young men are."

Alfred grumbled that he was listening.

"I would hire my skills out to whoever paid enough. I'm not evil. I never found a situation where I was pointing a gun at a woman or a child." Gil pondered as he slowly breathed in, then out.

"Go on." Alfred grumbled.

"That makes me wonder sometimes. Would I have stopped someone from killing an unarmed man or a woman? Would I have done the right thing when I was that immature, and that drunk? I don't know the answer to that. I might have been afraid to stop it. I'm pretty sure I would never have done it. But what if I was drunk and angry? You know?" Gil looked to Alfred for an answer.

"We all do stupid shit when we're young and drunk." Alfred said. "I'm the one you're supposed to be talking to."

Gil sat forward, taken aback. "Yeah?"

"Yep, I, ah, I'm not getting much sleep."

"Well, you lost your family. It's normal. And we're all hell bent on destroying the bastards who did it."

Alfred stroked his voice box and said, "I'm not sleeping because I had a man hung on very little evidence once. He was a bad man, I do know that, but I knew better. I don't know what happened. But, I think that maybe my loss was payback. It's payback for a death of someone who could have been innocent. And I didn't take the time to make sure. Makes me wonder, is it my fault? Or is it the times we live in? We're all killers, except maybe Cole. That's probably why he's not in this anymore. Frank has killed more men than the killers we're chasing. Frank's a gun-shark. But, from here on out, it's *who* we kill that's important. In our sick minds it's the right thing to do."

Gil said, "It has always been like this. For good people to survive, you have to have good people who are willing to kill."

The two cowboys paused in thought.

Gil said, "I tussled with one of the men who did this. The man who stabbed Cole."

Alfred bit down as he listened.

"These bastards ain't killing to get back at you for nothing. These demented gunmen are killing for killing's sake. Trust me, you're not involved. I've got some talents, some good and some not. But one talent is that I can sense motivation in evil men. Your family just settled on the wrong land in the wrong time." Gil shuffled his feet. "I wanted to talk to you because I'm not walking away from this."

"What do you mean? I ain't leaving either, that is, till it's done, and every one of them is bleeding in the gutter."

Gil's face was hard and scared with serious. "I mean, I'm not going to just ride away from this when it's over. My wife, Tami, knows I'm not coming back. I want you to go to her when this is done and tell her that I'm a free soul. That I did what I said I would do."

Alfred gave a brief nod.

Gil continued, "Tami now knows what I am. When I killed the Kingston Killer, I showed a side I had thought was long gone. But I'm okay with it because I know what I have to do. I am here not to find the killers of your family really." Gil turned in his seat and waved his hand. "I'm here to help, sure, but I'm here to save your lives."

Alfred listened more carefully to Gil than he had ever listened to anyone in his life.

Gil said, "I saved Cole that night. When I did, I smiled because my soul was relieved. I know it's going to happen. I am here to give my life for a higher purpose, and I am here to give my life for someone else. In some form, or shape, or something. I am now supposed to use all that I have experienced. You see, there is a reason I did what I did, and it all leads to now, where I use my talents to end this. And to give my life to save you and Frank."

Alfred rested his hands on his knees.

"Understand?" Gil smiled. "Maybe?"

"I understand. But I will do everything I can to keep you from giving your life for ours. We're all gonna walk away from this."

Gil sat relaxed. "Maybe, but it's okay if I don't, too."

"I will," Alfred said. "I'll visit your wife. Frank, too. He'll go."

Gil smiled. "She already knows." He pulled his pocket watch—it rested small in his big hand—and smiled at a picture of his wife and placed it back in his pocket.

A click, a squeak, and then a slam resounded down the steps from the upstairs. Ruby squeezed tightly to the back wall of her cage. Two steps of men's shoes followed by a woman's came down the stairs.

Abruptly the door to the cellar lurched open. A man and a woman entered. As the man stepped in, he lit a lantern that threw light and shadows onto the walls of Ruby's prison.

They didn't speak as they stirred about without much direction. Ruby was safe, for now, behind the bars of her jail, with the two intruders casting their shadows across her empty food and water bowls.

Ruby recognized them but she didn't know what they were planning. She shook nervously as she tried to retract herself into the two walls that formed the corner that she wished were a door to freedom. Her once beautiful red coat was not shiny any more. It had become dull. Her hair was spotted with clumps that clung together with muck, and her fur was losing its thickness as she slowly shed. She wasn't hungry anymore.

The man was the woman's boss, and he was also Ruby's jailer. The woman was the one who'd killed the man in the black bowler hat.

Plenty Sky stood at the center of the sterile brick-walled room. The only exits were the door they had entered and a slender rectangular window high up near the ceiling on the far wall.

"Damn it," Boss blurted. He took a step forward and gripped Plenty's jacket and shirt in a clump in his fist and jerked her to within inches of his face. "Did you destroy everything?"

Plenty said, as if aroused, "I told you I did, didn't I?"

It was quiet as Boss glared at Plenty. She didn't flinch. He kissed her open-mouthed. She kissed back and grabbed his face between her hands. She shoved her thumb in his mouth. He took it. She sharply shoved him. She wiped her mouth with her sleeve. Boss stepped back as he sucked in oxygen. He paced the room twice.

Plenty said, "Boss?"

"That's right, Boss, and don't—"

"I said that I cleaned up the office and that I understand the situation."

"You have too much power, Plenty, and do you know why?"

Plenty didn't answer.

"It's because you know who I am." He pointed his thumb at his chest.

"Nobody knows who I am," Boss said firmly.

He turned, strode up close to Plenty, and whispered, "I am aware that you're quite handy with that skull-splitter, but trust me." Boss instantly had a blade in each hand. In front of her, face to face, he touched the tips of his blades to her, pushing them firmly into her sides.

Plenty trembled, and her checks glowed red.

Boss said, "As I was saying, don't give me a reason, and we can keep this relationship at status quo."

Plenty's full lips separated, and her wet tongue stroked her shiny teeth. The pointy incisors touched a deviant nerve.

Boss said, "You are one sick chick." Boss recoiled from their silently violent embrace, and as quickly as they'd arrived the blades were gone.

Plenty brushed her hair back off her forehead. She laughed and said, "I'm sick? It's *your* love of blood that has you on the run from these murderous cowboys."

"Correction. I can't stand the sight of blood." He turned and paused and wrung his hands and said, "Torture and death, well, that's another story."

Plenty shook her head. "At least you left town to satisfy your craving. But something followed you. Didn't it? It followed you home. Something savage followed you home."

Boss turned back and said, "How'd you dispose of the room?"

Her voice grew louder with each word. "It looks like a storage room now—just as you ordered." She cocked her head and quietly now, as if she were using an alternate personality, she said, "I removed everything, even the two-way mirror, and I burned it all to ashes. I kept nothing." She glared at him.

Boss pushed his chin up and out. His leer flared sharply towards Ruby. Ruby winced and whimpered and turned this way and that looking for an exit that wasn't there.

"Why do you keep her around?" Plenty asked.

Boss said, "Because she saw everything." He slipped his hands into his pockets and added, "She's preciously . . . fragile."

"Where's the other one?"

"Dog food . . . he was done amusing me."

"You have an odd manner about you."

Boss ignored the comment. Out the side of his mouth he said, "I hate doing business out of a house."

"I don't know." She looked around. "It's kinda cozy, I think."

Boss attempted to ignore her but flipped a cross sneer, he said, "I've got way too many irons in the fire. Maybe you knowing who I am will help. I need an assistant. Operations in Chicago are getting too large to keep my identity hidden. Eventually, everyone will know who runs this town."

Plenty grinned.

"I should burn that hotel to the ground with that son of a bitch inside it."

Plenty asked, "How'd he beat you?"

He shook his head. "I don't know. It was so dark. That's what's so screwed up about it all. I couldn't see anything except shadows, but no matter what I did, that man saw it coming. I was as fast as I've ever been, it didn't matter."

Plenty listened.

"He's a force to be reckoned with," Boss said.

"Did he get a look at you?"

"I think he would have if I hadn't had my face masked. He could see everything."

"Why do you mess around with those knives? That Texas Ranger should be dead. You should have opened up a heater into him without pause."

"You've got your methods, and I've got mine. One down, that's what matters."

"But still three to go."

Boss pointed and said, "You need to increase our odds by disposing of him. I need to keep my distance."

"Maybe we should let Goth help. He's desperate to meet with you."

Boss rubbed his chin. "He's desperate in more ways than you'll ever know."

Plenty put her hands on her hips and said, "I can't tell if you love him or hate him."

"Both."

"Can he be trusted?"

"I only know him from the job he was hired to do. I found him through a connection in Kansas City. Kinda hoped he'd get caught. I knew the Kingston Killer would get caught. He fancied himself as a glamorous gunfighter for hire. His narcissism was his undoing."

"You think they got anything from Uncle?"

"No, he only knew enough to get himself killed."

"So, you want to meet with Goth?"

Boss paused in thought. "Yes."

"How about his brother? You want him along?"

Boss stood straight, put his hands in his pockets, and said, "Let's make this interesting. Arrange the meeting."

Plenty grinned. "Done."

CHAPTER 10

Frank and Becca returned to the hotel to inform the others of their plan to arrange a meeting. A meeting with the Police Department's ex-psychologist, Dr. Lore Ethos.

Frank, Becca, and Alfred were to leave the hotel for Detective Stranger's home to plan their investigation. The reason for going to the detective's home was due to the fact that Frank felt the group may have eyes watching their moves at the Palmer House hotel. It wasn't safe there.

Gil left the hotel when the conversation between Frank and Becca diverted to that of their lost baby. He stuck around just long enough to find out that he was not going along to the doctor's house. They needed someone Dr. Ethos wouldn't recognize if need be. Before stepping outside he threw on his long coat in preparation for the cool weather and possible drizzle.

Gil's eyes flattened as he looked down the long alley to Handsome Sam's bar. Without looking where he stepped, he strolled down the alley, and his boot splashed in a puddle of dirty water. As he paused at the entrance he heard a voice.

"How's it goin', Cowboy? Wanna go for a ride?" Gil looked up at a woman standing on her balcony smoking a cigarette. "I've got some spurs. But you have to promise to use them." A grungy grin grew across her jowls.

He said nothing and entered the bar.

Gil sat at the bar, sideways so he could see the entrance. He ordered a whiskey, a double. Sam poured it fat and Gil took a long pull. Sam refilled the glass.

A tall woman in an overcoat walked into the bar and looked around. Her coat covered her body, but it hung off her in all the right places.

He whispered, "Of all the damnable breaks."

"Stay away from that one," said Sam.

"Always do."

The tall woman took a seat at a table on the far end of the narrow pub. After Gil was halfway into his third drink, the door swung open and Detective Fulsome entered. Gil threw his hand in front of his face and turned away. When Fulsome scanned the room he didn't recognize Frank and Alfred's partner. He quickly took a seat at the table with the curly-haired woman.

"Sam," Gil whispered. "Who is that woman?"

"Her name is Plenty Sky."

"What do you know about her?"

"She works for *all* sides."

Detective Fulsome and Plenty moved close to each other to talk.

Gil prodded Sam for more information. "Explain."

"Look, I don't get involved with anything that goes on here. If I did, I'd not only be out of business, I'd have skipped the coroner because nobody would be able to find my decaying corpse."

"Frank said that I could count on you if I was in a jam."

"Savage? He said that?"

"Yeah."

"That son of a bitch." Sam rubbed the back of his neck.

"Anything at all that you can give us. It might be important."

Sam paused again and then said, "When I say all sides, I mean she works with all the mob types like the Irish, Italian, and some I've never heard of. There's even word on the streets about an Eastern European mob coming to play here. Doesn't matter what city either. New York, Timbuktu you name it."

"What is she doing talking to Fulsome?"

"Hey, I said I stay out of it. But I'll repeat myself, she plays *all* sides."

Gil rubbed his chin as the muscles in his face fretted.

Plenty and Fulsome abruptly stood up. The detective tossed some coins to the table and they walked out together.

Gil left some money on the bar and said, "Is there another way outta here?"

"Yeah," said Sam. He threw his thumb in the direction of a narrow hallway around the side of the bar. "Go down this long hall and it takes you out to another alleyway."

"Thanks."

As Gil swung around the bar, his revolver exposed itself from under his coat.

He popped outside and moved briskly up the alley toward the main street. Peeking around the corner, Gil caught sight of Fulsome and Plenty walking across and then up the street; they were moving away from him. He followed but at a distance. A few people bustled about up and down the street amongst the horse-drawn carriages. Their shadows ebbed along the brick and concrete structures.

Fulsome stopped and pulled Plenty into the niche of a building. With his back to a wall he held Plenty close to his chest and kissed her. She let him for a long moment, then she pulled her head back and slapped him. Fulsome slapped her back, and then she kissed him—hard.

Gil ducked into a cleft in the side of a brick three-story structure and watched. Plenty pushed herself clear of Fulsome's embrace and stalked off. Fulsome smiled and tilted his hat to the back of his head and walked away in the opposite direction. Gil pulled his hat over his eyes and sat down in the crevice of the building until the detective was clear. Then he crept out slowly and followed Plenty Sky.

Plenty sprang over a mud puddle, allowing her long coat to flap open. A double-barreled handheld shotgun attached to her hip hollered out to Gil to watch himself.

As a carriage pulled up, Gil moved fast in order to get closer. He was able to move without being seen. Plenty stepped up and into the back seat. Gil sprinted up the street. Just as the driver snapped the reins that coaxed the horses forward, Gil heard, "Aye, ma'am, Astor District."

Frank sat with a tall glass of bourbon and soda with two cubes of ice. The room smelled of years of smoking and no ventilation. He sat at the end of a leather-bound couch pulling on a bow tie, and Becca sat on the opposite end. He jerked about as he attempted to get comfortable. Vance Stranger held a broad smile as he poured a glass of Scotch.

"Not used to the tie, are you?" said Vance.

"Never understood why anyone would dress like this," Frank said.

"Oh, I think it's nice," Becca said.

Vance asked, "Where did you get the glasses?"

"They belong to Cole." Frank slipped the glasses up onto the top of his nose and attempted to focus. "He is truly blind without them."

Alfred entered the room through the front door. "Here you go." He tossed a circular metal container of pomade to Becca. She stood and caught the small tin and opened it and smelled the contents. Her face contorted. "Is this used on horses?"

Vance had a brow up. "Frank, I need you to be honest with me."

"Of course."

"We found a dead body in Lake Michigan."

"Okay."

"It was a man by the name of Lake Lagoon. He's from New York. We got a telegraph not long ago that he is an assassin of some kind."

"Yeah?"

"Now, we found something on his person." Vance walked to the coat rack and pulled a piece of cloth from a pocket and unraveled it. "It's a very sharp letter opener."

Frank jumped from his seat as Vance showed him the knife.

Frank said, "That emblem, there. What's it look like to you?" He pointed.

Vance said, "It's a cross and a crescent moon."

Frank turned the blade around and said, "Look . . . I believe it's an upside down cross and a waxing crescent moon." He fell back into his seat with a long gaze.

"What's it mean?" Becca asked.

Frank's gaze wandered to Alfred. "Not sure about the meaning of the symbol but I don't think it's good. There was a mark on the back of Alfred's daughter's knees. It looked like a knife had been heated up and then applied to her skin to make a brand. It was that same marking that's on that blade."

Alfred choked and grumbled, "So is he the one?"

Vance said, "His whereabouts during the time of your family's death are unknown."

Frank said, "The evidence has him linked to it. Whether he did it or not, I don't know. If he did do it, why?"

Alfred said, "I've never heard of him."

Vance said, "That name he goes by is very likely not his real name."

Alfred said, "If he's the man that I think he could be, I'll never know for sure. But what I do know, is that letter I got was sent from Chicago, not New York."

Frank nodded.

"So," said Vance, "do you think he was there?"

Frank said, "Maybe. The killing upstairs was done by someone who knew what they were doing. But to go around branding victims with some sort of Anti-Christian symbol is not something an assassin does. A professional assassin gets in and out clean and fast."

Vance shrugged.

Frank said, "Okay, we've got to move. What's the skinny on the good doctor?"

Becca put her hand in the can and scooped out a glob.

Frank jerked away from her approach. "Hey, not so much."

"Oh, calm down." Becca began to apply the pomade to Frank's hair, slicking it back with a black comb. His hair lay straight, flat, and with a wet shine.

Vance said, "Dr. Ethos used to work for the department as a psychologist. At first he was there to help our officers with distress and the like. But over time we found him helpful in identifying the traits of certain criminals. Why they did what they did, that sort of thing."

Becca's nose rumpled as she combed Frank's hair back.

Detective Stranger took a sip from his drink. He set his glass on a table and put his hands in his pockets. "Well, we started to see some erratic behavior."

Frank asked, "What kind of erratic behavior? Anything specific?"

"He started to take on some of those less desirable personality traits. To put it lightly."

Frank and Alfred both shot the same quizzical look as Becca wiped her hands clean on a towel.

"That's as best as I can describe it. He skulked around the station when he wasn't supposed to be working. He was caught manipulating some of our prisoners' files. It was like he was trying to sabotage some of our cases. When I learned of it, I made the mistake of firing him."

Alfred's voice vibrated the cubes in his glass as he said, "Mistake? How is that a mistake?"

"I think in hindsight I should have kept him around in order to find out the who, and the why. But after looking over some of my cases, they seemed to have been either drug related or they had some kind of a connection with the mob."

Frank asked, "Which mob?"

"It was, well, all of them. But there was a case on an Eastern European country gaining some ground here. Don't know the country. One thing odd about the doctor. I used to sometimes hear a hint of an accent every now and again. Anyway, I've tried keeping an eye on him, but I came up empty handed. At one point I was told to stay away from him. I stayed away but always kept an ear to the streets."

Becca said, "Dr. Ethos is known to have a hand in delivering opium and other exotic drugs."

A knock at the front door interrupted the conversation. Alfred opened it, and Stage Sturgus entered. He was wearing his newsboy hat and a long black coat. Frank stood and extended his hand. "Thanks for coming, Stage." Frank introduced Stage to the others.

Stage said, "I hope I'm not too late." He rolled his hat in his fingers.

Frank said, "No, you're just in time."

"Mr. Savage, I thank you for the opportunity to help."

"Becca is going to tell us what we're here to do."

Becca said, "Stage, you're going to be the carriage driver. You will escort Frank and Alfred to the home of Dr. Lore Ethos."

"Okay."

"He's a man with connections in the city."

Frank added, "And it'll be my job, along with Alfred's, to find out about him. Maybe he can give us some information, or maybe we can find out if he is someone who might be involved. Or rule him out altogether."

Stage asked, "What do I do when we get there?"

Frank answered, "You'll stay with the horses. Keep an eye out for anything suspicious. You smell something offensive, make a note of it and let us know. But don't interrupt us unless it's an emergency."

"Copy."

Frank said, "I'm ready." He sniffed the air, looked up toward his hairline the best he could, and wrinkled his nose.

Stage guided the carriage down the gloomy streets of Chicago with Frank and Alfred riding in the back. His hands were surprisingly steady. The wheels rolled quietly along the flat road except for the occasional snap of a pebble under the carriage's weight. With a light tug of the reins, Stage stopped the carriage in front of a large white house surrounded by trees and bushes. A row of equally large-sized homes lined the opposite side of the street.

Frank said, "Keep your lights lit."

"Yes, sir."

"I don't anticipate being too long."

Frank and Alfred walked up the long walkway that led to the front door. Alfred wore ragged clothes that Becca had picked out. His hands shook from the overdose of coffee Frank had forced him to drink. As the two walked, they got into character.

Frank rapped on the white wood door with the shiny metallic knocker. There was no light when they heard a door inside the house open and then close. A dim glow seeped out the window adjacent to the door. It seemed to come from the back of the room, growing brighter and whiter as it moved closer.

Without making a sound, the door opened, and a man in a robe and carrying a lantern stepped into the doorcase. He said, "Hello, gentlemen."

"Yes," Frank said. "Are you the doctor? I mean, are you Dr. Ethos?"

The man said, "And who wants this information?"

Frank stepped forward a half step. His face poked out from the shadow into the light. "And does it matter?"

Dr. Ethos chuckled.

"Doctor, I'm Professor Harris and this is my brother-in-law. I think Mr. Thomas from the apothecary arranged our meeting. At least, I hope you're expecting us."

The doctor was quiet then said, "I am Dr. Ethos. Come in, please."

Frank held Alfred up by the arm as they walked in. Dr. Ethos struck a long match and proceeded to light the lanterns in the room. It took him a few minutes. The light exposed a large entrance with a staircase that curved down the left and right sides. Frank and Alfred entered a room that mirrored itself.

On the left was a living room with a high ceiling and a large glorious red couch and a fireplace. On the right was the same living room with the same high ceiling and the same glorious couch and fireplace. In the middle of the double staircase was a double door with brass handles.

"Left or Right?" Dr. Ethos asked.

Frank said without hesitation, "Right."

Lore Ethos led them to the right and said, "You know what that says about your character."

Frank, again without wavering, said, "And you know I don't care."

Lore said, “I’m sorry. My fundamental character is one of knowledge.”

“Sorry, Doc, not in the mood.”

Alfred grumbled, “Where’s the stuff?”

Frank patted him on the back as he set him down on the glorious red couch. “Soon, my friend.”

“Coffee or Scotch?” Lore said.

Frank stood to examine the doctor. Lore had a fat nose and a puffy ashy face except for the balls of his checks. It was as though someone had punched him in the nose and the color from the blood had shot into the round knobs of soft tissue covering his cheekbones. Frank looked into his dark black eyes. It reminded him of looking into the hollow barrels of a side-by-side shotgun.

“Soulless,” mumbled Frank.

Lore’s head snapped back.

How had that come out? Frank owned it and said, “I gotta say, Dr. Ethos, your eyes are black and soulless.”

The doctor said, “Scotch and coffee, aye.”

“I beg your pardon.”

The doctor said nothing more.

Frank inspected the room as Lore poured from a pitcher three cups of coffee. He then followed it up by introducing a large shot of whiskey to each. Frank eyed the stranger in order to make sure nothing else was added.

Dr. Ethos handed Frank two steamy cups, and Frank gave one to Alfred who hurriedly drank the hot beverage down.

Lore said, “That coffee was boiling just a moment ago.”

Alfred grumbled, “The stuff.” His voice grated through the air as he spoke. His legs and arms shook.

Frank said, “You know why I’m here. Can you help?”

“Well, you—” A puzzled look took hold in the features of the doctor’s face, and he stepped back and set his drink on the cart.

Frank’s eyes went to the drink cart that sat in the opposite room with the same liquor bottles on it. There was even coffee brewing. The only thing missing from the other room was the three men.

Lore put his hands inside his robe’s pockets in a jerky motion and then abruptly his arms seized.

Frank held his drink and didn’t budge. They locked gazes, one onto the other, and held the stare. Frank had one sleepy eye hanging low, unassuming. The other open and ready to gather, ready to respond. Lore stalled his motions and shook his head side to side with a twitch.

"Has Mr. Thomas ever steered you wrong?" Frank asked.

"No."

"I'm here to help my friend. My sister's husband is addicted to opium."

"Go to Chinatown."

"I don't want to exasperate the addiction. I want to control it. I have a theory that I can help him overcome his addiction, and I need your help."

It was quiet, then Frank said, "If you can't help, just tell me so, and we'll leave. No harm, no foul."

Lore's eyes opened upward then he shut them and held them closed before staring at Frank's shoes. He looked up with just his eyes and said, "Maybe I can guide you to someone who can. What are your intentions?"

"I need enough to satisfy his cravings, that's all. Nothing more, and nothing less. No, I am no copper."

Dr. Ethos pursed his lips like a kiss and made a smacking sound as he thought and analyzed. "Alright. I've got a bit of a taste here." Then he blurted, "It'll cost you. It should get you by, for now at least. Then—"

"Then what?"

"I've got a contact for you—he's a Pole."

Frank's scalp perked with this information.

Lore walked backward one step and then executed a very crisp military about-face.

Alfred stayed in character as Frank scanned the room. The ceiling even mirrored itself on the other side of the room. "You have an interesting home, Doctor."

Lore Ethos shuffled through some drawers in a dresser at the back of the room. The same dresser rested in the same spot in the other living room. He said, "It's my design. I kept having these dreams of looking into a mirror and seeing someone else. I mean-" He turned as he stopped speaking. He carried a small bottle in his hands. "Do you have the cash for this?"

"Yes."

Lore continued, "What do you suppose that means?"

"Your design or the dream?"

"The dream."

Frank thought a moment. "You don't recognize yourself anymore. You question who you are, I imagine."

Lore grinned. "Very good."

Frank accepted the bottle and paid the doctor for the opium.

Lore said, "Give it to him."

Frank stalled. Slowly he maneuvered to stand between Alfred and the doctor.

Alfred looked and winked and said, "Yes, yes." His voice grated through his lips, enhancing his character's plight.

Frank twisted the cap off and set it on the coffee table. He pulled a pipe from his jacket along with a packet of tobacco. Frank poured some tobacco into the pipe. He broke up the opium and rolled a small ball between his finger and thumb. He put it in the center of the tobacco and lit it. Alfred puffed off the pipe and smiled as he sat back and stared upward in a daze. His eyes spun into the back of his head. Frank twisted the cap back onto the bottle.

Alfred whispered, "It helps."

Frank asked, "Where can we go for our prescription?"

Lore said, "I've a contact for you. His name is Lake Lagoon." He wrote something on a piece of paper and handed it to Frank.

Frank didn't feel surprised, let alone show any shock. He nodded and reached for Alfred and helped him from the couch.

Lore said, "Don't come back here again."

Frank turned to analyze the expression. There was nothing. He had no idea what was going on in the doctor's mind. That scared him. He said, "I won't. Thank you."

Frank helped Alfred to the door and down the path to the carriage where Stagecoach Sturgus impatiently awaited their return. Dr. Ethos watched them ride away down the long dark street.

"Hey, everything go okay?" Stage asked.

Alfred grumbled, "Shit, this stuff is giving me the mother of all headaches."

Frank answered, "I think so. The doctor's a tough one to figure out. We may have a clue I wasn't expecting, but I'm not surprised. Did you see anything?"

"It was quiet," said Stage, "but it was almost too quiet. I did notice a light go on and off in a room upstairs. No, it was more like someone walked by an open bedroom door with a lantern and the light shined out the window. It was for only a second. If I had blinked, I would have missed it."

Alfred rubbed his head. “Someone else was home. I heard a creak in the ceiling.”

Frank worked the night over in his mind as Stage took them back to the hotel the long and winding way.

CHAPTER 11

Goth's milky face glowed under the streetlamp-lit sky as he leaned against a brick building with his back to the wall and his arms crossed. Rocco paced back and forth while rabidly chomping and sucking on a cigarette. He stopped to extract a flask from inside his coat and stood motionless only long enough to slug down a swallow of rotgut. Rocco mopped up the dribble from his chin with his sleeve and resumed his nervous patrol of the backstreet's trash containers.

Goth interrupted his brother's nervous tics. "Shut up."

"But—"

"What?" Goth's forehead crinkled up tight, challenging Rocco to challenge him.

Rocco was down to the last nub of his smoldering butt as he worked at the tobacco. He looked down and shook his head and blew a thin stream of smoke into the night's haze.

He mumbled, "So, I get to meet the man who has inspired my one and only brother. I can't wait."

"I hate sarcasm."

Rocco huffed and turned back to pacing.

Goth's fist tightened until his forearm pulled up to his chest. He turned to the side to hide it. He said, "Rocco. Stop it. Stand here." He pointed at the wall to his side with his good hand.

Rocco took a place by his brother without saying a sour word and without throwing a dour glance. He had pushed Goth as far as he could. Any further could be dangerous. Even for family.

A mist was rising menacingly and rolling smoothly from the dewy street. The fog melted into the beam of light emanating from the tops of the lampposts. It blanched the alley from the ground to the row of second-floor apartment balconies.

A disturbance in the mist flowed out and upward to the sky. A man drifted in from the middle of the disruption with a woman at his side. Slowly the two bodies grew closer. Goth and Rocco waited quietly.

The man stopped in front of Goth and said, "I heard you wanted to see me."

Goth said, "I thought you might have a need for someone like me."

Plenty said, "If he needed you he would have asked you to come along."

Boss said, "Now, Plenty, there's no need for any of that. Besides, Goth was being tested."

Goth grinned.

"I knew if he followed me, than he surely must want the job. I don't like infirm knots in my organization. Not like that dumb bastard the Kingston Killer. You have to want to be here." His eyes moved to Rocco. "But, I am surprised you brought someone along." With a ghostly motion his head turned to match the direction of his eyes.

Rocco stood straight and put his hand near his gun.

Plenty said, "Shh." With a sadistic twinkle in her eye she pointed down with a flash of her gaze.

Through the thickening mist Plenty's shotgun-pistol seemed to hover just under the feathery murky soup.

Rocco's eyes bounced back and forth between the gun in Plenty's hand and the breasts on her chest.

Plenty breathed a laugh and said, "Don't look at me as if you have more to offer than what I'm looking at."

Rocco swallowed.

Boss sighed. "What's the baggage?"

Rocco said, "I'm—"

"Whoa," Boss interrupted. He shook his head and pointed. "Your breath stinks, kid. I wasn't talking to you." Boss dropped his chin to his chest and said, "Watch your step. You don't want to become a burden to me. You're lucky your presence hasn't caused me to kill you and your partner."

Goth seemed unfazed as he said, "This is my brother, Rocco. He can be trusted."

Boss and Plenty calculated Rocco. Boss said, "You don't want to end up being an unsolved case floating down the river."

Rocco looked to Goth for support.

Goth said, "Shh."

A clack from the hammer of Goth's drawn pistol sliced through the air.

Plenty smiled and holstered her cannon.

"I've a job for you," said Boss. "I'm actually astounded that you showed up when you did."

Goth said, "I was hoping you'd say that." The pallor in his face dissipated as his excitement grew.

"I've got an annoyance that needs to be . . . disposed of."

"That's my job."

"Right. My hideout at the Palmer House has been discovered. There's a sheriff by the name of Alfred Kincaid and another man by the name of Frank Savage."

Goth's head drew back.

"There is a third." Boss pondered a moment and then said, "He's one to watch out for."

"And Savage isn't?" Goth said sarcastically.

"There's something different about this one. Can't put my finger on it. Anyway, the hotel is no longer my base or a meeting place for that matter. Consider it compromised. We can give thanks to the Killer for that. You can find Savage and the others there."

"I can handle it."

Boss stepped up close and said into Goth's bony face, "This isn't a farmer's family. There isn't going to be unarmed children or old ladies locked in a box."

Goth gritted his teeth. "What's that supposed to mean?"

"This is the real deal. If you're not careful you'll find yourself and your smelly-faced brother splayed out on the carpet of a long dark hallway in the Palmer House bleeding into its foundation. Got that?"

Goth peered at Boss. What Boss offered might distill his desires, so he kept quiet.

"Any questions?"

Goth asked, "Any requests on how it goes down? That being said, I hope you're not too particular."

"Just be careful, and if you get caught, you don't know me."

"I don't get caught. They get dead. End of story."

Boss said, "I can't say it's been an aesthetic delight, but it's been . . . interesting."

Boss and Plenty silently disappeared into the fog. Goth and Rocco waited until they were gone. Rocco's hands began to tremble, and he turned to his brother. Goth lowered his head and frowned at the earthbound cloud.

Rocco said, "There's no turning back. Is there?"

Goth said, "That was never an option."

The sun had only just begun to communicate its ascent. Stage had all but arrived when he abruptly departed out the back door of the hotel. He was moving quickly with his head rotating about his neck.

Goth Furse slapped Rocco across the jaw. "Wake up."

Rocco blurted, "What the fu—"

"Shut it."

"Damnit, you don't need to do that crap, and you know it."

"Look." Goth pointed at Stage who walked briefly in their direction before he took a sharp turn up the street.

"Who is it?"

"Recognize him?"

"No . . . maybe, I don't know." Rocco squinted. "Maybe, yeah. So?"

"That's the punk kid of that old lady in the box."

"What do you think it means?" asked Rocco.

Goth rubbed his cheek with the knuckle of his fist as his brain worked the puzzle. "Get the horses."

"I'm on it."

Rocco ran up the road as Goth whispered, "You're my lucky break, my friend."

Goth started to follow Stage on foot. He was only one block along when Rocco rode up with the horses. Rocco was on a black and Goth leapt onto the sorrel.

"We can stay back a ways, like this." Goth slowed the pace with a tug on the reins. "I can see ahead for about five blocks. I reckon that this boy is gonna guide us to our first victim."

Rocco gripped his reins. The leather made a scrunching sound as he squeezed tightly to the straps. He trotted behind as they slowly followed the young grandson of their latest victim.

They had been riding for about ten minutes when Stage took a sharp turn into the front door of a three-story townhouse.

Goth signaled with his head toward the back of a row of houses and said, "Let's hole up over there."

Goth guided his horse around a moving cable car. He steered them behind the buildings. Their lookout positioned them cattycorner across the road with full view of the townhouse.

"We'll keep an eye out. Wait for dark. Then I'll go in," Goth said. "Alone."

Rocco was silent as his eyes shot sharply to a window on the top floor. He extended his arm and pointed. "Look."

Frank Savage was standing in front of a window that exposed a hallway. Stage was saying something as Frank nodded. Frank then handed Stage a piece of paper.

Goth grinned as Frank shut the door. He said, "That's Savage." Less than a minute passed and Stage took off running up the street back towards the Palmer House.

Rocco moved to nudge his mount forward as he barked, "He's gonna get away."

Goth grabbed him smartly by the sleeve of his jacket. "No. We aren't after him. As tempting as it is for me, we have to stay focused. There'll be time for fun later."

Rocco stepped his horse back and dismounted. "Unless they've changed the definition of fun, I don't think I'm having the kind of fun you're having."

They tied the horses to a wood fence. Goth glanced over his shoulder. A large slimy smile smeared itself across his face. His pulse quickened just a bit as he saw a woman walk by a window in the apartment.

Goth's fist actually loosened up a bit as he thought of his future. The tension in his muscles released just enough that he noticed.

Becca held a cigarette between her fingers as she cased the top drawer of her dresser for a match.

"Need a light?" asked Frank.

"Sure."

Frank stood on the opposite side of the room in his pants and no shirt. He lit a match as he leaned up against the wall and held his ground. Becca smirked as she was forced to walk across the bedroom to the burning match.

With her smoke lit, Frank pulled her in and kissed her. There was a rap at the door.

Frank inquired, "Who is it?"

"Mr. Savage, it's me, Stage."

Frank maneuvered around Becca and pulled his pistol from the holster that hung from the coat rack and slowly opened the door.

"Hey, Stage."

"I got word that Mr. Fulsome is off duty at ten o'clock this evening."

Frank pondered what he heard for a moment. "You have a pencil and some paper?"

"Yeah, gimmie a second," Becca said. She handed Frank a piece of paper and a pencil from a table by the window.

Frank jotted a note that instructed Gil and Alfred to meet him at nine. He handed the paper to Stage and said goodbye.

After closing the door Frank rested his forehead on it in thought. Becca watched from the window. Neither of them said a word for several minutes.

Frank turned and sat on the bed. He looked up and smiled and patted the spot next to him. Becca took her seat and looked into his eyes.

Frank said, "I'm sorry I wasn't here."

Becca stroked his hair. "It's okay, I understand what you're all about." She smiled.

Frank laid his head in her neck as they hugged. He smelled her hair.

Frank whispered, "I missed you."

"Me too." She caressed the back of his head.

"Today is our last day."

Becca's eyes drooped. "I know. You will say goodbye this time."

Frank didn't say anything and stood and went to the washroom. Becca rested her hands on her knees and sighed.

A few moments passed before Frank came back into the bedroom and blew out the light. The two lay down under the sheet and blanket.

They fell asleep on their backs holding hands. They slept.

Frank's eyes opened then lurched and searched. He bounded from the bed. He clasped the mattress and threw the bedding, with Becca, to the floor. The door smashed open. Becca slammed to the hard ground with the mattress on top of her. Frank sprang to the open door just as a fiery blaze blew out the barrel of a gun. He threw his weight into the door. The sharp edge slammed into the arm that spit sparks at an empty bed.

"Ah." Goth screamed. "Son of a—"

Frank pulled the door back as the gun clanked to the floor. With his fist firm and dense, Frank smashed Goth on the eye. The blow sent him back into the hallway.

Becca slowly worked her way out from under the mattress and bedding. She scanned the room for Frank's gun.

Goth pulled his permanent left fist back by his ear and hit Frank solid on the nose. Frank stepped back and caught himself in the doorframe with outstretched arms. Goth took the opening and pulled his left gun cross draw. Frank kicked the weapon out of his hand. Goth's clenched fist came again and Frank ducked.

In the move to duck, Frank's ankle buckled.

"Ah." Frank fell and Goth ran down the hall toward the stairs. Frank attempted to stand and fell from the weight on his sore tendons. He pushed on his ankle with his thumbs then threw his body down the hall after Furse. As Goth got to the edge of the stairs, Frank rammed into his back. The two fighting cowboys tumbled down the stairs and came to a forceful thud at the midpoint landing.

Simultaneously they stood and slung punches. Both adversaries managed to hit their opponent in the face. They both stepped back and shook their heads to regain their sense of direction.

For a brief moment they stared at each other, trying to focus. Then Frank propelled a right just as Goth sent a left. The two fists hit in midflight.

Goth allowed himself to fall down the stairs in order to escape. Frank reached out and grabbed hold of Goth's boot. The boot slipped off and fell. Frank quickly snapped up and picked up chase.

With solid blows they smacked each other again, belt after belt, as if they were taking turns on rounds of drinks in a bar. Each blow was followed by another heavy wallop until; finally, Frank blocked a swing and smashed his closed fist into Goth's stomach. Goth spit vomit onto his clothes and fell backwards. As he tumbled, he rolled over his back up onto his feet. Frank followed with a swing and a miss. His ankle let go and he fell.

Goth ran down the last flight of stairs with Frank a half flight behind him.

As Frank ran out the back door, an object flew toward his head. He ducked barely enough that the blow wasn't solid, but the brick connected just the same, sending him to the ground in a stupor.

Through a sparkly cloud Frank watched Goth run up the back road away from him. Frank stood to continue his pursuit but he lost his balance in a dizzying rush of blood to the head that made the earth spin under his feet. He attempted to run straight but his path curved and he fell.

Becca sprung out the door with gun in hand. As she knelt down to help, he snatched the pistol and armed it. Frank proceeded to aim at what looked to be two Goths running away.

"No, Frank," Becca said. "You might hit someone. You know better than that."

Frank uncocked the weapon. He sat with his head resting on his knee. "Damn it all to hell."

Becca rubbed his back. "You'll get him."

"I know, but—"

Becca was quiet.

"I got complacent," Frank said.

"You didn't know. They shouldn't have known you were here."

"Yeah, but still, and now you're involved."

"I can take care of myself."

"That doesn't mean I won't worry."

Frank caught his breath and allowed Becca to help him inside. After a look-over Becca decided Frank had to go to the hospital.

Alfred attempted to speak. A low scraping croak seeped out between his glowering lips. He smashed his fist on his knee.

Gil shook his head. He was reading through Frank's notes studying the happenings at Alfred's daughter's home. He focused on the picture Frank had drawn of a circle and a cross, attempting to place it. It was not familiar.

Stage barked, "Mr. Kincaid." He huffed and handed Alfred the note Frank had given him only moments earlier.

Alfred rubbed his voice box as he read. "He wants, Frank wants—" Alfred croaked again. "Nine o'clock at Becca's. We'll have a little talk with Detective Fulsome."

Gil took the note and rubbed his chin.

Stage inquired, "Can I go?"

It was quiet as Gil thought. His large hands pressed on his temples.

"Stage, you stay here with Alfred."

Alfred's head snapped up. "Wha—" His voice cracked.

"Rest yourself. You need sleep."

"There's no Godda—" Alfred cringed with the pain from his throat.

"Quiet down, you crazy S.O.B.," Gil said as he set down Frank's notes. He then lifted his mattress and withdrew a pistol. "You have not slept and the only thing you have had to drink is that burning oil you keep in that flask."

Gil called him out, and Alfred was busted. Alfred consented to a thick gristly laugh.

Gil handed the gun to Stage. "You know how to use this?"

He slipped the weapon into his belt and said, "Yes, sir."

"I want you to stand guard in the hall." Gil turned to Alfred. "And you are to drink some water and eat something and go to bed. That's an order. You are about to fall over from exhaustion."

Alfred studied the bed while his arms hung loose at his sides. "Okay."

"Besides, Frank and I can handle Fulsome. We're gonna need you, and you're no good to anyone right now."

Alfred acknowledged the comment with a dulled grunt.

Gil looked at Stage.

Stage said, "You can count on me."

"Okay then. I'll step out for a bit and meet with Frank at Becca's at nine."

Gil scanned his partners' faces. "Are we all on board?"

Everyone agreed.

Gil grinned and threw on his long coat. He stepped from the room with a sharp turn, throwing up the edge of his slicker with a wave. Stage took his post in the hall, and Alfred quickly went to sleep.

Gil wandered the streets of Chicago as he contemplated seeking out a drink. He decided it was best to stay as lucid as possible.

An alley captured his attention. He lit a cigarette and walked halfway into the narrow pathway. He leaned on the building and expelled smoke over the brick wall. His mind wandered to an earlier time:

A fourteen-year-old Gil. A mama's boy. He was walking home from school with a friend. He always walked home and always by the same abandoned shack and always with his friend, but never was he followed, until that day.

At the dinner table with four chairs, Gil sat across from his sister. She was seventeen with a cute face. She was friendly, and she smiled more than Gil.

Dad was a quiet but strong man, a hardworking type who knew he had to provide for his family. He taught Gil to always treat a woman with respect and to work hard and to help his neighbors. It was important to follow the guidance of the Lord, and to work the land was an honorable way to make a living.

Gil's mom had light hair and deep laughter lines around her eyes. Gil adored her and his sister.

Gil's sister, Jessica, watched out for him at school. He wasn't a big kid. He was healthy but skinny and prone to being bullied. Gil was learning to take care of himself. As time went on he found strength he didn't know he had, and his sister didn't have to step in anymore—unless Gil was hurting someone.

The creak of the farmhouse's foundation was normal and comforting, but steps in the middle of the night were not.

Gil woke to the sound of a sharp but muffled cry that was quickly followed by a muted but distinctive shotgun blast.

"Mom, Dad?" gasped Gil.

Jessica ran into the bedroom.

She whispered firm and clear, "Get up. We've got to move."

The thumping of boots grew and filled his ears. Gil leapt from bed as Jessica gripped his arm to pull him out.

Jessica ordered, "Out the window."

The door flew open with a force that knocked it off its hinges. A man sprang from the lightlessness. Gil couldn't see except for a fist as it hit Jessica. The blow shocked her so that she hit the floor with all her weight. Blood smeared out over her face.

Gil went into shock. He couldn't move. A flash of teeth snarled back. Gil's pause was just enough. He eventually forced himself to move toward the villain who had broken into his home. But it was too late.

The two reached out to attack each other as Jessica ran toward the man. She was screaming blue murder. "Don't you touch him!"

An explosion of gunpowder spewed flames. The flash was in Gil's face. He yelped out from the burn of the blast on the surface of his eyeballs. The blast dropped Jessica to her back.

Gil closed his burning eyes and gripped the intruder's forearm. They fought. The man tried to get out of Gil's tightening hands but couldn't.

When Gil opened his eyes he could now see perfectly. He could see the horribly ugly and dirty evil face of a killer. Gil fought as he watched Jessica take her last breath. With that breath—with the last breath she would ever take—a discharge expanded inside Gil's body. He squeezed so tight the killer's forearm that his grip cracked the bone, sending broken bone to protrude out through the skin. The killer's gun fell to the floor.

Gil's thumb was up and into the assassin's eye with no mercy. The killer hollered out from the pain. Gil didn't stop until his thumb was buried to his wrist. The dying man twitched with a frantic fury until an abrupt wilt arrived and he withered into death . . .

It was a memory that reinforced who he is and how he became a man who kills. A man who can see in the darkness when others cannot.

Gil leaned on the wall. His ash was long. He didn't drop the spent cigarette until it burned his finger. He ran his hand over his face and rubbed the stubble on his chin. It was time to go.

The sun was out of sight now as Gil rounded the corner of the alley. He walked to within two blocks of Becca's apartment. There were two horses and a man standing behind the building. He picked up his pace. As he got closer he could see that the man was armed and looked out of place. The man stood by a sorrel and a black. Gil didn't recognize him. A pistol report resounded from the apartment building.

The sorrel scuffled away in a half circle. The black yanked against the man's pull and whinnied.

"Settle," the man said.

Gil ran. He didn't make a sound. His hat flew off his head. He threw his arms out and back. His coat slipped off and floated to the ground. His .455 break-top was still strapped tight about his ribs under his left arm.

The man turned and noticed someone was coming in his direction. It didn't register at first. But when it did, he panicked and stepped up into his saddle. He hollered, "Go, go, go." He kicked hard sending his black down the dark street.

Gil thundered up behind the tied-up sorrel and jumped into the saddle with a leaping step. He pulled up the reins and spun the horse and swiftly took chase.

Their hooves sounded like thunderous explosions off the solid buildings. Rocco was a block in the lead, but Gil was accelerating. The streets were dimly lit by gas lamps that sat atop posts at the street corners.

The chase accelerated into a hard turn to the east. Rocco's horse skidded on the pebbly ground—he and the horse almost went over. They kept their footing, barely. He glanced over his shoulder. He blurted, "Oh, bitch."

Gil flowed behind him effortlessly on the sorrel and took the corner with ease.

Rocco began panting louder than his horse was breathing. He pulled into another much-too-hurried turn; they miraculously stuck to the street.

The buildings were growing farther apart as Rocco led the black into a park. An unlit park.

Gil noticed and grinned and whispered, "Thought as much."

There was no light as Rocco pulled on his black. He was continuing to slow as Gil rode up behind him. Rocco then heeled his horse, thrusting them into the park. Tree branches, hidden in the shadows, whisked by his ears. Some smacked his face.

Gil, with curt and precise guidance, led his sorrel, with controlled movements, around the bushes and trees. He continued to gain ground.

Rocco pushed his way forward, sending them up and over a small flat ridge that had a slight drop-off and led to the lake. A soft gleam bounced off the waves rippling onto the beach.

Gil noticed that Rocco's horse galloped cumbrously through the soft sand that paralleled Lake Michigan. He edged his own horse over to the shoulder of the beach line, progressing as if sailing smoothly over the firmer ground.

The sky blended into the dark ground. Rocco began to rustle through his bag that lay across the pommel of his saddle. He was searching for something.

Rocco's horse was slowing as Rocco continued to grab at a bag in his lap. Gil noticed a flash that illuminated outward from the border of Rocco's frame. It was only for an instant. Then it was dark again, except for a spark of some sort flying out in an arc toward Gil and the sorrel.

Gil pulled back just as something landed in front of him. Flames blazed, crawling outward like a thousand spiders leaving a nest, brightly lighting the beach. Gil reacted and sent his horse around the flames. He squeezed his eyes tight then opened them. It was fuzzy for a second, and then he could see again as he readjusted to the savage darkness.

"That crazy bastard," Gil said.

Having lost some ground, Gil adjusted and was once again quickly gaining. There was another flash. He snatched out his pistol and aimed it at the black body in the middle of the flash and pulled the trigger tight into its guard. The gun's discharge blinded Gil for a moment. As soon as the shell spit out the barrel, he knew that it would find its intended target.

Rocco felt the blow, but no pain. He dropped his bag full of kerosene and was staring into fire that licked his eyes. He screamed out like a child as the gas ignited on top of the head of the horse he was riding.

Flames of the fire flowed off the head of the horse in an almost instant stream over Rocco's body and into the night sky. The scream that the black let out sounded human.

Gil had a new purpose. He was no longer intent on catching Rocco. He had to save the horse.

Rocco continued to cry out as he tried to cover his face, never thinking to guide the horse into the lake.

Gil yelled, "Go into the lake, you dumb bastard."

The black, unaware of what had happened, slightly curved his path into the shallowest section of the lake. Its hooves splashed in the water as its head bucked this way and that. The water reflected the firelight. It was as though sparks were flying off the black's feet.

Gil nudged his sorrel closer as Rocco lost his grip and fell. His foot caught the bindings under his horse and he fell under its back hooves. He was being stomped to death.

Gil worked his way close enough so that he was able to leap to the black. He pulled hard on the horse's mane. The black dropped hard to its side into the water. Gil flew forward and rolled with the impact into the lake. He stood up and jumped on top of the black's head as it tried to stand. He splashed water on the burning horse until the fire was out.

Gil stood the injured horse. He then inspected the eyes as best he could. The smell of burnt hair infiltrated his nose. There was scarred flesh and dried blood, but the fire had never gotten to the horse's nose, mouth, or eyes. The black kicked its hind legs from the pain and cried out. Gil talked to the animal to coax him down. He tore off his shirt, dunked it in the water, and draped it over the head and over the mane.

"Shh, shh, sorry boy. Shh, you'll feel it for a while, but you'll live. I'm so sorry."

Gil held tightly to the black as he stared at the motionless body of Rocco.

Gil yelled, "You had better pray to the Lord above that you're already dead. Cause if you ain't, I'm gonna cut your head off and bury it in the sand."

Rocco's body didn't answer.

An hour passed with frequent applications of the wet shirt to the wounds. When the black began to calm down, Gil slowly led him to the soft sand and laid him down with the wet shirt over the burn.

Gil stepped over to Rocco and felt for a pulse. There was nothing pounding against his fingers. He turned him over to see that Rocco's head was charred and caved in. He spit, "Lucky you."

CHAPTER 12

Cole cracked a joke. It broke the ice. Alfred chuckled, Frank grinned, and even Stage allowed his first smile since his grandmother had been shot by Goth Furse.

A doctor and a nurse were tending to Frank's wounds.

"What made you shave your beard?" asked Frank.

"Uh," muttered Cole. He looked over at the nurse who was smiling.

"I always wondered why men grew full beards, now I know why," quipped Frank. "Hiding something."

The nurse interjected, "I think he looks handsome."

Frank grinned. "Oh, I see." He winked at Cole.

Frank waved Becca over as the doctor applied a bandage to the knuckles of his right hand. He whispered something into her ear. She kissed his cheek and said goodbye to everyone. On her way out, Gil, along with Vance Stranger, walked in.

Frank asked, "So, what's the scoop?"

Gil nodded at Frank.

Vance said, "The man's name is Rocco Furse."

Cole asked, "Goth's brother?"

Vance answered, "Yep. Although, he doesn't have the reputation his brother has. The records show he was only arrested for crimes when his brother was involved. Other than that he had stayed out of trouble."

Stage asked, "What's the story on Goth?"

Alfred said, "He's a total psychopath." His voice was grating but seemed smoother.

The doctor said nothing as he began to clean up the wound on the side of Frank's head.

Frank said, "Goth was one of the killers who murdered Alfred's family. The reason we're here. And, more than likely, he's the one who killed your grandmother."

Stage's face was tense.

The nurse began to wrap Frank's ankle. He winced.

"How's the horse?" asked Frank.

"He'll live," Gil said. "The fire burned mostly hair and some of the skin, but his eyes, nose, and mouth are relatively untouched, which is important. He's being tended to by a doctor in the shed out back."

The doctor and nurse finished up and left the cowboys and the detective and Stage to talk.

Frank stood from his chair and with a measured and sober pace picked up Goth's boot. He studied the heel. He said, "Stage, come here."

Stage walked over.

"You see these, these bolts that hold this plate in place?" Frank pointed out a silver heel plate on the back of the killer's boot.

"Yeah."

"There's a bolt missing. I found that bolt on the floor of Alfred's daughter's house, in the living room."

Stage's eyes grew wide.

Frank stepped over to Cole's bed and handed it to him. Stage followed.

Frank asked, "Recognize the sole?"

Cole examined the sole for no more than two seconds and said, "Yes, this boot walked in the back door and walked about the living room. Its trail ended in front of the trunk."

Frank listened.

Cole said, "And it was also in front of Stage's house."

Stage ground his molars.

Cole asked, "So, what have we got? Where do we go from here?"

Frank paced the hospital room, working the stiffness out of his sore ankle. "Uncle Baldy and the Kingston Killer are both dead. And they are unrelated to each other. We have two more to get, Goth Furse and the mastermind of the whole incident. Goth, we know but have no idea about his whereabouts, and the second—we don't know who he is."

Alfred inquired, "That body the detective found in the lake?"

Vance said, "Mr. Lagoon."

"Yeah, you think he killed my little girl?"

Frank rubbed his chin. "Maybe, I doubt it, but that's not the end of the trail if he did. If he killed your daughter, I believe he was working for someone else. We need to find that person."

Alfred said, "And kill him."

It was quiet a moment.

"I don't like that Fulsome character," Alfred said.

"Nobody does," said Vance, "but I don't think he's that powerful to arrange something of this magnitude. He does things for money or maybe sex, not a revenge killing."

Frank said, "As far as we know he has no direct connection to your family. All we have is a connection to Plenty Sky, who may have a link to the local mobs. Our little excursion on Astor Street never panned out, except for Lake Lagoon's connection to drug sales."

Gil asked, "That was who again?"

Frank said, "Dr. Lore Ethos." He dropped his chin to his boots. "I think he's a strange character, eccentric, and he may be a mob leader. But I don't see an association between him and Alfred."

Vance interjected, "His history is rife with oddities but I have gone through everything I have—I've got nothing linking Lore to Alfred's family or to that letter you received from Chicago."

Alfred nodded.

"Dr. Ethos has no family. No wife, no kids, his parents are in Europe somewhere. He actually has absolutely no ties to anyone. Anyone living, that is."

Gil listened and waited. Every cell in his body lurched about with impatience. Astor District had been Plenty's destination. And Dr. Lore Ethos lived on Astor Street. It made his stomach tighten up. His eyes darted around the room. His blood spattered under his skin like grease on a fire.

Frank said, "We all need some sleep."

Cole interjected, "I want to come."

"Me, too," said Stage.

Frank said, "No and no."

Cole mumbled something inaudible.

Frank pointed at Stage. "You're in this too far as it is. I want you to stay somewhere safe. Do you have family or friends you can stay with?"

Stage emphatically said, "No."

Frank was quiet.

Stage's shoulders relaxed as he looked down and said, "Yes."

Frank smiled and put his hand on Stage's shoulder. "I promise, if we need you, I will call on you. And don't follow us."

"Yes, sir."

"You've done a great job, Stage. We will work better if we don't have to worry about you."

Gil said, "You guys head back without me." He looked back and forth between Frank and Alfred. "I'm gonna check on the horse one more time."

Gil stepped from the hospital room backwards and walked briskly down the hall. He went out the back door of the hospital to a shed with light sneaking out the cracks of its wood planks.

A doctor and a nurse were standing by the door looking over the injured black who was lying on a couple of mattresses. He had a white bandage on his head.

"How is he?"

The doctor said, "We were just leaving. He should sleep well and at least somewhat pain free. I gave him some relaxant and painkillers—"

The doctor was interrupted when the black's head popped up.

The doctor grumbled, "Huh?"

The black stood up on wobbly legs and slowly walked over to Gil. The doctor tried to hold him back, but he bucked and shook his head and pushed through.

Gil patted his shoulders. "Well, now, you need your rest. I want you to lie back down."

The black blew out his nose.

The doctor, with a raised brow, said, "He shouldn't be awake, let alone walking around."

Gil said, "You can go, Doc. I'll take care of him."

Gil glanced over his shoulder to make sure the doctor and the nurse were inside the hospital.

"I want you to stay here, okay?"

Gil stepped back slowly and reached out to close the door. The black followed without reluctance until he was outside. He used the weight of his body as momentum to push through. They stared at each other. Gil had his hands on his hips. He shook his head. His eyes smiled.

"Okay."

Gil walked away and the black followed.

After a few blocks, Gil checked his revolver and holstered it in the leather shoulder harness under his arm. The black, with a white bandage on its head and over most of his mane, followed his new companion.

Gil said, "You really shouldn't be a detective."

The black was quiet.

"You're not very good at trailing people. You don't have the talent for it. You keep wanting to go ahead of me."

The black trotted. His movements were casual.

Gil smiled and said, "How about I let you know where I'm going? I'm going to Astor Street. Now you can just meet me there."

The horse got up close as if to hear him better.

"You know where that is?"

He snorted.

Gil grinned. "Okay, you can follow me, but when we get there, I need you to be quiet and wait outside. Alright?"

He snorted again.

A couple of men stepped from a bar and Gil asked them, "Where's Astor Street?"

"You walk east two blocks and you're there."

"Thanks, oh, and do you know Dr. Ethos's house? Maybe you know where that might be."

The two men showed their nerves, then the second man said, "Listen, mister—"

Gil interrupted, "I ain't getting you involved. Please, it's very important."

The men looked at Gil then at the black that followed him.

The first man said, "Shit, you're gonna find it anyway. Take a left on Astor, go up two blocks, and it's the biggest, whitest house you've ever seen."

As the two men stumbled away, Gil said, "Thanks."

Gil began his trek once again with his new horse following close. As the streetlights grew farther apart, Gil was able to see more clearly.

Gil said, "Well, here it is."

The black snuggled up close for attention. Gil patted and stroked the animal until it lowered its head.

Gil said, "I'm goin' in."

The black nodded.

"You gonna stay here?"

The horse shimmied and snorted.

Gil smiled.

A light flickered on and off in the basement of the large white home. The crisp glow streaked and stretched across the yard from the window. The shadows moved quick and disappeared.

Gil studied the picture of his wife in his watch. "Well, darling, here I go."

Gil, with intention, walked away from the black. His new friend stayed in place at the side of the road and watched him approach the front door.

Gil looked into the dim first floor. He then stepped back to observe the windows on the second level. He walked around the side of the house and peered into the one window in the basement that emitted light.

The wind whistled by his ears as he squinted to focus into the room. It was bright. It was a square, clean, and benign room with a cage, and a trembling Irish Setter in the corner.

He whispered, "Ruby."

A woman walked by and blew out the light. Gil could see well now. He watched her exit up a set of stairs.

"Screw it."

Gil walked to the front door and knocked loudly.

Nothing.

Gil banged again, this time with his fist and not the knocker.

Nothing.

Gil kicked the door. Then it opened. A man holding a candelabra with three lit candles said, "Yes, and what is so important?"

Gil acted drunk and said, "I want to talk to P-Plenty."

"Plenty who?"

The light from the flames caused the man's head to glow. Gil was forced to avert his eyes.

"Listen, either you gets me to see Plenty, or I put a slug into your chest." He hiccupped. "Deal?"

It was quiet, and then the man went to close the door. Gil pushed his way in and knocked one of the candles to the ground.

The man said, "What's the meaning of this?"

"And who might you be?" Gil pointed a crooked finger and stumbled.

"I'm Dr. Ethos. And I don't appreciate you squandering away my evening with this malarkey."

"And I am going to torment you until I get to see *my* Plenty." He pointed a thumb at his own chest and smiled a crooked and silly smile.

"Punch-drunk simpleton." Dr. Ethos stepped away and walked to the center of a grand double staircase and opened the door.

He said, "Plenty?"

"Yeah, that's what I thunk," added Gil.

There was nothing for a long moment as Gil scanned the room. On the left wall he noticed the room was exactly like the right side, that is, except for one difference.

The light was scant enough and beaming upward at just the perfect slant to reveal the evidence he needed. On the left wall some of the bricks were placed at a slightly funny angle. The angled bricks cast a slight shadow upward on the wall. The shadow formed a crescent moon. Gil's whole body turned sharply to the right. And on the right wall the bricks cast a shadow of an upside-down cross.

Gil narrowed his eyes and stood straight; he pulled out his gun. Quietly and with authority he marched toward Dr. Ethos.

He said, "This is for my friend, Alfred."

Gil pulled his gun and swung his arm up and then down, crashing the barrel solidly onto Dr. Ethos's cranium, sending him to the floor. There was a squeak that came from behind a second before he felt a blow that sent him forward over Dr. Ethos.

He stumbled over the doctor, fell into the open doorway, collapsed onto the first step, and then dropped across step after step until he hit his head on the wall at the bottom.

Gil squeezed his eyes.

Ruby whimpered.

A flash of bright light bloomed from the upstairs living room as a figure drifted down the stairs. Gil rolled away and lifted his gun from the floor as he moved into the basement. He opened Ruby's cage and ducked into a corner in the back of the basement under the window.

The light was brightening, and he took aim.

After a moment the light went out.

This allowed Gil to relax. He could see everything in a crisp blue.

He whispered, "Thought as much."

Ruby lightly barked as a form slid into the room.

Gil grinned and said, "Put the blaster down. Slow but now."

Plenty pulled taut on her firearm. The pellets hit the air and finished in the wall.

Gil attempted to identify who his attacker was but to no avail.

Moving to his side, he walked toward his opponent. He stopped abruptly and said, "Walk away."

Plenty grumbled, "No."

Gil pulled his gun up just as Plenty leveled hers. Gil's shell struck her in the knee. She fell with hardly a sound.

Gil said, "I'm not here for you."

"I don't care," she croaked.

She fired again, but Gil could see the aim of the gun and was well clear of the blast. Plenty drew her second shotgun from a holster strapped to her body and fired again. Gil was nowhere near. Then a bright flash of light came in from the upstairs. Gil squinted at the blaze, it was too much light for him, and Plenty could now see her target. Gil fell down as the buckshot scrapped his back. Most of the pellets hit the wall with less than a handful cutting across his body.

Gil bounced up onto his knees and with one shot he put a bullet in Plenty's head. Ruby spun in place as Plenty slowly released her life and slid to the ground.

The light grew brighter. Gil covered his eyes with his free hand. Then it was dark again. As Gil attempted to regain his vision, a figure walked into the room. Gil shook his head and leveled his gun, then the light was lit again. Gil stepped back covering his eyes.

The man said, "Son of a bitch, you're better off in the dark."

Gil shot at the voice and missed. The man smoothly flung a knife from his vest. The blade became lodged in Gil's shoulder.

Ruby whimpered and lowered her head. She moved to exit the open cage but dared not.

Gil ignored the pain as he pulled his trigger expelling his shell into the wall.

Another small sharp blade sliced into Gil's other shoulder stopping with its tip in the bone.

Gil fell to his knee, lost his balance, and slipped to the floor. He lay on the raw surface as he tried to regain his wits. The man jumped and snatched a blade from Gil's body and turned him onto his stomach and stuck the knife an inch into his back. Gil couldn't move his legs.

The man whispered, "Oh, ouch, right? That's your kidney."

Gil winced.

Ruby cried.

The buried dagger went deeper into Gil's back, slowly until the blade was completely embedded up to the handle.

Gil felt his eyes tear up.

His attacker said, "Get ready to bleed out. You'll go to sleep first."

Gil's hands went to his back. He breathed in deep then exhaled.

Some blood welled up around the knife and was absorbed by his shirt. The man stood and inspected his hands. He put on a glove to remove the blade from Gil's back. He breathed in and chuckled out, and walked toward the stairs. "You're welcome." He stepped over Plenty and around her blood stain. He left the light on the table by the door and went out.

Ruby slowly exited her cage and walked up to Gil who locked eyes with her. She lowered her head to touch his hand with her nose. The man returned out of nowhere and pulled on Ruby's collar with a jolt.

"No. It's much more poetic if he dies alone." He laughed and walked away. He forced Ruby to follow. Gil's hand reached out to her as she was snatched away.

Gil was overcome with guilt. His spirits lifted slightly as his right eye focused on the back of a long tan coat. On the back of it, and just above the hem, there was a blood smear, Gil's blood, of a half circle and a cross. It was a faint but visible marking that Gil was able to leave behind. A warning that just might help the others. Someone could see it, that is, if the light caught it right.

It got dark as his attacker exited up the stairs, even though the light was still there. Gil stared at Plenty's dead body. He then set his eyes on the blood on his fingertips. He breathed deep and slow. The fluids slowly leaked from the cut in his back.

He stared at Plenty's face and at the blood that flowed out of her wounds into the deepening puddle filling quickly from her draining body. Emotion shot through him. The muscles in his face cried out and a blood bubble took shape on his lips as they vibrated the words, "A woman."

Gil's heart broke only a moment before his eyes closed.

A light drizzle splattered on the glass. Frank sat up straight, cried out, and jumped to his feet. He focused his eyes, finally realizing where he was. He had been sleeping for two hours before he spooked himself to consciousness. He checked his watch, put his hat on, strapped on his holster, and made sure it was all clear out the window. He slipped his slicker over his shoulders and popped up the collar.

Somberly he walked to Handsome Sam's pub. Inside, it was empty except for Sam who was cleaning the bar.

"Has Becca Devlin been in yet?" asked Frank.

"Nope, haven't seen hide nor hair of her," said Sam.

"Scotch and soda."

"Thought you were a bourbon man now."

Frank thought a moment then said, "Doesn't fit my mood."

Sam poured a Scotch and soda on ice. Frank took a sip. The door swung open. Frank ordered a second drink and sat down at a table with Becca. She shivered.

"Want something hot?" asked Frank.

"No. I need something strong." She took a drink from Frank's glass.

They sat quietly, avoiding eye contact.

"Gotta keep you out of this," Frank said.

Becca sat motionless.

"I'm going to say goodbye . . . tonight."

In that instant a stream of tears erupted from her eyes. She found it difficult to breathe.

"You understand, don't you?" Frank put his hand on hers.

"I do, I do, really."

"I-I'm-" stuttered Frank.

Becca waited.

"I've got to kill some men. And . . . I don't need you to get hurt. I don't, I can't, have thoughts of you running around inside my head. It'll get me killed and maybe you, too."

Becca grabbed his hand tightly and said, "Can't you at least say goodbye to me this time? Can't you come to me, if only for a moment? Just for one kiss? I need to know you're alive."

Frank sat and stared at their clasped hands. Emotion was peaking inside. He softly blurted, "You see, you see what you do to me?" His voice shook. "No, I've got to say goodbye right now and forget about you. Not forever, but I can't be thinking about you. Understand?"

"I understand you don't want me to get hurt." A frail anger began to seep into her tone. "I understand that you don't want to get yourself, or your friends killed. But I do not understand why you can't come to me when you're finished."

Frank sat in thought. "It's just, it's what I do. It's the only way. My instincts would know if I was coming to you and I wouldn't be able to not think about you."

Becca pulled her hand away. The only sound in the pub was the clinking of glasses being put back on the shelves behind the bar.

Becca said, “I should have known better.”

“It’s not like that. I do . . . I will see you again. But I have to get some things done first. And I don’t want you to be a part of it.”

Becca stood. Frank held her hand as long as he could as she walked away.

Becca said to Sam, “Is the back-alley door open?”

“It is.”

Frank watched Becca turn and move to the side of the bar toward the back exit. He stood and walked to the other exit, equally as slow.

The tavern grew darker as Frank approached the door. He reached out and gripped the handle as he put his hat on. He didn’t turn the knob. He held it and pressed his gaze into the bleak red wood. In the dim rusty glow of the lamps, the door appeared bloody.

Frank turned slowly.

Becca was walking down the long vestibule toward the back door. As she moved she slipped into her dark overcoat. To Frank she was nothing more than a shadow. He couldn’t make her out, but he knew she had stopped.

Frank walked away from the front door and into the deep dark passageway, and, after what seemed like forever, he stepped up behind Rebecca. She didn’t turn to meet him.

“Why can’t you do as I ask?” she asked.

“You know I’ll come back again.”

Becca rested her chin on her chest. Frank put his hands on her shoulders, which instantly released their tension with his touch.

“You hurt me so much before,” Becca said quietly. “The way you left. Now you’re going to do it again.”

“I was in pain, too.”

“You could have at least said goodbye.”

“We’ve been over this. You told me to go. Why I never said goodbye, I will never understand.”

Becca moaned.

Frank was quiet.

With her back to Frank, Becca said, “Say you’ll come to me when it’s over, and then I’ll know you’ll come back.”

“I can’t.”

“And why not?”

“I don’t know. This isn’t the same. It was a mistake for me to do what

I did, but this is different."

"You've killed people before." Her heart skipped a beat.

Becca turned the handle on the back door and it swung open exposing the back alley. The rain had slowed its assault on the city as a light drizzle made the air feel wet. Shallow pools of water reflected the light from the gas lamp hanging above the door.

"I'm not sure I've ever gone out solely to kill someone. This time I am," Frank said. He spoke delicately into her ear when he said, "I do love you."

Becca stepped into the alley. Frank's hands slipped off her shoulders with his fingers stroking her back as they fell. She walked into the middle of the alley and sidestepped and stubbornly strolled away.

"Becca," Frank said.

She didn't stop.

"Becca, please. I will come back."

She kept walking.

Frank leapt forward moving briskly until he caught up with her. He swung Becca around and put his hand on her face. She stared into his eyes. He rested his thumb on her chin and pushed down, parting her lips.

Becca sighed.

Frank gripped her hair as he found her mouth. He held her tight to his chest as they kissed firmly. Becca clutched the sides of his jacket. He squeezed her hair tightly in his fist.

Frank pulled her head back firmly, but tenderly. He said, "Let this be my goodbye."

Becca's eyes glistened. "How will I know that you'll be okay? How will I know that you're not dead bleeding in some street somewhere?" Louder she said, "How will I know that you'll be alive?"

Frank kissed her again and then said, "That—I can promise."

CHAPTER 13

The sun was just shy of cropping up and over the horizon. Stagnant dark air hovered behind the large white house on Astor Street. A horse was attached to a buckboard. On the buckboard was some rope and under the coil of rope some thick horse blankets. Two of them.

Goth bumped his head on the topmost edge of the back doorjamb as he attempted to step out. "Shit." He rubbed the annoying pang and bent over to pick up his hat. He had Plenty over his shoulder. She was wrapped up, but blood still leaked out and her hand hung in view.

Gil's black waited at the side of the house. He sniffed and hugged himself up close. The horse rested his body against the wall. Restlessly his muscles vibrated with a rippled spasm under his shiny inky coat. The white bandage still clung to his face and head. A splotch of blood peaked through.

Goth mumbled as he crossed the backyard toward the buckboard. He loaded Plenty and wrapped her up with a blanket. Walking back to the house, he didn't see the black who was hiding out. Concerned and watchful.

After a few moments Goth stumbled out with Gil over his shoulder. "Son of a bitch, I ain't getting paid to clean up. I'm getting paid to—" He was halfway to the back alley when he heard a rustle and a growl. He turned in time to dodge the charging black. He stumbled with Gil but held tight. He pulled his weapon.

The black broke out of the still gloom. Goth fell back from the impact.

Goth scratched his head. "What the hell was that all about?" He holstered his weapon, readjusted Gil's body, and walked him to the buckboard. The black shot out of the dark again. Goth dumped Gil on the board and tried to move out of the way, but the black slammed into him with his chest. The blow sent Goth six feet into the air. He hit the ground so hard both his pistols loosed themselves and skidded out of reach.

The shock of what had happened began to tighten his right fist. He stared out and about looking for the black but saw nothing. His right hand shook as it continued to firm up. "Oh, no." He couldn't let it get like the other one.

The killer slowly got to his feet and paraded the area for his weapons, glancing over his shoulder for the black. The sun was breaching the horizon just enough that he was able to find his guns. But no black.

Vance breathed in through his nose. The air was clean from the rain and cool from the passing of the front.

Vance Stranger and Detective Fulsome walked up the steps to the police station. Neither was speaking. There was always an uncomfortable silence that floated between the two detectives.

Vance turned sharply in front of Fulsome to stop his entrance into the building.

Fulsome pulled away. He put up his hands. He said, "What the hell you looking at?"

Vance pushed a firm index finger into Fulsome's chest and said, "You on a special assignment?"

"What?"

"You heard me. I swear to God you best tell the truth. Are you working undercover for the chief?"

Fulsome's eyes squinted from the vivid sun that slipped out from between two clouds. His face was tight. He blurted, "If I was on an undercover mission, then that would mean it's none of your damn business. Wouldn't it?"

Vance interrupted him with another jab to the chest, hard. "That's not an answer," Vance growled.

Fulsome continued to travel backwards and away from Stranger's advancing charge.

Fulsome said, "What is your—"

"I've got someone who wants to have a word with you."

"About what?" Fulsome pushed Stranger's hand away with an annoyed glare.

Vance said, "He wants to hear about your connection to Plenty Sky."

Fulsome's face popped with surprise, then his eyes bugged out as a firm hand grabbed the back of his collar and pushed him into the front yard of the police station.

"Hey, what the hell?" Fulsome stumbled and attempted to turn around, but Alfred's grasp was too strong. Alfred led them around the corner of the building. He slammed Fulsome backward into the wall under a window. From that window Frank looked down at Alfred and nodded.

Vance took post behind Alfred.

Fulsome pointed and yelled, "I am done with you. No way in hell I'm working with you again." He straightened his clothes.

Vance shrugged. "I got no issues with that."

"You never go by the book, do you?"

"And spending your free time with Plenty Sky, a known criminal, is appropriate?"

Fulsome snarled and huffed.

Alfred said, "You mealy-mouthed son of a bitch, you're gonna answer our questions whether you like it or not."

"Prick."

Frank rifled through Fulsome's desk. His fingers hunted through its contents quickly but meticulously. Every so often he would glance out the window to check on Alfred's progress.

Fulsome ran his hand through his hair and adjusted his collar and tightened his tie. "My private life is none of your business. No matter who I decide to spend my time with. I told you that yesterday, you nosy bastard. So you didn't get what you wanted and now you sic this behemoth on me?"

Alfred grunted.

Fulsome said, "Do you ever *not* break the rules?"

Vance rubbed his chin in thought.

"Yeah, didn't think so."

Vance snapped, "Kelly, if you weren't the mayor's bastard child, I never would've accepted you as my partner."

Alfred's head tilted. Quizzically he said, "Kelly?"

"Don't call me that," said Fulsome. He caught his breath in the silence.

"Just answer the man's questions," said Vance.

Alfred asked, "Where were you last night? And what is your connection to Plenty Sky?"

"That's none of your business."

Vance interrupted with a sardonic grin, "I'm sorry. This may not be the best of tactics but we have a man missing. So, answer—now. Tell us about Plenty, we already know you two have some sickish relationship going on."

Fulsome paused and then said, "She's, well, I don't know. I met her after I'd been drinking."

Alfred said, "Go on."

"She's got me running after her like a dang puppy." His face flashed red with a swell of emotion.

Alfred noticed.

"She played hard to get at first—that is until I got her in the alley behind Sam's. And ever since, that's what we do. She gets off on doing it in the darkest and dirtiest places."

Alfred's shoulders relaxed.

Vance stepped in and said, "Those are the worst kinds of relationships. Do you know what she does? You're a detective for crying out loud. Were you even the slightest bit aware that she's been running errands for the Chicago mobs? She's got her big tits working overtime on you, buddy. What have you told her?"

"Nothing, I swear." Fulsome shook his head. "How did you know about her and me?"

Vance shook his head. "Gil saw you with her at Handsome Sam's and followed you."

"Where's Gil?" asked Alfred.

Fulsome's eyes darted about. "How should I know?"

"He's missing. He never came back to the hotel last night."

Fulsome thrust his hands out with palms up. "I swear—I have no idea."

Vance said, "I hope for your sake that you didn't lead her to him. Otherwise I cannot guarantee your welfare."

Alfred added, "It doesn't matter if he did. We wanted someone to come out of the woodwork after us. That was the plan." Alfred rested his hands on his hips in thought and pitched his head with concern.

Frank stood in the window and shook his head no.

Fulsome caught Alfred looking into the window. He turned to see Frank in his office. "What the hell? That's my office."

"I'm pretty sure that's why he's in there," Alfred said.

"Damn you all."

Vance asked, "Where can we find—"

Frank interrupted Vance by pulling open the window. Frank's eyes dripped with sorrow. "I just got word." He stuttered. "They found two bodies, a man and a woman."

Vance asked, "Where?"

"Behind the Palmer House."

Vance turned up the collar on his coat and walked away.

Alfred slouched. He eyed Kelly Fulsome. "Just when it was getting fun."

Fulsome trailed behind Vance with an annoying banter of complaints. "I'm only here because I have to be."

Vance tossed outward with his fingers as if he was listening but he didn't care.

"This goes down by the book," said Fulsome.

Vance turned and said, "By the book? You are so wrapped up in the smallest most minute of details that you can't see the big picture. You've got no clue."

"I've never seen anyone work outside the law like you do."

Vance ordered, "You might not want to do that again."

"Well, honestly, you're scaring me."

"Well, if I find out you had anything to do with Gil's death, you pedantic bastard, you're going to get the lead from the business end of a gun." Vance snapped away abruptly and moved toward the back of the hotel.

Frank stepped up to the Palmer House. He pressed on his temple with the palm of his hand.

Alfred carried a thousand-yard stare. He was gripping his axe. He mumbled, "I told him I wouldn't let this happen."

They walked around the building to the alley to find three uniformed officers, two of which were attempting to get a black horse under control.

Frank overheard a maid say to an officer with a pencil in his hand, "If that horse hadn't made such a stink, we wouldn't have found those two till next week."

"Whoa, fellas," Frank said. "What's the problem?"

One of the men held tightly to a rope around the black's neck. The horse pulled up firmly and stood on his hind legs.

An officer blurted, "Every time we try to load the body into the wagon this damn horse charges us."

Frank said, "Step away."

"What?"

"You heard me. Step the fuck back." He pointed at the man's chest.

The officer in charge said, "I don't think that's such a grand idea."

Frank gave a gaze that only gave the men one option. They let Gil's black loose, and, reluctantly, they stepped back. The black lowered his head to Gil. Frank watched and rubbed his chin.

Gil's body was half wrapped up—his upper body was uncovered.

Frank asked the officers, "Did you uncover him?"

"No, that's how he was when we got here, with that, that beast hanging over him."

The black wanted Frank's attention. He snorted. Frank walked over and knelt down. He put his hand on Gil. Frank lowered his cheek to Gil's face. The hairs on the back of his neck came to attention. "My, God."

Fulsome uttered, "Plenty?" He stared down at the blood. He pushed his way over to her body. His eyes teared up and his knees started to give.

Frank held Gil's large blood-covered hand. He ordered, "Get the doctor." He threw off the blanket and examined Gil's body as carefully as he could. He found all three stab wounds and some buckshot in his arm. He covered the deep wound in Gil's back with a handkerchief from his pocket. He barked, "Water, now."

Fulsome bore down on Frank with his stare. Tears shot out of his eyes onto Plenty's still body as he screamed, "It was your man." He pointed sharply at Frank. "He did this." He held Plenty's head in his lap as tears and spit fell from his shaky chin.

Frank ignored him as two medics took his place at Gil's side.

"He has some knife wounds," Frank said. "One deep in his back. In his kidney, looks like. All wounds appear to be clotted over."

Fulsome started hyperventilating. He let go of Plenty's head. It settled gently to the ground. He stood and walked away.

Frank grabbed his arm to stop him. The arm jerked abruptly from his grip. Tears streamed down Kelly Fulsome's cheeks. He barked, "What?"

Frank asked, "What did Plenty carry?"

Fulsome swallowed, slowly he uttered, "She carried two single-handed shotguns." He pointed at her body and sarcastically said, "They're right there—detective."

Two handheld shotguns lay at her side inside her coat. Frank inspected the guns to find spent shell casings.

Frank quietly asked, "Who does she work for?"

Fulsome walked away. Frank followed fast and spun him around. "I'll give you two seconds." Frank rested his hand on his pistol. "One, to let your life flash before your eyes." He pulled back the hammer. "And the other, to answer my question."

Fulsome's lip fluttered. "Shit." His eyes shot to the sky as he swallowed. His voice box bobbed up and down. He fought to keep his eyes open.

Frank read the tone on his mug and stood down. "Listen," Frank said calmly, "I know what how you're feeling. You spend all your life crawling on your hands and knees in garbage looking for an answer to a question you know exists. But you don't know what that question is and it haunts you. Then one day a ray of light comes down on you from above and lights up the street. So, you follow it."

Fulsome said nothing and yielded a quick nod.

"As that beam flows across your face, it comes to a rest. So, you hold onto that beam of light, even when you know that too much of it is going to burn you. But you don't care, at least, not for that moment. So what, you got burned. We're not here to judge you. We just want to catch this bastard."

"I don't know why I care so much about her," Fulsome said. He glanced at her body. "I don't know who she works for. I promise I don't have a clue. But I did follow her once. She was in the Polish neighborhood. I saw her go in and come out with a package. And then I lost her."

Frank asked, "Go in where?"

"Into a building across the road from the church."

"What church?"

"It's the unfinished one. They're still working on it. They're trying to build the second tower."

Vance stepped up and added, "The Saint Stanislaus Kostka."

Frank asked, "Which building?"

"There's a row of apartment buildings. I don't remember which one," said Kelly.

Frank waved at Alfred and said, "I think we'll check on Cole and get Gil to the hospital, and then we'll see what we can find. Ready?"

"Ready," Alfred said.

"Those buildings have everything going on inside. Everything illegal, that is," said Vance. "You'll find a lot of gambling. That might help get you in. Flash some money and they'll let you in. We can't go with you. Not with what you're going to do."

Alfred stepped up.

Vance continued, "We have no jurisdiction there. There is no law but the law of the streets. If you thought Deviltry was a violent town," he shook his head, "wait until you see this place. It's the wild west of Chicago."

Frank called to a boy off the street. "Hey, Kid, you want twenty-five cents?"

The boy responded, "Absolutely."

"Take this black to the Palmer's stable. Here's a dollar to have him brushed and fed." The boy grabbed the reins and the black reluctantly followed.

Frank turned sharply to Vance; he pulled his gun and inspected the chamber and said, "Just tell us how to find it."

Standing face to face over an oval-shaped wooden table, Lore lighted a lantern as Goth smoked.

The ceiling was high—so high only a wood rafter could be seen extending from a dark shadow. A large cross hung on the wall. The building was made from dark brownstone.

Colors of purple and green glided across the floor from the tall, broad, stained-glass window. This was supposed to be a place of worship.

In the wide and airy room were rows of pews. Ruby was tied to one in the first row. Along the side wall was a set of stairs, with no handrail that led to a second level above the cross.

Lore said, "Keep the dog. Lock her up. We've got work to do."

Ruby whimpered when she heard Lore talk of her.

Goth smoked.

"Nice touch leaving the bodies at the hotel. That'll draw 'em out."

Goth's left fist hung tight and casual at his side.

"Get some help."

"I don't need any," said Goth.

"Just the same."

It was quiet.

Lore changed the subject and said, "You got an itch to scratch?"

"Yes." Goth gritted.

Staring at Ruby, Lore said, "Well, maybe you can come up with a plan that will allow you to scratch that itch and get Savage."

"I know what to do."

Lore asked, "Do you remember the murders you've committed after you've done them?" He leaned forward with his fists on the table.

"Yes," said Goth.

"Do you know what you're doing as you're doing it?"

"Sometimes."

"You *are* insane."

"Sometimes."

"Any remorse?"

"None. Never."

The hospital was quiet. A few nurses and doctors bustled about between the rooms on the first floor.

In less than two seconds it grew busy as a half dozen doctors and nurses swarmed around Gil. They shot down the hall with him gliding along on top of a gurney.

Frank came to rest in the doorway of Cole's room.

"Where in the hell?" Frank said.

Alfred peeked into the room. On the ground was the bedding.

Frank ran down the hall, his gun flashing in his hand. "Where's the guard? Somebody tell me where Cole and the guard are." He hollered, "Was he moved?"

Frank took a nurse firmly by the arm. "Where's our friend?"

Befuddled, the nurse stammered, "I don't know. Isn't he in his room?"

The whites of Frank's eyes turned red. "Honestly?" He turned away in anger and yelled at a frantic Alfred, "You inspect that side." He pointed, and Alfred began inspecting room to room.

"Anybody see anything suspicious?"

A handful of nurses and a couple of doctors came out to see what the ruckus was about. They all shook their heads.

Frank busted in on an elderly man sleeping in his bed. He yelled again down the hall, "Alfred, check outside."

Alfred moved out.

A nurse said, "Sir, you're gonna have to keep it down."

"If I don't find my friend it's going to get a hell of a lot noisier in here."

"Frank," Alfred barked from outside.

Frank darted outside.

"He's okay, Frank."

At the side of the building Cole stood leaning on two crutches wearing his robe and a holster wrapped around his waist. A cop in his uniform hung close by. Cole was staring into some bushes next to the hospital.

Frank whispered, "Jesus." He holstered his gun.

"Hey, come here," Cole said. "I knew someone was looking in on me last night." He smiled at Frank. "Sorry. You don't need to worry about me."

On the ground by Cole's hospital room window was a set of boot prints.

"I was having a dream last night that someone was watching me."

"You recognize the prints?" asked Frank.

Cole rubbed his hairless face. "No, but I was thinking that that doesn't mean much. It still could've been Goth Furse. You've got one of his boots. It stands to reason he got new ones."

"Could be anyone," Alfred grumbled.

Frank stared at Cole and said, "Will you please tell someone the next time you go out. I had three heart attacks just now."

"Sorry."

"I want two men on call right here from now on," Frank said to the guard.

"Yes, sir."

"And, you." Frank pointed at Cole. "I want you on the second floor tonight."

Cole said, "Good idea. I'll get them to move me." He patted Frank on the arm. "I didn't know you cared so much."

"We almost lost someone today, and still may." Frank paused then said, "I don't want to risk another."

Cole glanced around.

"Gil is two skipped heartbeats away from leaving us," Frank said.

Cole was quiet.

Alfred grumbled in his throat.

"Not sure what happened to him. He went off alone. I think he knew something that we didn't."

"I haven't had a chance to buy him a beer for saving my life," Cole said.

Alfred added, "He was trying to save ours."

Frank said, "Cole, keep an eye on him."

"Yes, of course."

"You keep that blaster near, you hear? Sleep with your convincer on top of your mattress. Some eggs may come poking around here for you two in the middle of the night. And be ready to go home and in a hurry. We'll come back when it's finished."

Cole delivered a crisp salute.

Frank said, "I don't know how they knew which hospital you were staying in."

Alfred opined, "Somebody spilled the works."

"Maybe," Frank said, "so, sleep with your lids open."

Cole asked, "How are you gonna find them?"

"We're headed into the Polish neighborhood. Based on a tip from Fulsome."

"You trust that gink?" asked Cole.

"It's all we've got."

"What will you do when you get there?"

"Once there we'll find someone to put the screws on."

Alfred grumbled, "And splash them—all of 'em."

CHAPTER 14

A sweaty and burly man with hair from the top of his lip to the base of his neckline chuckled gleefully. He was wearing chaps. He spoke with an odd twang. “And what makes you t’ink I’m a gonna let you two yahoos in our fine estab’ishment?”

Frank turned to Alfred and threw up his hands palms up. He glanced back with one brow raised. He said, “Well, I think it might be worth your while.” He pulled a wad of bills from inside his coat pocket.

Frank’s coat covered his six-shooter. Alfred’s slicker was hiding his axe.

The man glanced at the money and rubbed his chin.

Frank wisecracked, “Chaps?”

The man squinted. “I lives outside o’ town. If it’s any of yur business.” His eyelids fluttered nervously like a flirting waitress.

“No, no. I reckon it’s none of my business.” Frank shook his head. He paused a moment as the man inspected them up and down. He stopped on Frank’s chest. Frank crossed his arms and flashed his hand and said, “May we come in?”

“Well, it’s a nice idea. But I ain’t gonna let you two into the wolves den wit’out some . . . pre’tection. Wit everyone armed it’s easier to keep da peace. Sounds funny, I know, but—” He shrugged his shoulders, laid his palms on his desk, and said, “It works.”

Frank exposed his gun, and Alfred unveiled his by briefly lifting it from its holster.

“Fine, fine. Goes ahead.” He waved his hand up a staircase behind him.

“Thank you.”

The building was old but still in decent condition. Not nice enough, however, to be a home or a place of business, a legitimate business anyway.

They stopped on the third deck for only a moment.

Alfred asked, "Shouldn't we have asked him about Ethos?"

Frank put his hands on his hips. "I'm going to be honest with you. I'm going off the cuff here. I have no idea how best to get what we need. It just wasn't the right time."

Alfred nodded and whispered, "I trust your instincts."

"Let's see how it goes. This place is like Dodge City, and that means people talk when they drink. Maybe, just maybe, we won't have to ask any questions."

"Understood."

"But, be ready to drink . . . a lot."

Alfred smiled. "No problems with that request."

"Stay lucid though. We've got two to go." Frank stuck out his thumb. "Goth Furse." He then added his forefinger. "And an unknown. Our leads are anyone who works with Dr. Ethos, Plenty Sky, or has knowledge of your family or Stage Sturgus."

"Got it."

"We listen for any other names that might trigger a connection, like Uncle Baldy."

Alfred said, "What if we find out Lake Lagoon is the culprit?"

"He may be." Frank thought a moment. "I still feel he was working with or for someone. And when we find that someone and Furse, no one walks. Right?"

"That I'm the most sure of."

"Okay, let's go."

They slowly worked themselves up two more flights of stairs. Alfred rubbed his throat with one hand and rested his thumb on his axe with the other.

Frank said, "Ready?"

"Yep."

Frank knocked.

"Come in."

Frank swung the door open to five men. Four sat around an oval table and the fifth stood in the corner.

The man in the corner was short and dirty and hunched at the shoulders. He was hugging a bag of what seemed to be trash. He was wearing shredded short pants and long brown socks that stopped an inch below the knees. He rocked slowly. He appeared to be slow. He said, "Nuts and bolts. Bolts and nuts." He was harmless.

Frank scanned the room, table first then towards the back. As his eyes hit the back of the room he noticed a woman in a small kitchen readying food. Also harmless.

"Nuts and bolts . . . bolts and nuts," said the man in the corner.

A dealer at the head of the table wore all white. "Don't mind him," he said. "Strangers make him nervous. He'll get used to you. He's family so I keep an eye on him."

The man in the corner said, "It sure is warm out . . . nuts and bolts." The comment was intended for Frank and Alfred.

Alfred said, "Yep."

Frank said, "Yes, sir, it sure is."

"Nuts and bolts." He grinned and nodded and looked down.

A gambler in buckskins sat next to the dealer. He said, "He's loopy. And I don't like him here."

The dealer scowled at the remark. Staring down the man in buckskins he said, "He stays. Period. And you know that."

The man in the corner blurted to the lady in the kitchen, "It sure is warm out."

She gazed out at the table with no response.

The undercover detectives squared their shoulders to the card players. Sizing up the men, Frank sensed that each one of them could be deadly in their own way. All dangerous.

The dealer sported two nickel-plated pistols, one under each arm.

The gambler in buckskins had two twelve-inch hunting knives. One was sheathed in a back harness and was poking out over his right shoulder while another was even more accessible in his belt. Frank assumed that there was at least one more in a boot under the table and out of sight.

Next to the man in buckskins was a man Frank recognized. Frank knew his face due to the fact that he was wanted for the murder of an entire posse. A posse that hadn't even been on the hunt for him. He killed them just because.

Frank had seen his wanted poster in the stacks of hundreds he had studied.

The fourth was a creepy-looking fellow with yellow eyes and a handlebar moustache. He was armed to the teeth. He carried two twelve-inch buntline specials, and he had a sixteen-inch buntline with a detachable shoulder stock pointed at Frank.

The dealer said quietly, "Put the gun down, please."

The man with yellow eyes slowly laid the gun on the table.

The dealer said, "Off the table or leave, please." He turned to Frank and said, "You have to add please to orders—they're less offensive that way. It keeps one from getting their head blown off for no apparent reason." He chuckled. "You know how it goes." It was quiet then he said, tainted with anger, "I think he forgets who owns this place." He leered out the corner of his eye.

The yellow-eyed man laid the gun at his feet. He didn't avert his eyes away from the newcomers. He mumbled, "He ain't so scary anymore."

The dealer ignored the comment and said, "My name is Jared Jenkins. This man to my left is Trip Stag. And that gentleman is-"

Frank interrupted, "Hook Ruse."

Hook snapped straight with a sour stare.

Jared chuckled again and said, "Well, now, that isn't the name *he* gave us."

"It's him nonetheless."

Jared smiled. "Okay, Mr. Ruse it is." He turned his eyes to the man with yellow eyes and said, "That man won't give his name."

It was quiet.

Trip said, "Just ignore Mr. Nuts-and-Bolts over there. He's slow and annoying. He watches us play cards."

"It sure is warm out."

"It sure is," Frank said. "May we join you in the next game?"

Yellow Eyes squinted, Hook grunted, Trip shrugged his shoulders, and Jared said, "Definitely, gentlemen. Take a seat, please."

Frank and Alfred removed their hats and took a seat at the two remaining chairs across from Trip Stag and Hook Ruse.

Frank said, "I'm Frank, and this is Alfred."

Alfred grumbled, "What's the game?"

Mr. Yellow Eyes squinched at the grating in Alfred's voice.

Trip spoke up as Jared tried to speak. "Five card stud."

Frank said, "Fine. Can we exchange our cash for chips?"

Jared snapped his fingers, and the woman from the kitchen scurried out with a box of chips and made the transaction.

Hook stared hard at Frank and blurted, "How you know me?"

Frank casually took his cards up in line with his gaze and said, "I'm a . . . business efficiency expert."

"What the hell is that supposed to mean?"

Jared said, "Come now, what's it matter?"

Hook snapped, "Get off his foot so he can answer my damn question."

It was finally quiet as everyone went through their cards.

Frank had three eights.

"Answer the damn question." Hook's hand moved to the edge of the table.

Frank smiled at his cards.

Alfred whispered through the corner of his mouth, "How is it that you're not dead yet?"

Frank's smile melted to a fierce grin that molded devilishly well into the venomous anger he called forth from his gut. "It's surely a shame your Pa had too much to drink that night."

Hook's hand jerked briefly then stopped.

Jared held both his pistols in his direction. "You too? You've forgotten who owns this establishment?"

Hook looked back and forth between Jared and Frank with darting eyes.

Jared said, "Now, Mr. Ruse, settle into your chair and get comfortable. This isn't Tombstone. I think you're forgetting that you've been winning today. And quite handsomely I must say. It would be a shame for me to have to shoot you. Then we would all get to split up your pot. And I so hate cleaning blood off of money. But, it is something I'm willing to do if you force my hand."

Hook relaxed his arm, Frank released the hammer on his gun, and Alfred holstered his axe.

"Nuts and bolts. Bolts and nuts. It sure is warm out."

Frank rolled and lit a cigarette as he matched Hook's glare.

Trip grinned. "It's quite an adventure up here, Jared. It's been worth the trip even though I'm losing, yes sir, sure has."

The table waited.

Frank asked, "Trip, you look to be a mountain man. What's your story?"

Trip answered affably, "Yep, spend most my time in Montana, Lewistown. But I'm a traveling man. I like to see the world. Was hunting with some friends of mine a couple months ago. They mentioned they had family in Chicago." He took a pull on his cigarette and dropped some chips at the center of the table to match the bet. "I just got to thinking that I've never been to a big city. Mind you, I've been to Omaha and even Denver but nothing like this. So I said to myself, I have to visit here someday, and so I did."

Jared rounded up the pot he'd won and dealt the next hand.

Trip scanned his cards then Hook Ruse. Hook barely acknowledged his cards as he continued to throw his attention at Frank. Frank blew smoke across the table into his face. A sliver of a grin appeared to pop out from the corner of Frank's mouth.

Trip asked, "I'm curious. How do you know our mysterious Mr. Ruse?" He tipped his head towards Hook.

Frank's eyes narrowed. "That's an interesting story."

"How about them branches . . . mmm-mm," said Goth. He eyed his female prisoner through the smoky haze. "You're a nice piece of gingham." He grinned and with his clenched fist he tapped the top of his cards that rested on the table face down. His left eye squinted in delight at the two whimpers that filled the room.

Cigarette, cigar, and pipe smoke floated from the floor to the ceiling, making it difficult to breathe let alone see.

Goth mumbled to himself, "This game sure is fun."

"Which game you talking about?" Gabe asked.

Gabe was a timid and skinny and fragile man. His pipe showed the damage of uncontrolled nervous chewing. The stem had been nearly gnawed shut.

Gabe's eyes flinched as he realized he shouldn't have said anything. This realization came just a moment after the words went spilling out of his mouth.

He wasn't too bright. But Goth cut him slack. Gabe reminded him of his dead brother, Rocco.

Across the table from Gabe was the third and final player. He was a very large and extremely bulbous man. His eyes were just barely visible under his low-hanging and protruding forehead and his bushy unkempt eyebrows. He didn't move a muscle except to pick up or set down his cards and chips.

Ruby sighed but didn't move. She was tied to a chair. She nuzzled her nose into the two tied-up hands at the back of the same chair. Blood trickled off the middle finger of the left hand. Off the left hand of Goth's new prize - Becca.

Becca directed her gaze to the ground as she tried to breathe through a broken nose. Her mouth was stuffed and tied with a handkerchief around her head. Her whimper was slightly audible. Her mind raced in an attempt to understand how she'd arrived at this place. It had happened so fast. One moment she was walking up a street, and then the next—here.

Goth lengthened his spine and said, "Game, game, which game? Why, this game, of course." He smiled and whacked his tensed fist on the table.

Becca jerked, and Ruby stood up and spun in place, yanking on her collar.

Goth said, "You have no idea what I'm thinking about. Do you?" He turned his stare from Becca to Ruby. "But you'll find out." Ruby stared back; she was fed up, and she released a low angry grumble from her rib cage. Her upper lip crept up over her fangs.

Goth didn't notice through the haze. He said, "If you don't stop staring at me, I can't be held responsible for what might occur."

Behind Becca was a window with strips of cloth hanging where there had once been a curtain. Through the window, and across the road, one could see there was a church steeple with a large cross, still under construction.

Goth turned to Gabe. He put his good hand on his shoulder and squeezed hard. "You are so like my little brother."

The movement caused Gabe to jerk in his seat.

"Relax, man." Goth slapped his back. "You're officially adopted. We're family now."

Gabe looked up through the tops of his eyes and stuttered, "Sure thing, M-Mister Furse."

"Hey." Goth grabbed the back of Gabe's head and pulled his face to within an inch of his own so they were face to face. "I'm your brother now. You call me Goth. Okay?"

Gabe, at a loss, worked hard to keep his cool. He swallowed down some puke that had seeped up into his throat. "Oh, okay."

Goth smiled and tapped the back of Gabe's neck aggressively with the pads of his fingers. "That's better. Even your breath smells like Rocco's. Now, where were we?" He sat back in his seat and picked up his cards.

The bulbous man laid his cards down. His eyes didn't move. The muscles of his face were exceptionally still. A lack of concern permeated his movements.

Goth sat forward. "Well, I guess Mr. Freakshow calls. You in, Gabe?" He admired his own ability to make Gabe uncomfortable.

Gabe's hand shook. "Uhh, sure."

Goth said, "Now, Gabe, how can you be in? You haven't even looked at your cards. Silly kid, yep, you're like my little brother. Just like him."

Becca squeezed her eyes tight then opened them wide. She could feel the fresh bruise spreading and deepening. She inspected the room, looking, searching, studying.

Ruby stood valiantly at her side.

Frank placed his bet. He was the new winner, but he didn't care. Just win enough to stay in the game.

Alfred fought the urge to twist about in his seat.

Frank rolled a cigarette and relaxed into his chair with his left elbow resting on the table. His right never wandered, but remained close. Never far from his pistol. He said, "Well, does everyone want to know the story of Hook Ruse?"

Jared studied his cards and said, "I certainly do."

Trip smiled as Hook pushed his seat away from the table.

Frank added, with a cool blasé tone, "Careful."

Mr. Yellow Eyes took a drink and said, "Another."

The woman in the kitchen returned to the room and poured a beer into Mr. Yellow Eye's mug.

Jared said, "Oh, where are my manners? What's your poison, gentlemen?"

Frank said, "Bourbon whiskey for me."

Alfred grumbled, "Moonshine."

Jared said to the woman, "Run out, get the man some bourbon from my kindred spirit next door. Tell him to put it on my tab."

Frank said, "Tennessee whiskey's fine."

"No, no, need to stock up anyway."

The woman poured Alfred a clear liquid and ran through the kitchen to a set of wooden stairs out the back.

Goth took a sip of whiskey. Gabe was beginning to calm down as Goth's head suddenly snapped. He drew his gun.

Gabe said, "What?"

Goth put his gun to Gabe's lips and said, "Shh."

Gabe's eyeballs crossed as he stared at the muzzle resting on his mouth.

A squeaky groan vibrated through the walls. Step by step it grew louder. Becca was quiet. Ruby kept her gaze on Goth Furse.

Goth anxiously watched the back door.

There was a knock.

With a feigned cheerfulness Goth said, "Who is it?"

It was a woman's voice. "Mr. Jenkins wants a bottle of bourbon."

Goth eyed Gabe. Gabe nervously tilted his head and his right leg bounced up and down on the pad of his foot.

With sarcastic exuberance, Goth glared and said, "Come in."

The door swung open with care. The woman said, "Okay?"

Gabe stuttered, "C-come in."

Goth's gun was still on Gabe's lips, muffling his response.

The woman scurried to a bar in the corner of the room and pulled a bottle of bourbon from the shelf. Goth followed her curiously with his eyes.

Becca tried to get eye contact with the woman. But as the woman moved about the room, she didn't seem to notice her or Ruby—or she didn't want to know. The woman shuffled hurriedly back to the door. She began to close it behind her and swung it open again and said, "Mr. Jenkins said to put it on his tab."

Gabe said, "O-okay."

The woman went out, outwardly careful to close the door without making a sound.

Goth chuckled, then realized that he still had his gun pointed at Gabe's closed mouth. Righting himself he said, "Oh, sorry, my man." He holstered his gun and settled back into his seat and studied his cards. "Yep, just like, Rocco."

CHAPTER 15

After the woman poured Frank's drink, she slowly stepped up behind Jared Jenkins. He angled his head back towards her as she leaned into him and covered her mouth with her hand over his ear. She whispered as he nodded.

When she finished he whispered back, "Thank you, my dear. You may take your lunch break now."

She bowed and stepped into the kitchen and sat down on a wooden chair and opened up a sandwich from some wax paper and began to eat. She chewed with her mouth firmly closed and with earnest. She sat with her back straight and her legs together. She faced the table as if watching a play. Content, almost vacant.

Trip Stag eagerly waited for Frank to tell his story as Hook Ruse continued to expel an uncomfortable aura.

Mr. Yellow Eyes said, "I call."

Frank said, "There was a young man out East who had made it to America as a baby when his parents came over from Ireland. He was a typical boy growing up. His parents raised him with a strong Catholic background and an emphasis on education. But there was always something in Skinny Charlie that made him feel restless. He couldn't sit still in school. His mind would wander, daydream. Thoughts of excitement out West, because of the dime novels he had read, would occupy his thoughts. Charlie decided at a young age that he would seek out excitement and adventure as soon as he could."

"This worried his family as well as his friends, for Charlie was timid, shy. He couldn't talk to a stranger, let alone a girl. So one day, his friends, a group that ran errands for Charlie's father's store, sat him down and tried to change his mind. They told Charlie that it was rough out there and that to head out alone would be crazy, insane, if not suicidal. They pushed hard as they tried to sell him a story, and he wasn't buying. They said that his mom would be devastated if he left the family."

"Well, like I mentioned earlier, Charlie was a smart lad and knew exactly what his friends were really telling him. That he couldn't do it. Now, Charlie was shy and quiet, but his resolve was not to be questioned. Even his closest of friends knew this, but they still felt it was worth a try. They didn't want to see their friend leave to go on an adventure, especially since he didn't invite them along."

"Needless to say, the conversation only made Skinny Charlie that much more determined to not only leave, but to make a success of himself in the free world that lay ahead."

Frank took a pull on his cigarette and watched Hook for any change in emotion.

Trip laid his cards out on the table to show everyone that he had won the hand. He smiled. Not because of the pot of money he was collecting, but because he noticed Hook shifting about in his seat.

Hook grunted, "You long-winded bag—"

Trip Stag chuckled as he interrupted, "The man *will* finish. Let him."

Hook grumbled an obscenity.

Trip's smile turned stern and said, "You don't scare me."

The nuts and bolts man in the corner had not moved or spoken since Frank had started telling the story of Charlie. Even his ear was turned in order to capture every syllable of Frank's story.

Jared said, "Well, well, I don't think I've ever seen him so captivated."

The man in the corner stared eager-eyed and said, "It sure is warm out." He seemed happier.

Jared said, "His vocabulary is not extensive. He's just letting you know that he wants to hear your story."

Frank continued after tipping a sip of bourbon. "So, Charlie cautiously and deliberately saved his money. He researched and prepared for the trek that lay ahead of him. He knew exactly how he was going to work his way into and through the Rocky Mountains. The train would take him to Pennsylvania. He had prepaid for his passage on a wagon train from Pennsylvania to Omaha. And he had sent letters ahead that arranged for goods and supplies including two horses and a donkey that would take him the rest of the way."

"Charlie said his somber goodbyes to his mom and dad, and they watched teary-eyed as he boarded the train. His parents relaxed and smiled when the train pulled from the station. Charlie was hanging out of the window all the way to his waist. He was frantically waving his arms and smiling from ear to ear. They were so proud."

Frank emptied his glass.

The man in the corner was smiling.

Jared held his cards. "You making this up?"

Frank said, "Not one word."

The man in the corner said, "I like Charlie."

Frank won the hand. "The first few days of the trip went famously. Skinny Charlie was no longer Skinny Charlie, he was just Charlie. And he introduced himself that way to the others on board his car. He slowly opened up to a middle-aged couple who were headed back home to a farm in Kansas. The art of conversation flowed easier for him because Charlie was quickly growing more and more confident, and the couple found him to be very charming once he warmed up to them. As the days passed, even his timid movements became more bold and outgoing. He walked with ease and approached others with more eagerness than ever before.

"They were only a half day out of Allentown when the nice couple invited Charlie to go to Kansas with them. He was flattered to say the least. Charlie told them he had made arrangements ahead of time to get to Colorado. The nice couple explained that he could exchange his ticket to Nebraska for a ticket to Kansas and that he could send a telegram ahead to Omaha to cancel his order for goods and horses. They also let him know that a good job in town could easily be arranged for such a smart and hardworking man. Charlie smiled and told them he was very appreciative, but he was going on as planned."

"Well, the train came to a stop and the three friends stepped to the platform. They smiled and shook hands and hugged. Then out of the fog of the steam engine, they heard a woman's voice. 'Uncle Terry, Aunt Molly,' the woman's voice cried out. 'Over here.'

"A young, beautiful, spunky redhead emerged from the fog, and she was running with open arms. Charlie's heart leapt from his chest and floated in air as he watched the girl give her uncle and aunt a hug. Dale was her name and she was adorable, and Charlie was smitten. He stammered about with a twinkle in his eye. Dale was also on her way to Kansas. She grinned wide, and her uncle noticed. Terry said, 'Charlie here, he's going to Kansas with us.'"

Frank paused to roll a cigarette. The man in the corner pulled up closer and sat in a chair. He whispered, "I like Charlie."

Frank continued, "Dale was excited to see that Charlie was joining the group on their trip to Kansas. Charlie nodded and followed Terry to the ticket counter to exchange his ticket for a ride to Kansas."

Trip said, "No way, he just changed his mind on the spot?"

Frank said, "I'm not sure if he changed his mind or was so taken aback by Dale and the attention she gave him that he just followed the three like a little lost puppy."

Jared added, "For some reason I don't see this ending well."

Frank said, "After a couple of months in Lawrence, Kansas, Charlie earned the respect of the town and the love of Dale. In the same week, Charlie was elected as a member of the city's council, and he married the love of his life. Charlie was then able to secure a nice home that would provide a comfortable living for his wife and, God willing, their family. His new job was that of the town's only lawyer. He worked hard to provide for Dale, who was very appreciative of her new husband."

"On Sundays they would go to the second church service and then follow Uncle Terry and Aunt Molly back to their home on their farm and have lunch. Sometimes, if the weather was good, they would sit outside on the back patio and watch the horses play in their pen and drink beer and maybe a little wine. Then, one sunny afternoon—"

Hook interrupted, "You and I both know where this is going."

Frank said, with a raised brow, "Oh, do you? Really?"

Hook's neck was bright red, and his hands bounced around nervously on the table. His arm slid towards his sidearm.

The sound of Trip's blade leaving its sheath was quick but well advertised. The shine caught Hook's eye as it came to rest within striking distance. Trip said, "But *we* don't."

Hook stopped moving and sat motionless. His gaze bounced between the knife and Frank.

Frank's voice was cold as he finished the story. "One sunny afternoon a local ranch hand by the name of Jason came to Charlie's office. Jason was seeking out advice on a pay disagreement that he had with his employer. But something caught his eye on his way into the office."

Trip whispered, "Dale."

Frank pulled up straight and put some space between himself and the table. He said, "Yes, Dale. He loved her beautiful red hair and infectious smile. Jason proceeded to get acquainted with Dale. But she didn't appreciate his advances, so he backed off—for the time being. But as

Jason's case with his employer progressed, Charlie realized that he was dealing with a no-good individual who had been lying to him, so Charlie told the man he could no longer represent him. Mr. Ruse didn't like this."

Trip Stag came to attention but didn't move his knife.

Hook Ruse didn't say anything. His left eyelid twitched as his jaw clenched.

Frank said, "Well, Jason Ruse quickly became Hook Ruse. A man known around the area as someone you could not trust. He always ended up 'hooking' someone, didn't you Hook?"

"I didn't think anyone would care about some local tomato from out East. And that's all she was," Hook said.

"I'm not finished," Frank said. He pulled himself up with his fists on the table. "Hook began harassing Charlie and his new wife Dale. It got so bad that Charlie and Terry had to chase him off their land with shotguns. Once the mayor found out, he had the sheriff escort you out of town. The city chased you out of town. That pissed you off, didn't it, Hook?"

"They had no right, but I left as I was ordered and never went back."

"No, no you didn't ever go back." Frank's pulse began to show in his neck and a hideously vengeful smile slowly spilled over his lips. His voice was commanding. "Yeah, it was just your luck that the town's attention was taken over by a bank robbery. And subsequent to that robbery, a posse was formed by the sheriff, and guess who was on that posse."

Trip Stag had grim cemented on his face. He barked, "Charlie was in that posse."

"Yes, he was. Along with five others. Charlie and the sheriff split out on horseback after the two lowlife robbers. As they stalked their men, Hook found an opportunity."

Hook barked, "I wasn't anywhere near."

"Oh, you were near. You were so near you slaughtered all five of that posse from a ridgeline five miles outside of town. And in the middle of your murdering rampage, you took the time to tie a shot-up and bleeding Charlie to a tree and torture him."

Hook stood up fast and yelled, "I never did no such thing."

"Your mistake, asshole, was that you were watched the entire damn time."

Hook's eyelid cramped. "Huh?"

"Yeah, the two robbers heard the gunshots as they attempted to backtrack to throw off the posse. They watched you from the same ridgeline where you'd shot those men."

Hook looked back and forth across the table. Sweat dripped from his face.

Frank said, "You're an unsolved case. How lucky for me."

The man in the corner pointed at Hook and cried, "Charlie, Charlie, you killed Charlie." Tears began to stream down his weathered face. "Poor Dale, oh poor Dale."

Frank shook his head no at Trip. Trip Stag understood the order and relaxed his grip on his knife.

"Poor, poor Dale."

Frank said, "Well, Hook, answer one question. Whose outhouse did they scrap you out of?"

Hook's hand dropped to his waist. Frank actually waited until the gun was coming up and out of the holster so there would be no doubt. Frank's steel flew into his hand as he leaned over the table. His pistol's violent arc came crashing down across Hook's face. Frank rapped Hook, plastering a gash diagonally across his forehead. Hook released his gun as he dropped. He cried out; blood gushed from the deep wound.

The man in the corner fell from his chair and ran to the corner of the room. "Nuts and bolts, nuts and bolts, nuts and bolts." He buried his face in the corner. "Poor Dale, poor Dale, poor, poor, Dale."

The room was quiet as Frank caught his breath.

Alfred said, "I am so happy you're on my side, for the love of Pete."

Jared said, "*Case*, friend? Here's some dope, this is not the place to be doing business, especially some kind of case. Do you know whose town this is?"

Frank wiped the blood and skin from the forward sight of his pistol and holstered the weapon. He said, "No I don't. Why don't you enlighten us?"

Jared said, "You might want to leave town. Just friendly words of advice."

Alfred kept watch over Mr. Yellow Eyes.

Frank said, "It's not in my nature, so instead of your boss coming to find me, why don't you tell me whose town I'm in." This time it wasn't a question.

Jared looked quizzically at the two gunmen. His gaze came to rest on Alfred's axe. Jared said, "Shit, it's not like I'm giving anything away. Dr. Ethos runs this place. Take it up with him."

Hook sat on the floor and covered his face with a handkerchief. It quickly grew red with blood.

Frank said, "I would love to tell Dale I shot you." Frank studied the man as he recalled why they were there. "I've got no time for you. We've got bigger fish to fry. Get the hell outta my sight."

Hook reached for his gun.

Frank growled. "Idiot."

Hook left the gun where it lay. He stood and moved toward the door as Frank eyed his progress. Blood dripped to the floor.

"If I even smell you again, you won't wake up," Frank said.

He whispered, "I'll hunt you down another day."

Hook stumbled down the stairs and fell out the front door.

Frank looked across the room and into the kitchen. There was a wooden chair and no girl.

Frank asked, "What did that girl say to you when she came in?"

Jared fumed with fear.

Mr. Yellow Eyes tensed up like a cocked pistol.

Alfred pulled his axe with his left and rested his right on his gun.

Trip Stag, with a calm demeanor, said, "Mr. Jenkins, unless your memory is as short as a fish, you will recall the speed at which this man can draw a gun and split open another man's face. And, if your memory is that short, just look at the blood on the floor."

Jared calmly breathed in and then out. Mr. Yellow Eyes held tight to his cards.

"Nuts and bolts."

Frank said, "It sure is warm out." He faced Jared a moment and then stepped around the table.

Mr. Yellow Eyes's hand leapt towards his buntline that lay on the ground. His cards fluttered to the floor. In that moment Jared reached for a gun in a shoulder holster under his jacket. Frank forcefully punched Jared's hand as it found the gun. His fingers were smashed into the metal.

Alfred swung the wooden end of his axe sharply across Mr. Yellow Eye's jawline. Everyone heard the thwack that left Mr. Yellow Eyes asleep. He settled to the ground and lay like a pile of dirty clothes with his front teeth poking through his upper lip.

Trip Stag chuckled and said, "If they weren't so stupid, you'd think they'd get wise." He shook his head and sheathed his knife.

Jared held his sore fingers.

Frank said, "Go on."

"She was just saying that there was a strange man there, someone she'd never seen before, and a woman tied to a chair, and a dog."

Frank had always believed that anger could throw someone off their plan—it was a distraction, a hurdle, and over the years he had learned to control his temper, not eliminate it, but use it. He was able to manage his aggressive nature in most all situations. This was not one of those.

"What?" His fingers armed the trigger of the gun in his hand. "Where?"

Alfred stepped on Mr. Yellow Eyes's unconscious body and went into the kitchen. He opened the back door, exposing a building across a small courtyard. The structure was a twin of the one they were in. He yelled as he pointed to the third floor that was just a short distance away, "There."

"Can you watch these two? Keep 'em occupied for a tick," asked Frank.

Trip Stag stood up, pulled two knives, smiled, and said, "It'll be a pleasure."

CHAPTER 16 - THE BIG HATE

As Goth laid his cards on the table, a small bell jingled with a startlingly aggressive yank. The bell, bolted to the wall, had a wire that ran up from a hole in the floor. The wire jerked up and down forcefully until the bell was pulled from the wall.

Goth smashed his tight fist onto the table.

"Shit, they're here." His tone was angry, but he grinned.

Goth jumped from his chair and flew across the room. The bulbous man didn't move, and Gabe just sweat as he mumbled.

Goth grabbed Ruby's leash and jerked it from the chair. He began to untie Becca's hands. She screamed, and he slapped the back of her head. Ruby snarled and bit down on his hand. He slapped Ruby. With a hand loose, Becca pulled away from her seat and lifted the pistol from the bulbous man's holster. She closed her eyes and ran across the room.

The bulbous man didn't move.

Goth screamed, "Give that to me."

She began shooting as she ran. Goth ducked, tugging Ruby along with him. "I ain't supposed to kill you, but don't think I won't, you silly bitch."

Gabe cried out as he took cover under the table with his hands over his head. He began to pray out loud. The bulbous man didn't move. He laid his cards on the table and scooped up the money from the middle of the pot. He actually had the best hand.

Becca's lead flew harmlessly over Goth's head as he ducked and moved across the room to the back wall. He pulled his gun, armed the hammer, and pulled the trigger. As he squeezed the metal taut, Ruby yanked back hard on the leash that was still in his armed hand. The bullet smacked the table leg, sending wood splinters all over Gabe who fainted at the bulbous man's feet.

Goth ran toward the back door as Becca exited out the front. She shot one last time into the ceiling as she hurried down the stairs screaming.

Frank ran into her on the staircase with gun drawn. She fell into his arms.

"Frank, Frank, I'm so sorry."

"Baby, calm down." He held her.

"He's horrible, just horrible. I'm so, so sorry. I didn't go home. I was gonna follow you and he, he, oh, he is so horrible."

Frank put his fingers on her chin to examine her nose. That anger that Frank was able to control, well, it was beyond being suppressed. It exploded in him like a cannon.

Frank rumbled. "Who is he?"

"Goth."

"I've got to get him, but—"

"Go, go. I'll be okay."

Frank filled shells into her gun. "Get Detective Stranger," he said.

"Okay."

As Frank went up the stairs Becca said, "Where's Alfred?"

"The back way."

"No, no, there's another way out, another set of stairs."

Frank ran back down, he picked up Becca and escorted her outside.

Becca pointed. "There."

He looked up at the church. "That's it."

Alfred ran around the corner and slid to a stop.

Alfred barked, "He didn't come out the back way."

"I know."

"Something is going on in that church," Becca said. "I heard him talking about it."

Alfred said, "Let's finish this."

Frank took Becca by the arm. "And don't follow me this time."

"As you wish, but please be careful."

He kissed her lightly on her lips.

Goth barked, "Can I kill this God-dang dog now?"

Lore Ethos's head hung at a forty-five-degree angle as smoke swirled around him. The sun shot in through the window and revealed half his face and body. The other half was hidden in the shadow of the window frame. He stared down and out to the empty street below.

The concrete walls were dark and the ceiling was dome shaped.

Lore puffed on his cigarette and without averting his gaze said, "If you want to see the sunset tonight you won't."

Goth huffed.

Lore said, "You know-" He lifted his nose to the ceiling and waved his cigarette hand in a circle. "This church was designed after one in Krakow." He waited for a response.

He got none.

Sarcastically, he continued, "You know—Poland?"

Goth scoffed. "Big deal."

"Yeah, big deal."

"Savage is coming. Let me put this dog down and—"

"You know your orders, and they will not be repeated." Lore was fixated on the street below. "I'm tired."

"*You're* tired?"

Lore sighed.

Oak choir stalls adjoined a baroque altar standing at the end of the center aisle. Above the altar was a painting of Mary and baby Jesus and a saint. The rows of benches were sprawled out across the large sanctuary.

The two cowboys ducked down behind an oak pew. The large gothic stained-glass windows allowed some light of varying colors to shine in. Along the walls were wooden walkways hanging from the incomplete ceiling. A few beams of light shined into the church at different angles lighting the dust that floated through the space.

Frank whispered, "Nice hiding place."

Alfred's voice rippled. "It won't stop me none."

Flapping wings sounded somewhere.

Frank's head pivoted about examining the church. He said, "There looks to be some rooms along the second level . . . over there." He pointed. A cement staircase along the wall led to the second floor.

"Makes sense."

Frank asked, "Any ideas?"

"Let's go up one at a time. We can cover each other that way."

"Okay, I'll go—"

"No," Alfred said. He rested on his right knee. His bloodhound eyes were somber and still. It always seemed to Frank that Alfred was on the edge of tears. "I'll go first."

Frank understood.

Alfred crawled on all fours behind the pews. His slicker slid along the floor.

Frank rested his pistol on the top of the pew and pointed it up the stairs. His hat was pushed back off his brows. He glanced quickly over his shoulder. No one was there.

Frank whispered, "I should've shot that bastard Ruse."

Alfred looked back just as Frank noticed a light flickering from the space under one of the doors. He said quietly, "Second door. I see something." He pointed up and held out two fingers.

Alfred pushed himself to his feet. He walked stealthily to the wall. With his back to the wall he lifted his gun. The silence of the sanctuary was disconcerting.

Frank gave an okay signal to show all was clear. The light moved again, causing a flicker of a shadow on the wall.

Alfred moved carefully as he calculated his every step. He scanned each stair before placing a foot on it. As he set his foot down, he relinquished his weight to the stair slowly. Step by step he worked his way closer.

Alfred reached the top step and knelt down. He tossed his head to Frank to start his trek and to assure him that he was covered. Frank checked his six again and smoothly worked his way to the stairs.

The two cowboys exchanged a nod just as a loud bark busted the dead air. A gunshot silenced the bark.

"Ruby."

Alfred ran to the door and Frank sprang up the steps. He led with his boot kicking the door in. Lore Ethos lay up against the wall with a bullet in his heart and his eyes open. His bloody hand jerked about on the wound. Initially he was fish-eyed but his shock shortly gave way to nothingness.

Frank went in and went to the window. "I don't see anyone."

Alfred leaned over the body. "No gun." He opened up Lore's vest and pulled a letter opener. "Here."

Frank inspected the opener. It had a cross on a moon carved into the blade. He scanned the room. Concern dripped from his pores. He glanced up. Above the window was another working plank nailed to the high ceiling. Then he turned to the body.

"The exit is lower in the back. He was shot at an angle, from above, looks like."

The two men visually examined the plank. A pulley was attached and above the window the wall was wood, not cement.

Alfred pointed up and said, "See that? That's a temporary wall. It's different."

Frank grabbed the rope attached to the pulley and yanked it down. "It's not gonna hold both of us."

Frank stepped onto the plank and Alfred used his weight as he worked the rope to raise the plank along with Frank to the wooden parapet. Frank pushed firmly on one end of a wooden barrier to the outside world, and it smoothly swung open allowing sunlight into the room. He looked down the outside fortification of the church. Wooden platforms were built into the side of the building all the way to the ground. Each platform was quite a drop—but it could be done.

Frank settled to one knee and rubbed his jaw.

Alfred tied off the rope, and swayed slightly with his eyes closed.

A whimper floated up from the street below. Then it was quiet. There was no sound until Alfred opened his eyes. Then there was a bark.

Every cell in Frank's body burned.

"Savage," said a voice. It answered his body's screams. It was followed by another sad whimper from Ruby.

Frank's spine compressed as his muscles tightened.

"Ruby," Alfred said.

"Yep," Frank said.

Frank looked down to his friend and eyed the axe blade that now stretched from his arm. He had a vision of Alfred's daughter. She was asleep. That's what he told himself.

Alfred breathed heavy, and a tear fell off his chin.

"Unfinished business," Alfred said.

"There always is."

Frank removed his gun from his side. He double-checked that it was loaded and holstered it. Without a spin.

A report coiled up from the street immediately followed by an outcry from a shocked woman.

Someone screamed out again. "Savage."

Frank said, "It's Goth Furse."

"I reckon so," Alfred said.

"This one's as good as dead, my friend."

Alfred nodded. "I'll be right behind you."

They both felt vacant and still.

"I know."

Goth Furse screamed out, his voice breaking high, "Savage, my little brother is dead 'cause of you, and now I'm gonna kill you. Damn you to hell, Savage. Damn you straight to hell."

Frank turned to the makeshift balcony and studied the street.

Goth's narrow shoulders hung loose as he held a pistol with his good hand and pointed it at Ruby's head.

Ruby tugged hard at the leash wrapped around Goth's crippled cinched-up fist. Her teeth began to show as she growled and eyed the gun.

The silent street waited for Frank Savage. A vision of his own little one, the one he and Becca had lost, formed a fuzzy image in his thoughts.

Frank had tunnel vision for the moment—and that made him vulnerable. Goth could have someone with him and Frank would never see him. But would it stop Savage from killing Goth Furse?

Frank stepped outside through the opening out onto a wooden rail of the second level balcony. He jumped to the hard ground below. He ignored the platforms that stair-stepped to the ground. He landed firm and remained steady as he stood straight. His gaze was riveted on Furse who laughed in a sadistic and angry outburst.

Furse barked, "I suppose you know by now." He laughed.

Frank hammered his glare into Goth's face with no mercy.

Goth reeled back a step and cocked the hammer on his gun.

Frank walked briskly, moving straight and steady toward the man he was hell-bent on killing. Step by step his boots dug in deeper with each impression. His mind was swimming in pain. He bit his tongue, hard. Blood surrounded his teeth. The mordant taste in his mouth sent adrenalin through him. Frank's vision grew narrower as he walked. His arms swayed, only slightly, keeping his hand near.

Goth said, "I suppose you know it was I who killed the precious little one."

Frank didn't hear, "the precious little one.' Frank heard, "your precious little one."

Goth grinned and said, "I liked it. No, no, I loved doing it. The others said no, don't do it. But I just did it because I wanted to hear her scream and cry out for her daddy. Once the Kingston Killer started laughing, I couldn't stop laughing. I laughed louder with each shot."

Frank bit down so hard his jaw cracked and he busted a molar. He could feel the veins in his neck bulging.

Goth hollered, "Tell your friend to say goodbye to his pain-in-the-ass dog."

Frank heard a single high-pitched whistle. Ruby heard it, too. She turned sharply towards her captor. Goth's gun blurted fire sending a shell down her back and slicing open her skin. A fluff of red fur sprang out from the wound. She latched onto Goth's thigh and buried her teeth into his flesh, puncturing his artery. She didn't let go, even when Goth jerked back and cried out and hit her with the barrel of his piece.

Frank didn't slow his pace, or speed up.

Goth looked into Frank's stare and drew his pistol on him.

Frank forced his gun out with malice. He aimed carefully and fired his shot. Then, without pause, he holstered it.

The bullet hit Goth's pistol. The impact caused the powder in the remaining cartridges to explode. The gun shattered to pieces, shooting shards of metal into his neck. Goth screamed out as he stared at the fingers of his right hand, all of which were spread back into open fleshy wounds that rendered them useless.

Two sharp whistles resounded, and Ruby let go of the bloody leg and ran past Frank in a blur.

Frank walked steadily toward Goth as if in a trance. Blood trickled from the corner of his mouth.

Goth yelled again as he tried to open his clenched left fist. He screamed at his hand. The fingers slowly separated. Blood flowed down his leg, and spurt from his destroyed right-hand fingers. His clenched fist relinquished to his will. His eyes bulged in disbelief. He grinned. "Yes."

Frank walked closer uninterrupted, undaunted.

Goth grabbed his second pistol with his new hand.

Frank moved purposefully, but he did not rush.

Goth held his weapon level to his would-be executioner.

Frank stepped sharply to his left. The bullet whizzed by his ear.

Goth pulled the hammer a second time.

Frank moved briskly to his right. The shell put a hole in his shirt and scraped his arm.

Goth tried to arm the gun one last time, but the smile that he'd held fell from his face. Blood gurgled out of a hole in his neck as he tried to speak. "No."

Frank pushed his gun forward and fired into Goth's shoulder, sending him to his knees. Goth dropped his weapon. His fingers snapped shut like a vice one last time.

"What?" Goth wept.

Frank stopped and held steady and aimed for the forehead.

"Savage, don't," a voice said. It was Fulsome.

Detective Vance Stranger looked on.

Frank's pupils surged to cover his whites.

Fulsome stepped forward. He reached into his coat. "Savage, he isn't armed," Fulsome said.

Ruby growled.

Alfred stood by with his red-handled axe.

Fulsome recognized the anger painted across Alfred and released his grip on his revolver and stepped back.

"Look at you, you wild-eyed bastard," cried Goth. "You are no better than me. No better than me. Pull it." Goth screamed, "Pull it and your soul will be dead like mine."

Frank didn't move as a tear instantly dried up. A gust of rage rolled over him. His chin dropped slightly, and his eyes flashed murder. Frank waited then said, "You know . . . I'm okay with that."

Goth blurted, "Why—"

Frank shot Goth Furse. The lead ball spread the back of his head into the street. The devil went limp and crumpled to the ground.

The street was mostly vacant, and those that were there said nothing. Becca stood off to the side and began to move toward him. Frank shook his head and she stopped.

Frank swallowed hard and put away his gun. He took a picture with his mind that would forever be locked away in his memory. He doubted that he would ever recall that image, intentionally. He walked towards the two detectives. Alfred knelt down and pressed a handkerchief to the cut across Ruby's coat.

Fulsome stepped forward and said, "Savage, I'm gonna have to arrest you."

Frank moved quickly as Fulsome went for his gun. In a flash Frank reached out and disarmed the detective and unloaded the ammunition at his feet and dismantled the gun.

Frank said hoarsely, "The next time you pull a gun on me, you end up like him." He pointed to the corpse he had left in his wake.

Detective Fulsome scoffed and sharply swung away from Frank. As his head turned, an odd grin leaked from the corner of the detective's eye. Fulsome's jacket floated upward and around his body. And on the bottom inside edge of Detective Kelly Fulsome's coat was a visible mark. A mark that was a dark, blood-red smear of a circle and a cross. Gil's warning was clear.

Frank turned sideways, pulled his gun, and reloaded his spent shells. He holstered it and said, "You're about to want for nothing."

Fulsome stopped and stood motionless for a moment. He slowly turned his head to the side.

Frank held his glare with a tight frenzy—a controlled anger. He reacted to the slight motion that was barely perceptible from the elbow hidden under Fulsome's coat.

Frank's gun was level as Fulsome spun around with knives in hand, one of which was about to fly from his quick fingers, but Frank's bullet ended in Fulsome's stomach first.

And Alfred's axe landed in Fulsome's chest at the exact same moment.

Frank readied for another shot as Alfred stepped up and kicked Fulsome to his back.

Fulsome sucked at the air and attempted to stab Alfred's leg. Alfred kicked the blade from his hand.

Alfred stood over the man who had slaughtered his family. He stepped on Fulsome's shoulder with his boot and worked the blade loose from the sternum as if removing it from a block of wood. The blade scraped as it left the bone.

Fulsome's lips sputtered spit, and his wound spurted blood. He croaked out, "Don't you want to know why?"

Alfred raised the axe above his head and with the big hate he said, "No."

The blade moved swiftly through the air, and when it stopped, it sent a splatter of blood up and onto its handle.

The acid of what had happened splashed over Frank's brain. It lit his vision so he could barely see and slowed his thoughts. A swarm of commotion attacked his nerves. He whispered, "Finished—for now."

Alfred and Ruby and Frank and Becca walked back in silence to the hotel. They patched up Ruby and fed their horses along with Gil's black.

Stage and Vance had a talk and a smoke out underneath the hospital sign. A watered and fed Ruby nudged the hospital door open. Gil's eyes were open and Cole sat at his bedside facing both the door and the window with his convincer firm in his grip. Alfred had a tear floating on top of his lower eyelid. Frank sighed as Gil smiled. Becca held firmly to Frank's arm and smiled at Gil.

Cole chuckled, "I guess we've got the same kinda blood."

Gil said, "Yep, Cole's blood runs thick through my veins. I can feel it. I'm all sluggish."

Cole added, "You complaining?"

"It was a one in four chance it would work. So far so good." Gil waved his thick hands as he spoke.

"How is it I still owe you a beer?" asked Cole.

Gil smiled and said, "Because you just do."

"I still owe him a beer even though we're even-steven now."

Frank said, "I wouldn't argue with him if I were you."

"I reckon not."

Frank nodded to Gil. "Your wife should be here tomorrow."

Gil smiled. "Thanks."

"It looks like you have yourself another horse," added Alfred, "That black has been pacing around nervously since you've been in here."

Gil said, "I do, don't I?" He chuckled. "And I guess I'm very lucky I was born with no left kidney."

Frank said, "And so are we, my friend."

THE END

AN AMERICAN SAVAGE

The long rectangular table separated the two men. The room was empty except for the table, two cowboys, their chairs and their smoke. The walls were flaking paint and plaster.

Frank's eyes became more sullen the harder he tried to smile. His attempts at true happiness were to no purpose. Not anymore.

Inspector Derek White spoke first: "What happened to retirement?"

"One last job," said Frank.

"Isn't there always one more?"

"I reckon there is, my friend."

The door opened. A young man entered with a round tray with two glasses and one decanter. He placed the tray on the table, filled the glasses with rye-whiskey and went out.

Derek pulled a rolled-up red leather map case from a pocket.

He said, "London."

Frank nodded.

"You might not get paid for this but you have full authority. As always, of course."

Frank nodded, tossed back the rye.

"How do you feel?" asked Derek.

"I feel like I'm experiencing a slight case of burnout."

The cleaver blade was straight-backed and just shy of a foot long. It was a Bowie knife and it shined, but it had blood caked into the crevice where the blade touched the handle.

A simple rectangular box sat on the table. It had a circular glass hole in its side. It was wood with an imitation leather cover, and it read: Kodak.

He smiled as he placed the blade into its sheath and the camera into a leather satchel.

A voice said, "J.R., it's time."

J.R. had dirty blonde hair that swooped over his forehead. A failed attempt to cover a thick scar that ran down his forehead. It wasn't a bulbous scar; it was concave, deep, overt.

He ran his fingers through his hair before putting on a dusty Homburg hat. A pair of work gloves hung from the pocket of his denim jacket.

Three men, appropriately dressed for a day on the farm, joined J.R. as he excited the three-story brownstone flat. People milled about the English street. Some were selling trinkets and others were selling men's suits. The four strange Americans, masquerading as Scots, huddled at the base of the steps.

"Cheerio, gentlemen," said J.R. Attempting the local dialect.

The three men laughed.

"Cheerio, is right. Gauld, they's talk funny over here," said Falene.

"Lose the chew," said J.R.

Falene spit a chunk of tobacco into his hand and put it in his pocket.

Falene didn't know he carried a woman's name let alone realize how stupid he was.

All four men were dressed in worn-out coveralls, but that was just the part they had to play.

J.R. was well aware that he carried the group on his shoulders, in more ways than one. But they would do.

"Are you ready, Boss? This is gonna be fun," said Jenkins.

Jenkins was smarter than his brother, Falene. But he had an uncontrollable temper.

J.R. smiled.

The fourth of the group was the oddest but was the smartest. He would often fixate and lose his concentration at the most inopportune times. Whenever Stinson would speak, he would say it twice. His compatriots knew one thing: don't ever, ever touch him.

"That Thymes stinks, it stinks," said Stinson.

"That smell is water, something you're not used to," said J.R.

J.R. had figured that the day would come when he'd have to put Stinson down like a rabid dog. It wouldn't be a problem.

"How much gold did you say? How much? It was a long-ass boat ride to get here. A long-ass ride," repeated Stinson.

J.R. eyed his newest member to the gang. He knew what the question really meant. He answered, "It'll be more than you can handle, even four ways split."

"What if it ain't there?" asked Jenkins.

"If that scenario plays out . . . then there'll be hell to pay."

Jonathon was an average height for a sixteen year old, brown-eyed, and strong. The girls liked his smile. He wore a cream button up with the sleeves rolled up, a grey vest and black cowboy boots. At school he was the only teenager still wearing cowboy boots. He handled the ribbing by knocking down the big kid in math class.

Chores didn't bother him. Jonathon was proud to take care of the grounds while his father managed the offices. It was the job that his dad used to do for a bank.

Great Cumberland Place had more than enough offices, and his dad had about ten employees to keep track of, along with the task of making sure that the embassy ran smoothly.

Jonathon, along with his father, his grandfather, and their 64 kilogram Saint Bernard, Theseus, lived in the basement of the large grey and white building. A large white wood fence set the border to the property. On occasion they could hear Big Ben announce the time. More and more cars had begun to take the place of horse drawn carriages in the streets.

Jon was excited about this change but his grandfather would complain of the noise that the new form of transportation made. He'd also remark that the smell of gas was more sickening than the smell of horse dung.

Jon had put off his break long enough. It was a bit of a walk to the Tower Bridge, but he would visit it often on his breaks, though not today. He wiped the sweat from his forehead, and pulled a pulp novel from his back pocket. The title: *The Complete Adventures of Frank Savage*. A book he had read twice. It was volume two, volume one was worn out.

"I could run to the Tower Bridge," Jon whispered. "But running in boots is not fun." He chuckled to himself. It's something Frank would say, he thought.

"Jonathon," said Grandpa.

"Yes."

"Where's your father?"

"I think he's walking his route." Jon checked the time from the watch in his vest pocket. "It's almost four so he should be getting ready to send everyone home."

"Oh, alright."

"What do you need, Grandpa?"

Grandpa had his wits about him, especially for his age. He said, "There's some men here looking for work. I don't like them. I want your father to tell them to be on their way." Grandpa was a good judge of character.

Jon nodded, put his dime novel into his back pocket and stepped out of the parlor. He walked out the back door and up the steps to the backyard.

From this position Jonathon could see his father talking to two guards. The guards checked the papers of the four strangers and allowed them in under the orders of his father, Aaron.

"Jon," said Aaron.

"Yes, Pop."

"I want you to escort these men to the shed and show them where the tools are. They're gonna work on the loosening balusters and newel of the main staircase. They'll sand and varnish every inch after they're done with that. I'm gonna go to the office and get some employment sheets. These gentlemen are gonna be with us this weekend and until they're through."

"Yes, Pop."

J.R. extended his hand. Jon shook it.

"Hello there, lad," said J.R. "We be down here from Scotland looking for work. Your kind father has graciously allowed us on. He's quite the guvnah, he sure is."

J.R. carried his satchel tightly to his body. The others all had bags over their shoulders as well. The bags bulged in odd directions.

Jon recognized the scar that lay over the man's brow. It shocked him that the picture in his book that he carried in his pocket was so accurate. Was it possible? It had to be *him*. The man Frank Savage regretted not killing when he had the chance.

Jon glanced down. It was there. A foot long Bowie knife attached to J.R.'s belt. He kept his cool and said, "Why, yes sir, you and your men will be a very welcome addition these few days." I don't know these other men, he thought.

J.R. nodded to Stinson.

"Yes, yes," said Stinson. "I'm on it, I'm on it."

Stinson's narcissistic stench stunk up the place even after he had trotted off toward the back of the building. J.R. put his arm across Jon's shoulders and with an aggressive pull he led him to the shed.

Jon almost asked where the other man was going, but he changed his mind. A mind that raced. His eyes darted about looking for his father, or grandfather, or guards.

"Jenkins," said J.R.

Jenkins's face puffed with a stime of anger. He nodded and walked away to the back entrance following the understood, but unspoken, order.

Before J.R. could nod again Jon opened the door to the shed and stepped out walking backwards. J.R. was about to call to him but turned to Falene instead.

Jon could hear that the two men were whispering but he could not make out what the orders were. He picked up his pace, away from the back entrance, around the side of the large embassy and to the front gate. The two guards were missing. There was a blood smear along the inside wall of the wooden guardhouse.

Jonathon ran. He ran up the street. A tear streamed down his cheek, it was from the dry air that flowed across his eyes and the adrenaline that shot though his body.

It *was* him. The man from his book. The two missing guards and the blood confirmed it. He would call for help and get back before it was noticed that he was missing. Just two blocks to a phone and then two blocks back. Jon had never run faster.

A tall broad wood desk sat atop an elevated wood base. It allowed the burly sergeant dressed in blues to look down from his perch like a judge overlooking his courtroom. He twisted his handlebar moustache.

The sergeant opened a drawer, popped open a metal can, used his index finger and thumb to take up some wax. He applied the wax to the tips of his stache. He then pulled a white handkerchief from his pocket, wiped his fingers, and polished the badge on his chest and the row of silver-dollar sized buttons that ran down his shirt. A black Sally-rod lay on the desk by his hand.

The saloon-style doors swung open as a short, somewhat rotund female officer entered in a huff.

"S-se-sergeant," she said.

"What in the bloody-hell, calm down there, lassie," said the sergeant, "and gather your senses about you."

The woman held a clipboard and stepped up to the desk.

"Lassie, take a seat."

"Yes, sergeant."

She sat, held the clipboard in her left and dabbed sweat from her forehead with her right. It was quiet.

The sergeant's eyes meandered to the ceiling in a calm contempt as he waited.

He could not wait any longer. He said, "Lassie, now don't just sit there hording information, out with it."

"Yes, sergeant."

She held up the board and read, "A call arrived from the Detective Bureau. A young man by the name of Jonathon Downey has reported four strange men at the American offices of Great Cumberland Place."

"That's the embassy," he said.

She nodded as she paused to breathe.

"Well, go on."

She read, "He reported - Jonathon that is - he reported that two guards had gone missing at the four men's appearance upon the grounds. The men are masquerading as downtrodden and looking for work. They say they are from Scotland but the young man reports that the men are American and that the leader is a man by the name of Jason Ruse, a notorious outlaw from Missouri."

"And how does this young lad know that this man is a notorious outlaw?"

"He recognized him from his dime novel, sir."

"Bloody hell, we're supposed to believe a--"

"Sir, we have no choice."

The sergeant twirled his mustache and threw down a solid scowl.

"I know, but it gets better."

"Better?"

"The detective agency has ordered us to inform their American contact here in London."

"And who may that be?"

"A Mr. Frank Savage, sir. And, he has full authority."

"You have any more information on this, Mr. Savage?"

"Not much, I've an address."

"Well, it looks to me like fact is grandeur than fiction. Alright, off with you and round up this American Savage and keep me advised."

The officer went to exit, and turned. She said, "Oh, sergeant, there is a description."

"Go on."

"He's a . . . a cowboy."

The sergeant said, "Ah, bloody hell."

"For crying out loud, I'm over 50 years old, I shouldn't be here," said Frank. "Can't believe I let that guy go. Shoulda shot him in the brain pan."

His wife rubbed his broad shoulders. She carried an uncomfortable smile. His dark skin cracked at the corners of his dark eyes.

"I know, Baby," said Becca. "I know."

"Are they just gonna wait?"

"Yes, I did offer them coffee but they chose to wait outside. They did say it was urgent."

Frank nodded as he slipped on brown-red boots, western style pants, and a tan felt cowboy hat. He stepped up to a dresser that had two holsters. One holster was for two guns. He grabbed it and threw it about his hips.

Frank drew each gun for inspection and then slipped into a long dark trench coat.

"Don't forget your glasses," said Becca.

"Oh, yeah, dad-blasted things."

Frank slipped the glasses into his shirt pocket and followed his wife down the stairs and hollered out the front door, "One moment, gentlemen." He ran his hand over a three-week old salt-and-pepper beard.

One of the men spoke in order to hurry him. Frank stepped back into their view with a stance and stare that informed the man to shut up. He did.

Frank found his long barreled 20-gauge shotgun and a handful of shells. Double-aught buckshot.

He kissed his wife and went out.

"Don't be long," said Becca.

Frank turned, winked, said, "Back before sunset. Have the steaks and rye ready."

"Last one, Baby?"

"Last one, Sweetness."

Frank didn't follow the two detectives.

"Mr. Savage," said one of the men.

Frank stopped, turned, and said, "Yeah."

"Mr. Savage, we have a carriage. Individual riding isn't allowed anymore."

"Son, what's your name?"

He shuffled uncomfortably. "Bernhard, sir."

"Well, Bernhard, it *is* for me."

Bernhard remained quiet as Frank leapt into the saddle of his Sorrel.

A stakeout was set up in a pub across the street of the embassy. In the pub was a small cadre of detectives and two police officers and Frank.

"Brief me," ordered Frank.

"Four men," said Bernhard, "led by--"

"Jason Ruse," interrupted Frank.

"Yes."

"He's why I'm here."

"Oh."

"How many hostages are there?"

"Well, I'm surprised you don't already know. Anyway, there are estimated to be eight: two guards, three grounds-keepers, three female office workers, and a Saint Bernard."

"And how many dead?"

"We know of two dead guards," said a police officer. "Other than the two we believe are inside, hopefully they're still alive."

"Where did you get your intel?"

"A young man by the name of Jonathon Downey," said Bernhard.

"I want to talk to him," demanded Frank.

"He's back inside. He escaped to make the call and went back home. His father and grandfather are inside as well."

Frank understood why the young man went back in.

"How'd he know? How did he know who these men were?" asked Frank.

"Volume two, of your book," said Bernhard. "He's an avid Savage fan from your dime novel stories."

Frank nodded. Two dead men meant two more lost lives he had to carry around. That's two deaths that could have been prevented if he had just used a lead bullet in the brain of Jason Ruse instead of a steel gun-barrel over the face.

"What's the plan to round these men up?" said Bernhard.

"We don't round them up," said Frank.

"Say again."

"I go in and kill them. Then you come in and clean up the mess."

"Sir, that's not how we do things in London. This isn't Wyoming."

Frank reached into his overcoat pocket and took out the red leather map case that Agent White had given him. He handed it to Detective Bernhard. "Open this once I leave. Take a look at the photos."

Frank laid his 20-gauge on a table. He pulled a rolling paper and a small bag of tobacco. He quickly rolled a smoke and said, "I don't want to look at them ever again."

Bernhard said, "And why are you here again?"

"I'm here to kill Ruse. He's been holding up banks, trains, you name it. And he destroys all witnesses. He seems to find a way to conveniently dispose of his gang in the process as well."

"You're an assassin."

"Something like that."

"How do you do it? I mean, how do you live with yourself?" asked Bernhard.

"Don't get much sleep. I remind myself of the men I take out. These men I kill, they have butchered innocent people. The type of filth I hunt, they do it again and again without malice. And they always keep on doing it, that is, until I stop them. I made the mistake once by not killing this bastard when I had the chance." He pulled on his cigarette and said,

"I consider that decision a faulty resolution that I have since resolved to correct."

One of the officers stepped up and said, "Sir, aren't you a bit old to be doing this?"

"I reckon so."

"So, why? Why are you?" asked the detective.

"They haven't found my replacement."

"But they are human beings and they deserve a fair trial."

"If they were human, I'd agree with you. I don't hunt human beings. These killers don't just rob and kill. And they will, without hesitation, kill Jonathon and his family."

Frank finished his cigarette, tossed it to the floor, walked to the bar, poured a shallow glass of whisky, tossed it back, said, "Ruse has the nasty habit of cutting off his victims heads with a foot-long butcher's knife. Then he takes photographs of the bloody result with a camera. It will not happen today."

Bernhard handed Frank three photos. "These are pictures of the Downey family. I don't have information on the other hostages, or the perpetrators. But I imagine a bloke like you knows who and what he's chasing."

Frank examined the pictures.

"Why are they at Cumberland Place?" asked Bernhard.

"For the gold. One hundred thousand dollars worth of gold bars are hidden in the vault in the lower level," said Frank.

"Well . . . haven't you been told?"

Frank's anger spilled forth. He knew what was coming. "Told what?"

"That gold was pulled weeks ago when word got here that it was in jeopardy."

"Son of a bitch."

Frank took off his coat, hat, gun-belt and laid it all next to his shotgun on the table. He looked as his watch.

"I'm going in. There's no time. From my estimate they just figured it out, that the gold is not there. They will start by torturing, and then they will kill everyone, one by one in an attempt to find out where it is."

As he stepped out, Frank said over his shoulder, "I'll give them a fair trial."

Bernhard yelled out to Frank, "What are you gonna do?"

"I'll think of something. I've gotta be home for supper. Just be ready to clean up, and more importantly, stay out of my way."

Falene had already allowed his stupidity to show in all its glory, and Jenkins had lost his temper more than once. The gold was not in the vault and someone had to pay, it might as well be everyone.

Jonathon hung close to his family as he attempted to rein in his dog.

Jonathon said to himself, "Maintain situational awareness."

He looked around the room analyzing everything that could be of importance. He then glanced out the window. There he was. Frank Savage stood on the other side of the fence.

Jenkins was barking profanities as he paced back and forth from the hostages to the window.

Frank waved his hand that he was going to climb the fence. Jon nodded. As Jenkins began his trek back to the window Jon yelled, "Why don't you leave? The gold isn't here."

Jenkins flared his eyes and stepped toward the young man. He barked, "You shut the hell up or I'll shoot you and your pop square between the eyes. It's here, I can smell that it's here and someone is gonna fess up or--"

J.R. yelled from the upstairs balcony, "Shut up, Jenkins."

Stinson stomped his way down the steps. "I'll get them to talk, just watch, just watch, I'll get them to talk."

Frank was thankful for the opening. He leapt the fence and snuck into the shack. Rummaging through the tools, he managed to find what he needed.

"What am I doing here?"

He heard a woman scream.

Jenkins held lookout duty by the east window as Falene stood guard with blood at his feet. Stinson pulled Jonathon, screaming, up the grand staircase.

A shadow fluttered across the yard, outside, next to the building. Jenkins whispered, "What in the hell?"

He moved out the side entrance to see a man in overalls kneeling by the flower bed that ran along the building. On the man's back it read: Gardner.

Jenkins hollered, "Hey, you, what are you doing here?"

The man stood and turned, his hands were covered in dirt. His face carried a beard and glasses.

"Well, son, what the hell does it look like I'm doing?" said Frank. He walked towards Jenkins with some leaves in his hands. "You see, I'm inspecting the tomato plants for caterpillar infestation." He held up a portion of a tomato plant. "You see here." He pointed, and adjusted his glasses. "The yellowish brown part here is telling me I've my work cut out for me."

Jenkins fumed, but decided to keep quiet. He acted somewhat hospitable. He said, "Mr. Downey asked me to come out and get you. He wants to talk to you." His cheeks formed an awkward smile.

Frank brushed the dirt off his hands and then his overalls.

Frank asked, "What's he wanna talk about?"

"Mmm, I think there's a back-pay issue, yeah, he owes you some back-pay."

Frank scratched his head. "Well, okay."

Jenkins scanned the yard, holding his gun from view. He looked down the back alleyway as they stepped into the building.

Once inside Frank came to the realization that he had overestimated the amount of time it would take for everything to go south.

A young man's screams framed the chaos. Falene stood over an unconscious guard lying in a pool of blood. Three women were weeping, one with blood on her face and another with her dress torn from her body.

In between Frank and Falene was a dead Saint Bernard. Head bashed in. Hair clung to the barrel of Falene's six-shooter.

Aaron Downey lay at the foot of the steps, beaten. Face bashed to bits. A fight he lost in an attempt to save his son from being dragged upstairs. Grandpa Downey sat on a step holding tightly to his left arm. His mouth agape as he sucked in air. Over and over he tried. His chest was visibly tightening.

Falene screamed, "Who the fuck is this?"

Jenkins backhanded Frank. He ordered, “Down to the ground.”

Frank eyed his captor in defiance. He whispered, “Jenkins, you’re such an asshole.”

The man’s eyes, enveloped in hatred, bulged in disbelief. He lifted his pistol.

Frank’s temper exploded like a keg of dynamite in his guts. He pulled a spade from his pants-pocket and plunged it into the belly of Jenkins until the sharp tip of the gardening tool pierced the spine.

A Colt .45 had been released from the dying man’s grip and was one inch from the wood floor when Frank had his palm on the butt.

Falene proved his stupidity and pushed his own gun toward Frank.

Frank was faster. The bullet entered between the nose and the left eye. A shard of skull popped up sending a tuft of hair into the air. Falene was dead but still stood. Blood spilled out of both ears. He just stood as his eyes rolled to the back of his head.

Frank pointed at a guard and the three women huddled together and said, “Help Grandpa Downey, he’s having a heart attack. There’s help at the pub across the street.”

Frank turned, ran, hurdled over Aaron, and swiftly shot by Grandpa as he vaulted up the steps.

Frank leveled his gun in anticipation. Sure enough, Stinson, in all his arrogant predictability, came out of the upstairs office face first and two guns drawn. Frank shot him in the face.

The sounds of women screeching bounced off the walls. Aaron hollered out to his dad to hold on. Then Jonathon screamed out: “Nooo.” It wasn’t necessary, but the crying and screaming was that added sense of dread that Frank used as ammunition.

At the edge of the door Frank stopped. He inspected his gun and quickly glanced in. Ruse had Jon face down on the desk with a Bowie knife just barely breaking the skin on the back of his neck.

“Who’s out there?” said Ruse. “The police? I wanna make a deal.”

Frank sneered: “A deal?”

“Yeah. I won’t harm the kid and--”

Frank interrupted, “And what? We promise to kill you quickly?” Frank peered around the corner of the door.

Hook hammered the knife into the top of the desk and yanked Jon up and pointed a gun to his head.

“I can see you, you bastard,” said Ruse.

Frank stepped into the room with his gun hand hanging at his side. "Hello Hook, nice scar."

"Damn-it, Savage, I thought you'd either died or quit looking for me." He pushed up a smile that was fraught with fright.

"Honestly, Hook, that was quite doubtful that that was going to happen. But you knew that. I've unfinished business with you," said Frank.

"What I ever do to you? All I did was accept this scar across my mug courtesy of your gun."

Frank pondered the situation, then said, "This reminds me of a situation I had with a man once. What the hell was his name? Oh yeah, Conrad Bovis, that was his name."

Jonathon looked at Frank, and he winked. Frank allowed a splinter of a smile.

Frank said, "Did you know him, Hook?"

"How the hell--" When Hook opened his mouth Jonathon used everything he had and yanked down, back and away. That was all the confusion that was needed. Frank moved smooth and fast, and fired into Hook Ruse. Blood was splayed over the look of confusion that was pasted to his grimacing mug. He fell back up against the wall.

"You okay, Jonathon?"

"Yes, yes, sir," said Jon as he held the back of his neck.

Frank moved behind the desk toward the bewildered Hook Ruse. Frank lifted the blade from the desk. He knocked the man down to his back. Frank solidly held the blade that came to rest above the heart of Hook Ruse.

Frank said, "I've a message for you from Dale. You remember Dale. The woman you made a widow."

Hook panicked and began kicking about.

"Here's the message," said Frank.

With his body weight Frank sheathed the knife slowly into Hook's chest. The blood vessels of Hook's right eye broke. The white of his eye filled with blood. The tip of the blade punctured through and into the wooden floor.

The cowboy stood and turned and said, "Go see to your family."

Jonathon nodded and ran to the door. The dime novel fell to the floor. He stopped, turned, picked up his book and said, "Thank you, Mr. Savage."

"I couldn't have done it without you, Jon. Now, let's save your grandpa."

THE END